Romancing Retha

By Cinda Brea

Acknowledgments

First, I give thanks to God. Thank you to my good friend Linda Sampson for encouraging me to write this book, though it was so long ago I doubt she remembers. Thanks to my sister Freddie Jacobs for sharing her vivid imagination and for willingly reading my first finished copy of this novel and providing me with honest feedback. Much appreciation to my niece Ida Smith for her image and her feedback. Thanks to my children Aaron and Cecily for their support during this process and my daughter Bettrina for allowing me the time to write and providing inspiration. I also want to thank my family and friends for the wealth of writing fodder many of you unknowingly provided. And I truly want to thank my best friend and partner in life Julio Brea for all his patience and support throughout this process and over the years. I love you.

Cover art by Shally Brady. Thank you, Shally!

Table of Content

Chapter 1 -- A Change is Coming

"How do I get myself into these things?" Retha asks out loud as she pulls up in front of her sister Jessie's home a little past six in the morning on her first unofficial day as an unemployed civilian. Once again, she has spread herself as thin as a small pair of dollar fifty cent panty hose on a queen size body. She promised herself weeks ago to take it easy, enjoy life, and not stress during her time off. So why is she still so busy in support of her military family? This will likely be her busiest day in months.

Retha hasn't even taken the time to celebrate her upcoming freedom from the United States Army; that will have to come later. First thing is to disengage from her military mindset and rest. The Army, with all its danger and uncertainty, had in many ways represented security but after two short hitches in Iraq, Retha is ready for something less dangerous, less exciting, just plain dull.

As Retha climbs out of her car and heads up to the front door of her sister's two story ranch, a tiny trickle of fear wiggles down her spine. The emotion has nothing to do with her surroundings. She is as comfortable in Jessie's neighborhood as her own. She is uneasy about the inevitable change.

"That you Retha?" Jessie asks, opening the door with a sleepy scowl that turns into a full blown yawn. "Why didn't you use your key?" Jessie turns and walks into her kitchen without waiting for an answer. "I set the coffee pot on auto before I went to bed last night. We can have a quick cup before you guys leave. I had to wake that boy up twice. He's getting ready."

"I can never remember the code to your alarm and besides Robert says he changes it every three months. I didn't want to scare you coming in here with the key. I thought you might still be asleep." Retha makes herself comfortable in a kitchen chair while Jessie pours the freshly brewed elixir and hands her a cup.

Retha sips her coffee like the arabica addict she is and groans. "Ooh! Good coffee. I wish my coffee was as good as yours."

Jessie looks at her baby sister with criticism seeping from her being before voicing the advice Retha can predict. "Wash your coffee pot and your coffee will be fine."

Retha smiles. She has long since learned to ignore these comments from Jessie. She takes another sip from her cup as she longs to go out back and lounge on Jessie's patio, leisurely enjoy a great cup of java that doesn't cost three bucks, and chat until the morning sun is fully risen. "When's your husband coming home, anyway?" she asks Jessie.

"Robert will be home tomorrow," Jessie answers as if her husband's return is of no consequence.

Retha decides to feign offense at Jessie's reference to her housekeeping. "What makes you think I don't wash my pot, Jessie? I wash my coffee pot."

"Hi, Auntie Retha." Retha and Jessie's eleven-year-old nephew RJ drags into the kitchen looking and smelling like an eleven-year-old boy out of bed too early on a Saturday morning, half dressed and half washed.

"Hey, baby. You ready?" Before he has a chance to answer, Retha continues. "You need to go back up and comb your hair a little bit better. I don't want people looking at me like I'm neglecting you."

Knowing his aunts all too well, RJ pulls an afro comb out of his backpack and heads toward the door, snatching an orange on his way.

"We'll get something to eat on our way," Retha informs Jessie before she can insist on RJ eating breakfast.

Jessie waves a hand as she heads off to bed. "Lock the door and set the alarm on your way out."

"Can we stop at McDonald's?" RJ asks before they clear the front door. Retha knew that question was coming. Her nephew is as predictable as the rising sun.

Work, obligation, and responsibility are terms Retha did not plan to use for a while. Use or not, her weekend is full of all three. Her brother, Raymond brought RJ to San Antonio from his home in Houston for the weekend while he headed off to Vegas with a new lady friend. Retha has volunteered her morning to the Fort Sam Houston Youth Activities Program which is holding a well-publicized and well attended youth Olympics on MacArthur Field. A large number of sports celebrities consisting of basketball, ice hockey, soccer, and a few baseball players are slated to show up to sign autographs and work the events with the children. RJ is a baseball player and a huge fan of the sport. As soon as he heard about the games, he declared he wanted to attend. Since Retha will work the games from morning until noon, she has the pleasure of her nephew's company on an autograph-seeking quest.

Fortunately for RJ, Retha's friend Staff Sergeant Jeremiah Rojas has a brother who plays shortstop for the San Francisco Cyclops. Richard Rojas, a South Texas native, is an active participant in the Youth Activities Games nearly every year. Jeremiah has promised RJ a personally autographed baseball from his brother and possibly several of the other baseball players.

Retha will work her butt off for that autographed baseball. After she finishes volunteering at the games, she will go home and pick up a partially prepared meal she started the night before. Retha will finish cooking the meal at Jeremiah's home before he and his guests arrive later in the evening. Afterwards she will go home and prep for a Sunday dinner party at her home. At this point, all Retha can do is pray for Monday morning and rest.

When Retha agreed to "help" cook dinner for Jeremiah's brother, she had no idea she would be on her own. Also, she didn't realize the dinner would be on the same day as the Youth Activities Games. When the command volunteered Jeremiah and his friend Sergeant Raheem Matinfar to work the games the entire day, the meal fell solely on Retha's shoulders. She doesn't mind – at least not much. Jeremiah is a good friend and a good soldier, one of the best she has ever worked with. He hardly ever asks for anything by way of a favor and is completely unselfish with his own time. Retha is prepared to run herself ragged to indulge her friend's seldom spoken wishes.

Besides, taking care of soldiers was Retha's job as a noncommissioned officer and the part of the Army she will miss most. There are many aspects of military life she will miss but she had to make the change. After so many years of getting up early and getting home late; running physical fitness training; so many changes of station and jobs and supervisors and soldiers and commanders and first sergeants; so many training exercises; after two too many combat tours; after so much anguish and even fear; after no good reason for a childless, love-filled marriage and after losing all she had to live for, Sergeant First Class Retha Lindo is calling it quits.

She will hold on to many of the friendships she has formed over her twelve-year career. That is why she volunteered at the games.

They are an excellent source of recreational funding for the children of military families and under-privileged children in the neighboring communities. Twice before Retha helped organize the games but always remained behind the scenes when the event took place.

Last year she was so far behind the scene that she was in Iraq trying to avoid rocket propelled grenades. She had failed but she was lucky. No, she was blessed. Retha had been thrown from the vehicle and rendered unconscious but her wounds were minor. The most serious was a piece of shrapnel embedded in her upper thigh, the outside fleshy part. Thank God for those heavy thighs she had always wanted thinner. Others in her group had not fared so well. Her platoon sergeant, Sergeant First Class Jeff Mason, lost a leg and young Private John Travis lost his life. With such traumatizing memories Retha can only be thankful she will never deploy again.

So working the games is Sergeant First Class Lindo's last official duty as an active duty soldier. Her ad hoc tasks keep her running around the soccer fields the entire morning putting out fires and ensuring each station has the staff, equipment and supplies needed. Thankfully, her friends Rojas and Matinfar are helping her keep watch over RJ during the games.

When her shift ends, Retha feels a little guilty about leaving so early in the day. Lieutenant Colonel James Freeman, the officer in charge of the games and a good friend, does his best to add to her guilt by acting as if he cannot manage without her. Retha ignores his efforts and briefs her replacement and several other members of the staff. She says her goodbyes and heads in the direction of her last RJ sighting.

Upon spotting her nephew, she can tell he is not nearly as happy to see her as she is to see him. It is clear he is not floating on the cloud she had expected to rein him down from. "What's up man?" she asks with little genuine concern. She is accustomed to his moodiness though surprised to see it on this occasion.

RJ walks toward her with his lips pressed together and stretched across his face, a sure sign that things have not gone quite his way. "I got some really good ones, but I didn't get over there in time to get Daniels to sign. It's your friend's fault."

"Daniels is not here." Retha has to stop and look around in awe. Jaren Daniels is one of the few baseball players she watches play.

Her brother-in-law, Robert, is a huge New York Liberty fan and Daniels is one of the star players on that team and in the league.

"Yes he is too; I saw him!" RJ points to the area where, Retha assumes, he saw the baseball star. There is nothing but grass growing at that spot now. "I was too late to get his autograph!" RJ adds with sheer disgust.

"Ah, man you gotta be kidding!" Retha empathizes with her nephew as she affectionately palms his head. RJ moves his head away with a scowl. He is unhappy and does not want to be consoled. He continues to complain about Jeremiah's failure.

"Yep, Jerry said Daniels didn't decide to come until the last minute but he didn't tell me until Daniels was leavin' for lunch."

That's an autograph I would not have been disappointed to get myself. "Shoot!" Retha stomps her foot lightly and looks around again in a futile half-hearted attempt at spotting the superstar. "Daniels is a great player but I like to look at him; he's my screen saver," Retha confides jokingly with her nephew.

"I know," RJ responds with his head hung even closer to the ground. He gives his aunt a pitiful sideways glance. "If I could'a got Daniel's autograph, I would'a gave it to you, Auntie Retha." He looks up at her for an earnest affect. "But I didn't know he was gonna to be here."

Retha has to smile at the pledged sacrifice. "That's sweet baby, but I wouldn't take your autograph." Retha often speaks to her younger nieces and nephews as if they are babies. They all say she is a little weird but like her for all her personality. She makes each feel special and each believes he or she is her favorite.

The favorite for the day and his weird aunt walk slowly toward her car, hoping to lessen the effect of the humidity which has gotten increasingly thicker on this not-too-warm November day. RJ keeps looking over his shoulder hoping to get another glimpse of the players and in particular the Liberty outfielder, Jaren Daniels. Retha feels a twinge of pity for her nephew but ignores it. He has racked up a nice booty of autographs from the other players, including several San Antonio Spurs. The disappointment of missing out on one single signature will soon be overshadowed by those he has captured. In order to get his mind off of the one autograph that got away, Retha takes off running at a full pace. "Come on! I'll race you!" she yells.

RJ accepts the challenge and bolts after her yelling, "That's not fair. You cheat!"

Retha has a good head start and needs it because RJ is fast. As they near the parking lot Retha looks up and wants to drop dead right there in her tracks from embarrassment. Standing at the end of the parking lot, all alone, is the sole possessor of the most sought after autograph of the day, Mr. Jaren Daniels and he is watching their foot race with interest. Retha tries to slow down without coming to a screeching halt. She slows up, turns around and starts running backwards all while trying to capture RJ's attention as he sweeps past her. After passing Retha, RJ stops on a dime and bends over with laughter between gasps for air, because he has finally beaten his elderly aunt in a foot race; his day is complete. He is still not aware of the baseball player.

Retha walks up to her nephew, takes him by the shoulders and turns him around. She points to the athlete who is still watching them with what seems like a great deal of amusement on his face. "Ah man, your screen saver!" RJ exclaims. "Can I go ask him to sign my card?" Retha walks a little closer with RJ and then stops and stays back by a few car lengths. She feels shy about meeting the man, maybe because she is dirty and not a little sweaty.

RJ shyly approaches Jaren Daniels and asks for his autograph. The ballplayer smiles as he speaks with yet another awestruck fan. Retha watches and notes that television and still photography do not do the man justice. She notices him glance in her direction and gives him a slight wave. He doesn't bother to return the gesture but Retha senses he is talking to RJ about her. After a minute or so, RJ turns. "Auntie Retha, Mr. Daniels says you can come over. He won't bite you."

Before Retha can catch herself she blurts out her response. "Nooo, but I might bite him." RJ's head moves back and Retha imagines his raised brow which is one of his many "you're weird" expressions. She is too embarrassed by the ridiculous comment to even look at the ballplayer. She yells for RJ to hurry up and leave Mr. Daniels alone, then turns and heads to her car where she sits and waits.

RJ jumps in a few minutes later and asks his aunt why she didn't come and meet the famous baseball player. "Because I might have wet my pants," is not an answer one should give an eleven-year-old, so she tells him she thought he would enjoy it better if he met the ballplayer alone. RJ proceeds to tell his aunt that he thought Mr. Daniels really wanted to meet her because he kept looking over at her. *He was probably wondering who the lunatic was.* Retha holds back her laughter.

"He asked if you were my mother and I told him you were my aunt and then he said 'Why is she standing over there. Is she scared I might bite her?' And I said 'No, you're her favorite.' That's when he said to tell you to come over and that he wouldn't bite you. But when I told you what he said, you said."

Retha cuts her nephew off, not wanting to hear her words repeated. "Yeah, yeah, yeah, I know what I said." She wants to slide down into a hole but there isn't one around big enough to hide her. *Oh well, who wants to meet gorgeous, sexy ballplayers when they're all hot and stinky?*

--

RJ leaps from the car and runs into Jessie's house before Retha turns off the car engine. When Retha walks in, Jessie and her friend Stacy are seated at the kitchen table listening to RJ recount the events of his morning. He reviews each in great detail and before Retha can stop him she hears "…and Auntie Jessie, he wanted to meet Auntie Retha but she told him she might bite him if she got too close and then she walked away. I guess she didn't wanna meet him, so he just talked to me some more. He's really cool, tall too."

Retha stands peering into Jessie's open refrigerator pretending she is engrossed with finding food. All the while she wants to strangle her nephew and kick herself for not bribing him before they got to Jessie's. Jessie and Stacy look at Retha with dumbfounded disbelief on their faces. Jessie tells RJ to go upstairs and check on his cousin. As RJ takes the stairs by twos, Jessie turns to Retha for confirmation. "I know you didn't. That baby better be lying on you and please close that refrigerator door."

"Please! Don't even go there." Retha tries to act disinterested as she closes the door and gets a water glass from a cabinet. "You know how RJ gets confused and embellishes everything."

"So which is it? Is he confused or embellishing? Did you tell one of them damn baseball players you might bite him, Retha?" Jessie asks in dismay.

Retha is busted. She bursts out laughing and confesses. "Jessie, it came out before I even knew what I was thinking. Girl, he is so fine, I started feeling dizzy just looking at him. You better be glad I didn't faint or pee on myself or something."

Jessie and Stacy join in and laugh with Retha while shaking their heads in disbelief. When the laughter dies down and Stacy catches her breath, she gives Retha the advice she has wanted to share for some time. "Honey, you been alone long enough. It's time you get a love life."

Chapter 2 -- The Sweetest Love

Retha Gray grew up in the small town of Seaside on the beautiful central California coast. Tragically, her parents, Donald and Wanda, were killed in an automobile accident when Retha was seventeen years old. For as long as Retha can remember, the Army has been an important part of her life. Wanda and Donald met and married during Donald's first assignment at Fort Ord which was just over the fence from the house that would later become the family's Seaside home. Donald traveled the world during his Army career while Wanda and the children kept a comfortable home in Seaside. Wanda was a Solomon and she had sisters and brothers living nearby. For years she was very comfortable and happy with Donald coming home long enough to develop a relationship with his youngest child and getting her pregnant with the next one before leaving on his next tour. Wanda had no wish to pack up her ever-growing family and travel with her husband.

Retha and her siblings were so influenced by the military that Andre, the oldest, and Retha, the youngest joined the Army. The second oldest girl, Ida, enlisted in the Air Force and baby boy, Jermaine, the Navy. Another sister, Madelyn, married an Army man. Jessie, the oldest girl, and Raymond, the second son, are the only two of the seven Gray children who did not join the military or marry a military member. Retha had enlisted less than a year after graduating high school.

While still in her advanced training Retha met Joe. Dark and early one Monday morning Retha, faking illness to get released from the day's training activities, stood in a long line of soldiers waiting outside the Fort Jackson Troop Medical Clinic. It was her first trip to the clinic and the first time her eyes set upon the likeness of Staff Sergeant Joe Lindo. Sergeant Lindo walked into the screening area of the clinic and everything came to a halt for Retha. She had to tell herself to stop staring at the man. The sergeant had dark brown skin, perfectly even gleaming white teeth, and beautiful deep brown eyes. He stood nearly six feet in his battle dress uniform and combat boots and was meticulous from top to bottom. Sergeant Lindo supervised the clinic's morning sick call with command, skill and efficiency, and interacted with patients and staff from colonel to private with ease and self-assuredness.

As fate would have it, the clinic was short staffed so Sergeant Lindo assisted with the day's patient triage. When he called Retha back for her screening, she cursed her bad luck for two reasons: she looked like death and she was certain he would know her illness was an act. Sergeant Lindo started out stern, direct, and professional. Retha immediately noticed a slight accent and asked his nationality. He informed her he was originally from the Dominican Republic but grew up in New York City. Retha relaxed a bit with that information and told the sergeant that her brother-in-law, Robert, is also Dominican and that Robert's family lives in Boston. When the sergeant finished the screening, he leaned back in his chair and stared at Retha without a word causing her to slouch deeper into her seat, feeling uncomfortable with his close scrutiny. She wished she had done her hair or at least put on her lip gloss. *God, I hope I'm not ashy*. Retha kept her eyes down and did her best not to look at the sergeant.

He finally spoke. "Private First Class Gray?"

"Yes, Sergeant."

"So you feel very sick today?"

"Yes, Sergeant."

"I tell you what. You look like you need some rest so I'm putting you on 24-hours quarters. How does that sound?"

"That sounds good," Retha mumbled.

"Can you handle that?"

"Yes Sergeant. Don't I have to see the doctor?"

"Not if I say you don't. This is between me and you, Private. So, you're in D-11-4, First Sergeant Jacobs, right?" he asked as he wrote in her medical record.

"Yes." *Oh shit*! Retha trembled inside. *Why is he mentioning my first sergeant*?

"I know him well. I want you to do something for me. I want you to promise not to discuss this with your little buddies over there at the company and I want you to promise me I will not see you in here again unless you are sick, okay?"

Retha's eyes turned to saucers. "Sergeant, I really don't…"

The sergeant cut her off. "I understand you really are tired and need some rest."

Retha was embarrassed but felt much better when Sergeant Lindo changed his stern expression to a smile. "Sergeant, I want to thank you."

"Don't worry about it Private Gray. I'm certain you will get the opportunity to repay me some other time." Retha wasn't sure if the sergeant was flirting or not but she sure hoped he was.

--

One year later, Retha and Joe were married and on their way to Germany. Retha was experiencing the most wondrous time of her short life. Joe was divorced and the father of a nine-year-old nicknamed JJ, short for Joe Jr. The Lindos started trying to have children on their wedding night and agreed that when Retha got pregnant she would get out of the Army and stay at home for their children. That pregnancy never came. Retha had numerous fertility tests and nothing seemed wrong medically. Joe's tests were also normal.

Joe was not Retha's first sexual partner but he was her first lover. With Joe she learned that making love is a continuum, not simply the physical acts of foreplay and intercourse. Joe made love to her with his eyes, with his words, with his deeds. He courted her all the time. He knew to walk up behind her and kiss her on her neck. He knew she loved for him to touch her very gently. Retha felt she was truly blessed to have a man who loved her as Joe did. Though very young, she was wise enough to realize not many men knew how to love a woman and make her happy in their love.

Joe was full of love and everyone loved him, especially women. He was perfection in Retha's young eyes. He was a gentleman who treated every stranger like a good friend; whereas, Retha was shy and reserved with people until she got to know them. Their tour in Germany was challenging for her. She was young and insecure with a mature streetwise and worldly husband. To make Retha's transition into her new life in Germany more complicated, she and Joe were assigned to the same unit and worked in the same building. She worked in the Personnel Administration Center and Joe was an operations sergeant in the Battalion Operations Office. Everyone in the medical battalion was familiar with the Lindos and had an opinion about them. Many were amazed that an experienced professional soldier like Joe would marry a girl like Retha. It was not uncommon for Retha to hear other soldiers talking about what a fine man Staff Sergeant Lindo was or have a fellow soldier ask "Oh, is that your husband?" after making a verbal blunder. Several female noncommissioned officers showed open disdain toward Retha and flirted shamelessly with Joe.

Joe had twelve years active duty under his belt and several longtime friends in the same battalion. A couple of these men had left their wives in the States and were living the lives of single men. Joe spent much of his free time with these men and it was not long before Retha started to pout and complain about Joe leaving her alone while he hung out with his "low life friends," as she called them. Things came to a head one Friday afternoon when Retha walked up on Joe and Staff Sergeant Wilma Jenkins, an alleged card playing buddy, having a cozy conversation in Joe's office. Both stopped talking long enough for Retha to have her say and leave but Retha decided to take a seat and join them. Joe was slightly intrigued by his young wife's possessiveness. Taking a cue from the looks Joe bestowed upon Retha, Staff Sergeant Jenkins knew she was fighting a losing battle and got up to leave but not before getting her dig in. "So, Sarg, am I going to see you at Lee's for cards later?"

Joe rendered a casual salute without taking his eyes from Retha's which were getting angrier by the moment. "I'll be there," he answered with an ever so slight smile.

The battalion headquarters building was fairly empty on Friday afternoons so no one heard Retha light into Joe after Sergeant Jenkins sashayed her fat ass out of the office. "While you're out playing cards with your friends, what am I supposed to do?" Retha complained.

"You can come with me if you want but I know you don't like playing cards that much."

"I don't want to go and play cards and I'm tired of you going out and leaving me all the time."

"Don't start with me now, Retha. If you want to come, you're welcome to come. You know you don't like my friends and don't even say I leave you all the time. I go out maybe two, three nights a week and it's not like I stay out late."

"How would you like it if I went out two or three nights a week and partied with my friends? You wouldn't like it at all. If you keep leaving me I'm going to start leaving you too."

Joe found Retha's threat exciting. He liked for her to push back at him. He also wanted Retha to have more friends and not spend so much time waiting around for him. He decided to push the envelope to see how Retha would react. "You need to get out and spend time with other people. Then maybe you won't be so worried about what I'm doing."

Retha could not respond; she was irate. She left his office without another word and headed back to her own. By the time Joe stopped by her office to pick her up at the end of the day, she appeared to have forgotten their earlier argument. Joe considered staying in with Retha or taking her to dinner or a movie that evening but, instead, once again extended an invitation for her to accompany him to the card party. Retha, who had hoped he would change his mind and spend the evening with her, graciously declined the invitation.

"You gonna be alright here?" Joe asked later that evening as he hesitated in the doorway of their home, contemplating his departure. He had never asked her that question before although he had left her alone in their little German village many times and for many hours.

"I'll be okay. I'll find something to do," Retha responded nonchalantly.

Joe was not completely out of the driveway before Retha was on the telephone calling one of her coworkers. Specialist Charmaine Jameson worked in the Personnel Administration Center with Retha and was one of the few people with whom Retha had rapport. Charmaine and her road dog, Jasmine, had invited Retha out dancing at a Frankfurt club.

"Yo' husband gonna let you go out with us?" Charmaine had questioned Retha earlier that day upon hearing Retha's tentative plans to join them.

"I do what I want. I'm not his child," Retha answered, sounding like an adolescent.

"Ooh, you must be mad at him. Well, if you wanna go, call me before eight thirty because that's a long ride out there to pick you up and it's in the opposite direction from the club."

"I'll give you some gas money."

"Don't worry about the gas. I just wish I knew why you all the sudden wanna go out partying with us."

Retha didn't answer and hoped she wouldn't have to go out with her single coworkers to give her husband a taste of his own medicine but found it necessary to follow through. Her mother had always said, "You can show a fella better than you can teach him." So, after calling Charmaine, she showered and put on the skimpiest dress she owned. She applied more makeup than usual, Joe's favorite scent, and made her way out to a Frankfurt club filled with American soldiers and German men, a single woman's dream.

Retha and her friends didn't leave the club until well after three in the morning and she entered her home forty-five minutes later. Joe was wide awake waiting for her. Retha walked in as if she went out dancing without him every weekend.

Joe didn't speak for nearly ten minutes until he had to let it out. "So, are you going to tell me where you've been?"

"I was out with some friends," Retha answered as casually as possible before heading into the bathroom to dress for bed.

When she entered their bedroom, her husband continued his questions. "Did you stop to think I might worry about you?"

"No, no I didn't."

"So you don't care if I was worried?"

"I'm sorry if you worried. I didn't mean to worry you."

"So, what now, Retha?"

"What do you mean?" Retha asked, perplexed.

"I don't want you going out like this. It's not right for you to go out to clubs without me. What are you looking for out there?"

"The same thing you're looking for when you go out without me."

"I don't go to clubs without you. I don't go out partying."

"So would you prefer I meet some friends and start hanging out at their homes when there are single men hanging out there also?"

"What? Do you think I've got a woman or something? Is that what you think? Because if you do, you're wrong."

Retha's emotions bubbled over as she stood beside their bed and pointed her finger at Joe. "I don't think you should hang out with geographical bachelors who shack up with women while their wives are back in the States and have all kinds of single bitches at their homes. If you haven't done anything yet you're setting yourself up to do something. I'm not going to be treated this way. I like to go out dancing. I don't like playing cards. I don't go out dancing because you don't think it's right for me to go out without you and you don't like to go out dancing. So why the hell are you sitting up at your whore mongering friend's house playing cards when I don't think that's right?" She was yelling and crying and slinging snot by the end of her tirade.

Joe had pushed the envelope way too far and he was sorry. He considered his response carefully, knowing Retha was right. He had been married to his first wife for five years and she had never been so honest with him, not even when the marriage ended. "So what if I take you dancing once in a while and you go and play cards with me occasionally?"

"Not at those whorish assed friends of yours houses."

"Okay, we won't go there. I'll find me some new card-playing buddies. Some my wife approves of. Just don't do this again."

"And I want you to start showing me a little more respect. Some of those women at work act like they hate me because of you. They're always in your face laughing and talking and then they don't even speak to me."

"Whatever you want Retha but please don't do this again." Joe took Retha to bed and tried to apologize by making love to her and he made sure no one ever had cause to question his feelings toward his wife again.

～～

The couple got the assignment of their dreams after Germany, Fort Sam Houston in San Antonio, Texas. Retha's sister Jessie, her husband, Robert, and their children had lived in San Antonio for years. Retha's Uncle Sugar and his two youngest sons, Gerald and Nathaniel, and several distant cousins also lived in the city. Joe and Retha purchased a home in San Antonio and planned to settle in for a few years before moving again but Joe was soon placed on special assignment, one that advanced his chances for promotion. The Lindos were in Fort Sam a little over a year when Joe shipped off to Iraq.

Retha remained in San Antonio and managed to stay busy with work and her family. Her sister Jessie's three children were: eighteen-year-old Mykol, twelve-year-old Elizabeth and the youngest, eight-year-old Catrina who is deaf-blind and developmentally delayed. The family received respite assistance with Catrina but they needed more help because she required constant care and supervision. With the additional help Retha provided, Jesse and Robert enjoyed time alone together whenever they felt the need.

Joe also liked being close to Retha's family. He and Robert became brothers and they address and refer to each other as "brah-in-law," a reference Madelyn's Georgia-born husband, Philip, had started years before.

Jessie was Joe's favorite among Retha's brothers and sisters. Jessie and Retha are similar in appearance and stature. They both stand five-feet three-inches in their stocking feet. Jessie carries a little more weight than Retha but she is thirteen years older. Jessie is a stay at home mom after over eighteen years in the insurance industry. She does her share of volunteer work and puts in a little time at her Uncle Sugar's restaurant. Jessie is usually right in the thick of whatever is happening with her family and often running things. She tries not to be a control freak but just can't help herself. She can't help giving her opinion either. Joe knew if he went to Jessie with a situation he would get an opinion and usually one he agreed with. Jessie was Joe's favorite because he and she thought alike and he was certain Retha would be in good company with Jessie.

By the time Joe returned from Iraq, Retha was on assignment to that same war zone. The couple spent two months together before her deployment. Retha's first hitch in Iraq was far less dangerous than Joe's had been. She spent all her time in the Green Zone, worked in a relatively comfortable office environment, and had many of the comforts of home. By the time Retha headed back to the States she had no plans to continue her military career. She wanted to be with her family and make her family with Joe larger.

As in all good marriages, Joe and Retha were best friends. Their lives were full but Retha desperately wanted children. She and Joe had discussed adoption earlier in the marriage but kept waiting for a pregnancy. As the years flew by, Retha became more receptive to the idea of adoption. No sooner than the couple made the decision to start looking into the adoption process, Joe was suddenly and unexpectedly offered up by his command for reassignment to Fort Hood, Texas, with immediate deployment back to Iraq.

Joe reached Iraq without a problem. He contacted his wife immediately and informed her that the conditions were not nearly as dire as they had been on his previous tour and he was doing well. He gave her a list of things to send. Retha was relieved and gathered the items he requested: more socks, junk food, camera, pound cake, DVDs, books, and most importantly a bible. He had left his bible on a military vehicle and would likely never see it again.

Retha started a prayer and running regiment that worked well and allowed her to focus on things other than Joe. She helped her Uncle Sugar in his restaurant, one of her favorite pastimes, and spent lots of time at Jessie and Robert's house. Often Catrina would go home with her for the weekend or an entire day, affording Jessie and Robert some needed quiet time together. Retha started sending Joe literature about the adoption process and the experiences of other adoptive parents and children. Retha also began to seriously consider in vitro fertilization which she had adamantly refused before.

Although Joe did not have a weekend, he usually called on Fridays, if at all possible. Friday represented one less week to be in country and one week closer to heading home. One Friday evening Retha made her regular stop in at Jessie's after work, picked up Catrina to spend the night, and then rushed home in time to catch Joe's call. When she arrived at her home she noticed a strange car parked in front of her house. She got Catrina into her home and then peeked out her front window just as two people exited the vehicle and started toward her home. Retha felt a numbing fear in her throat turning into hysteria as she watched the figures turn up her walkway. She ran into the kitchen and dialed Jessie's number with trembling hands. Robert answered. "Robert, I need you and Jessie to come over here, now! They're coming to my door." The doorbell rang a second time.

"Who? Did you call the police?" Robert asked in a panicked voice.

"I don't need the police. I need my sister. It's Joe!" Retha walked to the door with the phone in her hand. Robert could hear her ask, "Yes, who is it?"

"Sergeant Lindo, It's First Sergeant Rivers."

Retha opened the door to find her first sergeant standing there in his dress uniform. "Top, why are you here? Why are you here?" she screamed.

"I'm so sorry Retha. I'm here as a representative of the United States Army to inform you that your husband, Master Sergeant Joe P. Lindo was killed in service to his country…"

Retha started screaming. She could hear Jessie yelling over the phone "Retha, Retha, I'm on my way baby, I'm on my way!"

Retha remembered very little of that night. She heard the first sergeant tell her that Joe's vehicle had hit an incendiary device planted in the road but beyond that she knew no particulars. She later learned that four American soldiers had been killed that day. Joe survived the first attack and tried to pull another soldier from the demolished vehicle. As he worked to free the soldier, a grenade struck the vehicle, finishing the job the first had not. She is comforted knowing that Joe will always be a hero; no one can take that from him.

~~

Retha was numb. Her sisters pleaded with her to take medication to help her sleep but she refused; she felt drugged enough. She walked in a fog and laid in her bed or the guest bed at Jessie's house for days. She tried not to think and then she thought too much. She tried not to feel. She wanted to die. Why couldn't she go with Joe? She wondered if she would find him if she died right away? Why had he left her? What was God doing? Retha had thought she and Joe were favorites of God. Her mother had always told her God has no respect of person but Retha thought God would protect her from more hurt. How much more could she bear? She felt like she had just lost her mother and father a few days ago, then Joe.

Aida, Retha's mother-in-law, saw the degree of Retha's pain and decided to remain in San Antonio for a while after the other members of Joe's family returned home. Retha had always liked Aida but after Joe's death she started to love the woman. Aida tried to provide comfort when there was none to be had. "You are young. You'll love again. Not the same love. No love is the same. Joe loved you too much to want you to stay alone. You remember that. He loved you so much at first I wondered what you, such a young girl, had done to him, but soon I could see why for myself. I thank you for being a good wife to my son and giving him the good life he deserved. He was so happy with you."

After Aida's speech Retha broke down and cried again. Aida cried with her. The two women embraced on the sofa and shared their tears until Retha sobbed herself to sleep with her head in Aida's lap. Aida sat there with the salted tears streaming down her face. What they had lost was too great to comprehend. Aida knew they had to leave their loss to God.

One month after Joe's death, Retha returned to work. Her position within the Army's medical teaching academy consisted of teaching administrative procedures and regulations to Army medical officers. The command released her from all her instructing duties and assigned her to the teaching department's operations and administration branch. No one other than a newly assigned branch chief seemed to expect any work out of her. Major James Freeman kept her busy with projects that distracted her from her loss.

Being in the house alone was the hardest part but Retha craved that solitude which allowed her mind to dwell on Joe. One day about seven months after Joe's death, Retha answered the phone and heard a "Hello" in Joe's voice and pitch. Retha nearly fainted with joy. She imagined there had been a mistake and Joe was calling her. It turned out to be JJ sounding more like his dad than his dad had.

"Abuela said she hasn't talked to you lately. You probably should call her because she really worries about you, Mom." He had started calling Retha "Mom" several years earlier and his mother, Marta, seemed to take no offense in sharing her son.

"I wish she wouldn't worry about me. I'm doing okay. How are you and the rest of the family?"

"I'm fine but Abuela is tired. She seems exhausted since dad's death."

"I'll call her later. Does she need anything?"

"No, she's okay just still a little out of it. I start college next week you know. I promise to come see you during the Christmas break. I told Mami I am spending at least one week with you, okay?"

"Okay. What about your mother? You think she might come with you?"

Marta got on the phone and she and Retha talked for quite a while longer. Retha promised to pay them a visit and invited Marta out for the holidays. Marta accepted the invitation.

The conversation with JJ made Retha aware of her desperation for a relationship with Joe. Nothing filled the emptiness. At times the pain was so intense she curled up in the fetal position and cried. When Jessie found her crying one afternoon, she pulled Retha to her knees and told her that Joe would be brokenhearted if he saw her so unhappy. Retha realized that the most painful thing about death when you love and are loved must be leaving the people you love behind and worrying about their sorrow, their pain, their loneliness, their ability to have a good life after you have gone. She knew that if Joe had a sense of her pain and anguish he would be unhappy. After that conversation with Jessie, Retha worked hard at feeling less miserable.

Genuine joy did return. She started to laugh and not feel guilty about laughing. She started to laugh without thinking about how much Joe would enjoy whatever it is that caused the laughter. Retha grew up around lots of family laughter. Her mother's family, the Solomons, joke and laugh about everything. The worse the situation, the more humor they find when they recant the tale. Solomons truly take life very seriously but they are so in awe of God that they know not to take themselves too seriously. So they laugh. Solomons, especially Grays, don't laugh out of malice at the misfortunes of others. They laugh at themselves and each other most of all. They laugh at what they consider remarkable behavior, like Cousin Purvis and his wife going on *Divorce Court* or the time Uncle Sugar took Retha's brother Raymond on a thug bombing mission. Thankfully, the mission failed.

One of Retha's favorite offbeat recollections is about the funeral of her Aunt Faye's second husband. Aunt Faye was fifteen years older than Retha's mother, Wanda, and lived in Los Angeles, about three hundred and thirty miles south of her family in Seaside. Three carloads of family from Seaside drove all night long to make it to that funeral. They all piled into Aunt Faye's little two bedroom home and showered, dressed, and ate before the service. As expected, Aunt Faye was upset at the death of her relatively new husband. Wanda, being the helpful younger sister she always tried to be, gave Aunt Faye a Phenobarbital tablet to calm her nerves. So Aunt Faye, who was stoned from the barbiturate and her relatives, most of whom had completed a three hundred mile car trip just a few hours before the service began, sat and slept throughout her dearly departed husband's funeral service.

Uncle Sugar pulled out many of these old ridiculous stories and told them whenever Retha was around. To Retha it seemed the whole family was dedicated to cheering her up and getting the old Retha back but the old Retha was gone forever; she left with Joe.

Joe had provided well for his family. Jessie always told Retha to be fair with JJ and his mother. "Make sure you consider that baby like you would your own child," Jessie would say. So Retha insisted she and Joe take out extra life insurance policies that more than tripled the amount Uncle Sam offered. Joe had balked but Retha insisted. Retha's father had always pressed home the value of life insurance, particularly for poor folks. "No sense in being broke and in mourning," Donald had always told his family.

These monies provided Aida with the additional income Joe had always provided. College for JJ was not a financial issue and he had a large trust fund for later in life. Marta was able to focus on her own financial future instead of spending every extra dime on JJ. These are good things and maybe lessen the trauma of a lost son, father, husband, and friend, though they do nothing to alleviate the sorrow and the emptiness.

Retha doesn't have to rush into anything now that she is out of the Army; she has the luxury of taking her time. Her home was paid off by mortgage insurance and she has plenty of money in the bank and investments. The Army will pay her a death indemnity check as long as she doesn't marry. She can live easily on that check and her savings for the remainder of her life. Other than a substantial investment in Uncle Sugar's Place, she will use the funds in her investments and those from Joe's life insurance only in the strictest emergency.

Yes, Retha reached financial security at too great a cost very early in her life and for a long time after Joe's death she did not consider her life worth living. She did not stop wishing for her own death until she survived that attack during her second tour in the besieged nation of Iraq.

That last tour in Iraq was just as cushy as the first, but she often found herself leaving the safety of the Green Zone for one reason or another. Things had settled down so much that many of the soldiers who were not out fighting the insurgency took on a false sense of security. So when the RPG hit the Hummer Sergeant First Class

Lindo and her fellow soldiers were traveling in, they were taken completely off guard.

When Retha became conscious she was in the hospital with a stitched up outer thigh and a badly bruised forehead. It took all her strength not to yell and scream when she heard that Private Travis had lost his life. He had been in country exactly two weeks. Sergeant First Class Mason, who lost his lower left leg, had been evacuated out of country to Ramstein Air Force Base in Germany where he was stabilized and then sent back to the States for further care. At the time of the attack, Retha had less than a month left in country. She received numerous counseling sessions after her injuries, yet continues to have nightmares about the attacks on Joe and her. One thing was certain to Retha after that tragedy, she wanted to live.

Chapter 3 -- Friendship

The day before the Fort Sam Houston Youth Activities Games, Jeremiah was astonished when his brother informed him that they needed to swing by and pick up Jaren Daniels who would join them for dinner. Richard often spoke as if he and Daniels were good friends. As dynamic as Richard is, Jeremiah found it hard to believe that his brother was a close friend to Daniels who, by every account, is a star on and off the field. But there they were, on the eve of the Youth Activities Games, sitting in El Mirasol, one of San Antonio's best Mexican restaurants, laughing and talking with none other than the New York Liberty outfielder.

Jerry, as his close friends and family often call him, listened quietly as his brother grilled Jaren about his sudden decision to volunteer his time to the games. "Man the way you sounded, I didn't think there was any way you could get out of going to that wedding. What really happened? They didn't call it off did they?" Richard took a drink from his Corona.

"Hey, if I tell you I'm gonna do a thing then I try to do it but I don't like to get involved in a lot of complicated crap, that's all." Jaren's reminiscence irked him slightly and it showed. "No they didn't call off the wedding, at least not as far as I know. I don't know the groom or the bride. I was going with a friend. I hated to drop out but hey, she deserved it." He leaned back in his chair, picked up his brew, took a swig and looked away indicating he was finished with the subject.

Since Jaren and Richard work on opposite coasts, it had been awhile since they spent time together. Jaren had forgotten Richard's persistence and love of gossip. "Nah dude, you didn't just drop the babe at the last minute like that did you? Here she probably bragged to her friends that she was bringing you and you're a no show. That's embarrassing." Richard leaned forward and looked his friend straight in the face as if to make sure he was not an impostor. "That ain't like you. Must have been some serious shit for you to do something like that -- you being such a gentleman and all." Richard grinned wickedly, quite satisfied at the chink in Jaren's armor.

Jeremiah enjoyed watching and listening to his brother badger Jaren about his personal life. Jaren sat there with a slight smile on his face and allowed Richard to delve into things that were none of his concern. After several attempts at changing the subject, Jaren opened up and told his friend what he wanted to know. "You know it can get hard to meet genuine people when you're in our job. The last thing I need or I should say what I can't stand is when a person pretends we are a couple. Vanessa had people thinking I was about to propose to her. We don't have that type of relationship. I don't like being used. That says something pretty bad about a person who would act like that. Wants me walking around holding on to her like I'm a piece of jewelry for her to show off. Hell no. Screw her!" Guilt was biting Jaren; otherwise he would not have been quite so hostile.

At that point, Richard had leaned back and thrown up both hands indicating surrender. "Okay man, chill! I just hope you don't want your money back. That's the biggest damn donation we ever received. That colonel damn near shit his pants when I gave it to him. Thanks."

"Well, at the time, I thought that was the least I could do. I felt bad about not coming but wanted to help out. I mean as many times as you've helped me in the past, I owed you and this is a good cause. When I couldn't make it last year, I told myself I'd be here this year. So, now you got all my money and me too."

Richard let out a sarcastic laugh and looked at Jeremiah. "All his money. Listen to this fool. He's full of it." Changing the subject he moved on. "So listen, my brother's got one of his girlfriends cooking dinner for us tomorrow night at his place. He says she can really cook. You know he's single too so he's got it like that."

Jerry decided to join the conversation. "She's not my girlfriend. I told you she's just a good friend. She used to be my boss, but she can cook, so you guys better loosen your belts. Hey, how about going deep sea fishing with us Sunday morning?" he asks Jaren.

"Deep sea fishing in San Antonio?" Jaren looked confused.

"Man, don't show your ignorance," Richard joked. "What you got to get back to? Come on and stay over another night and go down to Corpus with us early Sunday. We chartered a boat all to ourselves. It's great out there on the ocean. We try to go every year. How about it?"

Jaren had considered the invitation for a moment and concluded that Richard was indeed right. He didn't have any good reason to get back to Tampa. He had planned to carry things to the next level with Vanessa after they had partied at the wedding reception. He had not doubted for one minute that he would wake up in her bed Sunday morning. Once he figured out that she was much more interested in his status as a ballplayer and his money than him, he lost all patience with her. He might have accepted her pretenses to her acquaintances if she hadn't hurt his ego. He sure wasn't going to sleep with a woman that didn't want him for much more than to show off. "Sure, why not? Me and my dad have been talking about going out but never get around to it. This'll be a first for me. I hope you got a reliable boat."

The brothers answered together. "The best on the Texas coast."

~ ~

While the Rojas brothers were out entertaining each other and Jaren Daniels, Retha had very wisely started cooking up food for Jeremiah's dinner the next day. Luckily, Jeremiah and his brother are simple men and prefer plain home cooking. Jeremiah told Retha that Richard loves barbecue and that is what he always wants when he comes home to Texas.

Retha cleaned the pork ribs and put on her own special rub. That way all she would need to do is grill them when she returned from the games. She made a potato salad, mixed up her baked beans so she could just pop them in the oven before dinner the next day, made homemade rolls, and baked Jeremiah's favorite German chocolate cake.

During her labor of love, Retha's school buddies, Simone and Brenda, called. Retha explained that she was busy in the kitchen but they had news and wanted to chat. There was no way to get them off the phone short of hanging up on them. Retha, Brenda, Simone and their other friend, Michele, have been close friends since junior high school and their bond is tight. All four live in different cities. Brenda lives in Dallas, Simone in LA, Michele in Seattle, and, of course, Retha in San Antonio.

"Who you cooking for anyway? They should be cooking for you. You the one getting her freedom," Brenda voiced her always available opinion.

"Jeremiah," Retha answered.

"Who?" Simone was baffled. Brenda remembered Jeremiah well, though. "You know that cute young Mexican sergeant she be hangin' with."

"Oh him. Brenda, you think everybody's cute."

"He is cute. Just a little too young and the wrong color for me."

"Did y'all call me to argue? Because if you did, I don't have time." Retha tried to get the ladies back on task.

"Well excuse me, Miss Thang. We called to give you your escape from Alcatraz and graduation present, Miss Summa Cum Laude." Simone moved on with purpose.

"Did she graduate summa cum laude? Retha did you graduate summa cum laude? I did not know that!" Brenda is impressed.

"See, I'm smarter than y'all thought but that was with my BA. I'm happy to have finished my MBA. What's my present? It should be damn good, considering that it's for two degrees."

"You better be glad we remembered at all. Besides I sent you a card for that first one. I didn't know you were one of the laudes, though. Girl, if I had known that, I would have spent more on the card." Brenda had burst out laughing with gusto before getting back to the reason for the call. "We want you to go to New York with us in January. We're buying your ticket as part of your graduation gift."

Retha was pleasantly shocked but the appreciation of her friends' gift did not immediately manifest itself. She hesitated for a moment. "What are y'all going to NYC for in the dead of winter, to see Bennie and Jackson and what is the other part of my gift?" Retha asked, a little concerned by the sacrifice her two financially strapped friends were making.

Simone explained, "Well yeah, but mainly for us to get together again and have fun and celebrate your graduation and your freedom from Uncle Sam. We're working on Mitch too. Do you know how long it's been since the four of us got together and partied? We need to have a good time like we used to when we were at home. That is the other part of your gift, the four of us all together. We know how much you love the city in the winter, so it's our gift to you. It's also the only time we can all get away. It's a new beginning trip for us."

Retha hardly knew what to say after hearing her friends' generous invitation. She had reservations, mainly because Brenda is extremely tightfisted with money and Simone has been on a tight budget since her recent divorce. She agreed that it would be fun to get together with her friends and knew she couldn't turn down their offer.

"It'll be a blast Retha. Why you so quiet?" Brenda asked.

"It's a great idea. You guys know I'll go, but I can't let you pay my way."

Simone stopped her. "No. This is our gift to you. We want to do this and if you don't let us, you'll be taking away our pleasure. Let us be, what's the word, magnanimous."

"Well, I sure don't want to take away any pleasure you guys might derive from being mag whatever. Guess I'll just have to sacrifice and enjoy your gift, so long as you don't expect me to reciprocate. Now I'll have our trip to look forward to and I won't be so distraught about unemployment, cleaning my house, and Uncle Sugar working me death. Thanks you guys. You are both so sweet and thoughtful. You know, just to show you how much I appreciate your gift, I'll travel broke so y'all can pay for everything and be even more generous."

Brenda stopped Retha in her tracks. "Oh no, the airfare is about all we can afford. As it is we'll have to stay with Auntie and Uncle Jackson." The Jacksons are Simone's Aunt Bennie and her husband Willie Jackson who live in Manhattan on West Eighty Eighth Street. *Ah, there is a snag in the plan right there, no hotel; don't complain.* They will be cramped staying in the Jacksons' home. But, Retha could smell Zabar's as thoughts of the city rose in her consciousness. She listened to her girlfriends for a few minutes longer before telling them she had to go, explaining that she would mess up or burn up her food if she stayed on the phone a minute longer. Brenda and Simone reluctantly let her off the call with promises to talk later.

Retha never has much to say when they are on three-way. She has always been the quiet one of the bunch. "Reserved" is the term her coworkers used to describe her. Her friends have other not-so-nice terms for her.

Often Retha feels slightly inadequate in the personality department when it comes to her old friends from school, but a rock concert might seem dull compared to Brenda. Brenda never holds back and is completely fearless when it comes to her life. Actions, opinions, relationships are just there for the living and giving with Brenda. Her personality is so abrasive; one would never know that her true art is music. Girl can blow. She sings and plays piano for her church choir and often performs with a local Dallas band called "them nappy headed boys." She earns her living as an MRI tech.

As with many women, Brenda is not content unless she is involved with a man, resulting in relationships with very, shall we say, challenged men. Brenda jumps into these relationships headfirst and when she is seriously involved she never looks at another man, no matter how challenged her lover. Her friends get blow by blow accounts of each of these relationships – the sweet, the sour, and the strange. Brenda will remain madly and deeply in love and deal with quite a bit of crap until suddenly she stops and turns cold as an Arctic winter. Her lover never sees the change coming. It is always the same. The dumpee will hang on for months trying to break the ice but once Brenda freezes up on him, he will never sense her warmth again. That is exactly what happened with her ex-husband, Marshall. He had been a bit more challenged than most. It has been four years and he is still trying to get back inside Brenda's front door.

Michele is no less complicated than Brenda. Michele is full of book sense but has a dumb aura about her. There are few subjects Michele cannot discuss. She can lay down pertinent facts on everything from Bach to basketball, blues to botany. She plays trombone and has read both Baldwin and Browning. Michele cannot name one Seattle professional sports team. She can, however, describe in great detail any play on any field including golf and ice hockey using all the correct jargon. Mitch, as her buddies like to call her, says whatever comes to mind, though very polite about any possible insult she may verbalize unintentionally. Michele is the only one of the four that is currently married. She and her husband, Sean, have two children, six-year-old Julia and four-year-old Jordan. After Jordan's birth, Michele gave up her career as a high school teacher and coach to stay at home with her children. Brenda refers to Michele and Sean's marriage as a free-for-all because Sean has had a couple of affairs. Michele doesn't fool around on her husband but she is one of the world's biggest flirts. Michele's friends wonder why she and Sean stay together and give little credence to the couple's love for each other.

Simone is the unconditional leader of the four and that's mainly because she unconditionally accepts a lot of crap from the others and ignores their stupidity. She is the professional's professional. She is the administrator for a large Los Angeles-based realty investment and accounting firm. Simone's bosses, peers, subordinates, friends, and family all go to her to talk, moan and groan, and get her objective opinion. She can be trusted with anything. She is one of those people that can gossip without malice. If you get the dirt from Simone, it sounds almost clean. She never appears too reserved like Retha, overly abrasive like Brenda, or disinterested like Michele. Simone is just right. She always has plans and knows the best places to go and things to do. If her plans don't turn out for the best, she doesn't worry that people didn't enjoy themselves, she moves on. Simone is in the process of moving on in her life right now. She and her husband of six years, Gregory, are recently divorced. Retha and Brenda have decided this is an area where Simone has fallen short, not her marriage, but her communications skills. She has not discussed her marital problems, separation, or subsequent divorce with either of them. As Retha explained to Brenda, "You don't be married to a son of a bitch for six years and not give a rat's ass when it all ends. That can't be normal." Of course Brenda was in complete agreement with Retha's assessment of Simone and both were quite happy to find fault in their friend.

As different as they all are, the friends always have a good time together. They disagree, never resolve an argument, chide each other, get deep off into each other's business, and keep on loving and liking each other anyway.

Chapter 4 -- The Meeting

After leaving the games, Retha tries to get away from her sister Jessie's home without her nephew. As she backs the car out of the driveway, RJ dashes out of the front door and heads straight to the passenger's side of Retha's Explorer. "Auntie Jessie said I can go with you 'cause you might need help."

Retha had known RJ would want to hang out with her as much as possible over the weekend because Jessie's husband, Robert, is out of town on business and son, Mykol works weekends. Mykol is still a big kid and he loves to take his younger cousins on when it comes to video games. He and his wife Nicola have recently had their first baby. *Jessie thinks she slick. She doesn't want to be bothered so she sends this little pushy munchkin with me. That's okay. Mykol will be off this evening and he promised RJ a trip to Dave and Busters to play games. Hopefully, Nicola won't throw a wrench in that plan.*

Retha and RJ stop by her house to pick up the food and haul it to Jeremiah's. Once there, she gets the fire started and allows the meat to cook while she prepares arroz con gandules, tosses a salad, makes a couple of salad dressings, and puts the beans in the oven to bake. Everything is finished and ready to eat by five.

While she is cooking, Jeremiah's Aunt Maria storms in from Hondo. Maria raised the Rojas brothers since they were in elementary school. She is not too happy with her nephews because a trip to her house in Hondo is not part of Richard's three-day Texas itinerary. Maria's accent seems thicker than usual because she is upset with her nephews. "Dis, dis como tu disay 'sobrino?'"

"Nephew," Retha answers, knowing Maria knows the word in English but is too agitated to take the time to think it up.

"See, nepew, muy grande baseball player. He fine tine fo de games pero no tine fo me in Hondo. Oh, he can go dee sea fishing. See, mucho tine for dis but no tine to dri to Hondo to see me. So, I come here. Das okay. No big deal."

"Maria, let them do their macho male bonding thing and you come and hang out with me tomorrow. I'm having friends over for gumbo in the evening. Besides I promised to take you downtown the next time you came up. So we can do that early tomorrow."

Maria is happy to accept. Even before Retha invited her, she had planned to spend the day with her young friend while her inconsiderate nephews are off doing some stupid manly thing. She does not understand where they learned this selfishness. She raised them to be more considerate.

Jeremiah and Richard are devoted to their aunt but they refuse to give in to her manipulating ways as often as she likes. The brothers call her the master manipulator. Maria just returned from a two-month stay with Richard and his family in California only two weeks ago but is still upset that her nephews aren't visiting her in Hondo during Richard's three-day visit with his brother.

The ladies visit while RJ plays outside with the neighborhood children. Retha makes the mistake of telling Maria she does not plan to return later to meet Richard because she has to prepare for her own dinner party on the following evening. She should know that Maria the Master will not allow her to stay away. Maria is a pit bull when she sets her teeth into you and they are deep in Retha at the moment. "Okay, okay Maria. I will stop in for a few minutes to meet your Mr. Muy Grande Baseball Player." Retha surrenders as she backs out the door and causes Maria to laugh at herself.

Retha knows that more than likely Jeremiah's girlfriend Carla and her friends will be over for dinner. These women do not care for Retha who chalks their dislike up to immaturity. Carla, who is also in the Army, has started a rumor that Retha is a lesbian and has tried to date one of her friends. When Retha learned of the rumor she laughed and later asked Jeremiah to point out which of the ladies she was interested in so she would know. The fact that to most people's knowledge Retha does not date, adds credence to the rumor.

James Freeman is the only person Retha has dated in the past three years. She hasn't discussed the details of their relationship with anyone, not even her sisters. After Joe's death, James helped Retha regain normalcy in her world by showing her life was still worth her involvement. He made her laugh and she felt safe with him. Retha was not attracted to James but thought she would never desire another person sexually if she did not make the effort. She and James spent a great deal of time together and became good friends before they tried to be lovers. The sexual relationship between the friends ended quickly when Retha realized that as much as she desired sexual intimacy she needed to wait until she felt a connection that was more than trust, lust, or friendship. James remains a good and constant friend who accepts her decision and Retha is content being alone.

--

After a quick stop by Jessie's to drop off RJ, Retha gets home, washes her hair, and sinks into a soothing tub full of warm scented water with a glass of Pinot Grigio and a new Walter Mosley novel as her companions. The bath is sweetly divine and before long she catches herself dozing off. She emerges from the tub after more than an hour, puts on her favorite scented lotion, applies more curl moisturizer to keep her hair from turning into an uncontrolled mass of wild naps, throws on a pair of jeans, a sleeveless blouse and a pair of slide sandals. She finishes with a huge pair of silver hoop earrings that Jessie always complains make her look ghetto and a little lip gloss. Retha has to laugh at the amount of time she spends on herself trying to look like she hasn't spent much time on herself. *Must be a sign of getting older.*

--

Although Maria is not happy with her nephews, they are surprised and pleased to find her waiting for them. Maria is like the sweetest, most loving grandmother toward Raheem and flourishes hugs and kind words upon Jaren while barely giving her nephews her ass to kiss. Richard reacts to the cold treatment but Jeremiah is immune. Right now his mind is on one thing, the food on the stove smelling so damn good.

"Where's Retha?" Jerry asks, as he looks into the pots and pans on the stove. "Was she here when you got here?"

"Who you tink did dis. Retha, chee go to home. Chee no come back, 'til I tell her chee mus to meet chu brotha. Chee may no come. That woman, chee no good to Retha, ah Dios mio!"

Jeremiah shrugs off his aunt's complaints about Carla. There are many people and things in the world that others find worthwhile but Maria labels as garbage. Carla, without argument, question, or thought tops that list. Jeremiah does not try to make his aunt like his girlfriend or vice versa. He tries to keep them apart or to at least not be in the room when they are in the room together.

Maria goes on to complain about her nephews not visiting her in Hondo, their planned fishing trip the next day, not being invited on the fishing trip, why Richard did not bring his wife and children to visit, her most recent doctor's appointments, Retha working herself so hard and cooking two big dinners in one weekend, the weather, and just about everything including why we don't know the day and the hour of the second coming of Christ.

Jeremiah listens and when Maria takes a breath he responds to the one thing he has not heard many times. "So you're hanging out with Retha tomorrow, Tia?"

"Chee cook de gumbo for me. Que linda, that Retha, chee shu be me sobrina."

"She's cooking gumbo tomorrow?" Raheem asks. "She's gonna have to save me some of that."

Jeremiah slaps his friend's hand in agreement. Still wearing the uniforms they've had on all day, Jeremiah and Raheem head off to separate baths to get showered and dressed.

Maria settles Richard and Jaren down with huge plates of food. Her mood mellows while she laughs and talks with her nephew and his friend but sours again upon the arrival of Carla and two of her girlfriends. Maria may have soured but the ballplayers are pleased to see three nice looking young women arrive.

Maria introduces the ladies to Richard and Jaren and she offers the ladies dinner, which they decline. Carla makes futile attempts at warming up to Maria who leaves the room rather than respond to the young woman.

While Maria is out of earshot, Richard and Jaren overhear Carla tell her friends that "the dyke" cooked the food. Carla's comment heightens both men's curiosity about Jeremiah and Raheem's friend, the cook. It is not long before their curiosity is at least partially satisfied. Retha rings the doorbell as Jeremiah joins his guests in the family room. She walks in looking tired and hurried, hoping for Maria's sympathy so she can dash in, meet Richard, and dash out. Retha stands in the family room with her back to the kitchen as she greets everyone.

Jaren and Richard can only see Retha from behind but Jaren is certain she is the young lady he saw earlier at the games. Richard looks at Jaren with a question on his face. Retha is not what he expected. Jeans hug her curves, the voice is low and mellow, smooth dark chocolate skin, and a thick nappy mass of hair; *she's rich.* Richard gives Jaren an appreciative smile. Hearing Retha tell Jeremiah she just stopped by to meet his brother, he licks his fingers in turn, half wipes his hands on a napkin, stands up from the table where he has been sitting and eating for nearly forty-five minutes and approaches her. Retha turns and laughs as she misses colliding into his massive chest. She greets Richard like they are old friends and gives him a handshake and a peck on the cheek.

"Excuse my hands. They're a little sticky. We been throwin' down on the food you cooked. It's good. You don't know how much me and Daniels appreciate it. It's not often we get food like this and I'm not just saying that."

"Well, thank you. You're more than welcome. Jeremiah said you love barbecue." Retha's lips move but her brain is in a tizzy. *Did he say "Daniels?" No, it couldn't be -- no, not Jaren Daniels.* As calm starts to prevail, Richard steps aside to introduce her to his friend who has stood up at the table.

Retha does all she can to keep her mouth from dropping open and steady herself. She sees a smile of recognition on Jaren's face and can't help but smile back. Outward calm prevails as she walks over to Jaren and extends her hand. "I promise not to bite you," she says loud enough for everyone to hear. She and Jaren laugh at the private joke, leaving everyone else curious about the humor.

Jaren greets Retha but she's not sure what he says. She mumbles a response with what she knows is a stupid smile pasted on her face. Retha's insides are haywire and she finds it hard to stay calm. She needs to get outside to collect herself because she is short of breath. It's embarrassing and she prays no one notices her excitement. She stays a while longer and chats a little with everyone including Carla and her friends. It seems as if Jaren is watching her more than necessary. She wonders if there is something wrong with her appearance or if he is aware of the effect he has on her.

After ten minutes, Retha starts making excuses to leave. Maria protests loudly along with Richard, but Retha explains she needs to prepare for the next day's dinner. Jeremiah has his opening. "What's this about a gumbo party for my aunt that I'm not invited to? How you gonna play me, Sarg?"

"You know you don't need an invitation. You're always welcome. But I know you and Raheem plan to take your brother to the coast tomorrow. When are y'all leaving anyway?"

"Early in the morning, but you know what? We'll be back in time to show up at your place for that gumbo. That is if you mean what you say about me always being welcome."

Without waiting for a response, Jeremiah turns to Richard and Jaren. "Hey, when we get back tomorrow, you guys want to go over to Retha's and eat her out of house and home? She's cooking gumbo."

Retha stands very still with that same stupid smile on her face and prays they decline.

Richard practically yells, "Oh hell yeah!"

"If your gumbo is anything like this food, I'd sure like to try it," Jaren adds, smiling and looking directly at Retha, increasing her unease.

Retha turns and looks at Raheem. "You know I'mo be there," he replies.

~ ~

Retha gets home and starts preparing for Sunday. She straightens up her house and starts prepping her ingredients for the gumbo.

She knows a couple of her friends will be disappointed that men will be at their party; these dinners are for women. That way they can sit around and bad mouth men, drink a little, dance with each other and have fun. Later they put in a movie and swoon over the male lead, at least those into men swoon.

The plans for Sunday's dinner have changed considerably. Even before Jeremiah weaseled invitations, Retha had invited James Freeman. So James would not be the lone male in a house full of women, she had asked her friend Rachel to bring her husband, Jonathan, along. Rachel was disappointed but agreed. Jonathan and James have met before and enjoy each other's company. Now that Jeremiah and his friends are coming to dinner, Retha will not need to worry about so few men at her dinner party.

There is one problem. Retha does not want the ballplayers at her home, particularly not Jaren Daniels. Nothing short of a major accident will keep Jeremiah and Raheem away but there is a possibility they will be so tired when they return from the coast that Jaren and Richard may bow out and not show up for dinner. Disappointment at the thought – *What is it you want Retha, the man to show or not and what difference does it make anyway? Good God, he is just a man.*

Retha is more upbeat than she has been in a long time. She is moving around like a schoolgirl. She stops her busy work and sits down to get a grip. *Okay the reality is that I'm happy because this man excites me and it's been a long time since I've been excited over a man. I'm not going to let him bother me. Bask in his presence while he's here and get on with life. Jaren Daniels will never give me the time of day.*

--

Jeremiah and his friends leave San Antonio at three the next morning to get to Corpus for their fishing trip. Jaren and Raheem are deep sea fishing for the first time. Once they are on their way, sitting on the open deck and sensing the boat's sway in the water has the effect of clearing Jaren's mind -- it's revitalizing. He begins to reflect on the things he wants out of life. He seldom worries about long term goals because life is so good right now; he can't imagine it getting any better. Jaren has worked hard at learning from the past, living for the moment, and preparing for the future. He's improving on his game and that is the most important thing for him. Baseball – that's where it's at. He lives and breathes the game and he's getting better. He is a contributor and often he is the difference between a win and a loss.

Jaren's family is the one thing more important than baseball. His father, Charles is a good friend and role model who taught him the game. Susan, his mother cherishes him and in turn he cherishes her. Susan is a little pushy and a bit too involved in his life but Jaren believes she always means well. His younger sister, Rachelle, is his greatest love. She is a spoiled but level-headed college student who can get anything she wants from her father or brother but asks for very little.

He doesn't have a serious relationship with any one woman and is in no hurry to see that change. After all, he is still young so why should he rush into a stifling commitment. If a woman interests him and she is willing, he asks her out, maybe. He has lots of female friends and those friendships often get mistaken for more than they are but seldom by the participating parties.

Jaren stands up and allows the breeze to hit him in the face as he watches the Rojas brothers handle their reels. They seem to love what they are doing and competing with each other. It has been a great trip so far, simple and easy. He hasn't even been asked for an autograph since leaving the fields where the games were held. He enjoys the company of these down to earth Texas boys and their Iranian-American friend. Their hospitality has been unsurpassed. Aunt Maria reminds Jaren of his grandmother, manipulation and all. Jeremiah's girlfriend and her friends were fun to hang out with. At first they were a little hostile, but after the cook left they warmed up considerably and almost ate the house down.

Jaren smiles when he thinks about the cook as he and Richard have referred to Retha since meeting her yesterday. *She is a babe and funny, too.* Women have come on to him in every way imaginable but, before yesterday, one had never threatened to bite him. He is curious about Retha. Why are the other women so hostile toward her? Is it because Jeremiah and Raheem like her so much? Why did she cook dinner for them and not the aunt or the girlfriend? Retha ran herself ragged at the games on Saturday morning; Jaren saw her. He finds it hard to believe that she went home and cooked all that food after such a busy morning. She was pleasant and friendly but kept her distance from him; that was odd. Jaren is exhausted but not too tired to show up at Retha's for dinner. He likes her and wants to learn exactly what there is to like.

Chapter 5 -- Another Generous Offer

Retha's Sunday is more relaxing. She and Maria make a short trip downtown to El Mercado where they stroll through the markets considering many items but purchasing next to none. The ladies sit outside of La Margarita and drink frozen margaritas and talk for well over an hour.

When they enter Retha's home, she finds a message from Jeremiah beeping away on the answering machine. "Retha, hey where you at? You should be there cooking. Anyway, it's almost four and we're just getting ready to leave Corpus. We'll probably show up to your place about eight – eight thirty or so." Jeremiah yells at his fishing companions. "Could you guys hold down the noise? I'm tryin' to talk here." He speaks back into the phone. "Sorry about that. I hope you cooked a lot. These guys don't want to stop and pick up anything. They say they're saving it all for you." Jeremiah laughs. "Anyway, see you in a bit. Give Tia my love. Hey, tried your cell phone but as usual you didn't answer."

Retha hears the other men yelling in the background that they expect plenty of food. If they're coming, Retha wants them to bring big appetites. She loves to feed and entertain people; hospitality is her calling.

With the gumbo, she will serve rice, homemade corn muffins, and a tossed salad. Since she has extra guests coming to dinner, she asks Charmaine to pick up a few dozen chicken wings on her way over. She bakes a huge peach cobbler and has a full gallon container of Blue Bell Homemade Vanilla Ice Cream in the freezer. She will need to send the leftover cobbler and ice cream home with Jeremiah after she puts a little aside for her brother-in-law Robert, otherwise she will eat herself into a coma.

All Retha's guests are on time except the fishermen. Her friends start eating as soon as they drop purses, meet and greet each other.

Retha told most of her girlfriends that they would have men joining them but failed to mention it to Charmaine, who is indeed her closest friend in San Antonio, if you don't count family as friends. Charmaine looks at Retha with a raised brow and a tilt of the head upon spotting Jonathan and James when she arrives with her arms loaded down with chicken wings.

"Well, sister I would think if you were going to invite men you would at least invite enough for all of us. I might have been able to conjure up a date. What happened to the girls' night thang?"

"James is leaving in a couple of days. We have not spent time together in weeks. We've both been so busy trying to clear post and he's also been tied up with the games so, if it's okay with you, we'll suspend girls' night for tonight. I do owe you an apology though, because I told everyone but you that we would have men joining us this evening. And, oh, don't worry about more men. I'm expecting at least two to four more."

"Okay, as long as there's one for me. You just take me for granted. Got me hauling greasy-ass chicken wings over here like a crazy person but don't even bother to tell me I need to make myself presentable because old fine-ass James will be here. You must be a little threatened by a sister. I see you got your makeup on and what other men you talking about? Anybody I know?" Charmaine gives James a sultry wink as she harasses Retha.

"Jeremiah and Raheem for starts," Retha responds, slightly distracted by the bubbling over of her beautiful cobbler into her recently cleaned oven. "I hope that stuff doesn't run off that foil onto my oven. God knows I hate cleaning an oven, even a self-cleaning one."

"Hmm, Raheem. I better go put my makeup on." Charmaine makes a beeline to the powder room.

Each of Retha's female guests was caught off guard to find James relaxing in the family room. Their surprise does not stem from his gender but a general impression that he and their friend were no longer involved in any way. In recent months, Retha has barely mentioned his name causing a great deal of curiosity but her friends concluded that James and Retha had decided to go their separate ways. Charmaine is close enough to Retha to probe but she would not bother because Retha would give an unsatisfactory half answer or ignore the questioning all together. Retha likes to keep her business to herself. That way she doesn't need to explain things to people.

James Freeman is an intelligent, easy-going man who makes a very nice living in the military. He is nice looking with a friendly personality and dresses so well that on several dates Retha changed clothes after setting eyes on his attire. All of Retha's friends like him for her. Every thought tells Retha he should be the one. His aftershave alone is enough to turn the average woman on.

As much as Retha's female friends like James, her male friends are not impressed. The first thing Jeremiah and Raheem notice when they pull in front of Retha's raised ranch style home is James Freeman's truck parked in her driveway. Raheem does not hesitate in voicing his displeasure. "What the hell!"

"What's the matter?" Richard looks around for looming disaster as he asks.

Jeremiah explains, knowing exactly what's causing his friend's agitation. "Colonel Freeman, the one in charge of the games, is here. He's cool but he's always up in Sergeant Lindo's face. He's on his way to Korea so I bet he's pulling out all the stops before he leaves."

After comments Carla and her friends made the night before, Richard needs to quench his curiosity about Retha. "Your friend, the cook?"

Jeremiah isn't taking the cook reference any longer. "Her name is Retha or Sergeant Lindo if that doesn't work for you."

Richard continues, ignoring his younger brother's comment. "So, she a lesbian or what, she don't like men?"

"Nah man. She's not gay." Raheem jumps in. "She was married. She's had a rough ride. Her husband got killed in Iraq on his second tour. She just not interested. Dudes on post say she cold but she's alright. Takin' her time, just takin' her time."

"What made you ask if she's gay? Did you hear Carla say that?" Jeremiah sounds more than a little upset.

"Chill, little brother. I was just wondering why she's by herself, that's all."

Raheem rings Retha's door bell, ending the discussion of her love life. The fishermen enter Retha's home starving and ready to eat anything in sight. Each of them gives Maria and Retha a hug and proceeds into the family room/kitchen area where the other guests are assembled. Retha introduces everyone and tells the guys to help themselves to dinner. Maria insists on serving so Retha helps. There's a card game going on at the kitchen table, so the new arrivals sit at the dining room table.

Retha's other guests, particularly her friends Rachel and Jonathan, are in awe of the two ballplayers. Jonathan and James stop playing bid whist in the middle of the game and join the other men at the dining room table. They talk about the fishing that day and what a good time they had on the coast but mostly the conversation is about ball, baseball in particular.

The other women are so excited over the ballplayers that Retha relaxes, except for those times she tries to sneak a peek at Jaren and finds his eyes on her.

Once again Jeremiah and his friends sit and eat nonstop for the better part of an hour. Retha was worried about leftovers but that will not be a problem. Her guests sop up every bit of the main course. Even those who don't care for okra seem to enjoy the gumbo.

Retha's friend Cherri turns off the television and turns on the music. Between the music, card playing, friendly conversation, and laughter, comfort eases in and envelops all. Retha becomes so relaxed that she finds herself having a friendly exchange with Jaren, an action she thought she could not achieve while breathing. But barriers come down quickly between open-hearted folks and Retha speaks her mind and asks exactly what she wants to know. "How do you deal with people gawking at you all the time and women always trying to hit on you? It must get really boring and bothersome after a while."

Jaren smiles a smile Retha hasn't seen and she can't help but stare as he answers her question. "Well, the women hitting on me part never gets boring but other things do get to be a bit nerve racking. You never know how people will react to you."

He seems too genuine. This guy's too good to be real.

"Well, I know if my brother-in-law and RJ knew that I had you guys over here tonight, they'd both be here vying for your time and attention."

"So where is your family? Why aren't they here tonight?" asks Richard who has been sitting quietly listening to Retha and Jaren.

"My brother-in-law has been out of town for over a week and got back this evening. My sister wanted to stay at home with him. They've been married for nearly twenty-seven years but still act like they're on their honeymoon."

While Retha and Richard talk, Jaren looks around Retha's home and takes note of the other guests. Her friends are as diverse as her possessions. Her friends Charmaine, Cherri, and Jonathan are black; Flo is Samoan; Joy is Filipino; James and Rachel are white; and Lori is Mexican American. Jaren is certain Cherri and Lori are lovers. He hopes Retha is straight. Her friends seem like a good group of people that enjoy getting together for a good time.

After a while Flo and Charmaine get up and start dancing a popular line dance. Soon Jonathan jumps in because he wants to learn the steps and Rachel has given up trying to teach him. When Fleetwood Mac's *Dreams* starts to play, James pulls Retha out into the middle of the floor to dance to one of his favorite songs. They have danced their two-step numerous times and move well together. Jaren is caught off guard by the emotion that creeps over him as he watches the couple. He physically shakes his body in an attempt to rid himself of the strangeness. Thankfully, Richard grabs Maria and Jerry grabs Joy to dance. Now there are others he can focus on. "Man you need to work on your timing," Jaren yells at Richard.

"Let's see you do any better," is Richard's big-grinned reply.

Retha stops to catch a call from her friend Simone. She speaks loudly over the music so everyone hears her end of the conversation. One topic catches Jaren's attention.

"I'm not spending my money going to see the New York Knicks."

"The Knicks are okay. They're not the San Antonio Spurs, but they'll do."

"Hey, you guys can go see them without me. Hell, those damn tickets probably cost an arm and a leg."

"I don't think so."

"Oh yeah, girl, you know I'm game for that." Retha starts to throw her head back in laughter but notices several pairs of eyes focused on her and realizes she is being rude. "Listen, I've got a house full of company, so I'll call you tomorrow and we can finish arguing about this."

"Are the Knicks coming to town soon?" Rachel queries before the phone is out of Retha's hand.

"No. Remember I told you my friends are treating me to a trip to New York in January. They love the Knicks, so they want to go to a game. Simone's uncle is a big fan and took us to games when we were young."

Jaren sees Retha's visit to New York as a perfect opportunity to continue their friendship and repay her for all the hospitality she has shown him. "So, what, you don't like the Knicks?" he asks.

"I like them fine but I'm not willing to pay Madison Square Garden prices to see them."

Without giving it any thought he offers, "I'd be grateful if you'd let me take care of that for you and your friends. It won't be a problem for me at all. I'd like to do a little more to thank you for the dinner and all."

Retha is speechless but not about the tickets. *I may have an opportunity to see him again. This is too good to be true.* The room is very quiet; probably because everyone is a little surprised by Jaren's offer. "You don't have to do all that to say thank you. I love feeding people. This is one of the things I do best."

"Oh, I know I don't have to. Right now I can't think of anything I want to do more than get tickets for you and your friends." He responds with such a direct look into Retha's eyes that she gets lightheaded and has to look away. She hates the ecstasy welling up inside her because it has nothing to do with the Knicks and is all about the way Jaren looks at her. She accepts his kind and generous offer.

Retha knows that financially the tickets are no burden for Jaren but she hates being obligated and depending on a man she barely knows to provide tickets for her and her friends. She makes a snap decision not to tell Brenda or Simone about his offer until she is certain he will come through.

The rest of the evening goes well but toward midnight the weekend is taking its toll on the host. Hints to her guests that she is tired shoot over their heads. Out of desperation she pulls Charmaine to the side. "Girl, you got to help me out. I need to go to bed and these people act like they want to stay all night."

"What you want me to do? Those are some fine men you got off in there. I think Raheem is trying to get up enough nerve to ask me out."

"Well, just give him your number and have him call you. No. Really. Listen. Can you say how tired you know I must be and that you're going to leave so I can get some rest."

Charmaine acts insulted. "I know you and I have gotten entirely too close if you have the nerve to just ask me to leave your house. You must think I like you."

"Yeah and I love you too," Retha responds with a hug.

Charmaine looks at her friend with disgust and for the first time realizes that Retha is worn out. No sooner than they join the others, Charmaine does exactly as requested with all the bravado of a paid actor. She wastes no time gathering her things, talking to Raheem on an aside, saying her goodbyes to the rest, and heading to the door. The other ladies and Jonathan soon follow.

Retha realizes that James plans to outstay the others. He, Maria and her nephews, and their two friends are the remaining guests. Maria takes the hint and tells the men they should go so Retha can rest.

Retha can tell Jeremiah and Raheem do not want to leave James with her. *Tonight is James's last night in town and they must think he is spending it with me. Well, that is not happening but it's none of their business.*

Maria gets her four men to the door but not without a great deal of expressed gratitude and fanfare. After they file out and start down the walkway with Retha standing in the doorway waving goodbye, Jaren stops and comes back. "I need to give you my number. I was wondering if you have a pen so I can write my home phone on the back." Jaren gives her that open direct look that she likes so much. Retha leaves the doorway and returns with a pen. Jaren writes down two numbers and asks if he can get hers. "Sure," is all Retha can squeak out. He gives her another card; she writes down her numbers and hands it back to him.

"So as soon as you know exactly what day you want the tickets, let me know."

"I will and thanks again for the offer, Jaren."

"You take care and again thanks for everything. I had a great weekend."

"I'm glad. Have a safe trip home."

Jaren hugs her, turns and walks away.

James has Erykah Badu playing on the stereo and is relaxing as if he has no intention of leaving. Retha gets her second glass of wine for the night and makes her mind up that James can stay all night long if he wants but she will finally rest. Now she realizes how tense she had been while the baseball players were in her home. She enjoyed them very much but their presence drained her, in particular the tall green-eyed one.

James will not try to stay the night. He wants a romantic relationship with Retha but is willing to take it slow. He stays for another ten minutes, gives her a copy of his orders and tells her he will call and write. They update email info and Retha wonders why Jaren did not give her his email address. James places a very gentle and sweet goodbye kiss on Retha's lips. Retha's heart is heavy after James walks out of her home. It will be a long time before she sees her good friend again but hopefully their time apart will help resolve her feelings for him.

Charmaine, Jessie, and Rachel each had encouraged Retha to have a relationship with James. Jessie said Retha should give him a chance and make the best of it. Rachel had even encouraged marriage. "You'd never have to work again if you married that man. You know he's going to be a general. He likes you enough to propose if he thought you would accept."

"He won't see general if he marries a black woman. He'd be lucky to see full colonel."

"Don't be silly, Cohen is married to a black woman and was Secretary of Defense."

"His wife is so light, she could almost be white and I'm so black I'm hard to see at night. There is a difference."

Rachel was offended and told Retha she wished she wasn't so hard on white people. "We're not all that bad," Rachel pouted.

"White people are not the only ones who discriminate against people with dark skin. Black folks are guilty too," Retha informed her friend.

Chapter 6 -- A New Start

After such a busy weekend it is hard to relax. After such a busy life it is hard to take it easy. What it comes down to is that Retha does not enjoy doing much of nothing. She does not want to sit back and read or watch television, the two things she thought would occupy her time for at least a month after she got out of the Army. One week into her unemployment finds her house spotless. Nine days in and the garage is cleaned out and reorganized. Two weeks in and she has finished painting the kitchen and bathrooms. Sixteen days of freedom find her winterizing the doors and windows. Retha still has more time than she wants for watching television and reading. After her third week she can't find a movie she wants to see.

Thanksgiving comes, providing a sweet respite from the monotony of a life without demands. Retha practically lives at Jessie's from Tuesday through Saturday Thanksgiving week. Raymond and RJ are down from Houston and one of her other brothers, Jermaine and his wife, Phyllis along with their two sons, Anthony and Jamaal, are visiting from San Diego.

Retha's two brothers are characters more like their Uncle Sugar than their father, Donald. Raymond is the kindest of the brothers though he loves to tease and make fun of his sisters and younger brother. Raymond is a tall, thin man, the tallest of all the Gray family men. He is a drug and alcohol counselor, a profession he is well suited for based on his life experiences. He works out of a number of halfway houses in the Houston area. He takes after his Uncle Sugar in his love of women. Raymond has been married and divorced three times and is looking for wife number four. For reasons his sisters cannot understand, women find him irresistible. He does have an easy-going kind and gentle spirit and a smile that often disarms the women in his family. A stranger would never guess at the wild streak in him.

Jermaine is eighteen months Retha's senior. He is in the U.S. Navy and has lived in San Diego with his family more than ten years. Jermaine makes a point of visiting San Antonio once or twice a year and always stays in close contact with family members in other cities. People love Jermaine as much as he loves people. As they say, you get what you give. Jermaine is a big fellow; though only six feet tall he carries a solid two hundred forty pound frame and walks around looking like he eats nails for breakfast but has a smile and personality that can light up any room he enters. He is the life of the party and tries to take over wherever he goes. His brothers and sisters find it necessary to keep him in check.

The brothers have discussed Retha's future and waste no time telling her what they have decided. Raymond does the talking. "Retha, me and Jermaine was talking. You should think about moving to San Diego with Jermaine and Phyllis and the boys. San Diego is nice and there's all kinds of good jobs for people with your work experience. Prior military can land a job like that," Raymond emphasizes by snapping his fingers, "and make good money too -- a whole lot more than you can make in San Antonio."

"Why do you want me to move to San Diego?" Retha asks as she turns to Jermaine, "so I can babysit those heathens of yours? No, I love San Antonio and I want to stay near Jessie so I can help her with Catrina when she needs it. Besides, I'm going to work with Uncle Sugar for a while. He needs help. That place is a mess."

Jermaine speaks without looking away from the food on his plate. "Sugar's not gonna let you change his place. He likes it the way it is."

"Oh yes he is. I've got money set aside to fix that place up."

"How much money?" "What kind of money?" The brothers ask in unison.

"Not much," Retha answers evasively.

Raymond and Jermaine had not considered how much help Retha provides Jessie and Robert with Catrina. They cannot challenge Retha's commitment to Jessie. Neither cares for the investment in Sugar's Place but would not dare try to stop Retha from helping their uncle. Business out of the way, the brothers resume their Thanksgiving celebration.

Jessie's home stays full of people and activity for the remainder of the holiday weekend. Robert has invited a couple of single men from his job to dinner. He has bragged to Jessie, Raymond, and Jermaine that one of the guys is "smooth" and the other is a "really good guy." Robert is certain one of his coworkers will capture his sister-in-law's interest.

Retha enjoys her family but, in her opinion, Robert's coworkers add to the clutter. Her brothers and brother-in-law watch as Mr.

Smooth strikes out. After a few liberating drinks, Jermaine confronts Retha. "Talkin' about ice maiden, what's your problem? You plan on being celibate the rest of your life?"

Retha makes a mental note that Jermaine's usually big mouth is running even more freely because he is drinking. She tries to ignore her brother and continues talking to Phyllis. Jermaine is not a person to be ignored. "Okay, you better answer me before I get loud in here."

"You are already a little too loud for my taste. You might be forgetting who you are talking to, brother." Retha gives him a look that lets him know she is serious.

"Answer my question."

Retha rolls her eyes at her brother, sucks her teeth in disgust and growls at him as she walks away. "I'm not even going to dignify that question with an answer."

Phyllis looks at her husband and tells him off for harassing Retha, finishing her lecture with, "Would you like for her to leave with one of these guys and go and lay up with him? Would that make you happy?"

"How you sound? How you gonna ask me some shit like that?"

"Well that's what it sounds like. You need to leave her alone and give her time."

Jermaine knows Phyllis is right, as much as he hates to admit it. He waves his hand at his wife in a downward motion indicating he's disregarding her as he walks away to find more mischief to get into.

True to form, the family survives Jermaine and Raymond's meddling in Retha's affairs and enjoys the holiday. Retha is saddest of all when her brothers leave for home that Sunday. She doesn't go home until after Raymond and RJ climb into Raymond's old F150 and head off to Houston. She reluctantly grabs her purse and heads toward Jessie's front door.

"You leaving, baby?" her sister asks.

"Yeah, I think I'll head on home. Let you guys rest. I know Robert is tired of company."

"Since when did you become company? I'm gonna lay right here on my sofa and let the television watch me." Robert mumbles as he stretches out on the sofa, happy his home is nearly guest-free again. He doesn't mind if Retha stays forever, but Retha knows it's time to give Jessie and Robert time alone together. Two things Robert and Jessie love about visitors: seeing them arrive and seeing them leave.

Jessie walks Retha out. She sympathizes with her sister's loneliness. Many times she has considered asking Retha to move in with her and Robert, but Retha is an independent woman. "Are you bored with all this time off? Looks like you're workin' yourself to death around that house. What are you going to do with yourself? You ready to start at Sugar's? That's gonna be a challenge."

"I know. I don't think I can hold out any longer. This relaxing crap is not all it's held up to be. I'll talk to you later. Love ya." Retha gives Jessie a hug and light peck on the cheek as she turns to get into her car.

"Love you too." Jessie watches as Retha pulls off and wishes she could fill a bit more of the chasm in her sister's life.

--

Retha is committed to work part time in Uncle Sugar's restaurant. She had planned to begin after the holidays but starts helping out after Thanksgiving. In the past, when Sugar was shorthanded, Retha, Jessie, and Robert helped out around the place. Since Sugar pays his employees poorly and is generally a lousy employer, he is often short of staff.

Retha recently invested thirty thousand dollars in Sugar's Place to help finance equipment upgrades and the overall atmosphere. Sugar's needs a complete redo, but how to do that and honor the overall juke vibe will not be an easy task. Sugar's regulars love his place. Retha and Sugar have discussed the changes at length and agreed that the best course is to make them gradually. So far, the changes are coming along smoothly with Sugar making all the decisions. Now Retha will become an active participant in the management of Sugar's. As long as she stopped by to help on occasion and voiced an occasional opinion with no weight behind those opinions, Sugar could easily ignore her. Retha is no longer occasional opinionated help, she is a major investor.

Sugar has a well-established customer base. Customers return even though his place is often closed when it should be open. There are times when he rents out the entire restaurant for parties, providing take out service only for others. Customers do not dare complain to Sugar. If they do, he is subject to curse them out if he knows them well or talk about them like they stole something if he doesn't know them at all.

Many patrons are faithful because Sugar's is one of the best spots in San Antonio to get home-style Southern cooking. Many return because Uncle Sugar is a character. When Retha was a child he was her favorite amongst her aunts and uncles. After seven wives, numerous girlfriends, a couple of short hitches in jail or prison and recurring drug problems, Retha became leery of her uncle. She simply tired of the drama. It became easier to avoid him than watch him self-destruct. His two younger sons, Gerald and Nathaniel, also live in San Antonio.

Jessie has never given up on Uncle Sugar. She has been as close to him as her brothers over the years. Not long after Retha moved to San Antonio, Jessie got her on the phone and gave her "what for" for ignoring their uncle. Then Jessie flipped the switch by using one of their mother's favorite lines. "You know where you been but you don't know where you going." Retha had to assess her behavior. She realized she had not given her uncle the respect and deference he deserved. Sugar had always been good to the members of his family and a good neighbor. He may not have been the best role model for his children, nieces, and nephews but he always told them what was right. Except for taking Raymond along on the bombing mission of the local neighborhood thugs, he had never encouraged wrong behavior. Soon Retha and Joe started spending more time with her uncle. Joe, Sugar, and Robert would go out hunting and fishing together and often Mykol, Nathaniel, and Gerald would tag along.

At sixty-two, Sugar has settled down considerably, though he continues to hawk Retha's twenty and thirty-year-old friends to the point of embarrassment. He was a good looking man at one time, but hard living shows all over his face and body now. He can still talk a good game, so Retha's friends tell her.

Three weeks after leaving the Army, Retha finds herself averaging thirty to sixty hours a week at Sugar's depending on how much he needs her. Retha relieves Sugar of many of his responsibilities. She is eager to learn the operation, take charge, and make decisions. Within days the restaurant has a new vigor and a constantly changing look. The atmosphere is bright and upbeat and the place is nothing less than spotless. Retha's hard work is contagious. She motivates everyone around her.

Sugar's Place captured Retha's heart long ago. She doesn't believe she will ever cook as well as her uncle. That is God's gift to Sugar, his special touch with making food just right -- so right, you can call it nothing less than delicious or excellent. But Retha believes she can cook well enough and loves her uncle's place enough to make it better. Once she jokingly asked him to sell her the restaurant. Sugar laughed and replied, "I'll leave it to you when I die."

Retha laughed back. "It wouldn't be any fun without you, Unc."

Sugar is more than a little tired but the place is his livelihood and his life. Sugar's Place is where he and his cronies get together and "talk shit;" where they go in the back office and smoke a now occasional cigarette and play cards; where they watch the young honeys come in and wish — oh how they wish. They remember too: some memories good, some needing to be forgotten. Sugar is a big man at his place. No way he would give it up, at least not while he lives.

The time put in at Sugar's completely washes away Retha's boredom. The customers are interesting; many are characters much like Sugar. There is always a lot of laughter and storytelling going on. Retha is a blessing to Sugar. He prays she will not give up on his place or him.

Chapter 7 -- I Just Hate to Beg

The restaurant is hard work. Often Retha drags in at the end of the evening too tired for anything but a hot bath and her bed. These are her plans tonight. She considers unplugging the phone and waiting until morning to check her messages. "Lord, please don't let anyone want me to call them back," she mumbles as she pushes the play button and plops into a kitchen chair next to the phone. She flips through her mail while listening to the messages.

"Hey girl! Hey, call me so we can solid up these plans for our trip to the city. Oh, and guess who I called last night. Craig, the lawyer I told you about. He wants to take me out. I'm tempted. Anyway, call me. Brenda's on the phone too. Call me and we'll do the three-way thang. Bye."

"Bye Bye, Re. I love you," Brenda squeezes in at the end.

The New York trip is an event Retha doesn't think on much lately. For a few days she had been caught up in anticipation of the trip. She conducted a reality check and decided to put the trip in the proper perspective. There is nothing worse than getting all hyped up looking for a good time and finding disappointment. Of course the time spent with her friends will make the trip more than worthwhile.

"It's me, Jerry. I'm driving down to Tia's on Sunday morning and spending the day. She wants you to come too. It's just me and Carla." There is a long pause before he continues. "I need you. So, how about it? I'll be out for a while. I'll try and catch you at Sugar's or call you tomorrow. Why don't you turn on that cell phone? I can never catch up with you." That was Jeremiah inviting her to ride down to Hondo with him and Carla to see Maria. *Not with that cat along for the ride. I'll send my prayers with that brother*.

The third message causes her to drop all of her mail to the floor. "Yeah, this message is for Retha. This is Jaren. Ah, call me when you get in. I need the dates you and your friends will be in town so I can get the tickets. Take care."

Tired, who's tired? Jaren Daniels called her and he is getting Knicks tickets for her and her friends. She has tried to keep her mind off of Jaren since meeting him. Thinking about him is sheer fantasy and Retha refuses to entertain fantasy. She has a hard enough time keeping Joe out of her dreams.

Retha hasn't mentioned the tickets to Simone or Brenda because she wasn't certain Jaren would come through. He might have been trying to impress Retha and her friends or may have forgotten his promise. Brenda would have called Jaren a day or two after he left San Antonio to ensure he came through with the tickets, but not Retha. She seldom asks anyone other than her very close friends or family for anything in the realm of a favor.

She decides to tell her friends about the tickets but not specify Jaren Daniels as their benefactor. Retha is certain that if her friends learn that a pro ball player is providing the tickets, they will apply pressure. Brenda, in particular, if she is familiar with Jaren, will ask Retha to act out of character. It might start with questions like, "What, this dude like you or somethin'?" next, "He got any friends we can meet? Hell, me and Simone wants us a baseball player too!" and, "You telling me, he's gettin' these tickets because he ate yo cookin'? You don't cook that good, Re."

After the questions will come the serious pressure. "Shit girl, you need to take advantage of this. Hell, I would." then, "Listen Re, if you ain't gonna do this dude, let me. I'll rock his world. We'll have baseball, basketball, football, and hockey tickets 'til the next millennium, shit," and finally the guilt trip, "Why you got to be so goody goody? If this guy likes you we could all get over. You ain't got to give him none, but I sure in the hell can't see why you wouldn't want to and he got those pretty green eyes too."

Retha imagines Simone sitting back and listening as Brenda applies the pressure and every once in a while saying "I know girl," or "You know how Retha is."

Brenda has the ability to embolden her friends. The fear is that Brenda might push Retha into a situation with Jaren. The reality is Retha will not need much of a push. *Damn his eyes are beautiful.* Retha remembers Jaren's face as she comes back from her condemnation of poor unknowing Brenda. She chastises herself for blaming her own lustful thoughts on Brenda who has yet to meet the man. This seals it for Retha. Brenda and Simone will not know about Jaren until they get the tickets in their hands. Retha knows she can't take the pressure. She envisions herself in a New York court charged with sexual assault on a young famous baseball player.

She must return Jaren's call but is uneasy about speaking with the man. She considers taking her bath and drinking a glass of wine to relax before calling but decides against that tactic because she doesn't want to be tactical. She wants to be herself and not care that he called. Retha boldly snatches up the phone and dials his number. Jaren answers almost immediately with a simple, "hello."

"Hey, how you doing?" Retha nearly yells into the phone in an attempt at sounding at ease.

"I'm good."

Retha, hearing the question in his voice, enlightens him. "This is Retha. I'm returning your call. How are you?" *Oh, God I already asked him that.*

"Listen, let me call you back. Are you at home?" Jaren sounds rushed.

"Sure. Okay. I'm at home."

"Okay, I'll call you back."

"Bye," Retha blurts out as she hears the click of the phone on the other end. She pushes the button on the receiver and lays the phone down a little embarrassed and hurt. *He was short with me.* Before she can finish her thought the phone rings. She answers without considering that Jaren might be calling her back so soon.

"Hey!" he smiles with his voice in response to her "hello."

The surprise takes her breath away. She doesn't like the effect he has on her. An obstruction, has to be air, gets caught in her throat causing her to cough, and cough, and hack, and cough more.

"Are you okay?" Jaren asks with concern.

"I'm sorry." More coughing. "Excuse me." Still more.

Jaren politely holds on while Retha coughs and hacks her throat clear. He is certain she is the most laid back lady he has ever met. She manages to squeeze out a coherent sentence in a strangled whisper. "Excuse me. Something went down the wrong way." Now, she is truly embarrassed. *Maybe I should have had the bath and the wine first.*

"I need to get the information on your trip so I can get those tickets for you. I thought I might join you, if it's okay."

Oh shit! This is too much. Retha places her hand over the mouthpiece so Jaren can't hear her excitement. *Deep breath. Relax. Now breathe.* "Sure. We'd love to have you come with us. I hope my friends don't scare you off though. They can be a little out there. I haven't even told them that you offered the tickets."

"Why not? What's the big secret?"

"Well, I wasn't sure that you would remember and I didn't want to get their hopes up. They love the Knicks. I don't know why. I mean, I don't dislike the Knicks but I do love my Spurs."

"Back up. You thought I might not come through with the tickets after I told you I would?"

"I thought you might forget or something."

"Did you plan on reminding me in case I forgot? I gave you my number for a reason. As I recall, I gave you every number I have."

"I wouldn't have done that. That's not me. But we will be there Wednesday January sixth and we leave the following Monday. We don't have any set plans yet, so any night from that Thursday to that Sunday would be great for tickets. Jaren, I can't tell you how much I appreciate you doing this. I know you're busy. My friends are going to flip."

"I'm not busy this time of the year, just working hard to be ready for the season. I told you I wanted to repay your hospitality when I visited San Antonio. I had a good time out there, but it looks like I still need to find a way to thank you for all the hospitality you showed me. What can I do to get you excited? I haven't even met your friends and you're telling me how happy they'll be with the Knicks tickets, but I'm trying to please you."

Retha is so overcome by these words that she needs to lie across her bed to continue the conversation. Jaren's voice soothes her. *God, I like him,* she moans deep inside her head. *This is awful.*

"My friends are giving me the trip as a gift. They said we need to go and have a good time together. We all love visiting New York so the tickets are great and I know they will get a kick out of meeting you. They are not baseball fans so don't be surprised if they don't recognize you right away."

"I can live with that. I'm not real big on the celebrity thing. So you'll be here the first full week of January and any night Thursday through Sunday is okay for tickets. Now that we've got that out of the way, how have you been doing now that you're free from the Army? I hope you're not too busy to talk for a while."

Retha and Jaren talk for another forty-five minutes about their day-to-day lives, where and how they spent their Thanksgiving holiday, their plans for Christmas, and the Rojas family. Retha tells Jaren about Uncle Sugar's and her wish to have her own restaurant. Jaren shares his love of baseball and movies. The talk is light and easy and Jaren sounds willing to talk all night but Retha is fearful she might bore him so she reluctantly ends the call. Jaren promises to call her as soon as he checks the Knicks schedule to let her know the date of the game. He tells Retha to call him anytime and says if he is not available, he will call her back as soon as he gets the message.

The call and the conversation mystify Retha. Jaren is giving her a great deal of attention and consideration. She wonders if he is usually so generous. She understands why women and girls swoon over him; he is easy to like, even without the tickets. *Well, he said he wants to thank me for the hospitality and so I'll take that for what it's worth. Don't read into it and don't start daydreaming.* If it was hard keeping Jaren Daniels out of her thoughts before, it has now reached the realm of impossibility. Retha senses him in the pit of her stomach and other places much more private.

Retha considers calling Simone right away and telling her about the tickets but knows Simone will sense her excitement. No use in trying to act calm because that's a dead giveaway. She decides to wait a day or two before telling Simone.

A message from Jaren greets Retha again the following night. It seems he's getting tickets for Thursday night but wants her to call him. When Retha returns the call she is pleased to learn that the Knicks will play the Lakers that Thursday. They play the Cavaliers the following Saturday but Jaren thought she and her friends might prefer to see the Lakers.

Retha confirms his belief and thanks him again.

"Please, stop thanking me. It was no problem and I was glad to get the tickets for you and your friends. You sound like you are not used to people doing things for you."

"No, it's not that. I appreciate this. But I won't thank you again for the tickets if that will make you happy."

This call is more formal than the previous night's and causes Retha to descend a little closer to earth. Jaren ends the conversation explaining he is meeting friends for dinner. Retha calls Simone and tells her that a friend in New York will provide tickets to the Lakers vs. Knicks game.

"What friend is this?" Simone is skeptical.

"A friend of Jeremiah's I met a few weeks back."

"What does he do for a living that he can get tickets to the Knicks/Lakers game? How much are these tickets? I called Jackson and he told me he couldn't get any good seats to that game without cutting off an arm. He wasn't sure he'd be able to get seats at all."

"Don't worry about the cost. He's getting them for us," Retha answers, ignoring Simone's first question.

"So who is he?"

"I told you, a friend of Jeremiah's. I cooked dinner for Jeremiah and his friends twice one weekend and Jaren heard me talking to you about the Knicks and volunteered to get us the tickets. I didn't say anything about it earlier because he just confirmed he can get them."

"How many is he getting?"

"Three, for us."

"You think he can get at least one more? Michele has decided she wants to come too."

"Mitch is coming! Good. We are going to have a blast!" Retha is excited about Michelle joining them on their mini vacation until she realizes she will need to ask Jaren for another ticket. "Damn, this guy is going to think I'm trying to take advantage of him. He told me it was no problem to get our tickets. Hopefully he can swing another one as easily. If he can't, I'll stay behind"

"Ask him first, Retha." Simone advises her friend.

"I will ask. I just hate to beg."

"Jackson is going to be pissed when he finds out we got tickets and he can't get one. You know he likes the Lakers," Simone hints.

"I'm not asking for a ticket for Jackson. I'm sorry, but I just can't."

"I know. That might be pushing it."

The tickets are a dilemma for Retha. She has told Jaren that she does not ask favors of people and now she needs to call him back and ask for more tickets. She does not call that evening because he is out. She dials his number early the next morning and barely says hello before she asks if he can get more tickets. Jaren is quiet for a moment and Retha can hardly breathe. *He's disgusted with me. God, what if he's nasty when he says "no."*

"How many do you need?" Jaren asks without further comment.

Retha cannot tell by his voice how he feels about her begging for more tickets but he does not sound pleased. "Three, if possible." She sounds timid to herself and hates not having the courage to explain why she wants the additional tickets. She can't see staying with Bennie and Jackson who are hardcore Knicks fans and not at least trying to get tickets for them also.

"Should be doable. I'll call you if there is a problem." His voice is a degree warmer.

"Thanks, Jaren, a lot. I appreciate it." Her thank you sounds hollow. She hates the pitiful thank you more than asking for the tickets and wishes she had never gotten on the ticket merry-go-round.

Chapter 8 -- A Budding Friendship

Christmas is fast approaching and so is the blues. Everyone except Retha has forgotten that she and Joe married in December. It is impossible to let the date pass without special acknowledgement. Those closest to Retha get uneasy when she talks about Joe too much or seems to dwell on the past. Everyone wants her to get over losing Joe and it scares them when they see her pain is still quite acute at times.

The family is ready to celebrate. Jessie's oldest daughter, Elizabeth, is home from college and Catrina is out of school for the holidays. Raymond and Ida and Ida's sons will visit for Christmas. Jessie and Robert are full of Christmas cheer. Their home is decorated and the tree is up. Jessie has been planning her Christmas dinner since before Thanksgiving.

Jessie has also been baking nonstop since the first week of December. She bakes her Christmas cookies for friends, neighbors, and Sugar's customers. The customers love receiving their festively tied bags of homemade Christmas cookies. Jessie and Retha decorate the restaurant and have a good time doing it but Jessie is unsuccessful in getting Retha to decorate her own home. Retha is fine but not up for much holiday merriment.

On the evening of her anniversary, Retha opens a California Syrah, pours out a glass, toasts her husband, and sits down with plans to indulge in a good cry. It has been a while since she allowed the tears to flow for Joe, so she makes no attempt to ward them off. She is always lonely for him but carries a continuous façade of peace and strength. She doesn't like to wallow in the addictive sorrow that often envelops her mind, body, and soul. Oh, but the façade is so heavy that it wears her out, even beats her down. Then her old friend wins. Retha opens her arms and accepts the sorrow, allowing it to soothe and cover her like the finest down comforter on a freezing December night. This is one of those nights, but disappointment soon takes the place of her companion of sorrow. The tears do not flow freely and dry much too fast. The sobs don't sound real to her ears and the pain doesn't squeeze her heart like before. *Am I going through a ritual here? Am I losing my mind? Maybe I'm getting better.* Retha realizes that in a small way she wants to keep mourning Joe. She wants her heart to ache for him. *I can't forget*

Joe. She wishes there was one person she could tell about her husband, that sweet, beautiful man who kept her so warm and secure.

As the evening wears on and Retha lounges on her sofa in that healing place between sorrow and guilt, indulging in her third glass of wine, she decides to call Jaren. She hasn't talked to him in over a week. She called him once after asking for the last set of tickets. She felt she should call him without wanting a favor. Jaren was a little cool during the call and left most of the conversation to Retha. She decided not to call him again but the wine has the "Brenda Effect"; Retha is emboldened. She wants to talk to him and she wants him to talk to her as she rests in the mellow tones of his voice.

Retha thinks Jaren is certain to be out on a Friday night and says as much when he answers. "Oh, you're there. What are you doing home on a Friday night?"

"I live here."

Oh, he can be a smart-ass.

Jaren continues, not giving any sign of how pleased he is to hear from her. "If you didn't think I'd be home why are you calling? Were you trying to get my voice mail? If you want, I can hang up and you can call back and talk to the machine."

"Hey, I'm sorry I bothered you. You're not up to talking. I'll let you go."

"Wait a minute. I wasn't. I didn't mean to be rude. Can you hold on?" Jaren asks.

Retha doesn't respond. She considers hanging up but the urge to talk with him is strong.

"Retha, would you hold on a minute?"

"I don't want anything, Jaren. I was just calling to talk."

"That's fine. Don't hang up." Jaren clicks over and gets the young woman he has been chatting with off the line.

"Retha?"

"Yeah."

"Thanks for waiting. I can't believe you're calling me just to talk."

"I've called you before to chat."

"No. The last time you called to make up for the tickets. You didn't want it to seem like you only call when you want a favor."

Retha is surprised her motive for that last call was so transparent. Embarrassed and a little tongue-tied she changes the subject. "Well, to be honest you're my last resort. Today is my anniversary and nobody here wants to hear me talk about it. I'm supposed to be past all that now, you know. I got a little desperate and sad and needed to talk. When I get the blues my family and friends pick up on it and start to freak. They're afraid I might jump out of a window or off a bridge."

"I wish I could say happy anniversary but that would be way off base. So what are you doing tonight other than calling me?" Jaren asks with slight concern.

"I guess getting drunk; I'm on my third glass of wine. Two's my limit. Joe, that's my husband, always said I couldn't hold my liquor. I get real stupid after two glasses of wine."

"Maybe you shouldn't drink."

"Maybe, but I'm a bit of an alcoholic. I drink as a crutch and I drink alone. Always have at least two glasses."

Jaren laughs softly. "Sounds like a real problem. Why didn't you go out or have friends over?"

"I wanted to be alone here with my thoughts but I got too sad, so I'm calling you to cheer me up."

"I'll do my best," Jaren promises with amusement in his voice. On a serious note, he asks, "I don't mean to be too personal, but have you been interested in anyone since your husband died?"

YOU! Retha's brain shouts. "I dated one guy but as much as I liked him as a person there was no real romantic involvement on my part. We were moving too fast. I couldn't keep pace with the situation. I decided to be alone; that's best for me right now. I've been married all my adult life. I hadn't had protected sex in more than ten years until last year. You don't have to worry about that when you're married."

Jaren is a little shocked at her candor but chalks it up to the wine. It does answer a question he would never have dared to ask, at least not so early in the friendship. Retha has been sexually active since her husband's death. Jaren is surprised at his disappointment.

"So you don't think married people get STDs?" he asks.

"No, I'm not saying that. I just never worried about it when I was married."

"Well, welcome to the jungle. You were very fortunate. I haven't had unprotected sex since I got smart enough to know better."

"So, what, you've been practicing safe sex all month?" Retha jabs, causing them both to laugh.

"No, nearly all my adult life." Jaren happily shares his personal information.

"Yuck! What's the point? There's no intimacy. Sex without intimacy is like, like, like pancakes without syrup; popcorn without butter; rain on a sunny day; sleep without. . ."

"I get the picture." Jaren cuts off her symbolic critique of his sex life. "I'd rather be safe than sick or worse yet, dead. A little obsessed with food, aren't you?"

"Food's good. I don't understand, Jaren. You haven't met a steady girl that you can trust and that can trust you or are you too much the player for a long-term monogamous relationship? No thoughts of marriage, ever?"

"Marriage, no! I've dated a few women but they don't stick for one reason or another. Mostly it's the ball. I don't have time to be in a long-term relationship. You know women like the attentive lover. That's not me. Baseball, that's my baby. I really liked one lady but she wanted to get in the way of ball and that's not happening. She didn't make any demands on me. She dumped me when I couldn't see her regularly during the season. Never said a word. When I got her on the phone, she told me she was bored with the relationship. Said I didn't need her; all I needed was baseball."

"Was she right?

"Hell no! Well, partially wrong. I need my family but I didn't need her."

"Don't you get lonely?"

"Can't miss what you never had. I get lonely for baseball during off-season. Listen, you called to cry on my shoulder. Now you're trying to get me feeling sorry for myself."

"I didn't mean to get you started. But at least I'm okay now. I'm too busy feeling sorry for you. Damn, sex with a condom for ten years." They share a good laugh.

Retha catches her incoming calls but gets right back to Jaren. He on the other hand ignores all incoming calls except one from his sister Rachelle. Two hours later Retha ends the call complaining that she is about to pass out.

The next evening Jaren calls to check on her and they watch a college football game together over the phone. They talk several more times before the New York trip. About the only topic they stay away from are Retha's tours in Iraq. When Jaren asks about her time in that country she tells him about her fellow soldiers who were killed or seriously injured and how that war killed her husband. She tells him how she was injured, blessed to be alive, and that she does not like to talk about Iraq.

Retha has a new phone buddy. She loves their conversations but has no wish to be his pal. She worries that one of her friends will lay eyes on Jaren and make a move or even worse, he'll make a move on one of them. After all, he and Retha are just buds.

~ ~

One week before their trip to New York, Simone calls to inform Retha of a problem with the sleeping arrangements at Bennie and Jackson's place. Seems the Jacksons gave up their two-bedroom apartment for a one bedroom in the same building a while ago. They did not bother to tell Simone about their smaller living quarters when she invited herself and her friends to spend a few days in their home. More than likely they didn't mention the move because they were afraid Simone might change her mind about staying with them. Also, they see Simone and her friends as young girls who can sleep on pallets if need be.

Simone's solution is not working for Retha. Simone plans to sleep at her cousin's house in Jersey while the others sleep on the sofa and sofa bed in her aunt and uncle's front room. Retha hates the idea and reiterates her earlier suggestion that they stay in a hotel. Simone makes a conference call to Brenda and Michele so all four friends can discuss the sleeping arrangements.

Everyone except Retha agrees to Simone's plan. The others do not want to spend money they can use for shopping and partying on a hotel room. They will also save a great deal on eating out because Simone's Aunt Bennie will feed them well. Retha can't squawk too loudly because Simone is purchasing her airfare as a gift. Retha offers to pay half the total room cost but the others are dead set against staying in a hotel. Retha hadn't been happy about piling up in the Jacksons' small two-bedroom. Now she knows she'll be uncomfortable. Even if Simone sleeps at her cousin's home, Retha,

Brenda, and Michele will be cramped in Bennie's front room. Retha considers staying with Aida but she doesn't want to be running in and out of Aida's all hours of the day and night. Aida would stay awake each night waiting and worrying until Retha returned.

As Retha angrily winds up her sleeping arrangement discussion, Jaren beeps through. She gets off the phone with the ladies and starts raising all kinds of hell with him because he's there. She expresses concerns to him that she didn't mention to her friends, not wanting to offend Simone.

Jaren finds Retha's perturb humorous because he has never heard her upset. When she calms down, he presents a solution. "You know, if you don't want to stay with your friends, I've got plenty of room here. You're welcome to come and stay as long as you want and no one will bother you."

Retha is surprised. She had not considered an invite from Jaren and hopes she didn't give him the impression she wanted one. She quietly contemplates the offer while Jaren waits for her answer. "Thanks Jaren but it's probably best for me to stay at Bennie's. Besides, I don't want to put you out. I hope you don't think I was telling you all that because I wanted an invitation."

"Come on, Retha. I've got plenty of room. Why should you be uncomfortable over there when you can crash here? I'm out most of the time anyway. I'm not that far from West Eighty-Eighth so you can get to and from your friend's place with no problem. I'd like you to stay. It'll be like a sleepover," Jaren jokes.

Retha's mind is racing. *Why not? I mean, what have I got to lose? He's a nice guy and we're just friends. Yeah right. What if he doesn't like me after we spend so much time together or vice versa? He says he won't be around -- bummer! Maybe Brenda or Michele can stay too and Simone won't need to stay in Jersey. Is this right? Should I accept his invitation? Does he mean it when he says he doesn't mind or is he just being nice? Go for it. You know you want to stay at his place. Go for it! HEEEEEEY!* "Are you sure it's okay? I mean I don't want to push in on you."

"Believe me, I wouldn't offer if it was a problem."

"Would you mind if Brenda or Michele came along also? That way. . ."

"Wait a minute, hold up! I know you. I don't know your friends. I can't do strangers in my home. I don't want to sound mean but I wouldn't enjoy that." Jaren is serious and seems set on his decision.

"Oh. Well." Retha hesitates as she wonders if she should decline the invitation since he won't allow one of her friends to stay. "I understand. I do appreciate the offer. I guess you say I'm always asking for more. Well, hey, they didn't want to spend the money for a decent room so they can suffer." Without question and with little thought Retha accepts Jaren's decision not to have a stranger in his home. She had him scared for a moment. He would have conceded and allowed one of Retha's friends to stay if she had declined his offer because of his decision.

When they end the call, Jaren can't help his wicked thoughts. *What did that spider say to that fly?* He feels ashamed of himself. The shame does not last long though; Jaren is too pleased to deal with guilt.

Simone, Michele, and Brenda get the self-sacrificing diplomatic spin of how Retha plans to abandon them and stay with her friend Jaren during their New York trip. Simone is relieved. She and Brenda can sleep four to a Porta Potty as long as it's clean but Retha and Michele hate being cramped up. Simone had no genuine intentions of staying at her cousin's home in Jersey but knew she had to have a plan better than the four of them piling up in her aunt and uncle's front room if she wanted Retha to make the trip. Michele is usually easy to persuade but Retha can be difficult for difficulty's sake. Now the deception is no longer necessary.

Once again Michele voices her concern that they may be too cramped in Bennie's small place before switching her attention to what Bennie might feed them while they are in town.

Brenda's reaction is the most predictable. "How many rooms this dude got?"

"I think he told me three and the guest bedroom is bigger than his." Retha tries to remember.

"Hell, I'mo stay over there with you."

"I already asked him about that and he doesn't want any strangers staying in his home."

"What!" Brenda is dismayed.

"Brenda, he doesn't know me that well and I appreciate him letting me stay. Now Simone won't need to travel to Jersey each night, which she wasn't going to do anyway. You guys didn't want to spend money on a hotel. You said you'd be fine at Bennie's. So don't make an issue."

"I'm not making no issue but I can't wait to meet this uppity Negro. Re, he is a brotha ain't he?"

"No, he's purple. What difference does it make?"

"I can't believe he wouldn't want another woman staying with him. What is it? Either this dude is trying to get in yo draws or he's gay."

Retha simply groans in response.

Chapter 9 -- The Stopover

Brenda's home in Dallas is the first leg of the trip to New York for Simone, Michele, and Retha. Simone has been in Dallas visiting with Brenda for two days when Retha arrives early Tuesday afternoon, one day before their departure for New York. Michele will spend a few extra days with Brenda in Dallas on the return leg of the trip. Since Brenda is working, Simone meets Retha's flight. Retha and Simone will cook dinner at Brenda's while Brenda negotiates Dallas traffic to meet Michele's flight later in the evening.

Ah, there she is. Retha fights back tears as she watches Simone walk toward her at a fast clip, weaving her way in and out of DFW congestion as if she alone holds the deed to the terminal. Simone is not one to show a lot of emotion but Retha grabs her friend in a bear hug and yells anyway. "Hey girl! It's so good to see you." Retha's tears well up now.

Hugging and crying in the middle of the Dallas Fort Worth International Air Terminal is too much for Simone, though she's every bit as happy to see Retha. "Don't start!" Simone chastises in her sternest voice as she cuts her eyes at her friend and tries to suppress a laugh. "You're such a big crybaby. I will go off and leave you right here if you embarrass me, Retha," Simone threatens but holds on to her friend and releases her laughter as she recalls what a crybaby Retha truly is.

--

Retha is pleased to have an opportunity to talk to Simone face to face without interference from Brenda or Michele. In her opinion, Simone has sounded entirely too pleased about her divorce. As the friends relax in front of Brenda's sound system with a bottle of Chardonnay, Retha asks Simone about the end of her marriage and finds her friends openness a surprise.

"Greg was a person I settled for and he settled for me." Retha is aware of vulnerability seldom visible in Simone. "I always wanted a nice guy, one with things and position. After we had lived together for so long, I gave him an ultimatum. I told him he could leave me or marry me. You guys left me out here by myself. You and Joe had been married for years and Michele and Brenda weren't far behind you. I should have at least waited to see how each of you fared. Those other two didn't come out any better than me."

Retha is certain she has fared the worst of all but does not give voice to her opinion. "Why do you say Mitch didn't come out well? I thought Sean was behaving."

"She's being awfully quiet. It could be my imagination. I think Sean has chilled out. God knows she has forgiven him enough times. That shit gets real old real fast. I can testify to that."

"You and Greg didn't have the same problem Mitch has with Sean did you?" Retha asks.

"No, not us, but I watched my Cousin Gale go through that crap for years. That wasn't our problem. I." Simone stops and shakes her head and with an uncommon lapse of composure looks off at a distant place not visible to Retha before she continues. "I had this lofty image of what my marriage would be like and what my man would be like and materially Gregory fit that image perfectly but emotionally we didn't have any passion for each other. Our relationship was empty. I would think a man would try to find someone who satisfies his passion, you know, a person he could get emotional about."

"Why would you expect that of him?" Retha asks. "Did you ever play around on him?"

"No, girl, but I wanted to so bad. Believe me; I was tempted many times. I couldn't do that to our marriage or to him and still have an honest relationship. You know that's not our style, you and me."

"Humph, what makes you think I never fooled around on Joe?" Retha asks with a wicked smile.

"Because you told me he was a damn good lover. Refused to give me any details but you did say he was good."

"Yes, he was, but don't remind me. Are you telling me Greg wasn't a good lover?"

"Me and Greg weren't good together. We went months at a time without sex and neither of us cared. Hell, maybe that son of a bitch was playing around," Simone jokes but with a thoughtful look on her face.

"What about now? Is there anyone special, any one you're interested in? Seems every time we talk you mention a different guy."

"Girl, I've been looking, but it's hard to find a good brotha out here. I know we all get tired of hearing about the shortage of black men that want black women but it is true. I occasionally go out with my friend Christian; he's gay." Simone smiles. "Once we went out dancing and I was eyeing a good-looking brotha. Girl, Christian caught him and I went home alone. They did walk me to my car, though. He always calls me to make sure I get home safely when we've been out late. I have a better time with him than I've ever had on a date with a straight man. You got to meet him the next time you visit. I know you'll like him. Brenda was out last year and she met him, but you know how she is. She asked me why I was so desperate that I was hanging out with the competition. She makes me so mad at times. I wonder how we stay friends. Anyway black men are few and far between."

"So, why do you limit yourself?"

"Limit myself how?"

"Have you dated a white guy or a Latino or?"

Simone stops her. "Girl, I like the brothas, okay. I mean those other men want their own women."

"Now Simone, are you telling me you have never flirted with a man from another culture or nationality and that no one other than a brother has ever hit on you? Girl, you are so much like Charmaine. Stop limiting yourself. There are a lot of good men that are looking for a good woman. And some of them may not be looking but that don't mean you can't find them and show them what they're missing. You can't tell me that white men don't hit on you because they hit on me and I don't even have big boobs. I know you like who you like but please don't limit yourself like that."

Simone wonders if Retha's lecture on diversity has anything to do with her relationship with James Freeman. "Are you and the colonel getting serious?"

"No. I liked him a lot, still do, but he didn't excite me. I don't think it had anything to do with the color of his skin. We just didn't have that chemistry thing going on." Retha thinks for a moment before continuing. "Listen, I understand not wanting a sorry man, a stinking man, a hustler, or a criminal, even a stingy man but not being with a man because he's Chinese. That's stupid."

"Oh, so you calling me stupid."

"If it fits."

"Well, listen, believe me, if I find a man that turns me on, he can be blue and I'll be with him. TaRosa's boyfriend is British." TaRosa is Simone's younger sister.

"Is he white, Indian, black or what?"

"Oh girl, he is Prince fucking Charles British, you hear me." The wine is truly speaking for Simone now.

"Are they serious?"

"I guess. He's been trying to get her to go home with him on a visit, but she keeps putting him off. She's been telling me the same thing you have. She'll be glad to hear you're on me about opening up other avenues of opportunity."

Retha's query into Simone's personal life ends and the friends make a move to get dinner ready. The cooks prepare shrimp and chicken kabobs, a seasoned tomato sauce with linguine, and a Caesar salad. Brenda loves to complain and she will expect them to have everything ready when she and Mitch arrive but no matter what, Brenda will complain; it is her nature.

By the time Brenda and Michele arrive, the grill is ready to go, salad needs to be tossed with the dressing and pasta boiled. Brenda questions why the food is not on the table. Her friends ignore her. Michele is tired but laughing more than usual because she's so happy to be with her friends. While Brenda and Michele get cleaned up, the cooks finish up the meal.

Brenda's younger sister, Dara, joins the friends for dinner. Since it is unseasonably warm for a January evening in Dallas, the ladies sit out on Brenda's large plant-infested balcony for hours lingering over the meal and chilled bottles of Spatlese. The cool evening turns into a marvelous night filled with reminiscent stories of their youth. The Dallas sky is clear enough to count the stars and the night is quiet in comparison to the roar of laughter coming from Brenda's terrace. Dara can't get enough of their storytelling and neither can they. At nearly midnight Dara reluctantly calls it quits because she, unlike the others, must rise before the sun in order to earn a paycheck at the end of the week. The ladies crash at about two in the morning and rise early enough to make their midmorning flight.

Chapter 10 -- New York

Simone's Uncle Jackson is waiting for "his girls" upon touch down. Simone had tried to talk him out of picking them up but since he is now retired from all work outside the home, he has plenty of time to serve his family and does to capacity. Jackson is a retired New York City police officer who worked private security for a number of years after he retired from the force. His wife, Bennie, is a retired school administrator. Jackson and Bennie moved to New York City over forty years ago and never lost their southern friendliness, hospitality, or drawls.

Simone's friends have known her Aunt Bennie and Uncle Willie Jackson for years. At one time, the Jacksons made a yearly trek to Seaside to visit Simone's family. Their visits to the Pacific coast have become less frequent as the years have gone by. Twice during their teenage years, Simone and her friends spent weeks during the summer in New York with the Jacksons. Those were the best times the friends shared as girls. Over the years, whenever Retha came to New York to see Joe's family, she always made a point of visiting with the Jacksons also.

When the out-of-towners arrive at the Jacksons' home they are pleased to find Bennie waiting out in front of the building talking to a neighbor. There are hugs and kisses all around before Bennie starts her much expected ritual of critiquing their appearance. She starts with Retha. "Ooh baby, I'm so glad to see you have put some meat back on those bones. I was worried about you the last time you passed through here. When was that, summer before last?" she asks before moving on to Simone. "You still too little. You just like your mama, girl. You ain't gonna never gain no weight. I'm glad you lettin' your hair grow back out though. It sure is pretty." Turning to Michele. "Michele, come on over here and give me a hug, girl. You still just as pretty as a speckled pup. How those babies?" Last but definitely not least is Brenda, her favorite of Simone's friends. "I don't never have to worry about you being too thin. Girl when you gonna lose some of that ass?" They all laugh as Bennie swats Brenda on her behind. "You need to give some to Simone."

After her individual critique, Bennie addresses the group. "Y'all so beautiful and healthy looking. I can't believe you're still friends after all these years and so close. That's not a common thing these days. I'm so proud of how good you all are doing." "Good" means employed, not in jail, not walking the streets, homeless, or strung out on drugs. The friends appreciate the praise coming from Bennie.

Bennie has a soulful mouth-watering dinner of pot roast with new potatoes and carrots, collard greens, cornbread and a "slammin'" pineapple coconut cake waiting for them. The visitors eat like the pigs they often are.

Retha is so excited she can hardly contain herself. She wants to jump up and down and cheer. It takes her a while to realize that – yes, she is happy to be with her friends and to see Simone's aunt and uncle, and to visit with Aida and JJ and the rest of Joe's family. Yes, she is glad to be in New York to have a good time but the main cause of this elevated level of excitement, which she has never experienced before, can be summed up in two words, Jaren Daniels. The thought scares her.

Bennie notices the change in Retha from one moment to the next. "Retha, where that cloud come from, baby? You were glowing like a firefly a few minutes ago. What's the matter?" Retha shakes her head, smiles, and shelves her concerns for the present.

On the ride from the airport, Simone and Brenda spotted a new pub on Amsterdam around the corner from Bennie's building. Brenda suggests they all walk around to the pub and socialize. Jackson objects. He has an apartment full of young women and wants to enjoy them for a while before he has to share them with the rest of the city. "That damn place is way too high. I got a couple of bottles of pretty good stuff right here or if you want somethin' else, tell me and I can get it for you right there on the corner. I can tell you, it'll cost me a whole lot less money if we stay here where it's warm and then we don't have to be bothered with nobody."

Bennie rolls her eyes at Jackson, which she does with frequency since he retired and is at home most of the day and night. "How do you know how expensive the drinks are in that bar? When you been in there drinking?"

"What you think woman, I don't know what's going on in my own neighborhood?"

Simone puts an end to the discussion. "Uncle Jack, how you sound talking about staying here so we don't have to be bothered? Being bothered is one of our primary objectives while we're here."

Jackson sucks his teeth and Bennie shakes her head with a huge smile as she chastises her niece. "Simone, don't think you so grown you can do anything and act anyway while you here in town, miss."

"I'm kiddin', Auntie. A little bit anyway." Simone grins.

Bennie makes the final decision. "Get your coats and bundle up good, cause if you think it's cold now, wait till we come back around that corner. It'll be so cold it'll freeze a sneeze in front of your face."

--

"Hey, Jack!" The bartender waves and greets Jackson as he and the ladies enter the bar. A couple of patrons also acknowledge Jackson. He looks a bit sly and acknowledges his acquaintances. The group settles in at a table and order drinks.

A little later, Jackson notices a couple of guys he knows from the area and calls them over to meet his niece and her friends. Bill and George pull up chairs and settle in for a cozy visit. Bill is mesmerized by Brenda and invites the ladies to a little jazz club the following Saturday. Brenda tells him she will have to let him know after she and her friends discuss their plans. Jackson, sensing his friend's disappointment, invites the men over for a dinner party he and Bennie plan for that Sunday. The guys accept the invitation without hesitation.

The group sits in the pub for well over two hours. It is late and freezing when they return to the Jacksons' apartment. Retha visits for about another thirty minutes before she asks Jackson to get her a taxi. Jackson cries foul about the taxi. "No niece of mine is taking no taxi in New York City this time of night." He's a little drunk so all four of his guests are now his nieces. His condition is a good thing because he definitely cannot drive Retha to Jaren's.

Retha's friends along with Bennie beg her to stay the night and continue the good time they are having. "I can't. That wouldn't be right after I told Jaren I would be there tonight and he's made arrangements for me to get into his place."

Michele starts with the questions about Jaren again. "Who is this guy anyway? You haven't known him long enough to be staying at his place, do you think Retha?"

Brenda joins in. "She say he ain't trying to hit on her. I'm still trying to find out if he's gay."

Inebriated, Jackson must have his say. "Well, he must be one rich gay SOB if he can swing for six tickets to tomorrow night's game."

Bennie puts a stop to all the speculation and calls the taxi. Retha promises to return by noon the next day for a short shopping and loafing trip before the game. Thanks to the cold, Jackson is the only one who walks Retha out to the taxi. He takes down the taxi number and informs the brother driving the hack that he's a retired New York City police officer. He goes on to say how glad he is that the brother, who has a most distinctive West Indian accent, is a brother and not "one of them damn foreigners" and to please make sure his "niece" gets where she is going safely.

"Shooya mon, no problum," is the driver's polite response.

Retha has escaped her friends, leaving only Jaren's cell phone number with Simone. As the driver pulls away she gives him the address and in return receives a thoughtful glance through the rearview mirror. She tries to relax as the taxi rushes through the city streets. When they pull up to Jaren's luxury midtown apartment, a shiver of dread ripples through Retha's body. As she and the driver approach the steps leading to the building entrance, the doorman exits, briskly approaches, reaches to take one of Retha's bags from the driver and slaps the driver's hand before taking the other bag. The driver thanks Retha and the doorman and returns to the taxi smiling as he assesses his tip.

"Who are you here to see, miss?" the doorman asks in a friendly business-like manner.

Retha is flustered at losing control of the situation. "Ah, Mr. Daniels, Jaren Daniels." She answers the doorman's question. *I hope he lives here since my taxi is driving away.*

"Jaren, excuse me, Mr. Daniels told me to expect you and to treat you real good." Now the doorman has a big friendly smile spread all the way across his wide face.

Retha likes him and the information he imparted does not hurt his standing with her one bit. She can't help but beam. Retha is feeling quite special about now. "Thank you." She smiles back at her new friend. "My name is Retha. I see yours is Raymond. That's my brother's name. It's nice to meet you."

"Well thank you, miss. It's nice to meet you too."

Raymond escorts her up to Jaren's door and rings the doorbell. He had called Jaren and informed him of Retha's arrival as soon as the taxi pulled up. Retha's heart is about to beat out of her chest. She tries to calm down and not embarrass herself.

Jaren answers the door in an undershirt, jeans and flip flops. He looks divine, better than Retha remembers; everything about him is perfect. He gives her a huge smile and greeting "Hey girl, I thought someone stole you! I was getting worried." Jaren adds a "Thanks man" to Raymond and slaps his hand as Raymond had slapped the taxi driver's earlier. The doorman returns the thanks, bobs his head to Retha, and walks off. Retha enters the apartment and exchanges nice big hello hugs with Jaren. There is no shyness in their embrace. They are genuinely pleased to see each other.

Jaren grabs up her bags and starts off toward a hallway. "Come on and let me show you your room so you can get settled in. How was your trip?"

Retha is torn between watching him and gawking at his home. "It was good and uneventful." She answers once she realizes he asked the question. "I'm having a great time. My friends didn't want me to leave them." She takes in her surroundings. *This is a different world. My God, I thought he said his place was small – compared to what, the Taj Mahal?* Retha follows Jaren out of the gray slated foyer onto the deeply stained herringbone wood floors of the gallery. A short hallway off the gallery leads directly into the master bedroom, her room during her stay. Retha fights the sucking in her chest. The room is richly furnished with a cherry wood dresser and chest of drawers, a huge flat screen, two night tables, a queen size bed with cherry wood head and footboard, two overstuffed chairs with an ottoman, end tables, and a standalone mirror. A wall of three gigantic windows from floor to fourteen-foot ceiling makes up the west side of the room. The attached bathroom has double stainless steel sinks and a claw foot tub with separate shower. After wonderment, guilt creeps up Retha's spine as she thinks about her friends cramped up in the Jacksons' one bedroom apartment.

"This is a nice place you have and the room is fabulous."

"Yeah, it's supposed to be the master. I prefer the other room, so I made this one the guestroom. My room is simpler and a bit more modern. My mother outfitted this room. My parents sleep in here when they visit." Jaren puts down Retha's baggage and gives her a thoughtful glance before asking, "Did you want to stay with your friends?"

"To be honest, not really. I hate being cramped up. I didn't mind so much when I was younger but now I like as much space as I can get. I guess I've gotten selfish in my old age."

Retha follows Jaren out of the room and back into the front part of his home.

"You hungry? Want something to drink? I bought you a few bottles of wine. I'm told they are pretty good. Got to feed that alcoholism you know."

Retha can't help but blush remembering the call she made to Jaren on her anniversary. "That's not funny and no I don't want any wine right now. I've had more than my limit today. Thank you. I want to thank you again for letting me stay. I hope it's not an inconvenience."

"What's a little inconvenience between friends? I'm glad you came so we can have those deep conversations face to face. At times I wonder if you're bullshittin' me or if you're serious. Now I'll be able to look into your eyes and know." Jaren glances over at her and looks directly into her eyes for the first time since she arrived. Retha squirms, almost but not quite imperceptibly.

"So, you hungry?" Jaren asks his guest.

"I think I am a little."

Jaren shows her into his kitchen and points toward the refrigerator indicating for her to help herself. Retha can't help but envy his state-of-the-art kitchen. She stares at the thirty-six inch combination range with double oven, stone counter tops, subzero refrigerator and nearly drools. *What the hell is he doing with my dream kitchen? He hardly cooks at all.*

Jaren smiles slyly as he guesses her thoughts. "You like my kitchen?"

"Well, yeah. But what do you need a kitchen like this for?"

"Maybe you'll hook something up in it before you leave, huh?" he asks.

"I hope so," Retha answers quietly as she pulls grapes, a brick of Scharffe Maxx Swiss and some prosciutto from the refrigerator. She stands at the sink and washes the grapes before placing the cheese on a cutting board. Retha will never admit it but she's a little intimidated by the kitchen. Jaren stands across the room and watches her from behind as she prepares her snack.

"I'm surprised I can eat anything. Bennie cooked us a great meal but that was several hours ago. My appetite has gotten bad though."

Jaren notices that she's a little healthier than when he met her. The extra weight looks good on her. To him she is beautiful. He never considered himself an ass man but he has a hard time not admiring Retha's behind and her thighs. His thoughts are in turmoil. *Damn she's fine. This is not going to be an easy visit. Shit, shit, shit!* "I noticed you put on a little weight."

Retha turns her head and looks over her shoulder at him and instinctively looks down her back toward her rear, as if she can see her butt from that position. "Do I look fat?" she asks as she looks back up at Jaren with a furrowed brow and worried expression.

"Nope," Jaren answers as he turns and walks out of the kitchen with a huge smile on his face.

"You want anything?" Retha yells at his back as he departs. "You should be serving me you know. Bennie hooked her guests up. I have to come over here and fix my own cold snack. What kind of host are you anyway? Seriously, do I look fat?"

"Yeah, I'll share yours. If you had come to my place at a respectable hour I would have fed you a decent meal because I am a damn good host most of the time and believe me, you do not look fat."

Retha can't help but smile at his answer as she walks into the living room. When Jaren catches her eyes, the smile is unconsciously replaced with a flustered look as her eyes search for a place to rest other than his face. Retha can't help her reaction. He makes her feel good and uncomfortable at the same time. Every time he looks directly in her eyes, yes the cliché applies, she gets weak in the knees. *Goodness!*

"Got any good movies?" Retha asks in an attempt to calm herself.

"I thought you might be tired but we can watch a movie if you want."

"You don't have to stay up with me or I can watch in my room."

Jaren ignores her attempt at being considerate and starts going through his DVDs

Retha suddenly remembers she hasn't called the gang to let them know she made it safely. Brenda or Simone will dial her cell phone any minute if she doesn't call them first. Simone answers her phone. "Well, we were wondering if you were going to call or what."

"Just wanted to let you know I made it okay."

"How's your friend?"

Retha looks over at Jaren who is watching her. "He's good."

"Can I speak to him?"

"Why?"

"I just want to meet him and thank him for the tickets. What's wrong with you anyway? I'm beginning to think somethin's up between you two."

"Don't you start," Retha warns and hands the phone to Jaren. "Would you talk to my friend, Simone?"

Jaren raises his brow in a question but moves without hesitation to take the phone. Retha listens to his side of the conversation with a little uneasiness.

"Hello."

"It's nice to meet you too. Looking forward to meeting you and Retha's other friends in person."

"No need to thank me for the tickets. They were no problem to get and Retha has thanked me to the point of boredom."

Retha gives him a look of disgust. He smiles back at her with a smile that could melt Lady Liberty.

"Yeah, sure."

"No, I don't mind."

"Hi, Brenda." A very long pause.

"I will take good care of her." Another much longer pause.

"Sure."

"Okay."

"Okay, thanks. I'll talk to you later." Jaren puts down the phone with a thoughtful smile. "Your friends, which one were you trying to bring over here with you?"

Retha can't hold back her laugher. "Brenda!" she answers, understanding the reason for the question very well.

"Oh yeah, I definitely made the right decision on that one."

"Don't be nasty, Jaren."

"No, they both seem nice. Brenda, Simone, what's the other friend's name?"

"Michele. She's a little quieter than the other two. You'll like all three of them."

"Yeah, I bet."

The two friends settle in to watch their movie. Retha makes herself at home by stretching out on one of the sofas and Jaren sits on a floor cushion in front of a chair across the room. In less than thirty minutes, they are both on their way to another world. They take turns waking up and looking at each other. Jaren gets up and wakes Retha for bed. She accepts his proffered hand allowing him to lead her to her bedroom. Outside her room, she plants a kiss on his cheek, tells him goodnight and enters the room closing the door behind her. At the moment, standing outside his guestroom door offers Jaren considerably more warmth than his own bed. He wonders how long he can hold out.

Retha's mind never leaves her host during her shower. Her thoughts race. *This is miserable. I want to attack this twenty-nine-year-old. Hell, Stella was twenty years older than what's-his-name when she got her groove back. Three years is nothing. More the issue is that he may not be interested in me. He doesn't look at me like he's not interested. God, why does he look at me like that? I can hardly stand it. If I dabbled with him, would I be able to stand the pressure when he loses interest? Don't even go there Retha. Leave that alone.* Retha crawls into bed and passes into exhausted oblivion.

Chapter 11 -- A Good Time

Jaren's guest awakens happier than any mere mortal should. She lies in bed for a moment smiling to herself. She sees Jaren in her mind and smells him with her memory but dismisses him as the cause of her euphoria. *Better get up before those guys start calling for me.* After a good stretch, she bounds from the bed and heads to the bathroom to take care of those morning essentials. When she leaves her room she finds Jaren sitting on his sofa watching *Sports Center.*

"How'd you sleep? Okay." He asks and answers his question.

"Like a rock. I was tired after all that traveling. How about you? Did you sleep okay?" Retha asks as she turns her head toward the kitchen sensing the fragrant allure of java.

"I made you some coffee. I hope it's good because it's my first time."

His remark catches Retha off guard. She can't help but wonder if there is a hidden meaning but Jaren seems absorbed with the sports broadcast he is watching. *Just my dirty mind.*

"If it's not good, I'll let you know," Retha yells from the kitchen as she pours the blackest cup of coffee she has ever seen from the full pot. *Does he think I'm going to drink the entire pot by myself?* "Are you going to join me in a cup?" she asks as he enters the kitchen.

"I have no addictions. Not even coffee." Jaren smiles at her as he leans against a counter to watch his guest.

Retha starts to come back at him but stops after sipping on the coffee. *Damn, this coffee is good!*

"Listen, I've got to get out of here but we need to make plans for tonight. I need the address to pick you up. I'd like to take you and your friends to eat after the game, if you don't have anything else planned. I've got a place not too far from the Garden that I go to after games. Nothing fancy but it's pretty nice. Do you need to talk to your friends first?"

This deal keeps getting better and better. When does the balloon burst? "No, I know they won't mind. I'm sure they'd like that." Retha holds back the question that is at the forefront of her mind. *Why are you doing all of this?* She cannot figure out how to say he is being too generous. She is afraid to ask him why. Besides, she doesn't want to seem unappreciative. Telling herself to leave the gift horse alone, Retha gives Jaren Bennie's address and they make plans to meet at six that evening. To make that gift horse a little more bothersome, Jaren hands her a set of keys.

~ ~

A fresh pot of coffee is brewing when Retha walks into Bennie's apartment. She has a quick cup, her second cup of the morning. She sips on her coffee, smiles to herself and floats off into La La Land as she remembers Jaren making coffee just for her. Brenda, always dependable, snaps her back to the present by throwing her jacket at her so they can leave.

The ladies take off with no real direction. They have a late lunch in the Village at a little Italian eatery Bennie likes and shop in SoHo. They return to Bennie's right at five, thirty minutes past the time Jackson had allowed. Retha takes all the joy out of Jackson by taking away his opportunity to fuss. She declares there is no time for fussing and rushes everyone to get ready before Jaren arrives. She is excited to the point of agitation and stays on her friends to get dressed. She has Brenda pissed nearly all the way off with the rushing. "Shit, you'd think Clinton is coming to pick us up the way yo' ass is acting," Brenda complains.

Brenda and Michele are still in the bathroom getting dressed when the door buzzer sounds. Jaren is a full ten minutes early. Jackson rings the buzzer to let him in but Retha insists on opening the apartment door. Jackson complains about not being able to open the door of his own home but Retha ignores him. She can hardly wait to see his reaction when he meets Jaren. She is certain he will appreciate the meeting far more than the women and she is right.

When Jaren walks in, Jackson starts laughing. "Oh hell! Oh hell! I don't believe it! I don't believe it! I don't believe it. My man!" Jaren smiles and seems at ease with the reaction. "Bennie, Bennie, come out here, baby. You not gonna believe this!" Jackson yells.

Bennie and Simone exit the bedroom together. Bennie's hands go to her mouth as she lets out a gasp. Simone's mouth drops open. Brenda and Michele hear all the commotion and hurry out of the bathroom and see Jackson gripping Jaren's hand and patting him on the back while the ladies stand around making noise. Michele doesn't recognize Jaren but Brenda does and doesn't hesitate to ask, "Ain't that that baseball player?"

Retha introduces her old friends to her new friend. As expected, Brenda's thoughts flow directly from her mouth. "Re, I'mo kill you girl. That's why you been keeping everything so secret. What did you think we were gonna do to him?"

Retha laughs nervously and hurries her friends into the bedroom to finish getting ready. Once inside the room, Bennie grabs her things and returns to the living room, leaving the friends alone.

"Retha, why didn't you tell us?" Michele asks. "I've even heard of him."

"I wanted to surprise you guys and I didn't want a whole bunch of pressure like my friends like to put on me." Throwing an accusatory glance in her fellow Texan's direction, she adds, "Brenda."

"Don't even try it. That ain't no reason for you to keep us in the dark. There's no tellin' what we could have done if we had known you knew this dude." Brenda's hands are firmly pushing down on her abundant hips and she is ready to enter her "telling off" mode.

"See what I mean. Let's go." Retha starts to walk out of the room but stops and asks Brenda. "I know you're not really upset, are you?"

Simone interrupts Brenda's oncoming rampage. "Upset -- hell no, amazed; astonished; bedazzled -- yes. He is deliciously fine. Retha, are you sure you want to put him out there as just a friend?" Simone laughs as she tries to high five Brenda. Brenda shirks off the gesture, although the question does cause her disgust with Retha to wane.

The group files out of the building to find a stretch limo and driver waiting to take them to the game. Once in the limo, the ladies have little opportunity to talk over Jackson and Jaren who act like old friends. After a while, the driver is right in the middle of the conversation with the men talking sports.

They arrive at the Garden in plenty of time to take their seats before tipoff. The seats are the best Retha has ever had for a game. Jaren immediately realizes he should have gotten the tickets on two rows instead of all in a row. He lands smack in the middle of the group with Jackson on one side and Simone on the other. Michele and Retha are near the aisle with Brenda and Bennie on the other end. Jaren hadn't considered the possibility that he might not sit next to Retha. He knows it would be rude to switch seats now that they are all situated. He contemplates how he can maneuver Michele into switching seats with him. There are two seats next to Retha right on the aisle. As he is about to excuse himself and move into the empty seat to her left and talk with her for a few minutes, two young men slide in and take the seats. The strangers notice Jaren and render nods of acknowledgement before focusing their attention on Retha and Michele.

The game is a fast one with a close score but Jaren and Retha are distracted by their neighbors. Jaren doesn't mind that Jackson stays in his ear but the guy sitting next to Retha is working his worst nerves. The man is clearly making a play and Retha doesn't seem to notice or, if she does, she doesn't mind. She's laughing more than Jaren has ever heard her laugh. At one point, she lets her head fall back and laughs loud and hard. Michele is sitting on the edge of her seat and leaning forward so she can get in on the conversation with Retha and the two men. The laughter dies down enough for Jaren to hear Retha and one of the strangers discussing the game as if they are old friends on an evening out together. Jaren's spot has been usurped; he tries to hide his disappointment. His guests are enjoying themselves and that was, supposedly, his purpose for buying the tickets and bringing them out. He tries to relax and get into the game but all the playmaking going on a few seats away keeps him on edge. He gets a good game dialog going with Simone and Jackson. Simone knows the game. She is a sport and he likes her easy, direct, and friendly ways. She reminds him of Retha.

No one would ever guess that Retha could recite a great deal of the conversation that passes between Jackson, Simone, and Jaren during the first half of the game. Retha wants to join in their conversation, but can never find a way to escape her involvement with Michele and the strangers. During halftime the strangers leave their seats and Retha finds ease in talking to the rest of her group.

"So, Retha, you enjoying yourself?" Jaren asks with as much innuendo as he can muster without sounding like a rejected boyfriend.

Retha smiles without looking at him and replies with exuberance. "This is a good game!"

Jaren decides to leave the discussion where it lies. When the game starts back up, he is surprised but pleased to see Michele and Retha switch seats. Michele is now seated next to the men near the aisle. Simone asks Retha if she wants to switch seats and Jaren is slightly offended when he notices Retha respond with a wave of her hand and a, "no girl."

The game goes down to the buzzer but the Knicks squeeze out the win by three points over the Lakers. After the game, Jaren takes them to a small diner which he declares to be one of his favorite spots. The diner has good food and excellent music blasting, most of which Retha and her friends have never heard.

Retha and Michele go straight to the ladies room. Michele hates public toilets but she has been holding her bladder and figures the restaurant restroom is more sanitary than one in the Garden. On their way back to the table, Retha walks directly into one of the guys that sat next to them at the game. Now she understands why Michele was so inquisitive about where they were having dinner. Michele stops to talk to the guys so Retha stops also, more out of politeness than a wish to converse. Michele introduces everyone. Retha wonders where she was when Michele got their names, probably listening to Simone and Jaren's conversation. Michele's friend, Malcolm, gives her his card. The other young man, Akbar, hands Retha a card and asks her to call him. Retha takes the card but explains she does not live in New York and is not likely to have an opportunity to call. He asks Retha if she has a number where he can reach her. She tells him she does not give out her phone number. Akbar accepts Retha's refusal without further comment but continues to stare at her in a manner that makes her uneasy. Retha excuses herself and returns to her table leaving Michele to finish her conversation with Malcolm.

When Michele, with her null and void brain, gets back to the table she announces to everyone, "Retha, that guy is hot for you, girl. Malcolm could hardly talk to me because Akbar kept asking questions about you. They want us to go out with them."

Retha wants to slide under the table with embarrassment. She doesn't even bother to respond to Michele's excited outburst. She had told Jaren that her friends were lively but she hopes he will not have a bad impression of them when they go home on Monday. "Well, I've got their phone numbers. I don't see anything wrong with them meeting us out to dance," Michele continues, sensing that she has talked too much again.

At Michele's comment, Bennie and Simone watched for Jaren's reaction. It is obvious to the ladies that there is more than friendship between Jaren and Retha. Retha is doing a pretty good job of hiding her feelings but Jaren watches every move Retha makes and goes on alert at the sound of her voice. He could hardly respond to questions after Malcolm and Akbar entered the restaurant and stopped speaking at all while Retha and Michele were with the men.

Simone's brain cells are racing with excitement and worry. Jaren is one of the most sexually attractive men she has ever met. He is a little too light-skinned for her taste but everything else is so great that she has decided not to fault the brother for his coloring. He has the whole package. He is wealthy and a much sought after celebrity. These traits alone carry a certain degree of appeal. But Jaren has so much charm and personality it is hard not to gravitate toward him. His smile is genuine and beautiful and would leave almost any woman a little shaken. His green eyes are intense and so mystifying that it is hard not to look into them. He is tall, lean, and muscular and wears well-fitted clothing that show off his style and physique to their best advantage. There is nothing pretty about the man. He'd make a damn ugly woman but, goodness, he is a handsome man.

Upon first meeting Jaren, Simone thought she might get something going with him, but it is clear that he wants Retha for more than a friend. He looks at Retha differently from the way he looks at her friends and tries to catch her eyes at every opportunity. Retha blushes and avoids his stares. There are serious sparks flying between these two. Simone wonders if Retha believes she is fooling anyone because there is no way she is immune to Jaren's attentions toward her. Retha and Simone are very different in their dealings with men. If Simone was in Retha's position, she would be all over the brother, would make sure he knew she was game for whatever intrigue he wanted. But Simone has always been adept at the game. Simone understands "here today, gone tomorrow." Retha has never played the game, finds it boring, does not comprehend it, and does not want to learn the art of the game. Simone wonders if she should warn her friend to be careful. She fears things may go badly for Retha if Jaren is the first person she has an emotional relationship with since Joe. Jaren would be very difficult to forget after a breakup. This brother could break a sister down, way down.

The group finishes their dinner, pile back into the limo and arrive at Eighty-Eighth Street fat, tired, and happy. "Y'all come on up for a while. We can have a drink before you head home," Jackson offers. He has enjoyed the evening and wants it to continue. Retha reads Bennie's face. She is tired. All the ladies are.

"I don't mind stopping in for a minute," Jaren responds to the invitation and turns to Retha with a questioning look.

"I'm tired, Jaren. If it's okay with you Jackson, I'll pass," Retha begs out.

"Come on Retha. You'd think you was an old woman the way you actin'. Y'all come on up for a bit," Jackson pleads.

Retha spots Bennie subtly shaking her head behind Jackson. Retha hates to tell him no when he so obviously wants Jaren to stay, but Bennie is tired and Retha can't disregard Bennie. "Don't make me feel bad, Unc. You'll get to spend more time with Jaren before we leave."

"Girl, you just a party poop." Jackson gives in and then addresses Jaren. "Listen, brotha, I know you tired of us telling you this but I sure do thank you for tonight. And we havin' dinner over here on Sunday for these ladies and me and Bennie would be honored if you'd join us. She gonna cook some good food and Retha here promised me a couple of her sweet potato pies. How about it?"

Jaren doesn't hesitate. "Wouldn't miss it. I'll see you Sunday and we can finish that discussion."

The two men give each other death grip handshakes, the kind that mean respect, hit each other on the shoulder and part company.

Jaren has been very friendly and talkative with Retha's friends all evening though he has barely spoken a full sentence to her since they left the Garden. She wonders what caused the cold treatment he is dishing out. He talked to Simone more than any of the other women causing Retha a pang of jealousy. He doesn't speak a clear syllable during the ride to his place. Once they get inside, Retha knows she has been silent long enough. "So, did you like my friends?" she asks in an effort to start up a conversation. She holds her breath fearing he shows interest in Simone as more than a friend.

"They're great. I think I like Simone best. She's a nice lady."

"Nearly everyone likes Simone the best. You can't beat her as a person." *How diplomatic of me,* Retha criticizes herself.

"Did you enjoy your evening?" Jaren asks.

Retha cannot help but smile in response. "I had a great time. The game was awesome and that is a cool place you took us to eat. The food was fantastic." Retha is relieved. Jaren seems relaxed and not too smitten by Simone the Fox. Her gal pals have big things in store for the next day so she decides to call it a night. "I think I'm ready to crash."

"Retha let me ask you a question." Jaren follows her into the kitchen where she is getting her eighth glass of water for the day to ensure she doesn't sleep through the night.

"Ask away. Anything."

"Why do you always look away when I look at you? Do I make you uncomfortable?"

Retha answers before she thinks or she would not be so honest. "Because I like looking at you but I don't want to be rude. I don't want to stare. I bet people stare at you all the time." She gives Jaren a wicked one-sided smile. "You're my screen saver, you know."

"Your screen saver?"

"Yep. I have your picture on my computer screen at home. I had a different picture of you on my screen at work before I got out of the Army. Rachel too. You remember my friend Rachel. She has your picture as a screen saver too."

Jaren blushes. "Why do you have me on your computer screen?"

"Because I like looking at you. So when you look back, I feel like I've been caught taking a peek. I know I'm silly, but hey I'm just being a woman." Retha is honest with Jaren about this but she will not share her true feelings with him. She keeps her secret.

As honest as she is, she is taken completely off guard by his comeback. "I'm flattered. I like looking at you too but when you look away I wonder if you're uncomfortable with me or if there is a problem."

Jaren's honesty should be flattering also but it unsettles Retha. She can't make herself look at him. "I'll try to do better," she responds with her eyes turned downward. "I think I'm going to take a shower and go to bed now." Retha is flustered.

Retha places her glass in the sink before walking over to Jaren and bestowing a gentle kiss on his cheek. "Thank you so much for such a good time, not only for my friends but for me too."

Jaren is silent for a moment before he asks. "Is that the best 'thank you' you can give?" As he asks the question, he reaches around her waist and pulls her closer to him. Not allowing Retha time to react, he kisses her very lightly, barely touching her lips at first. Retha doesn't move; she can't. Jaren opens his mouth slightly and delicately runs his tongue across her mouth but Retha's lips do not part. He begins sucking ever so softly on her bottom lip until she allows her own mouth to open. Jaren pulls her closer and kisses her so deeply that she can't help wrapping her arms around his neck. They stand there kissing for what seems like several minutes. When Jaren's hands start to wander, Retha pulls away and steps backward. She visibly shudders after she does so.

"Are you cold?" Jaren asks with a smile on his face.

"No not at all, but I think it is time for me to go to sleep." Retha chooses not to use the word "bed." She does not want to leave him an opening to make an offer.

"If that's what you want." Jaren steps aside allowing her room to pass without going around him. "Pleasant dreams."

"Goodnight, Jaren."

Retha doesn't dream at all; she hardly sleeps. She is afraid Jaren might come in her room. She considers locking her door. She knows he would not try to have sex with her against her will; he wouldn't have to. So she lies there wide awake for hours. When she does doze off it seems like she only sleeps for a few minutes before the alarm goes off.

Retha had good reason to be concerned. Jaren didn't go to sleep for at least another two hours after climbing into his bed. He laid there the entire time contemplating going into her room. Two things kept him away. He thought of how embarrassed and hurt he would be if her door was locked. There was also the possibility she might have turned him away.

～～

Jaren rises early the next morning. He has a full day scheduled which includes attending his cousin's high school basketball game in Jersey. He wishes he hadn't booked himself so solid during Retha's stay but figures she will be out with her friends and probably have no time for him during the day anyway. He knocks at Retha's door but does not get an answer so he leaves her a note letting her know that he will be out most of the day.

Retha is in the bathroom brushing her teeth when Jaren knocks. She is relieved to find him gone when she comes out of the room. She is not sure how to act toward him since he kissed her. Should she go on as if it never happened? Should she try to talk to him about it? What? She isn't even sure what she wants, but she knows for certain that she does not want to get hurt. Panic wells up inside her. *Damn it Retha, it was just a kiss. You're a grown damn woman. Why the hell are you so worked up over a kiss? Why? My God why do I like this man so much?*

Chapter 12 -- No Strings

Retha's friends have a full day planned, so she packs her carryall and takes her clothes for the evening along with her to Bennie's. After a little too much shopping, a barely digested lunch, and more shopping, the ladies head to the Nederlander Theatre to catch a matinee showing only Simone wants to see. The evening is left for Brenda and Michele to plan. Simone and Retha beg the "wild pair," as they call Brenda and Michele, not to get them killed, arrested, beaten up, thrown out of any establishment, or cursed out. The "wild pair" promises it will be a nice boring evening like the two "fuddy duddies" enjoy. They fail to tell Retha or Simone that they have invited Bill and George and Akbar and Malcolm to meet them at the club later in the evening.

They choose a club highly recommended by Simone's elusive cousin Renee that offers a good selection of dance music. Jackson also gives his unsolicited approval of the club which draws one of Bennie's disgusted looks.

George, Bill, Akbar, and Malcolm are waiting at the club when the ladies arrive. Akbar is persistent but not a pest and he keeps Retha from longing for Jaren who she has been thinking about all day.

At about half past one, the partiers start talking about going to another club that stays open all night. Retha is finished. She is tired but more than that she wants to see Jaren. Simone and Michele will not make an issue of her leaving them but Brenda will. Retha has to be tactical with Brenda. She can't simply announce that she is going home unless she is prepared for fifty eleven dozen questions and complaints. Here goes. "Brenda, girl, I'm so tired and my feet are killing me. I need to go home and go to bed. You won't be mad at me if I don't go with you guys, will you?"

"How come you don't want to go? We're just getting started," Brenda says as if she did not hear Retha's explanation.

I'm glad I didn't use all my excuses at once. I know her too well. Retha holds back a smile at Brenda's predictability. "Well you know, I've got to get over to Aida's early tomorrow to help her cook food for tomorrow night, so I need to get my rest. I'm going to head on home when you guys leave here, okay sweetie?"

Brenda gives her blessing.

~~

Jaren spends a good portion of the afternoon at his aunt's house in Jersey. He calls Retha several times on her cell phone but gets no answer. He doesn't want to appear desperate though he is. When he gets home there is no sign of her. He checks her room and gets concerned when he realizes she has taken her carryall and her overnight bag. He hopes he did not offend her and cause her to leave his home for good but figures she would have taken everything if she did not plan to return. Again, Jaren thinks about calling her but feels that if Retha wants to see him, she will call. He wonders if she made a date with one of the men she met at the game the night before; the thought irritates him. He contemplates going out but fears he might miss her so he settles in with a movie.

As the time moves forward, his level of irritation rises. *She has to know I want to see her. What did she think I meant by kissing her? Why the hell am I getting so mad? I have no claim on this woman.* Jaren dozes off on the sofa while waiting but his phones keep ringing with calls and beeping with messages and waking him. With each call and message he gets a little angrier at Retha, mainly because she is not the person reaching out to him. He hears her at the door well after two in the morning. Not sure if he is still angry, he does know he is relieved.

Retha comes in quietly because she can't tell if Jaren is sleeping or just lying on the sofa. She walks toward him and gives a quick start when he suddenly sits up. "Hey, you scared me!" she nearly yells, caught off guard. "Hi," she continues not hiding her joy at seeing him.

Jaren attributes the happiness radiating from his house guest to a night out partying without him. "Hey. What, have you been gone all day?" he responds as disinterestedly as possible.

"Pretty much. What time did you get in?" Retha asks as she heads to her room to leave her things.

"About eight or so," Jaren answers with a frown as he takes in the length and fit of Retha's dress. He wants to follow her into her room but waits for her to return. "You and your friends go out dancing this evening?"

"Yeah." Retha plops into a chair and starts rubbing her feet. "We had a blast. This has been the best trip. Those two buddies of mine,

Michele and Brenda, they told these guys that Jackson introduced us to and those two guys from the basketball game where we would be tonight so we had plenty of dance partners. My feet are killing me. Michele and Brenda never get tired of dancing. They've all gone to another club to party but I couldn't hang with them; I'm too tired." She waits for a response from Jaren but gets none. "So, you didn't have any plans for the evening?"

"No Retha. I'm kind of a homebody. I don't do much partying."

"That's a good thing. I don't either, but I am enjoying my time here." Retha sits a few moments longer. Sensing that Jaren doesn't want to talk, she disappointedly gets up and heads to her room. "I'm going to take a shower." *Hell, he sure seems grumpy. Maybe he's one of those moody people. He was acting strange with me last night and then grabbed me and kissed me and now he acts like he doesn't want to be bothered with me at all. I could be out partying with my friends but I wanted to get here to see his ass. I'm so stupid.*

Retha showers, washes the smoke from her hair, and puts on a pair of satin-like pajamas. She is upset with Jaren for acting sullen with her and mad at herself for expecting more from him. She goes into the kitchen to get food to munch on and a glass of water before returning to the front room to sit down with him for a few minutes while she eats her grapes.

"So you had a good time tonight?" Jaren asks.

"Yeah, I did."

"I called and left a message for you to call me. I thought I might go with you tonight."

"Why didn't you call my cell phone?"

"I did. Twice. You're pretty bad with that cell phone aren't you? Did you miss me?"

Retha tries to hide the smile that takes over her face as she blushes. "I'm sorry about the phone." She drops her eyes even further. "I did miss you. Did you miss me?"

"Yeah, I did." Jaren cannot take his eyes off Retha and she cannot stand the tension; she has to get away. She takes her glass to the kitchen and heads off to bed. "Goodnight, Jaren. I'm going to bed."

She is almost to the door of her room when she hears him call her name. *Oh no.* Retha turns and finds Jaren a few steps behind her. "When are you going to spend time with me?" He asks.

"I didn't know you wanted me to spend time with you. You want me to stay up with you?" Retha can hear the excitement in her voice. Jaren is so close to her that she knows he wants more than her company.

"Come here," he commands in a very low voice as he reaches for her.

Retha takes the two steps between them as if she is powerless to resist his request. Jaren places his hand behind her head and gently pulls her damp hair to tilt her head back as he looks into her eyes. She can't help but turn her eyes away. "Look at me Retha." She turns her eyes back to his face. "I like your eyes but you never let me get a good look at them." Jaren holds her gaze as he lowers his mouth to hers. He doesn't need to nibble on her lip to get her to open her mouth this time. Jaren allows his emotions to come out in his kisses. When his hands start to roam over Retha's body, she doesn't stop him. He takes his mouth away from hers to whisper in her ear, "Sleep with me tonight Retha. Please!"

Retha's stomach joins her heart in her chest. "Jaren we're supposed to be friends. I want to stay friends." He kisses her face, her neck, her ears, her shoulders as he whispers "We'll stay friends; I promise."

Without waiting for an answer, Jaren takes Retha by the hand and leads her to his room and closes the door behind them. Retha has no thought, desire, or will to resist. Jaren stops next to his bed and kisses her as he begins to slowly unbutton her top. Once he has the top unbuttoned he stands back and stares at her naked breasts. Retha stands there awkwardly until Jaren returns her attention to him by reaching out and placing a hand on one of her breasts, gently rubbing his thumb across her hardened nipple. She enjoys the touch of his hands on her bare skin. Retha begins to unbutton his shirt so she can see and touch his skin. Jaren watches her progress with surprise at her sudden participation. Once she gets his shirt off, he guides her down on to the bed and glides his hands down her hips taking her pajama bottoms along with his fingertips. He runs his fingers along her scarred upper thigh and gently kisses the scar. Jaren's cool, easy lovemaking has Retha overly anxious. She reaches for him causing him to moan at her touch. He is so hard she wants to see and touch him unclothed. Jaren doesn't wait for her to help him with the rest of his clothing. He has held back as long as possible and is out of his pants so fast that Retha nearly bursts out laughing but she restrains her laughter so as not to spoil the mood.

The sight of Jaren's body puts Retha in another world completely. She wants to lie there and relish the sight and sense of him for a while but Jaren will not wait a moment longer. He has a condom on before she knows what he's doing. As he lies down on top of her, she accepts him and whispers, "No strings," more for her own benefit than his.

"No strings," Jaren moans in an answer as he enters Retha's warm melting body.

Retha has nearly forgotten what it feels like to be with a man she desires. She has imagined but having Jaren inside her is much better. Jaren lies there without moving for a full minute or longer. He kisses her deeply and then all over her face. Suddenly he groans loudly, "Retha, baby, I'm sorry but I don't think I'm going to be able to last long." She can feel him throbbing inside her as he starts to move. He feels so good, she has to bite her lip not to scream. It seems before they get started good Jaren loses control, groans long, loud and deep and collapses on top of her.

A more sexually active woman would be horrified but it felt so good to have Jaren inside her that Retha isn't upset that he finished so fast. It has been so long since she felt this level of sexually arousal that she is happy for what he has given her.

Jaren is embarrassed. He can't believe he lost control the way he did. He has thought about being with Retha every day and night since he met her. The thought of her has consumed him. How is it possible that he couldn't last three minutes inside of her? "Damn, what happened to me?" he complains.

"It's okay." Retha hopes he normally lasts longer. If he doesn't, that explains no regular girlfriend.

When Jaren rolls off of her, she grabs her top and heads to the bathroom. Not sure what Jaren wants and not wanting to embarrass him any further, when Retha exits his bathroom she picks up her PJ bottoms from the floor and starts to leave the room.

"Where are you going?" Jaren asks as he heads toward the bathroom.

"To my room, to bed."

"I thought you were going to sleep with me tonight."

Retha's heart leaps. She wants to sleep with him more than make love with him. It's been a long time since she curled up in the bed with a man. She happily climbs back into the bed as Jaren goes into the bathroom. He wastes no time when he returns. Without a word he unbuttons Retha's top and takes it off. She is ecstatic. He stretches out facing her, places his elbow on the bed, rests his head in that hand, and watches as he lightly strokes her breasts with his free hand. After a while, he leans forward and kisses and suckles each in its turn while running his hand all over her body, stopping at her upper thighs. Retha is so wet when he touches her that his own body throbs. His hand does delicious things slowly and deeply as she avails herself to his caresses. Retha stops him from touching her just before she releases on his hand. Jaren is in no hurry when he enters her this time. He starts easy, going from long deep strokes to nice small dips into her body. Retha can no longer hold back her moans. She has missed this type of lovemaking, this type of passion. She wants to hold on for a long time, hell forever, but soon finds herself letting go. She fights the urge and tries to think about something other than what Jaren's body is doing to hers but is lost to the building orgasm. She digs her nails into him but he doesn't seem to notice. Jaren lasts quite a while longer before letting go. Afterwards he lies there on top of Retha while she lightly kisses his shoulder. She is relieved that he can last longer than thirty seconds.

--

Retha panics, believing she's in the middle of one of her "me and Joe" dreams she had experienced for months after her husband's death. When those dreams stopped, she knew she was better. So when she awakes totally wrapped in Jaren's arms and legs it takes her a moment to realize she is here and now, not with a wished for Joe but a real Jaren. At first she is relieved but then torn for preferring to be with Jaren instead of dreaming about Joe. She rebukes herself and determines not to think of Joe.

Retha turns to face Jaren and watches him sleep for a few minutes before reaching down between them. He wakes and is ready for her in no time. She rolls over on top of him and lowers her warm open body to his. Jaren also wonders if he is dreaming because her sweetness is better than any he has experienced. Retha makes love to him and he lies there and enjoys it. He has never known a woman to make love to him as Retha does. His stomach muscles tighten much quicker than he thought possible. Life is marvelous.

Jaren gets up just after daybreak. He wants her again but is ashamed to wake her for that purpose. He decides to make Retha's coffee and use that as an excuse. He takes the freshly made cup of coffee into the room and no sooner than the smell finds Retha's nostrils her eyes pop open. The laugh on Jaren's face tells her how she looks, awful. Her thick kinky hair is squashed flat against her head on one side and in the back but standing straight up on the other side and top. She looks like she made love all night long. Embarrassed, she covers her head with the blanket but Jaren pulls the blanket back with a strong yank. "Damn, I guess what I see is what I get with you," he laughs. Retha stays lying on her stomach and tries to cover her unruly naps with her arms but when Jaren starts kissing her shoulders and her back she forgets about her head and the freshly brewed cup of coffee he used to lure her awake. She relaxes in his kisses and caresses. "Come here, Jaren," she coaxes. No need to ask twice. Soon, he is positioned over her back as she raises herself. Jaren can't help but gasp at how wet she is. He's amazed that she is as voracious for him as he is for her. *This keeps getting better and better*. Jaren smiles as they once again attempt to satisfy their appetites for each other.

Later, the lovers take a long relaxing shower together, lie across the bed and talk before dozing off in each other's arms. At precisely half past eleven, the sound of a ringing phone awakens Retha. She grabs the technological offender and passes it to Jaren who is nearly a zombie. "Yeah." There is a moment's pause and then, "AH SHIT, DAMN! Is he by himself?" A slight pause in expletives "Hell! Keep them down there for a few minutes. Give me five minutes before you let them up. Tell Aaron you woke me and I'll need a couple of minutes. Shit!"

Retha can tell by the conversation that a person or persons Jaren should have expected is or are downstairs for him. She gets up, grabs her things, and heads toward her room. "Where are you going?" Jaren asks. Retha glances over her shoulder at him as if to say "don't be ridiculous" and keeps stepping. Jaren doesn't want to be bothered but he made this commitment and can't back out. Why couldn't Retha make it hard for him, no not her, not her style?

He knocks on her door. "Yeah," she answers.

Jaren yells through the door instead of entering the room. "Retha, hey listen. I'm sorry about this. I forgot I scheduled this for today."

"Don't worry about it, Jaren. Get dressed."

As far as Retha is concerned, it's probably best they were interrupted because she would have stayed in that room with him until he threw her out. She is having dinner with her family today. She has not seen Aida yet and JJ is coming down from school for the weekend to see her. She is pleased that Jaren apologized. She listens for his guests and is surprised when she hears women's voices. There is also a man with them. So he meant he had a date scheduled, not an appointment, not plans, but a date. Jealousy is vicious. Retha goes from happy honey to jealous bitch in a nanosecond. She wants to confront him but decides to leave for Aida's and deal with him later.

Jaren's guests are his friend and teammate, Aaron; Aaron's girlfriend, Lauren; and her friend, Jennifer. Jaren has never met Jennifer so this is a blind date. He makes himself presentable and is his usual congenial self by the time he opens the door for his visitors. They have plans to drive over to another friend's house on Long Island for lunch. All kinds of excuses bounce inside Jaren's head to break the date but nothing he can live with comes to mind. He can't understand why he set a date during Retha's visit when he could have met Jennifer anytime. Why had he tried to convince himself that his interest in Retha was not that great? Now he wishes he could kick his own ass.

About fifteen minutes after Aaron and the ladies arrive; Retha emerges from her room ready to make her escape. Jaren's guests cannot hide their surprise and Aaron gives Jaren a look that is downright accusatory.

Jaren introduces Retha and his guests before asking her where she's headed. He considers inviting her along with them but realizes that would be a very awkward situation.

Retha responds with a smile. "I've got to get over to Aida's. I haven't seen her yet and I promised to spend the day. I thought you were going to knock on my door earlier. Some alarm clock you turned out to be." To his friends, she adds "Nice meeting you all. Maybe we'll see each other later."

Jaren follows her out and closes the door behind him not caring what his visitors think. "When are you coming back?"

Refusing any eye contact, Retha fumbles in her purse as she answers. "I'll be at Aida's all day, Jaren. Call me. See you later." She walks off without a backward glance. Her demeanor upsets Jaren but he is not certain why. She acts as if she could care less that he will spend the day with Jennifer. He shakes off his agitation and returns to his guests. He makes no attempt to explain Retha to them though Lauren asks numerous seemingly innocent questions about his house guest. Later, when they are alone, Aaron goes for the direct approach. "Is she single?"

"Why?" Aaron is more than a little shady and Jaren doesn't appreciate the question.

"Just curious. Man, what have you got, iron nuts? How can you have a woman like that in the house with you and not sleep with her?"

"I did. So, you don't even think about that woman."

"She is hot! How was she?"

"None of your damn business."

Chapter 13 -- Family Parties

Retha's mother-in-law cuts a long-planned visit to Delaware short by two days to spend time with Retha before her return to Texas. Aida had offered to cancel the trip entirely but Retha begged her not to, explaining that she would spend most of her time with her friends. Aida understood and was happy for any opportunity to see her daughter-in-law. The ladies enjoy an afternoon out picking up a few additional things for dinner. Aida prepares her mouth-watering stuffed roast pork, along with rice and beans, avocado salad, and fried plantains. Dinner preparation turns into a refresher cooking lesson for Retha who had long ago learned to cook this food but since she cooks it so seldom has lost that special touch in the preparation.

While cooking, they catch up on all the news in their families. Then Aida asks the dreaded question. "You know what I want you to tell me, Retha?"

"What's that, Aida?" Retha answers with a question, all the time knowing exactly what Aida has on her mind.

"How are things with you and the big officer? JJ says he go to Korea. I don't think he was for you. I think maybe you don' like him that way. You find someone special yet, any one that can make you happy like my Joe?"

"Aida, I don't want to be bothered. I meet men all the time. I mean I was in the Army. You need to stop worrying about me. You don't want me to rush into anything do you? Besides, no one could take Joe's place."

Aida shakes her finger at the side of Retha's head. "You don' need somebody to take my Joe's place. You need a man to take his own place. You not so young. Time for you to find a good man and have babies. Joe would want that for you."

Retha doesn't quite understand Aida's obsession with her finding a mate but she listens to the same lecture every time she talks with Aida. She thinks her mother-in-law may believe Joe is out there watching and will not rest until Retha is settled into a good relationship. The truth is that Aida loves Retha and wants her to be as happy as she was with Joe.

"I will Aida, but don't rush me. You want me to find someone good don't you?"

"You too smart to be with a bad man. I no worry about that, never hoppen."

Retha changes the subject by asking when JJ is due to arrive. She is eager to see him. Marta expects him around four and then they will come over to Aida's. Retha becomes more anxious as the time for his arrival draws near. When he and Marta walk in, Retha is astounded at how much he has changed; he is a man now. Eighteen months ago he seemed to be a boy, but not now. He reminds her so much of Joe. Not dark like Joe, but the same build and mannerisms. He even wears the same haircut on that beautiful nappy, curly hair.

They sit and talk about his school and things going on in his life. A superb athlete, JJ has chosen to limit his involvement in sports because his academics were suffering. His chosen field, physical therapy, is very competitive so he needs excellent grades. Marta is such a proud parent, all she can do is smile and occasionally encourage JJ to tell Retha an achievement he may have forgotten to share. JJ asks about the family in San Antonio and makes plans to visit again during the summer.

Retha can't help but ask. "Are you nice to the ladies?"

"Mom, what kind of question is that?"

"Your father was very nice to me and your mother says he was nice to her but that they were just too young. It is important that you treat women well." Aida and Marta nod in agreement.

"I like women a lot and they like me. Some of my best friends are women and yes, I am very very nice to the ladies. I wouldn't consider myself a man if I wasn't."

Retha becomes emotional and gets up and hugs him long and hard. "I love you JJ," she tells him.

"I love you to Retha, I mean Mom, very much."

Aida watches and listens with tears in her eyes. "Just like my Joe. The lucky one who gets him, ah Dios mio!"

"Hey, Abuela can you explain that to this one girl I've been trying to talk to at school?" JJ jokes with his grandmother and gives her a hug.

Retha, JJ, Marta, and Aida eat as soon as Aida finishes cooking. The rest of the family and Retha's gang arrive in shifts and eat in shifts. Soon, all of Aida's guests are crammed in the apartment, eating, drinking, listening and dancing to merengue and salsa.

"Was Jaren upset when you got in last night, Miss Thang?" Simone asks Retha when no one else is in earshot.

"No, why would he be upset? I didn't need to wake him; he gave me a key."

"Listen, you might be able to fool the average person with that 'ain't nothing happening between me and Jaren bullshit,' but I am not the one, okay. Y'all got the hots for each other."

"You think you can keep that to yourself?" Retha whispers.

"I told Brenda and Mitch that I think he likes you but at that time I wasn't too sure how you felt. That was before you ran off last night. You were trying to get to that man weren't you?"

"Maybe I was tired."

"Please don't set yourself up. He seems like an awesome guy, but he can have almost any woman he wants and yes, he would be a fool not to want you but he is a man. I don't think I can go through another hurt with you. Do you think you can handle a relationship with him and even more important, a breakup?"

"Girl, don't think I haven't thought about it. Don't worry; we won't be having a relationship. I hope we can stay friends. He has made it very clear to me he doesn't have the time. Baseball is his woman. You are too much like me. You just verbalized all my thoughts. I'll be okay."

"Okay. You not mad at me for getting in yo' business?" Simone asks as she nudges Retha's shoulder with her own.

"That's what I got you for." Retha smiles at her friend with a thankful heart.

~ ~

The topic of Retha and Simone's conversation is having a pretty nice time himself at a party across the river. Jennifer is beautiful, intelligent, loves baseball, and enjoys a good time. Jaren decides to settle in for the day and not worry about getting to Retha; tomorrow is another day. As much as he enjoys his present company, thoughts of Retha keep popping into his head. He wonders where their relationship could go with the season around the corner and her living in Texas. He wouldn't even be able to spend time with her on his few days off. Jaren decides not to get caught up. He has seen it many times before with teammates and friends around the league. So much drama and heartache with guys distraught over a bad relationship that started off really hot. He decides it is a good thing that Retha doesn't live close. It is best to let the intimacy end after she goes home on Monday. Hopefully, they can stay friends.

--

As the party at Aida's draws to an end, all three of Retha's buddies announce that they want to go over and see Jaren's place and hang out for a while. When JJ learns that they aren't calling it a night, he wants to hang with them. He is surprised to hear that his stepmother is not staying with the others at the Jacksons' place but with a male friend. He doesn't ask any questions but is anxious to meet Retha's new friend.

Jaren is at home with his guests for no more than thirty minutes when Retha calls and asks if she can bring her son and friends over for a while. Jaren hesitates for a moment before telling her that while she is in town his home is hers. Retha is a little formal with him. She is hurt he has not called her all day. When she learns he still has company, she cools even more. Jaren is tired of his guests and ready to be rid of them but they are not ready to leave. Jennifer has become enamored and it seems Aaron and Lauren will not take her away with them until Jaren proposes marriage or at least asks her out on a date.

Retha arrives with JJ, her friends, and a shopping bag full of food. She lets them in with her key. She hasn't told her friends that Jaren has visitors. Their entrance is a little awkward, but they get through the introductions and Retha and her crew all, except JJ, head toward the kitchen.

"What's in the bag?" Aaron asks before Retha completes her escape.

"Oh my mother-in-law cooked way too much, so I brought food for Jaren but he'll never eat it all. It's basic Dominican food: rice, beans, salad, and roast pork. Would you like some? I'm going to fry a plantain to go with it."

"I could eat." Aaron responds without hesitation, glancing around at his companions.

"What about you, Jennifer, Lauren? You ladies want to try some Dominican food?" Retha asks with a smile. The ladies decline.

"Jaren?" Retha asks as she turns and heads toward the doorway without a glance in his direction.

"Maybe later." Jaren catches the chill but smiles anyway, a little pleased that she cares enough to give him the cold shoulder.

JJ is way too cool to show how excited he is to be in the home of one of his favorite athletes. He stands and watches Retha and Jaren's exchange dumbfounded that his stepmother is acquainted with Jaren Daniels and a guest in his home. He can't help but be impressed.

Once in the kitchen, Retha fries the plantain to go along with the dinner. JJ and Aaron eat as if they haven't eaten all day. Brenda and Michele take an uninvited tour of Jaren's home. They consider entering his bedroom but talk themselves out of such a breach of decorum before migrating to the living room. After a while, Jaren cannot resist the kitchen any longer. He finds Aaron eating and making a not so subtle play for Simone and JJ advising his stepmother on her love life. "That's the guy I want you to marry, Mom. Colonel Freeman is a good man and I know he'd take good care of you. I'd never have to worry." Jaren nearly freezes in his tracks upon hearing JJ's take on Retha's future.

Retha smiles at JJ and asks, "Do you think I'd take good care of him?"

"What kind of question is that?" JJ asks, surprised.

"A woman has to take good care of her man also. It's not a one way street, you know."

"Oh, sure, I know that, Mom. Of course you would. You took good care of my dad. He was a happy man, a very happy man." JJ looks around at the others in the room as he nods his head with pride.

Retha cordially ignores Jaren. "Can I try some of that food?" he asks in an attempt to bring her out. Retha hands him a plate and starts serving food on it. She asks him how much of each thing he wants as she serves, but never once looks at him. He is a bit tired of the cold shoulder and ready for everyone to leave so they can be alone and thaw things out a little.

Jaren takes a seat at the counter with the others and quietly listens to JJ who does most of the talking. *The kid's not shy*. Jaren likes JJ though he cares little for the young man's take on Retha's future. He is surprised at the devotion JJ has toward his stepmother. It is easy to see that Retha loves him very much as well; she watches JJ like a proud parent. Retha seems to love all her family and friends deeply and Jaren likes that about her.

All Jaren's guests end up back in the front room where Brenda has taken over his sound system, playing a variety of jamming music. Soon the ladies start talking about going out dancing again. "I feel a party coming on," Simone hints.

"I'm game," Michele agrees as she stands and dances in one spot totally capturing JJ's attention.

"Me too." Brenda passes the motion and asks the downer of the group. "What say you, Retha?"

"You guys are going to be too exhausted to board the plane home on Monday and Bennie has that big dinner planned for us tomorrow evening. She expects us to help her."

"Don't you ever get tired of being such a downer?" Michele complains to Retha and then turns to Brenda and Simone. "What's that Jackson calls her all the time? Oh, yeah, party poop. I'm the one that's married with children. Come on girl. We may not get a chance to get together like this again for a long time. We are in New York and it's too early to call it a night. Besides, it's Saturday night!"

Retha sees Jaren watching her, so she purposely refuses to answer. Aaron asks where they plan on going and JJ names several spots off the top of his head.

"I thought you wanted to spend time with me, JJ," Retha protests, feigning hurt feelings.

"I do, Mom. Come on and go with us. It'll be fun." Retha still doesn't respond.

Aaron and Lauren join the plan to go dancing but Jennifer remains quiet until she asks Jaren his plans. Jaren is tired of the awkwardness and wants time alone with Retha. If he stays in, Jennifer will want to stay with him. He can envision Retha going to bed and leaving him up with Jennifer or worse yet leaving him with Jennifer and going with the others. He decides to be clear about what he wants. "What are going to do Retha? You staying or are you going?"

"I'm tired Jaren. I'm going to stay here and put in a movie."

"Downer!" Simone and Michele cry simultaneously.

"Party poop," Brenda adds.

"Well, I'm going to stay in too. You came all the way from Texas and we haven't even had time to talk. Jennifer if you want to stay with me and Retha you're welcome." Jennifer looks like she has been smacked upside the head. Retha feels that Jennifer doesn't deserve Jaren's snub and cannot help but roll her eyes at him. He looks defensive as if to ask "What did I do?"

"Jennifer, Jaren's got a lot of great movies. Let the wild ones go. We'll get him to pop popcorn while we chat and watch movies." Retha tries to make the best of a bad situation, not considering how awkward things will become if Jennifer, Jaren and she are left together.

"Well, you guys will probably be talking about old times and I don't want to be in the way." Jennifer directs these comments at Jaren who renders a tight-lipped smile but no further invitation.

"Girl, you won't hardly be in the way."

"Thanks but I think I'll pass. It's very nice of you to offer though."

Retha, put off by the way Jaren handled the situation with Jennifer, goes into the kitchen to clean up while her friends make their plans and prepare to leave. Jaren wants to follow her but thinks better of it. JJ comes and keeps her company, putting away dishes and food but never once asking where anything belongs. "Mom, does he have a thing for you?"

"What do you mean?"

"You know what I mean, Mom."

"Jaren?" Retha gives her stepson a look of disbelief. "We're just friends, JJ."

"Mom, you're beautiful and a lot of fun, but why would he pass up an opportunity to spend time with that honey to stay at home with you unless there's something going on between you? No offense but that Jennifer is a babe. And why are you mad at him?"

"What makes you think I'm mad at him?"

"I spent lots of time with you and dad and believe me I remember how you treated him when you were mad at him; I know you. This guy's got a thing for you, Mom. He did not like it when I said I wanted you to marry Colonel Freeman."

Beaming with pride, Retha smiles. *JJ is sharp; he doesn't miss much when it comes to the women in his life. He will make a good husband.* "And you're leaving me and going dancing with my friends."

"Don't change the subject, Mom. When you catch 'em you catch 'em big."

"Get out of here and please be careful and watch those old women you're with. They're desperate. They're my friends; I know." JJ lets Retha off the hook with a smile and a thumbs-up before returning to the party planners in the front room.

Once the partiers leave, Retha lies on the sofa and goes to sleep in a matter of minutes. Jaren is surprised that she is so tired. After letting her sleep for a while he gets her up. "Retha, let's go to bed." He takes her by the hand and leads her into the gallery. Retha turns to head toward her room but Jaren stops her progress with a strong hold on her hand.

"I'm going to bed, Jaren. I'm tired."

"You're sleeping with me."

"I'm tired." Retha whines as she pulls her hand away.

"I can tell. I'm not going to bother you. I'll let you sleep." Jaren recaptures her hand, holding it gently now.

"I've got to get my pajamas."

"I'll give you a shirt to sleep in."

"I need to brush my teeth."

"Use mine like you did this morning."

Retha gives in. When she climbs into his bed, she gets as close to him as possible without having him inside her. He wraps his arms around her as if they have slept together for years. "Are you going to spend time with me tomorrow?" Jaren asks.

"Will you help me bake the sweet potato pies?"

Jaren laughs. "Sure. I'm not sure I'll be much help, but I'll try. Then can we spend time together?"

"Yep."

"So your son wants you to marry the colonel."

"He's so sweet, Jaren."

"The colonel?"

"Well yes, but I was talking about JJ."

"I'm not much older than your son, Retha."

"Neither am I."

Jaren wants to ask her more about James Freeman but decides against it since she has begun to snore lightly. Soon he is on his way also, all wrapped around her.

--

Jaren and Retha are up and out early the next morning to buy the items they need to bake the pies for the Jacksons' that evening. They grab a few Danish, fresh fruit, and coffee for breakfast. True to his word, Jaren helps Retha bake the pies when they return. They bake an extra pie for Jaren's doorman Raymond and it is still warm when they deliver it to him on their way out later in the day. Raymond likes Retha best of all of Jaren's female visitors and the pie improves her standing immensely.

Jaren treats Retha to lunch and takes her shopping for gifts for the Jacksons, Aida, and Retha's family in San Antonio. He insists on purchasing the Jacksons' gifts. Retha buys a sterling silver and black onyx cross and silver chain for Aida. She recommends an intricately embroidered sofa pillow for Bennie and a bottle of brandy for Jackson. Jaren drives her to Junior's to buy a red velvet cheesecake for Jessie and uptown for a couple of bottles of Robert's favorite Dominican Rum for him and Uncle Sugar.

When they return to Jaren's later that afternoon, he tries to lure Retha into the bed but she won't cooperate. He begs her to take a shower with him but she refuses and locks herself up in her bathroom for a leisurely soak in the tub. Thus, a sullen Jaren accompanies Retha to the Jacksons.

Several of the other guests, including Aida and JJ, are present when Retha and Jaren arrive for dinner. They haven't started eating because Jackson was determined that Jaren should see every dish untouched before serving. Jaren and Jackson are like old buddies now. Those two, along with JJ find a corner and start having such a good time that Jaren soon forgets he's pissed at Retha.

Aida has lots of questions about Jaren. Retha explains that they are friends but Aida isn't buying it. "He watches you too much." There is no accusation in her voice, just observation. Retha wonders what JJ has told her mother-in-law.

Retha can hardly believe her traveling buddies plan to stay in after dinner on their last evening in New York. JJ danced their socks off the night before. Still, to no avail, JJ, Bill and George try to talk the ladies into going out for a while.

Brenda and Bill have developed quite a thing for each other. Bill has family in Dallas and has applied for numerous jobs in the area. He plans to move to Big D in the next few months. Brenda tells her friends that meeting Bill must be fate. She is certain he is her future

Mr. Right, the man of her dreams, and soul mate all bundled up in one.

When no one is watching, Simone triumphantly flashes Aaron's business card at Retha. "Now, that one seems a tad bit on the shady side to me," Retha honestly assesses. "He's fine and all but come on Simone, his girlfriend was out with you guys. How's he gonna hit on you? Drop the 'tad bit;' that dude is shady."

"I don't see where he's any worse than Mr. Perfect over there." Simone tilts her head toward Jaren. "He spends the day out with one woman and then runs her off so he can spend the night with you. Pot, kettle, black, okay." Simone's face reeks with attitude.

Retha doesn't try to defend Jaren. Thinking back on the events of the day before, she figures his behavior probably fits Wikipedia's definition of "shady" or at least her niece Elizabeth's definition of that word. Elizabeth is a college student and after "douche bag," "shady" is her favorite description of her fellow male college students.

The evening at the Jacksons' comes to an end too soon for Retha and not quick enough for Jaren. The goodbyes with Aida and JJ are prolonged and heartfelt. Retha tells JJ to keep close tabs on his grandmother and promises Aida she will not be too choosy finding a man.

"Remember, you will never find nobody like my Joe. Not even his brothers are the man he was, the two of them together." Aida indeed believes her two living sons are the best the world has to offer so Retha must settle for a lesser being than Joe.

By the time Retha and Jaren return to his building, Raymond has finished the entire sweet potato pie, except for the slice he shared with one of the building maintenance staff. When he hands the empty pie pan to Retha, she asks if he threw the pie away. He proudly declares he ate every bite except one "small slice" and it was without a doubt the best "potato pie" he has ever eaten. Retha is pleased with his declaration.

Retha and Jaren go straight to bed where she attempts to hide her distress about leaving the next day, fairly certain she will never see Jaren again. She tries to be free and easy and laugh and have a good time during these last hours together. Jaren takes a completely different approach; he wants to make lots of love. Retha is astonished by his sexual energy. He keeps her awake a good part of the night. When he is not making love to her he is talking to her. By the time she drags herself out of the bed the next morning, she wonders if he slept at all because he sure did not allow her much sleep.

Jaren offers to take Retha and her friends to the airport but she declines because Jackson has claimed that privilege. "Have you thought about staying longer, Retha?" he asks before rising from the bed.

"I can't," she responds.

"I figured as much."

They become very quiet. Each finds it hard to believe so much has happened in five days. Jaren is determined not to commit to anything, not even a phone call, and Retha is determined not to show how much she wants more from him.

Jaren walks up to the Jacksons' apartment with Retha and tells everyone goodbye. He feels like he's saying goodbye to longtime friends. He likes these people very much and, at Jackson's insistence, promises to come by and have dinner in the near future. He gives Jackson the phone number to his apartment and it is clear that Jackson is honored. As Retha's friends pile into Jackson's car, Retha gives Jaren a quick peck on the cheek and jumps in without a word of goodbye. Jaren stands and watches the car roll off. If Retha was alone in a taxi she might cry. She manages to hide her sadness admirably from all but Simone. Her friends peer out the window and wave at Jaren. As they pull off, Brenda whispers "I sure hope you hit that, Re!"

Chapter 14 -- Let the Games Begin

It is good to be home in San Antonio. Of course after five days in New York, Retha's city no longer seems like a city. Many San Antonians say she is a big town and they like her that way. The weather is warm so Retha doesn't need her lightweight jacket or sweater.

Once Retha unpacks, starts a load of laundry, feeds her face, and makes a few phone calls to family and friends, she settles in for a quiet evening at home waiting for a call from Jaren. The call does not come. So early the following day she calls him but Jaren does not answer. Retha leaves a voice message advising of her safe trip and thanking him again for his hospitality. She anxiously anticipates a return call. After two days, her anticipation turns to anguish which rapidly deteriorates to anger at the cruelty of his not calling. No call comes for ten days and Retha is astounded that after all the intimacy between them, Jaren doesn't think enough of her to return her call. By the time Jaren calls, Retha is no longer angry. She is hurt and embarrassed at her own feelings and resigned to not having what she truly wants, him.

Jaren makes the long awaited call for one reason, he cannot help himself. But he has waited too long for Retha to forgive him easily. His call comes through as she is finishing up a conversation with James Freeman who is calling from Korea. Retha tells Jaren she is on the phone with James and will call him back. She speaks with James for another five minutes but waits a full thirty before returning Jaren's call. Again, she gets his voice mail. Retha considers hanging up but decides to leave a message. She makes the message short and to the point. "Hey, this is Retha returning your call. It's seven thirty-five. Bye bye."

Jaren sees Retha's number on the caller ID. He wants to answer but hesitates. When he hears Retha's voice he reaches for the phone but her short cold message stops him. The message disturbs him nearly as much as having to wait for her call back. Jaren had struggled to make that initial call to Retha. He held his breath until she answered the phone. He got excited when he heard her voice sounding so happy but when she recognized his voice hers turned cold. He wonders why she even bothered to return his call. Based on her message, she does not want to talk to him and he sure does not want to explain why he waited so long to call. Jaren decides to leave well enough alone, ignores the call, and heads out for the evening. When he returns, he wants to call more than ever but it's late. The next morning he is up and out too early to call. Later, he decides to leave things as they stand.

When Retha realizes Jaren is not calling back, she has to fight off her tears. Joe is the only man, other than her father, she has ever cried for and she plans to keep it that way. She can hardly believe that Jaren, who had been so thoughtful while they were together, is so cruel and inconsiderate. Retha wishes they could at least try to resume the friendship they enjoyed before her trip to New York but has to accept the reality that the nice friendship was ruined forever by their intimacy. She decides not to allow her misstep with Jaren to get her down any more than it has. She tells herself there is no room in her grief stricken heart to start longing for a nonexistent relationship with a self-absorbed pro athlete.

~~

For the next month, Retha dedicates herself to Sugar's, working nearly every day. Even when the place is closed she's there working. The contractor completed the overhaul of the kitchen in no time, amazing everyone. Seventy-five percent of Retha's investment went into the kitchen. Sugar made up the difference with no problem. Retha insisted that the remainder of her investment go toward fixing up the overall ambiance of Sugar's Place. She gets Gerald, Nathanial, Mykol, Jeremiah, and Raheem to come in and help with much of the work; these guys work for food. Occasionally, Sugar stays and helps out but his health is not the best and he is often tired by the end of the day and needs his rest when the restaurant is closed.

With Mykol's help Retha develops an effective marketing strategy for Sugar's Place. They get a web site up and running, promote the business in all the local social media outlets, and purchase targeted television spots. Sugar's now has a Facebook page and within two months of putting the business on Urbanspoon, there are two hundred fifty-four likes and a ninety-eight percent approval rating.

As well as things are going at the restaurant, it doesn't take long for Retha to decide she needs extra income. She needs new windows in her home and minor remodeling. She also wants to take a long vacation to the Dominican Republic next year but does not make enough money working at Sugar's to save for a vacation or the home repairs. Always frugal, Retha decides to earn the money rather than use credit, her savings or investments. Without discussion with anyone, she applies at a large insurance company located on the other side of town. The company pays well and has excellent benefits.

When Sugar hears her tentative plan, he is not pleased. "I need full-time help not this part-time mess you pullin'. You hadn't been workin' two months and took a week's vacation. You work when you want. Nobody'd think you been in the Army. I know you didn't pull that shit on them."

Retha understands Sugar as well as anyone but she is surprised that he is so upset about her taking another job when he pays her so little. "Uncle Sugar, I'll work as many hours as you pay me for now. I'll just work most of my hours on the weekends."

"I'll be damned. If you don't want to work here, go and take your ass over there and help them white folks. I don't need to put up with this bullshit, 'cause if you stay here and can't be here when I say so but run off over there when they want you, I tell you what I'm gonna do. I'm gonna fire your ass. You ain't no mo' special than the rest of these folks here just 'cause you put a little money in the place. Had me spend up all that damn money. If I let you pull this shit on me 'cause you my niece, they all want to do the same thang and I'll be goddamned if I'mo let that shit happen. So you take yo' ass on over there if you want but don't be surprised if you wake up and ain't got no job here no mo'."

Retha doesn't say or do anything to make Sugar angrier. She ignores his ranting and threats.

Within one month, Retha starts a training course in property and casualty insurance. Sugar's other employees hate that Retha has taken on the additional job. Things have been running much smoother at the restaurant for the past few months with Retha riding shotgun and occasionally pulling the reins. Food items and supplies are on hand when needed. Sugar's has been opening and closing as scheduled. There is no more profanity, at least not within the customer's earshot. They now have set menus and daily specials so the customers know what meals to expect and Sugar can exercise the menu variety he likes at different times. Sugar's Place is always clean and now has an ambiance other than juke. The place has picked up many new regular customers who sit down and spend time in the restaurant enjoying their food; whereas, before many customers preferred take out. The employees fear that Retha's new gig will result in Sugar's reverting back to the old place. When they make their concerns known to Retha, she assures them she will stay on top of things.

To keep her commitment to the restaurant, Retha stretches herself thinner than ever. At first it is as if Sugar is doing everything in his power to make things difficult. He fusses out his employees and customers more than ever. There are days when he doesn't show up at all or comes in just prior to closing. He constantly challenges the way things run in the restaurant even though a particular practice or method is working well. He is having an adult tantrum.

Sugar's difficult behavior continues until Jessie tires of it. One Friday evening, when Retha is tired, Jessie volunteers to fill in at the restaurant. Jessie barely has an apron tied around her waist when Sugar starts complaining about Retha. "Oh so she couldn't get in here tonight. I don't expect her to keep comin' long. She tellin' everybody she gonna keep workin' here just as much as before, but I know better. Soon as she get her money out, she'll be gone. I sho' didn't know that girl was so obsessed with money. I don't know why. She got plenty. It's like she just need mo' and mo'. What gets me is that I didn't think she would quit on me like this. I sho' thought she would be more loyal. Goes to show you, family ain't no different from anybody else."

Jessie listens without comment until Sugar questions Retha's loyalty. Jessie very calmly calls her uncle into the little office in the back of the building and lets him have her infamous "what for". "I don't believe you, Uncle Sugar. Retha has been nothing if not good to you. She works here for a little of nothing. There ain't another person on this earth you could get to do all my baby sister has done for what you pay her. She has spent her own money buying stuff to fix this place up and got people to come in here and work on the place and it hasn't cost you half what it could have. You got more people coming in here to eat than I can ever remember and you know as well as me that's because of Retha. You don't pay her one quarter of what she's worth."

"Retha, Retha, Retha! You bad as these other folks round here. This place was doin' fine before Miss Retha."

"Old man!" Jessie snaps loudly. She stands her ground and takes most of her uncle's as she points her finger in his face and places her other hand on her hip. "If you don't stop fussing about my sister and stop raising hell with the people around here, you won't see me or Retha in here for nothin' but to eat a meal, on occasion! AND you can start making those monthly payments on her investment right away instead of next year. How about that?"

"You can't stop Retha from working here. Cain't nobody make that girl do what she don't want."

"Just try me!" At that, Jessie storms out, leaving the restaurant for the evening and leaving Sugar stunned, angry, and a wee bit scared. The last thing on the earth he needs is for his nieces to give up on him. They have provided an anchor in his life over the past few years. Sugar does the unthinkable. He sits down and reflects.

Retha shows up at Sugar's at seven the next morning to help prep for lunch and bake. She is amazed to find a new Sugar, a laughing Sugar, a sweet and somewhat passive Sugar. She comments to Jim, Sugar's main cook. "He must have got some last night."

Jim, well aware of the butt chewing Sugar took from Jessie, laughingly replies, "He got somethin' alright."

Jessie is proud of herself. She is a force to be reckoned with and more importantly, Uncle Sugar did not ignore her ultimatum. She never tells Retha about her intervention.

Everyone is overjoyed that Sugar has chilled out. Sugar stops fussing long enough to start talking to a young woman who waits tables and performs other miscellaneous tasks around the restaurant. Sugar becomes even sweeter. Twenty-nine-year-old Sylvia has three young children ranging in age from two to eight. Sugar courts the young woman with a vengeance. He sends food home from the restaurant, takes her to dinner and movies, shops for groceries and clothing for her children, takes the family on outings, and spends all his free time making a good impression.

The sisters make fun of their uncle's relationship but soon come to the conclusion that he and Sylvia are moving too fast. Sugar suffers with chronic stomach problems. He has an awful lower back problem and a variety of other ailments. His nieces try to get him to at least get his stomach problems diagnosed but Sugar is in love and getting young hot stuff as often as he can handle it. If he never had time for the doctor before Sylvia, he's too busy now. "I been dealing with my ailments since Christ was a corporal," is his blasphemous response. "I can't stop living because I'm sick." Boy did he keep on living, right in to the house with young Sylvia and her three children.

Chapter 15 -- A Late Night Call

Insurance training, coupled with pacifying Uncle Sugar by almost killing herself at his place, keeps Retha extremely busy. She tries to take Catrina for at least one evening on the weekend. Either she collects her niece on Friday or Saturday night after work or keeps her all day on Sunday. Catrina is seriously disabled but requires little hard work. After you help her bathe, eat, dress, brush, medicate, take her to the park, and massage her, she likes to be left alone. Occasionally, she demands attention but not often. Frequently, Robert and Jessie refuse Retha's offers to take the child, insisting she needs rest and relaxation also. Retha always protests that her niece is no trouble. Often it depends whose will is strongest as to whether Catrina stays with her parents or goes home with her aunt.

After a while, Retha's life is back to normal. She still misses Joe but is reconciled that she will always have that void in her life. Her disgust with Jaren has subsided also. She just wants to work and save her money and move on. She has little time to regret her faux pas with the ballplayer.

~ ~

"Why don't you have your phone set up for email and why don't you answer my text messages?" Jaren's sister, Rachelle has arrived in Tampa during his spring training. Although he dislikes the distraction, he enjoys his sister's company. She sounded down and desperate when she asked to visit for a few days; Jaren could not tell her no. Rachelle complains that their parent's Tampa home is too large and "spooky" so she usually stays with her brother when her parents are not occupying their Tampa home.

Jaren doesn't bother to answer his sister's question. Rachelle continues to scroll through her brother's phone. Jaren is one of the smartest people she knows but technology, unless it is sports or music related, holds little interest for him. "Set it up for me," he tells her.

"I bet you haven't even taken any pictures with this phone." she chastises as she opens the phone's photos. "Oh my, but you have. I'm surprised." She scrolls through the few photos on the phone and stops at one that catches her attention. It is a photo of Jaren with a group of people she has never seen. That is not unusual but he is really happy in the photo, as if these are good friends, not fans or mere acquaintances. "Who are these people, Jaren?" She shows him the photo and he smiles with both mouth and eyes. "Some friends." Then, tilting his head thoughtfully says, "I guess they are friends of mine, now."

Rachelle looks back at the photo and focuses on Simone. "So the lady next to you is not one of your girlfriends?" she asks with a sly smile.

"Nah. That's Simone. She's a friend. The old guy is her uncle. Let me see that again." He takes the phone and glances at the photo and remembers that Retha was the photographer. It seems like a long time ago.

Rachelle's curiosity is raised even more as she takes the phone back and looks at the photo again. Simone has captured Rachelle's attention. The woman is attractive and very clearly a fair-skinned black woman. Rachelle has never known her brother to date a black woman, at least not one that looks black. "Is she Latin?"

"She's black, I think. She acts black to me anyway. Why all the interest in Simone? She's not my girlfriend."

"She's pretty. I never see you with black girls or women, I should say." Rachelle's eyes are cast down self-consciously.

Rachelle is the lone brown-skinned person in her immediate family. Jaren and his parents are very fair-skinned. Many members of their mother Susan's family are so light people think they are white. Jaren and Rachelle's paternal grandmother, Charles's mother is a dark-skinned black woman who married a fair-skinned black man resulting in five fair-skinned children. Had Susan Daniels thought that her one daughter would inherit her paternal grandmother's dark skin, she would have reconsidered marrying Charles Daniels. Susan considers light skin superior and has always given Rachelle less consideration than her older brother because of the child's dark complexion.

"What are you talking about? I've dated black girls before," Jaren responds, a bit caught off guard.

"Not the ones that look black," Rachelle responds softly with her eyes still downturned.

Jaren gives his sister a hard stare. His black younger sister doesn't think he likes black women. "Like I said, me and Simone are just friends. I had a thing with a friend of hers named Retha. Retha took that photo. She's a hell of a lot darker than Simone." He gives a little chuckle.

"You liked her?"

"Yeah, but it didn't work out. She lives in Texas. We don't talk anymore."

"Good thing," Rachelle advises.

This gets Jaren's full attention and he turns off *Sports Center*. "Why do you say that?"

"Mom would not like that. She doesn't like dark-skinned black people."

Jaren notices his sister wipe a tear from her cheek. "What is this about, Rachelle?" he asks, moving to her side.

"Nothing. Forget about it." Rachelle has said too much. Skin color is a sensitive topic for the twenty-one-year-old and it hurts too much to discuss with anyone, especially Jaren who always receives preferential treatment from their mother. She goes to her room and closes the door, code for "Don't bother me unless the house is burning down."

Jaren is aware of disagreements between Susan and Rachelle over the years, but he has never seen his sister so sad. He sits and thinks about the conversation he had with Rachelle. He is never sure when he should attempt to talk things out with her or let her work them out alone. He wonders if he should talk to Rachelle about their mother. Does his sister believe Susan has a problem with dark-skinned people, black people? That is ridiculous. One of Susan's oldest friends is brown-skinned like Rachelle. Their Grandma Betty is very dark-skinned. Jaren has to back up because Susan cares little for her mother-in-law.

Soon Jaren's thoughts turn and he gets slightly piqued at Rachelle. "Damn. Now she's got me thinking about Retha," he mumbles under his breath as he throws the remote on the coffee table in front of him and rests his head back on the sofa.

Nearly two months after his little coup with Retha, Jaren finds little contentment with anything. He cannot recall being so anxious for the season to start. He has been in spring training for two weeks but he is no better. He is certain the full swing of the season will put him right again. The past off-season was his worst so far. Jaren took his annual trek to Puerto Rico with Aaron and several other friends. While on the island, he spent time with Ines, a young lady he has been dating off and on for several years. Every aspect of the trip added to his boredom.

Aaron was stupefied by his friend's melancholy and guessed that Retha was the cause. "You know what they say? A lot of those southern black women practice voodoo." Jaren resented Aaron's reference to Retha but merely smirked at his friend and changed the subject. Aaron has learned that Retha is not a subject for discussion.

After returning from Puerto Rico, Jaren started dating Jennifer. Jennifer is a good sport but as much as he likes her personality and enjoys her company, he has no passion for her. It has dawned on Jaren that sex is not enough; he needs to make love. There is no emotional intensity when he tries with Jennifer or Ines. Often he is lonelier after the sex. In the past, he saw no value in a relationship. He wants to get back to where he was before and hates to admit that the "before" is pre-Retha.

--

Jaren sits on his sofa and tries to clear his mind. He just returned from a teammate's home, where he was invited to dinner and to meet a lovely doctor named Helena. The people were pleasant, food good, Helena interesting and very interested. What should have been an enjoyable evening was mind-numbing like dozens of evenings before. Jaren showers and lies in bed but can't sleep. He reaches for the phone.

Retha awakens after the fourth ring and picks up before the machine. "Hello!"

"Hey."

Silence. "Andre?"

"No, not Andre."

Silence as Retha sits up before speaking again. "Jaren?"

"How are you?"

"Sleepy. What's going on?" She figures there must be an important reason for him to call her, especially at such a late hour.

"Sorry I woke you, but I haven't talked to you in a long time and wanted to hear your voice."

"Whose fault is that?" Retha straightens even more in the bed as her insides are reveling though she sounds calm.

"Are you thinking I'm at fault because I haven't called? What about you? You could have called me?"

"You didn't return my last call. But that's neither here nor there. What's up?"

She sounds flippant and Jaren is slightly put off, but he is so relieved that she hasn't hung up on him or rushed off the phone that he ignores the flippancy. "Nothing much new with me. Training is going good. I can hardly wait for the season to get into full swing. That break is too long. I think we'll go all the way this year. What about you? How's your family and those buddies of yours?"

"Everyone's good. Talked to Brenda yesterday. I may visit with her soon. Michele's great. She and her husband are having a baby. We kept trying to figure out why she was behaving differently. She was pregnant all along, but not talking about it."

"How many does that make?" Jaren asks with no true interest before moving on. "What about you? You still working at your uncle's restaurant? I miss our conversations. I can't find anyone to hold my interest like you."

Retha is all tingly but makes up her mind that she will not fall into one of Jaren's traps again. "Yeah, we did have good talks didn't we? I miss them too. I'm working another job now so I don't have nearly as much time to chat."

"I can't believe you gave up on your uncle's restaurant. I thought that was your thing."

"No, I still work at Sugar's part time."

"Are you trying to get rich or what? Sounds like you're working awfully hard. Where is this other job?"

Retha tells him about her new job at UP&C Insurance Company, explaining that she isn't sure if she likes the work because all she wants is to work at Sugar's. She shares her enthusiasm about the day to day restaurant operations. Retha can't help but brag about how busy the place has become and about all the changes she made. Jaren can hear the excitement in her voice as she talks about Sugar's. He never visited the place but heard it was a dump with good food.

Jaren realizes he wants to see Retha more than ever and Retha realizes she has let him off the hook for not calling her for the past two months. He drew her out far too quickly. "Jaren."

"Yeah."

"I've got to get my rest. Thanks for calling and listen the season will start and it will be great. You take care."

Jaren is dismissed and knows it.

"Can I call you again?"

"Sure, if you want. Bye."

Retha hangs up before hearing his response. Jaren is pleased the conversation wasn't any worse. He wants to see her. He lies in bed thinking about Retha and wondering why he screwed up until he passes out.

Retha lies in bed thinking about Jaren also. She wonders how to respond if he calls again. Maybe she is a game to him. Here she is doing so well and he calls again. She considers calling him back and telling him she prefers he not call. *Yeah, sure. God, give me strength.*

Before long, Jaren starts calling Retha weekly. During these calls, if he even comes close to speaking intimately she changes the subject or gets off the phone with a lame excuse. She never calls him. They are basically at a stalemate. If Jaren tries to move in another direction, Retha puts him in check.

Retha is pretty exasperated with the whole thing. She's glad he is calling, but she isn't giving him any room to get close again. Retha's behavior toward Jaren is not at all in line with her desire for him. She wants to be with him but is certain he will hurt her again. Instead of cutting him off completely, she continues to take his calls, telling herself that she will learn not to care for him except as a casual friend. She doesn't want to dislike him even though his behavior toward her after the New York trip was inexcusable.

After weeks of Jaren's calls, Retha's defenses give way and she decides she must see him. She takes a weekend trip to Dallas under the pretense of visiting Brenda. The sudden visit puzzles Brenda, especially since she is scheduled to work Friday and Saturday evenings. Retha declares she needed time away from San Antonio and refuses all of her friend's suggestions for entertainment. Retha slips off to the Liberty vs. Wranglers game that Saturday evening and gets little satisfaction out of seeing Jaren on the playing field. She sits alone and condemns her desperate behavior. *I bet this is how stalkers start.* She envisions herself lurking in an alleyway across the street from Jaren's building on cold winter nights to get a glimpse of him. Hopefully she'll never get that bad. The best part of the night is when the Liberty pull off the victory based on a game-winning RBI in the top of the eleventh inning hit by none other than center fielder Jaren Daniels. The nicest part of the trip is a late morning breakfast with Brenda on that plant infested terrace of hers.

Chapter 16 -- Faithless Old Faithful

Retha returns to the news that Sugar and Sylvia are now husband and wife. Everyone in the family is caught off guard and Sugar's sons are particularly unhappy over the marriage. One would think that Sugar is a wealthy man or at least very well off and Sylvia a very obvious gold digger for all the stink Gerald and Nathaniel raise over the nuptials. Sylvia is every kind of bitch you can think of: "money-hungry," "stankin'," "black," "fuckin'," "gold-diggin'," and "big-assed," to name a few. Sugar's sons are threatened for reasons no one else understands. Sylvia is wife number eight and the boys have never been so adamantly against their father's marriage.

Jessie, Retha and even Robert, who minds his own business, reason with the boys to be as supportive as possible. After all, what else can any of them do? The deed is indeed done. Defeated, the brothers welcome their newest stepmother into the family with a modicum of civility.

Life takes a new twist with Sugar's marriage. Retha's new aunt assumes a leadership role in the restaurant. Sylvia starts flexing muscle immediately and acts as if Retha is now working for her. Retha has never been anything but kind to Sylvia and is the one person that discouraged Sugar from firing Sylvia on several occasions when she was late or failed to come in at all. A response to Sylvia's behavior presents a genuine dilemma for Retha. She has no wish to make her uncle choose between his new wife and her. For one thing she is certain she will lose. She wishes Sugar would have, at least, informed everyone that Sylvia would be part of the management of the restaurant. Of course, he never informed the employees of Retha's role when she started working regularly and imposing her will so why would he do so in Sylvia's case?

Without a doubt, Sylvia is queen bee. Uncle Sugar rather enjoys seeing his niece take a back seat. Retha had basically relegated him to a lesser role when she came to the restaurant as an investor employee and now she is getting a taste of her own medicine. The problem is Sylvia does not have Retha's knack for the restaurant business, managerial skills, or experience working with people. Retha finds herself constantly putting out fires between Sylvia and the employees and correcting Sylvia's mistakes. Sugar is not at his best and is willing to allow whomever to reign as long as he has the final word.

One good thing about Sylvia's increased role is that Retha does not need to work so hard. She takes her back seat and allows Sylvia and Sugar to drive. Retha does put her foot down when Sylvia attempts to disturb her work schedule. Sylvia has no idea that the clout Retha yields is not familial. She is not aware of the amount of money Retha has invested in Sugar's Place, but Sugar has become very much aware of the instantaneous difference Retha's money and management have made. His end of day sales have nearly tripled in the past few months. So, when Sylvia approaches him with the subject of Retha's schedule, he stares at her as if she has slipped from sanity. "Retha work when Retha wanna work. You best leave that one alone." Sylvia pouts for a few days and barely speaks to Retha but she lets the subject rest, at least for a while.

Once the conflict at Sugar's dies down and Retha eases Sylvia into a training mode the place starts running smoothly again. Sugar and Jim, the cook, are old hands at food service and Sylvia is a quick study. So with a new hands-off attitude toward the restaurant, Retha finds she has more time to focus on her other obsession, Jaren Daniels. She has started watching Liberty games with her brother-in-law Robert every chance she gets. Jessie and Robert find it strange that she has become such a New York Liberty fan. Retha is obsessing over a baseball player and is too ashamed of her behavior to tell anyone, not even Simone or her sister Ida, with whom she usually confides all.

Retha wants no part of the obsession but is lost to it. Jaren calls two or more times a week now. Occasionally she doesn't take his calls but she can only hold out for a day or two. At times she forgets how she hurt when he ignored her and finds herself slipping into a comfortable place with him. Once he starts speaking to her in his quiet voice her alarms set off and she puts up her guard by ending the call. She loves that quiet voice of his; it is hypnotic. *Beware!*

Jaren is exasperated with Retha's apparent lack of interest. He suspects her behavior is an intentional barrier she has in place to keep him in check and he is not finding it easy to bypass. She is friendly enough on the phone but nothing like before her trip to New York. Back then they spoke freely and laughed long, hard, and often. He wants more from Retha but right now will gladly accept a return to that place. It was a warm, cozy and inviting place. He misses his friend and the stalemate continues.

It occurs to Jaren that Retha may be stringing him along while she carries on a long distance relationship with James. Once this thought enters his head it starts to grow. He does not want to continue calling Retha and have her one day announce her engagement. The possibility troubles him so he asks about James. "What do you hear from your friend in Korea?"

"Oh James, he's good. He should be home on a mid-tour leave soon."

Home! Where the hell is home? There with her? "Where is home?" he asks trying to hide his irritation.

"He's from Alabama and that's where his father and stepmother live. I think he'll spend a couple of weeks in San Antonio before he goes there. He owns a home in Schertz and I'm sure he wants to check on the upkeep."

"Are you and he friends or what? I mean is there more going on between you?"

"I told you about James and me." Retha decides to answer as honestly as she can, although she questions if Jaren should ask her about her relationships. She doesn't ask him about his.

"No, you never told me anything about him and your relationship. I don't mean to get in your business but I am curious."

"Yes, I did tell you. You just don't remember. I told you the relationship was moving too fast and I wasn't ready for that."

"So he was the one. I didn't know." Jaren had wondered if James was the man Retha had been sexually involved with since Joe's death. He hoped not. He gets angry though he has no right. He can't even think of anything else to say, but no need, Retha is far from finished.

"With James, I knew I was not ready to be involved but I thought maybe it was him, you know, that maybe I didn't have the feelings for him. Now I know that it will be a long time before I'm emotionally strong enough to be involved with anyone. I don't think I can handle a relationship. When I get to the place that I want or need to be involved, I hope I find a guy just like him. I think the people that make the best friends make the best lovers." Retha can sense Jaren squirm on the end of the phone. She didn't say what she said for his benefit; she meant it. She wishes she could want James like she wants Jaren. James would never hurt her. He would always be there. He is constant.

--

Routine can be tedious. Those of us content with our pay and benefits as sufficient compensation for the work we perform are fortunate. Of course there are the truly blessed who reap the rewards of both pleasure and pay for their jobs. As tasking as many functions are at the restaurant, changing menus; marketing; managing the employees; and dealing with customers prevent the tedium of routine Retha experiences daily on her insurance job.

Just in time to break the back of the overbearing monotony that is dominating Retha's world, her faithful friend James comes home on a mid-tour leave. Jessie is ecstatic to see James back in town visiting with her sister. Retha has always been amazed that Jessie developed such a liking for James. Jessie had even voiced the opinion that James would make Retha a good husband. Retha figures Joe Jr. probably got the same idea from Jessie.

During James's visit, JJ and Aida also come for a short stay. Retha enjoys having all of them in the house. JJ, like Jessie, hopes for progress in Retha's relationship with James. It doesn't take either long to realize that Retha's feelings and intentions toward James are unchanged. She loves James in that special way one loves a true friend, but she refuses to settle into a relationship with him for the sake of having a companion.

Retha gives a get-together while her house guests are visiting. It is a nice quiet party and does almost as much to improve her mood as her visitors. Sitting in her back yard on a not so hot midsummer night with her closest family and good friends lifting her spirit, she makes a vow to enjoy life in the present.

Two of the key contributors to her spiritual elevation, Aida and JJ, are on their way back home before Retha has time to tire of them. Joe Jr.'s eyes are brimming with tears when he leaves Retha for the airport. He senses his stepmother's loneliness and it breaks his heart. He remembers what his father was to Retha. He had been certain Retha was better but now, even though she smiles and laughs, it is like she has lost Joe all over again. When in New York, JJ goes on with life as if Joe is still alive living in Texas. He can't pretend when he visits Texas. He feels his father in the air and knows Retha does also.

Once JJ and Aida are well on their way, James sits Retha down for a good heart to heart. It seems James is finished with his wait for Miss Retha. He has met a lady in Korea and is in love. It is as if James hit Retha in the face with a baseball bat. She is happy for him but shocked and more than a bit jealous of his new love, *the bitch*. According to James, the lady shares his feelings and he is seriously considering a marriage proposal.

Retha congratulates James and says all the right things though she is in a thick haze of emotion as she speaks. The conversation does not seem real and her words echo in her ears. "Well, James I don't know your friend but she is one very lucky lady. I hope you and I can still be friends because you have been one of the most important people in my life since I lost Joe. Thank you for that. I don't know if I would have made it without your friendship. You helped me." Retha can barely hold back her emotions.

"We'll always be friends Retha and we have to keep in touch. I don't have to tell you there was a time when I hoped there would be much more between us but things will work out for the best for both of us. You'll find someone you want because you deserve the best. I mean that, the absolute best."

One person is not at all nice about James finding a new love. Jessie is more upset than Retha when she learns she is losing a prospective brother-in-law and says as much to Retha and James. "She didn't want me Jessie. I tried," James says with a smile and a touch of satisfaction at seeing and hearing how upset Jessie is at the news.

"You don't miss your water 'til your well runs dry," Jessie profoundly declares, throwing a scowl at her sister.

To Retha's relief, James only stays two days longer after his announcement. She does not understand why she is so upset about James finding a love. Until now she didn't realize how important it was for James to want her. Now she feels she may not be worthy of anyone. James has been her faithful friend whom she assumed would always want her. She doesn't want him as a lover but she does want him. He validated her. Retha is glad he stopped waiting for her and found his lady, but she is distraught that she can no longer arrogantly flaunt him as her old faithful. She is very much ashamed of her thoughts and has to constantly remind herself to be happy for her friend.

Wallowing in dumpee self-pity is the course of action readily available. Retha enjoys the self-pity wallow more than she will even admit to herself. Before getting James's news she had decided to loosen up on Jaren and respond more positively the next time he called but when the call comes she is relishing her self-pity. Self-pity is such a strong addiction that a call from the man that causes her soul to tremble at the sound of his voice does not snap her out of it.

"Why are you sounding so pitiful? Are you sick?" are nearly the first words out of Jaren's mouth. Retha is always taken off guard at how in tune Jaren is to her emotionally. She tells Jaren about James and her ambivalence about his new relationship. Jaren is jealous, offended, and hurt but overjoyed James is no longer a threat.

"So you like this guy that much?"

"No Jaren. Did you listen to anything I said? I mean, yes I like him a lot but not as guy I want to be with. I guess I thought he'd always want me. He lifted my self-esteem."

"Why, because he's white?"

"No, because he's a great guy. Listen, you don't understand. Forget it. It's just all about how self-centered I am and that's a little scary. I guess I experienced one of those significant emotional event things."

Jaren is quiet for a moment and then suddenly blurts out, "Why don't you come to Houston this weekend to see me? We're playing there and it'll do you good to get away."

"You want me to come to Houston?" The self-pity wallow just ended. Retha stands straight up in the middle of her kitchen floor with thousands of yellow caution flags waving all over the place. "You know Jaren I wouldn't mind coming to your game, but I don't want to make that drive to Houston and my brother will be out of town. I don't like staying at his place alone."

"I didn't ask you to come to see your brother. I asked you to come see me. Don't worry about the drive. You can fly up and I'll have a car pick you up at the airport. I'll get you a room in the hotel where we're staying. I'll take care of all the arrangements. How about it?" Jaren spits the information out fearful of her answer. He is nearly out of breath with anticipation.

"Why do you want to see me?"

Jaren doesn't answer for a moment. "Do I need to spell it out for you, Retha?"

"You want to have sex?"

No, I want to make love. I can get sex anywhere. Jaren doesn't dare verbalize his thoughts. "Look, yeah, I want you but more than that I want to see you and for us to spend time together, alone. I'm just asking for your time, that's all; I swear."

"Oh, I see." Retha hesitates for a moment in thought. "I don't think you'd want me there this weekend."

"Why not?"

"I won't be well this weekend."

"What do you mean you won't be well?"

"Just what I said, I'll be, well, not ill but . . ." She hesitates then continues. "A woman's thing, you understand?"

Jaren is dumbfounded. *No she didn't go there.* Retha keeps him off-balance.

Retha continues without giving him a chance to renege on the offer. "But I tell you what, you think about it and if the offer stands make the arrangements, call me, and I'll come. But if not, I'll understand. Okay?"

"Okay, sure," Jaren replies hesitantly.

"Bye bye." Retha hangs up. She cannot believe she told him anything so personal. *Well that may be the last time I hear from that brotha.* Her period will most likely be over by Friday at the very latest but if she goes to Houston, Jaren needs to be aware of the situation. Can't have him expecting hot passionate sex on Friday when she still might be on her period. As much as she had said, she can't see herself saying "Well Jaren, we can't do it on Friday but I should be all cleared up by Saturday and then we can do it." No, that would have been a bit much, even for her to say to him.

Jaren's mind is spinning when he hangs up the phone. He is astounded that Retha was so open with him. *How the hell am I going to make it through the whole weekend with her without sex? Oh, I could have made it without the love making, but no sex. Damn!* He still wants to see her, touch her, smell her, taste her. *One damn thing is for certain, if she comes to Houston, she'd better bring her black ass to New York the following weekend or I'm giving up on her ass. Friends -- she wants to be friends, if she doesn't show up in New*

York real damn soon that's all we'll be and I mean that shit. No sex!
Hell! What the fuck!

The next evening Retha receives an email from a travel agency
with all the details for her trip to Houston. She begins to panic.
Maybe she stepped in it. There is nothing she wants more than to be
alone with Jaren for the rest of her life other than Catrina's hearing
and sight and Sugar's restaurant -- well, maybe not the restaurant.
She's not up to a hot romantic weekend just to get dumped for
another two months or maybe permanently. *Maybe I should cancel. I*
want to be with him though. Hell, I'm going. I gave myself a certain
amount of protection with the period thing. He won't be expecting
any sex. Of course my period will be over on Friday at a stretch,
most likely by Thursday but he won't know that. Please, Retha, stop
fooling yourself. If you go you're going to sleep with the man and
much more than that. She is resigned to her fate.

Retha lies to her family and friends and tells them she is going to
Dallas. Since she had visited Brenda in Dallas the previous month,
those close to her are a bit put out by the trip.

"Hell, you might as well move up there. When was the last time
Brenda came down here to visit?" Jessie complains.

"You ain't doin' me or the business no damn good from Dallas. I
don't care what nobody tell you, it's best not to do business with
family." That's Uncle Sugar.

"Hey, Sarg, we were counting on you to help us cook on Sunday.
Did you forget we was throwin' a barbecue?" Raheem talking about
the almost monthly barbeque dinner Jeremiah and he prepare for
friends.

"You gonna miss Steinmart's fourteen-hour sale again. I told you
I got some really good buys at that last one you were too tired to go
on. What is in Dallas? You got a man up there?" Charmaine talks as
if Steinmart doesn't have a fourteen-hour sale every other week.
Retha does feel guilty for canceling on Charmaine for the second
time in three weeks. But Retha is on her way to Houston. Jessie also
wonders if Retha has found a man up in Dallas. If only they knew.

Chapter 17 -- My Best "Dallas" Trip Ever

By the time Retha arrives at her Houston hotel she is tired, hungry, and thankful Jaren had a car waiting at the airport so she did not need to drive herself in Friday evening Houston traffic. The suite's opulence causes Retha's jaw to drop. Jaren has sent flowers, fruit, and chilled wine but best of all there is a card signed by him with love. *If he's trying to impress me, he's doing a good job. Wonder what else he's got in store for me?*

After a leisurely shower, she helps herself to the fruit and waits for Jaren, hoping they can eat together. She pours a glass of wine before getting comfortable on the sofa. Retha hardly slept the night before due to her excitement and is dozing off when she hears Jaren come in. "Hey baby," he greets her with a huge smile.

"Hi," she responds as she sits up, stretches and then rubs her eyes.

Jaren leans over and kisses Retha on the cheek. *God, he smells good.*

"Sleeping already; you tired?"

"Yeah, I worked all day. I'm glad I flew. I don't think I could have made it driving. Jaren this room is great. I didn't need anything so nice. You'll spoil me. I won't want to go back to my raggedy home."

Jaren takes a seat in a chair across from her, leans back and crosses his long legs at the ankles.

"Oh, and thanks for the beautiful flowers and the fruit and wine. You'd better be careful or you might turn a girl's head."

"So that's what I've been doing wrong. I guess I misjudged you. If I had known all I had to do to get your attention was spend money on you, I'd have done that long ago." He smiles slightly while eyeing her in a way that shows he is serious. She becomes uneasy under his gaze.

Jaren is as hungry as Retha but neither wants to leave the room so they settle on ordering two special clubs and share fries. A little uncomfortable with each other, they talk casually over dinner. As soon as they finish eating, Jaren moves on to more important matters. "So are you better than you were the other day or are you still upset about your friend, the colonel?"

Retha is shamed-faced and tries to explain again. "It was so unexpected. I guess I should have suspected because he wasn't calling quite as often and our conversations had changed. I didn't know I was holding on to him the way I was." Retha takes a deep breath and her chest slumps as a sign of defeat. She turns her head away for a moment. "Let's talk about something else."

Their reunion is not progressing as Retha thought it might. Here they are, all alone in a hotel room, and Jaren hasn't touched her other than the peck on the cheek when he first entered the room. She had imagined him taking her up in a mad embrace, sitting on the sofa with her in his lap, and showering her with sweet passionate kisses; this is a bit of a letdown. She can feel the electricity in the air but they both seem afraid to move. Retha is now seated in an arm chair pretending to watch television while Jaren sits on a sofa and quietly watches her.

The tension is too much; she can't stand it any longer. "Are you tired?" she asks.

"Not any more. Come and sit next to me." He pats a spot on the sofa.

Retha moves next to him and kneels beside him on the sofa as she leans across his chest and kisses him very softly on the mouth. He is much more cooperative than she has been in the past and parts his lips for her as he pulls her closer. Jaren has a hard time not putting his hands on her body while kissing her. He finally pulls away. "I've got a gift for you." He goes over to his bag, retrieves an oblong box tied with a ribbon, and hands it to her. Retha gives him a skeptical look as she reluctantly reaches for the richly wrapped box.

"Open it," he prods as he sits back down next to her.

Inside the box lies a gorgeous three quarter inch yellow and white gold wheat linked bracelet identical to one she had seen in a jewelry store while shopping with Jaren in New York. Retha had never mentioned the bracelet to him but it had caught her eye immediately that day. She is beguiled.

"I hope you like it. I bought it the day you left New York. I kept meaning to send it but after making such a mess of things I thought I'd better give it to you in person if I ever got the chance."

"How did you guess I liked this one?"

"I knew something in that case caught your eye and the jeweler was certain it was that piece. He said you have a good eye, expensive but good."

"Jaren, this is too much. Why?"

"Because I want to make you happy." He leans in close and looks in her eyes. "So tell me, are you happy?"

Retha smiles. "Hmm, maybe spending money on me does work."

Jaren slides down on the sofa next to her and pulls her onto him. Retha rests her head on his chest. They lie there for a while before he asks if he can stay the night with her. Retha nods a yes. She is so overwhelmed by him, by his nearness, by the thought of him buying her a bracelet and keeping it for her all these months. She allows her mind to question if maybe he cares for her more than a little.

Later, she lies in the bed and watches him strip down to his underwear before joining her. The sight of him with so little clothing rocks her resolve not to make love to him on their first night together. She cannot help but stare at him. Jaren self-consciously asks why she is watching him. "I told you before, I like looking at you."

He smiles and climbs in next to her. Retha melds her body next to him and wraps her legs up with his. She has no mercy for the poor brother. Jaren takes a very deep breath and, in order to take his mind off their bodies starts talking very quietly about family and friends. They lie there and talk for a while before he changes the subject. "You live alone. Do you ever get lonely?"

"Sometimes for my parents, often for Joe and don't get scared if I say this."

"Scared? What could you say that would scare me?" he asks as he entwines his fingers in her thick naps.

"I get lonely for you a lot," Retha speaks into his shoulder, ashamed and afraid of his reaction to her confession.

Jaren doesn't comment but gently pulls away from her.

"See, you're running away. Where are you going?" she questions with a laugh, turns her back to him and moves her butt closer to him.

Jaren groans and tries to maintain his distance. "I'm trying not to offend you." They laugh but the air gets heavier when the laughter no longer lightens it.

"What about your friend, James? Do you get lonely for him?"

"I get lonely for James like I get lonely for Michele or any friend. He was, or I should say is, a good friend to me, Jaren."

Jaren is satisfied with her answer. "I've been lonely since I met you, Retha. I don't remember being that way before. I've missed you." He kisses her on the back side of her neck.

"So why no call for all that time? I figured I was just a long one-night stand. Is that what this is?"

"Nothing like that. I guess I decided it would be best if I ended it when you left New York but I thought about you all the time. I wanted to keep talking to you but I knew we couldn't go back to where we were before your visit."

They lie without speaking for a few moments.

"I got scared, Retha. I'm sorry."

Retha wants to shout for joy but all she says is "you're forgiven" and again gets as close to Jaren as possible before starting her descent into sleep. Jaren lies awake wondering how he will make it through the weekend without making love to her.

They order a late breakfast in the room the next morning before Jaren leaves for the park. Retha stays in the room as long as possible before taking off to the game. No telling when or if she will ever stay in another luxury suite and she wants to enjoy it.

She considers the things she and Jaren discussed the night before and wonders if he will continue seeing her after the weekend. Shame comes over her when she honestly assesses the situation. She has flown to Houston to be with a man and has no real clue of his intentions. She knows her mother would be ashamed and hurt by her behavior. Wanda and Donald raised her better. *I promise I will not let him use me. If he doesn't want a serious relationship with me, we can talk but that's all. No more sex – after tonight.* Retha tries not to laugh at herself.

The Liberty win the game with little effort and lots of action but Retha wishes she had a friend with her to enjoy it. After the game, she rushes back to the room and takes a long hot bath. She considers calling Simone but decides against it because she isn't ready to give a play by play of "Retha and Jaren."

Jaren comes in a short time later and waits for her to exit the bedroom. When she doesn't come out, he ventures in and finds the bathroom door ajar. "Damn, why is she doing this to me?" He groans under his breath. He tries to resist approaching the bathroom but when Retha hears him she calls him in. She is submerged in bubbles. Jaren sits down on the edge of the tub and talks for a while. It is obvious he is tired. "I think I'll sleep in the other room tonight."

"No! Why?" Retha protests.

Jaren tilts his head to one side and looks at her quizzically as if to ask "How can you possibly not know?"

"So are you leaving me now?"

"No, I'll stay until you pass out like you did last night. If you want, I'll sleep on the sofa. I'm not Superman, Retha. I didn't sleep well at all last night.

"I want you to sleep with me," Retha whines.

Irritated, Jaren kisses her on the forehead as if she is a child he is attempting to pacify before he leaves the room. Retha finishes her bath, oils, scents, and dries her body. She puts on a short nearly transparent teddy along with her bathrobe before joining Jaren. He is sitting on the floor brooding when she enters the room

Retha sits on the sofa next to Jaren, touching her outer calf to his upper arm. "Tired?" she asks.

"Very," is his moody response.

"Jaren, if there's something you want to do or someplace you want to go, you don't have to stay closed up in this room with me. I can go out and visit family. But you did invite me here."

"There's no place I want to go. I, hey let's just forget it. I'm not very hungry yet. What about you; did you eat?"

"At the park earlier, I'm not very hungry either."

Retha kneels down in front of Jaren and starts untying his sneakers.

"What are you doing?"

"You seem uptight. I want to help you relax."

"Retha, I can take off my own shoes."

"I want to. You told me you wanted to make me happy so let me do this for you. Let me ask you a question."

"Yeah."

Retha finishes removing his shoes and socks. She can tell he is excited. "So how many women have you been with since we were together?" not looking at Jaren, she pries.

"Don't you think you're getting too personal?"

"If you don't want to answer, I understand."

"Two! I've been with two, okay. Why the question?"

Retha stares at him but tries not to show how his confession saddens her. She doesn't answer Jaren who has a hard time returning her gaze. "What about you? Have you been with anyone since me?" He asks.

"You're the only one I've been with in more than two years."

Jaren is visibly relieved and becomes ecstatic when Retha straddles him and begins unbuttoning his shirt. She is slow and purposeful and aware of the change in her breathing as she touches his bare skin. She loves his chest and shoulders and the faint tuft of hair coming up out of the top of his jeans. She stands, pulls him to his feet, places a large bath towel on the carpet, and coaxes him to stretch out on his stomach. Jaren has a question on his face but obeys her without protest. Retha kneels at the side of his waist as she starts to massage his shoulders and back using aloe oil she bought for him. He moans softly as she moves to his lower back and waist. She works very slowly and methodically. She has him turn over and starts to undo his jeans which have an obvious bulge in the front.

"Are you trying to make me suffer?"

"You don't seem to be in any pain at all." Retha smiles. "I'm trying to help you relax."

"Do I look relaxed?"

Retha ignores the innuendo, gets his pants off with not a lot of assistance from him. She has him roll back onto his stomach. This time she starts on his thighs, works down his calves, and back up to his buttocks. He flinches when she puts her hands inside his briefs but doesn't complain. Jaren's breathing has quickened to a near pant. Retha can wait no longer. She removes her bathrobe and has him turn over onto his back. When she starts pulling down his briefs and hands him a condom he is happier than he can ever remember. He lies there and watches as she removes her panties, straddles him and lowers herself onto him as they both moan with pleasure.

Retha is a seasoned lover. She uses all her experience while making love with Jaren and he reciprocates beautifully. Every touch, every kiss is intensified and prolonged throughout the night. Each refuses to accept more than they give.

Retha and Jaren are realists and were certain that their time together in New York was part reality and part fantasy. Though they held high expectations for their reunion, neither expected the intensity they are experiencing in their lovemaking. Jaren thought that after making love to Retha the spell might break and he could place her in the category with other women with whom he has shared intimacy. Retha, on the other hand, is sexually deprived. She assumed that the first experience with Jaren was a bit of a fluke based on his status, her physical attraction to him, and her need to be fulfilled. Neither expected the other could live up to the sweet memories of their first meeting. They expected to enjoy each other but not the way they had on those frigid New York nights seven months prior. Both are surprised.

Strangely each has regrets when they exhaust the night. Jaren is jealous that Retha is so well versed in lovemaking and cannot help but wonder if she gained all her expertise while with Joe. His ideal woman has little or no experience in the art of making love. He always thought he would be the teacher. He wonders if Retha would be as free with any man and if she and James shared such intense lovemaking – had she even learned things from him? Jaren gets angry at the thought of Retha enjoying the intimacies she shared with him with another man, even Joe. Retha is ashamed of her own abandon. She told herself she didn't care what Jaren thought of her. They would share a night of sex, nothing more. Now she worries he might think she is a total freak. They lie quietly but not sleeping.

Jaren is the first one to speak "What happened, Retha?"

"What do you mean, what happened?"

"Well, I thought we couldn't make love."

"I'm fine. I finished Thursday."

"So, why did you make me wait until tonight?"

"I don't know."

Another quiet moment passes.

"Jaren?"

"Yeah."

"I didn't scare you did I?"

"Scare me how?"

"Being wild."

"God, no. I loved it. I just don't like thinking that you were ever that way with anyone else, even Joe."

"It's been a long time for me and I wanted you a lot. Before we made love in New York I didn't have much desire." Retha pauses for a moment before continuing. "I get jealous too when I think about you with other women. I knew you had been with other women since we were together and I hate that."

"Wait a minute. Retha, I'm a man, baby. I messed up but I tried to get back to you and you wouldn't have me. You wouldn't even discuss it. I'm not saying it's right but, well, I mean I don't know what to say."

"Do you have a special person in your life?" Retha knows she should have asked this question days ago.

"You."

"We never see each other."

"We need to fix that. How about you let me come to San Antonio to spend some time with you at the end of the season. We've got a couple of more months with the playoffs. Maybe you could come up to New York between now and the end of season and we could get to know each other a little better face to face instead of over the phone and in the bed. How about it?"

"I'd like that Jaren," is all Retha can get out. Her heart is racing like a greyhound's in the heat of competition.

Jaren tries to talk Retha into visiting him in New York the following weekend but she refuses, promising to visit as soon as she can get away. She stays for his game the next day and afterwards catches an early evening flight home, flying high.

Chapter 18 -- They Don't Sell That Shit in Bottles

No sooner than the team jet lands, Jaren dials Retha's home phone in an attempt to prove he will not repeat his previous skittish behavior. During their conversation he explains how busy he'll be over the next two months, emphasizing that Retha will need to work with him on "this relationship thing." After Jaren's call, Retha feels as if she is floating on a cloud.

Jessie notices a change in her younger sister who now has a happy aura about her. Nothing seems to faze Retha. Sylvia tries once again to make an issue of Retha's hours at the restaurant but Retha shrugs the issue off. "Sylvia, baby, I'm always willing to come in and help if you need me." Jessie is present during this exchange and looks on in amazement as Retha walks away without even a backward glance in Sylvia's direction. Retha is not a complainer but one thing she does kick up all kinds of hell about is Sylvia and the restaurant. So why not now? Jessie wonders.

Retha shows up at Jessie's one evening wearing her new bracelet which Jessie notices before Retha takes a seat. "Girl, where did not get that bracelet? That is gorgeous." The closer Jessie gets to the bracelet the more astonished she becomes. Retha does not buy extravagant things for herself nor does she wear costume jewelry, no matter how expensive.

"It was a gift from a friend," Retha answers nonchalantly. *What was I thinking to wear this bracelet in front of Jessie?*

"What friend gave you somethin' like that?"

"A guy in Dallas."

"What's his name? I don't know nothin' about no guy in Dallas." Jessie declares and looks over at Robert for confirmation that neither of them know about "a guy in Dallas" before she continues her grilling. "Are you dating this guy?"

Robert has turned off the television and is now tuned in to the conversation between his wife and sister-in-law.

"His name is Jaren." Retha answers quietly, wishing for an end to the questioning but sensing that Jessie is just getting started.

"How long have you been seeing this man? Why haven't you mentioned him before? When do we meet him?"

"Good God, Jessie! It's no big deal. Hopefully, he'll visit in the next few months and you can meet him."

Robert jumps in. "He must think a hell of a lot of you to buy that load you're wearing. That thing must have cost a mint. What does he do for a living, rob banks, sell drugs?"

Retha changes the subject but Jessie and Robert have their sensors up now. They will watch Retha like hawks until they find out what is happening between her and the Dallas guy. Joe's death and Retha's own experiences in the war cause her sister and brother-in-law to handle her like a frail child, fearing any additional emotional trauma might send her off the deep end. What or exactly where the deep end is they aren't sure, but they fear that place for Retha.

A few days later Jessie and Robert stop by Retha's home and find her down on her hands and knees scrubbing out corners and washing baseboards. When they ask why all the cleaning, Retha tells them that the house needs it. Jessie cannot take this. Retha hates housework. Jessie goes home and calls her sister Ida in Seattle. Once she gets Ida on the phone she dials her sister Madelyn in Germany in order to hold a three-way conversation. Seeing that it is two o'clock in the morning in Germany, a half dead, overly anxious Madelyn picks up the phone expecting the worst. And for a moment she believes that's what she is getting when Jessie announces, "Y'all need to pray for Retha!"

Madelyn goes into a tizzy. "What's the matter? What happened? Oh, Lord!"

"Would you shut up and let Jessie tell us what's going on." Ida speaks calmly and deliberately but holds her breath in anticipation of bad news.

"She's not sick or anything like that but I'm afraid she's got herself into something. It seems Retha is wrapped up with a man that me and Robert have never met and know nothing about. He could be is a drug dealer or worse because he is buying her expensive gifts and Retha is being closed-mouthed. I can't get a thang out of her. You guys need to talk to her. She tells you everything, Ida. Somebody needs to find out who this guy is and let me know."

Ida breaks in as Jessie takes a breath before continuing. "Girl, please! I thought something was up. So what if Retha got a man? It's about time."

"Amen, I know that's right." Madelyn adds. "You nearly scared me to death. I can't believe you called to wake me up with this mess."

"What's the matta?" Madelyn's husband, Philip, stirs and asks.

"Go back to sleep, baby; nothing's wrong."

"Okay, but I tell you she's too serious too fast. Me and Robert went over there and she was cleaning like company's coming," Jessie presses her point.

"Cleaning -- Retha?" Ida sounds shocked. Now the sisters are concerned. Retha is the youngest of the girls. Each of the three older sisters had experienced the unenviable task of either working with or supervising their lazy baby sister during household chores. None of the sisters wanted Retha to help them because they had to beg her to do her share and often ended up doing her part and theirs. Although Retha keeps her home clean, she despises housework and has been known to hire a cleaning team.

Ida suggests Jessie call Brenda and Simone. She speculates that since Retha met the man in Dallas, Brenda probably introduced them, "heaven forbid." Jessie suggests that Ida call Michele since the two of them get together occasionally. In the end the sisters develop no solid course of action for getting deep into Retha's business. Madelyn finally makes a positive observation. "The man can't be too bad or Retha wouldn't be messin' with him."

They all agree until Jessie remembers James Freeman. "We all say Retha's got good sense, but she makes me wonder. That colonel liked her a lot and she wouldn't give him the time of day."

"As I recall, they did date a time or two. At least that's what you and Retha both told me. I guess she didn't like him much," Ida reminds Jessie.

"Who y'all talking about, that white guy?" Madelyn asks.

Ignoring Madelyn, Jessie continues. "That man had everything going for him. Retha was a fool to let him get away."

"Hell Jessie, first you didn't like the idea of her dating him because he was white. You even said the man was too good-looking. Now you mad she didn't marry him. If she didn't want him she didn't want him," Ida argues.

Madelyn puts an end to the discussion. "Listen you guys, we have to accept the fact that Retha is a grown woman. Like I said before, she's got good sense. She's our sister ain't she? And her feelings are written all over her face. We'll know if something goes wrong."

Discussing the situation with her sisters temporarily pacifies Jessie so she lets the subject drop for a day or two but the mystery won't let her rest. Out of desperation she asks Sugar what he thinks about the change in Retha's behavior. Sugar gladly shares. "I don't know what got into Miss Retha but whatever the hell it is, I hope she keeps it. I don't get no back talk, no rollin' eyes, no smart mouth, nothin'. Believe me life is easier around here. And 'bout to work herself to death, always laughin' and jokin'. I cain't make her mad if I want to. She ignores all of Sylvia's foolishness and that's sayin' somethin'. I tell you whatever it is she got, I wish I could get me a taste. They don't sell that shit in bottles."

Jessie makes one more attempt to pry information from Retha but that proves useless. Retha does not want to seem a complete fool. If she tells her family she is involved with Jaren Daniels, they will swear she is asking for trouble. She expects Jaren will come through on his promise to spend time with her, but if he doesn't, it is best the family never suspect their involvement.

--

With the playoffs about to start, there is no way Jaren can break away and get to San Antonio. So, even though Jessie is staying closer to Retha than usual, one month after her trip to Houston, Retha manages a quick weekend trip to New York under Jessie's radar.

Before returning to San Antonio, Retha tells Jaren that her family does not know she is in New York. Based on Jaren's reaction she soon wishes she had not spoken.

"Why didn't you tell your family you were visiting this weekend?" Jaren asks with a frown.

"They don't know I'm seeing you. They don't even know I met you. It's best to keep it that way until you visit."

"Maybe you'd better explain this. Why don't you want to tell your family about us? What the hell's the problem?" Jaren does not appreciate being a secret. He is, after all, a little vain and can't understand why Retha is keeping her relationship with him under wraps as if it is shameful. Most women he dated tried to flaunt him like a piece of jewelry.

"There's no problem, Jaren. I just want to wait and not have them asking me a lot of questions."

Jaren guesses at Retha's reason. "You still don't trust me, do you? You think this is a game to me. I'm not that kind of a person, Retha. I wouldn't do that to you. I told you I was coming to San Antonio to spend time with you but there's not a hell of a lot I can do so close to the playoffs to make you believe me. I don't understand why you continue to see me if you think I'm that low. I mean, I don't get it. One of the first things I did when I got back from Houston was call my parents to tell them about you and that I want them to meet you. You think I'd do that if I didn't plan to come to San Antonio?"

Retha doesn't even attempt to deny her lack of trust; it's written all over her face. "I'd like to meet your family." She tells him in a pitiful attempt at changing the subject.

"Hey that's cool. I want you to meet them, but I don't want you keeping me a secret from your family. That's no way for us to start out. You need to tell them what's going on. I don't want to be nobody's surprise, okay. I think we have played out that scenario," he adds sarcastically.

Retha doesn't respond.

"Okay, Retha?"

"I'll tell them when it's time. There is no reason they need to know my business. When you come to San Antonio, that's when I'll tell them."

Jaren is thoroughly pissed off and is his sullen self when he puts Retha on the plane back to San Antonio. He believes Retha should be well over his past behavior. Of course, instead of behaving in a manner that will encourage Retha to trust him, he lets his anger dictate his response. He refuses to call her.

--

Susan Daniels had indeed received a call from her son upon his return from Houston. She was surprised because Jaren never willingly discusses the women he dates. Susan discerned that her son was serious about Retha. She also determined that Retha was not "a girl." The more Jaren told his mother about Retha, the less she liked Retha for her son. Later, Susan shared the conversation with her husband, Charles. "Seems she's a few years older than him." Getting no response from Charles, she continued. "She's a widow with a twenty-one-year-old son and she was in the Army for a number of years. She works in a restaurant now."

Susan has her husband's attention with her description of Jaren's most recent love interest. "Either you're making this sound worse than it is or this woman had a baby when she was ten years old?"

"The boy is her stepson, but I tell you Jaren likes this woman."

"Why do you say that?" Charles grumbles.

"He called to tell me about her. That was the sole purpose for the call. Usually I get bits and pieces of information about his girlfriends and he doesn't let me ask any questions. He wants us to know about this one up front. He's serious. He wants everything in the open."

"This too shall pass. I know my boy. Right now the only thing he's really interested in is baseball."

"I hope you're right," Susan responds.

--

Jaren's friend Aaron also recognizes that Jaren is serious about Retha. It is no secret that Aaron and Simone talk regularly, are having a quasi-coast to coast relationship, and have spent time together when the Liberty played West Coast teams. Aaron likes Simone more and more the longer she refuses to show any real interest in him.

"Daniels has got it bad for your friend." Aaron tells Simone out of the blue during a phone call one evening. Simone finds Aaron's statement telling, certain he must believe it to say it.

"Why do you think that?" she asks, hiding her surprise at learning Retha and Jaren are seeing each other.

"This guy walks around like he doesn't have a care in the world until he gets on that baseball field. Then he gets intense. But your friend, she keeps him upset. She's got his number." Simone is pleased to hear that Jaren cares enough about Retha to get upset. Aaron continues. "I think he feels like he's not in control of what's happening between them."

Simone does not like the fact that Retha is keeping quiet about seeing Jaren. Not being one to beat around the bush, she gets Retha on the phone and grills her. "Why are you being so secretive? I hope he's not trying to keep you under wraps because of that celebrity bullshit."

"It's not him Simone; it's me. If things don't work out, I don't want people around feeling sorry and worrying about me."

Simone understands. She is worried and with good cause. Jaren and Retha are playing games again. Jaren is angry for no good reason and Retha is passively awaiting his next move. They experienced calm in their relationship for one month. Considering that they have spent four days together in that one-month period it appears their future is doomed.

After Retha's visit to New York, Jaren had decided he was fed up with chasing behind her. He has never had to run after a woman and he does not like the dynamic. He wants Retha to want him as much as he wants her. So far, all the effort has been on his part. Still, with all his effort, she wants to keep her relationship with him a secret. His darker side tells him to cut her down a notch or two.

After not hearing from Jaren for nearly two weeks, Retha calls. His team has lost the first game of the Pennant Race and he is not happy. He has no idea how tense he is until he hears Retha's voice and the pressure melts away like the wax on the wick of a newly lit candle. Yet he stays upset with her. He barely participates in the call nor does he mention seeing her again -- not in San Antonio or elsewhere. Our girl's head comes out of the clouds when she puts the phone down. She has been on a slow but steady descent since her visit to New York. The call leaves her with both feet firmly planted on dry ground. When Jaren doesn't bother to call after the Liberty win the Pennant and go on to win the World Series, Retha sinks. The ground under her feet isn't so dry after all.

The day following the Series end, Simone calls to ask Retha if she is going to New York to celebrate with Jaren. "Aaron invited me up. I have to keep my guard up with this man because he is being way too nice."

"Aaron is cool. You be careful and have fun. I haven't heard from Jaren in over two weeks, so have fun for me too."

"You didn't call and congratulate him? Retha, he's the MVP!"

"The last time we talked it was like communicating with a damn sloth. Things are not good between us and I'm not going to act like everything is okay and go up to New York to get my feelings hurt. I couldn't bear that. I'd probably curse his ass out. I'm going to leave well enough alone. Congratulate Aaron for me, okay."

"Nothing for Jaren?"

"Not unless you want to tell him to kiss my black ass."

"Nah. He'd probably like that better coming from you," Simone jokes. She considers pleading with Retha to come along with her but knows futility when it comes to Retha. So she goes without her friend and enjoys her time with Aaron.

Retha makes up her mind to get on with life with or without Jaren Daniels. *I should have just enjoyed the sex.* She mentally kicks herself. *You can't make a man be what he is not.*

Chapter 19 -- Can I Keep Him, Jessie?

The first weekend of November finds Robert and Retha throwing a huge "surprise" forty-fifth birthday bash for Jessie in Retha's home. The best thing is that Madelyn is home from Germany and will stay in San Antonio until after the New Year. Madelyn's husband, Philip, is going on to Georgia to enroll their youngest son, Aubrey, in school. He and Aubrey will return for Thanksgiving and again for Christmas. Life will be one big fall party from November to January and Retha plans to enjoy it to the fullest. Retha and Robert are glad Madelyn is in town to help with the party preparations but she is such a perfectionist that they work twice as hard to meet her stringent standards.

As a child, Madelyn had given her parents more trouble than any of the other children. She wasn't truly any worse than the others. She was just open about whatever she did. Ida would say, "Maddie don't have sense enough to be sneaky." Once Madelyn made up her mind to have or do something that thing was done at all costs. Thank God she met and married a good man very early in life. After she married Philip, they got involved with the church to keep from killing one another. Maddie got her GED and went on to college and got her masters in psychology. Now she is a pillar of whatever community she lives in and she has lived in three different military communities over the past eight years in Germany.

The party planners had hopes of surprising Jessie but that proves to be impossible. As soon as she has an inkling they are planning a party for her, she tells them, "I hope y'all not tryin' to throw me no surprise party 'cause you know I don't like surprises."

Jessie's knowledge of the party does not cause the planners to skip a beat. They still ban Jessie from Retha's house during the three days prior to and the day of the celebration and she is not pleased. It isn't that she cares so much about the planning, though she is indeed a little curious. Her displeasure stems more from being deprived of Madelyn. Jessie feels it is not fair for Retha to take all of Madelyn's time preparing for a stupid party even if it is for her. She calls and complains to Ida who grumbles about how much she wishes she could be at the party and moans that she always misses all the fun.

When Robert escorts Jessie into Retha's home on the afternoon of her birthday, she immediately forgets her ire. Her eyes take in the results of her family's labor of love on her behalf. Furniture has been shifted to make plenty of room for guests to move freely throughout. All the blinds and windows at the back and sides of the home are open having the effect of a large continuous space with the inside and outside flowing into each other. Robert has strategically placed lawn tables about the yard with decorative lighting. Nicola's special decorative touch is everywhere. There are fresh flower-filled vases in abundance, along with plant baskets hanging from many of the open windows. Everything is beautiful. The buffet table is marvelously dressed and covered with scrumptious looking delicacies. She can see Madelyn and Elizabeth's decorating talents on her birthday cake. Jessie is brought to tears.

Mykol, Elizabeth, and Raheem are responsible for the music. Robert has pulled out many of his old albums and CDs and selected special cuts for Jessie. These songs include everything from blues to country.

Jeremiah arrives with Maria and his date, a new love by the name of Alisha who is much nicer than "that cat" Carla. He also brings a couple of his single male friends from work. Retha is pleased that Jeremiah had the foresight to bring his friends. She had feared there would be a shortage of men at the party.

Robert married the right woman. He and Jessie love to dance as do almost all the members of the Gray family. Robert pulls Jessie on the dance floor almost immediately once the party gets started. Brenda and several friends make it in from Dallas and jump right in the mix.

"Retha this reminds me of some of those parties you and Joe used to have, girl," Brenda yells as she and Retha get on the dance floor with Elizabeth, Robert, Madelyn and Sugar who is shaking a tail feather with the youngest and the best of them. Uncle Sugar was not well earlier in the day and thought he might not make it to the party but he did. By seven o'clock just about all the guests have arrived and the party is going full steam. Retha drinks a little more than her limit of wine and is partying almost as hard as Jessie and Robert.

The consummate hostess, Retha wants her guests to enjoy a perfect evening. She stays busy dancing, laughing, and talking with the partiers; replenishing food and drinks; and keeping everything picked up. She and Madelyn are refilling ice buckets when she hears

Raheem yell, "Jaren, hey man! Good to see you." Retha is baffled. *Am I hearing him right? Did he say Jaren? Jaren who? Which Jaren? I only know one.* She turns around to see who Raheem is addressing but Philip is blocking her view. She hears Raheem continue. "Congratulations on the Series and that MVP man. You deserved that. What the hell are you doing here?"

Finally Philip moves to the side and Retha's eyes confirm what she hears. The air leaves her lungs, her legs are like pipe cleaners, her head swims, and her stomach is queasy. *He came!* Her brain shouts and her heart leaps. Not sure what to do with her body, she does not move. *Thank God all mighty he's here!*

"I came to see your bud. Where is she?" Retha hears Jaren speak for the first time. She had never known his voice to have so much warmth.

"Retha, hey Retha, look whose here to see you!" Raheem has been drinking so he yells as if Retha is down the block.

Avoiding Madelyn's stare, Retha dries her hands and walks out of the kitchen into the family room area where Jaren and Raheem are standing. Brenda comes in from the patio and runs over and gives Jaren a hug. "How come you didn't tell me Jaren was coming, Re? You and yo' surprises." Jaren simply smiles at the friends.

Philip, more than a little under the influence, goes out and gathers up Jessie, Robert, and Sugar and tells them, "Come and see what Retha got." Everyone comes in from the yard to find out either what all the commotion is about or if what they have heard is true. Robert breaks into the room through anyone or thing that impedes his progress, walks up to Jaren, grabs his hand and introduces himself. This explains so much, the new-found love of baseball; the sudden devotion to the Liberty; the trips to Dallas; the mysterious boyfriend. Jessie looks at Retha in disbelief as it dawns on her that Jaren Daniels is the gift-giving lover Retha has been keeping a secret.

Retha takes Jaren by the hand and leads him upstairs to an empty bedroom where they speak to each other for the first time. No sooner than she closes the door, he pulls her close and wraps his arms around her. Retha eases in as close as she can get and takes a deep breath, relishing his scent and touch. After a moment, she pulls back slightly. "Why didn't you tell me you were coming?"

"I thought you might curse me out and tell me not to come. So I figured I'd take my chances and show up. Are you glad I'm here?"

"You know I am." They do not speak again for several minutes. Retha reluctantly pulls herself away from him.

"This is quite a party. What's the occasion?"

"My sister Jessie's birthday."

"I guess my timing isn't the best. I imagine we'll be partying for a while."

"We'd better go downstairs, but first I think I owe you an apology for not calling you after the Series. I wanted to call and congratulate you but I was being stubborn. I'm so sorry."

Jaren gently runs the back of his fingers along Retha's face, leans forward and passes a delicate wet caress from his mouth to hers pulling her close.

Once again, Retha backs away. "We'd better go." She turns to leave the room pulling Jaren out behind her.

As soon as Retha returns downstairs with Jaren, her sisters attack her and take her back upstairs and demand an explanation. Jessie jumps right into Retha. "What in the world is going on? Where did you meet that man?"

Retha can't help but quake inside under her older sister's interrogation. It is clear that Jessie is upset. "Remember, I met him last year when I took RJ out to the Fort Sam Youth Activities Games. I mean, I met him at Jeremiah's later that day but it was that same weekend."

"The one that almost made you piss your pants?" Jessie asks with a scowl.

"Piss her pants?" Madelyn asks with a frown at Retha.

"No, I didn't piss my pants." Retha can't help but smile at the reference Jessie has chosen to remember.

"But this is the same guy? You mean to tell me you been messin' with this man since last year this time? Retha, you got better sense than this, baby. Even the most naïve woman knows better than to get involved with a professional ballplayer." Jessie shakes her head in disbelief.

Retha sighs in frustration. The last thing she wants is to argue with Jessie on her birthday, a day of celebration. Arguing over Jaren would get his visit off to a bad start. Best to be open, direct, and honest or this could get worse. "Yes, this is the guy and no, I have not been 'messin' with him all this time. We mostly talk on the phone. We spent some time together when I went to New York in January."

"January! What's up with all the secrecy?" Madelyn is stunned and her shock adds to Jessie's perturb.

"Well," Retha hesitates. There is no way she can explain her involvement with Jaren since January in a positive light without leaving out details. "We didn't talk for a few months after I was in New York."

Jessie glares at Retha for a few moments before her intuition clears her brain. "You mean he hit it and then didn't call for months after that. Just what I thought. Why would you get involved with someone like this? I know you are smarter than this."

"Wait a minute." Madelyn stops Jessie in the middle of her hissy fit. "Just about every other woman in the world, at least in these United States, has had the opportunity to make a fool of herself over a man. Retha might as well join the crowd. So long as she ain't trying to marry the man."

Retha is not sure if Madelyn is helping or hurting her plight but Jessie does seem to soften a little. Still her words do not reflect any ease in attitude. "Just look at that man. I wouldn't trust him no further than I could throw him. Green eyes. Retha he probably collects hearts for the fun of it. I can't believe you fallin' for his bullshit. He already showed you what he's about."

"He is gorgeous ain't he girl?" Madelyn jumps in, completely ignoring Jessie's concerns. "Goodness!"

Retha wishes she could deny that she slept with Jaren or at least deny that he stopped calling after they made love but it is all true and she is a lousy liar. "Now you see why I was not talking about him, Madelyn. Listen to Jessie. She talks like he's the devil incarnate."

Jessie gives a "humph" but no one says anything for a moment. Retha appears so torn that Jessie can't help but soften. Seeing hope, Retha pleads her case. "He's not a bad guy, Jessie. Sure, we need to work some things out, but I like him a lot and I want to try. I'm not saying it is easy for me to trust him but I know he likes me too. We just want to spend time together. Like Madelyn said, I'm not looking for a husband. But Jaren is the only man I've wanted to be with since Joe died. Please don't make this any harder for me than it is. I mean,

Jaren didn't want to make a commitment to me, but his being here is a commitment. Can I please enjoy this?"

Jessie's lips are tightly pursed together and stuck out. Her arms are folded across her chest and she is squeezing them tightly under her breast. Jessie looks at Madelyn for support but gets a "you should be ashamed" look. Madelyn then rolls her eyes up before cutting them at Retha. Jessie gives a tight lipped grimace of a smile.

Retha jumps at the opening. She seizes her older sister's hand and jumps up and down like a small child. "Can I keep him Jessie? Please, please, please! Can I keep him, can I, can I, can I?"

The act causes all of Jessie's resistance to dissipate; she has to laugh at Retha. "I don't see how you could resist anything that man wants. If you enjoy being with him that much, I'll leave you alone because he's probably in as much trouble as you are. Just don't let him take advantage of you." Jessie peeps over her shoulder and lowers her voice. "Girl, he's got lots of money don't he?" They all laugh at Jessie's sudden change in focus as they hug each other and leave the room.

The party is jumping but Retha is finding answering questions pretty tedious. Mykol, Elizabeth, Brenda, Jeremiah, Maria, Charmaine, Raheem, and nearly everyone else at the party, including those she has not met before today, want all the details of her involvement with Jaren. To those close family and friends she promises she will tell them all about it later. To others she says she and Jaren are good friends. It is clear to everyone they are much more than friends. Jaren does not hide his affection for Retha or she for him.

Both Retha's brothers-in-law are pretty loaded by the end of the night. A little after one in the morning, they walk out with Jaren to help bring in his luggage from his rented car. They don't allow anyone else to accompany them because they need to talk to Jaren privately. Mykol tries to go along with his father and the other men but Robert and Philip tell him he might betray them to the women. Mykol is insulted but stays behind with hurt feelings. When Philip and Robert see how much luggage Jaren has, they figure he plans on being around for a while. They can't help but be a little sorry for him. Robert is the first to ask. "Man do you have any idea what you're getting yourself into? Are you sure you're ready for this?"

"What do you mean?" Jaren questions.

"These are not love 'em and leave 'em women. Not saying that any woman is." Robert glances back to make sure no wife is in earshot, before he continues. "But these women get hold of you quick. They make you not want to go nowhere else."

Jaren's subtle smile indicates he is aware of this fact.

Philip takes over. "We ain't trying to run you off, but you're a pretty young fella to be getting tied up with a woman like Retha. Retha will leave a brother wounded. She don't mean no harm. I know you don't have long term plans here or you would have given her a ring instead of a bracelet. But you might as well leave now if this is not where you sure you wanna be. God knows I love my wife but I couldn't go nowhere else if I wanted to. Thank God I never wanted to. I been hooked to this woman almost since I laid eyes on her. It feels good but those weren't my plans when I first got with her. Brah-in-law here is the same way. They might have some mojo on us. Oh hell, it's probably too late to save yo' ass anyway. Welcome to the family." At this the two nearly drunk men turn with their arms full of Jaren's luggage and laugh their way into the house.

Later, as Madelyn and Jessie drive home with their two inebriated mates asleep in the back seat, Madelyn asks Jessie, "Do you see the way that boy looks at Retha? Damn it makes me melt just to look at them. Remember when Robert looked at you like that?"

"I don't know what you talkin' about. Robert still looks at me like that."

"Yeah. Okay. Right. Well, do you remember when he looked like that and looked at you like that?"

"God almighty! Poor Retha, she's in so much trouble. I hope she enjoys it while it lasts. I told y'all we need to pray for her. She gonna need strength to deal with what Mr. Jaren Daniels is layin' down. That boy is too fine."

"She gonna need something," Madelyn quietly responds.

--

Retha's eyes pop open after two hours of sleep. She is exhausted but far too hyped to sleep. Jaren is with her, in her bed, not by accident or coincidence but by purposeful choice. *Now what am I going to do with him? He's going to get bored and leave within a week. I work all the time. God, please let him stay with me. Please,*

Lord. Retha prides herself in not wasting God's time with frivolous requests. Hopefully, the Lord won't be disappointed with such a selfish prayer from one of his favorite children. Retha lies there staring at Jaren as he sleeps. She thinks it's childish and shallow to take so much pleasure in his looks. She can't help herself. She watches him until her bladder makes her move. She creeps from the bed and heads for the bathroom.

"Where are you going, Retha?" Jaren mumbles, barely awake.

"Be right back."

Retha hurries into the bathroom, pees and returns to the bed, as always squeezing as close to Jaren as she can. He wraps himself around her and they drop back into a deep much needed sleep.

Chapter 20 -- That Scent Thing

It is nearly noon when Retha's eyes open to the sound of people walking and talking throughout her home. At first she assumes Brenda and her friends are the perpetrators but soon hears Robert's mouth and Jessie shushing him. Retha drags herself from the bed and heads into the bathroom to get presentable before putting on her bathrobe and checking on the noise in her home. She finds Jaren wide awake when she exits the bath.

Brenda and her friends are joined by Jessie, Robert, Madelyn, Philip, and Catrina. When they see Retha, Jessie gets defensive. "I tried to keep them away Retha, but Robert and Philip wouldn't mind and yo' sister wasn't much better. They said they wanna eat some of this food. Like they couldn't come over here later and eat."

"Daniels still sleep?" Robert asks.

"Who could sleep with your big mouth around?" Retha barks as she plops into a kitchen chair.

Jessie has pulled food from the refrigerator and has the microwave and stovetop going. Retha is relieved to see Madelyn starting the coffeemaker. Retha could have slept another two or three hours with no problem. Coffee might help dissolve the rocks under her eyelids.

After sitting for a few minutes, Retha gathers up her niece and takes her in the bedroom to meet Jaren. Jaren is surprised to see that Catrina is not the small child he imagined but nearly as tall as her aunt. Catrina leans on the bed and stares at him.

"Why is she watching me like that?"

"It's probably strange for her to see you in my bed and she's curious about you. When she recognizes you, she'll grab your hand to rub her face. I don't want you to be uncomfortable around her. She can be a trip."

"Don't worry about us. We'll get along fine," Jaren assures Retha and to Catrina he adds, "Won't we, Catrina?" He throws Retha a thoughtful glance. "Thanks for the heads up. I thought you said she was blind."

"She is, legally. She has no lenses and no vision at all in her right eye and a scarred retina in the left. She uses her vision very well, the little she has. She can't focus though, no lenses. Are you staying in bed?"

"I don't suppose you're getting back in here with me today are you?" Jaren seems hopeful.

Retha gives him her "don't be ridiculous look" as she takes Catrina by the arm in an attempt to lead her from the room. Catrina drops to the floor, signaling she is not ready to leave the room.

"I'm gonna take a shower and then I'll be out. Sounds like you've got a house full."

"Yeah," Retha answers with a tired smile as she wrestles Catrina into the hallway.

The remainder of the day is spent entertaining drop-ins. Even Sugar and Sylvia stop by so Sugar can have a talk with his friend Robert. When no one else is in earshot, Sugar questions Robert about Jaren. "I know Retha is somethin' special. All them girls is, but what this nigga got up his sleeve sniffin' round my niece? I don't trust him, truth be told. We cain't have nobody messin' over that girl. She a little bit mo' frail than them othas. Not sayin' she ain't tough, cause she is, but she been through a bit much already. If this fella ain't got good intentions, I don't thank I want him 'round here."

Robert nearly chokes in humor as he chomps down on one of the many chicken wings he has on his paper plate. "Sugar, man you don't even got to worry about Retha. Me and Philip talked to the brotha last night. He seems cool. He's the one you might need to worry about. He likes Retha. Matter of fact, I think she's got his nose open so wide you could drive a Mack truck up it. I haven't been around him much more than you have but he reminds me a hell of a lot of me when I met Jessie."

Sugar relaxes a little after getting Robert's assessment of Jaren and Retha's relationship. Still he keeps his ears open and barely misses a word that passes Jaren's lips but finds nothing to criticize.

As the day lingers on, Retha is so tired of guests she wants to take Jaren and abandon her home. "This is like a fucking open house," she complains to Brenda who ignores her friend and continues to laugh and talk with the rest of Retha's visitors. Brenda had planned to depart for Dallas in the early afternoon but, hey, these people are partying so she delays her departure until late evening. Just past nine o'clock, Rachel and Jonathan, who have been visiting for well over five hours without an invitation, are the last to leave.

Retha showers and settles in with Jaren for a long night of conversation. They talk for well over three hours, mostly telling stories about their families. Jaren describes his parents and sister in great detail for Retha. She can tell he loves his family and is beginning to sense his devotion to them. Retha gets comfortable and starts speaking freely about Joe. She is so open that she leaves Jaren wondering if she will ever get over Joe's death. They stop talking. The sweet closeness comes and then sleep.

Retha calls in sick on Monday and has Tuesday off. The couple spends those two days melding with little to no outside distraction. Retha's sisters have never quite figured out her work schedule since she has rotating days off. She lets them think she is working. Retha and Jaren stop in at Jessie's for dinner Tuesday night but leave as soon as they can get free.

Their time together is like surrendering to an addiction. Retha stays as close up under Jaren as she can. They sit on her sofa for hours and watch television, read, and sleep with Jaren lying flat on his back and Retha stretched out on top of him. They nap like this until Jaren complains of discomfort or not being able to breathe. Retha is like a small devoted child clinging to a much beloved parent. She tries to give him space but when she moves away, it is not long before Jaren pulls her back as close as he can get her. Retha is so excited inside that she is embarrassed. She chastises herself for being so happy. She tries to bring her emotions down to earth but can't contain them.

The intensity of Jaren's feelings for Retha are a mystery to him. He has never been so caught up by a woman before. He cannot understand what it is about her that has captured him so completely. Sure, she looks good, she is damn sexy, he loves her smell, they talk about everything, and she makes him laugh a lot. But Retha doesn't just make him laugh; he is happy when they are together. Even when he is pissed with her, he's still happy just to be with her. He likes that Retha likes him as much as he likes her. They are a good fit. He remembers Retha capturing his notice before he got close enough to see her well. *Maybe that scent thing is real*. The thought causes him to smile; it excites him.

--

Within a week of Jaren's arrival, it becomes clear to Retha's family that he plans to be a regular. By the end of his first full week in the city, Retha has a new garage door opener and Jaren, Mykol, and Jeremiah have cleaned out her previously junk ridden garage to make room for his newly leased truck. Jaren rents a storage unit for all the misplaced junk that previously lived in Retha's garage.

By the middle of Jaren's second week in San Antonio, Retha is uneasy. Jaren is a little too giving for Retha. He is generous to a fault. Retha has barely spent a dime of her own money since he arrived. When he offers to have a sprinkler system installed in her yard, she flatly refuses. "You've already done too much. It's not right for you to spend your money on my house. It makes me feel like I'm taking advantage of you."

"We're talking about a sprinkler system here. I mean how expensive can that be?"

Retha shrugs off the question but it is obvious to Jaren that she does not want him to have the sprinkler system installed. He recognizes this as a barrier Retha is putting in place and is offended. Offended or not, Jaren is not easily deterred once he sets his sights on something. "Look baby, I'm not trying to tell you what to do but all that going outside and moving the hose around doesn't make sense when we can have a sprinkler installed. I guarantee you your lawn will be much nicer and you'll probably save water."

"I'll give it some thought," Retha ends the discussion.

Confused as to why she does not want Jaren spending money on her home, Retha asks Jessie, Robert, and Madelyn their opinions. Madelyn goes first. "Mama always told me, if a man sees you have needs and he doesn't try to take care of those needs he is not a good man for you. Jaren is just trying to take care of things he can help you with."

"Retha, he ain't spent an hour's salary on you and that house," Robert pipes in.

Jessie is more in agreement with Retha. "Yeah well, I'm a woman and it don't take much to spoil me. How's Retha gonna feel when Mr. Deep Pockets is gone on his merry way and she has to come down to earth and make do on her own. But even more than that, you don't need to let him have too much control over your home. And as God is my witness, when a man is spending his money he expects to run things. Why is he so anxious to spend money on you? You'll end up obligated and going along with him because he did this or that for you. No, baby. Don't set yourself up like that."

On second thought, Madelyn agrees. "He sure doesn't seem to mind spending his money. Jess may be right, though. He might be trying to buy his way in."

Jessie and Madelyn's opinions have Retha's brother-in-law pissed off. Robert has not spent much time with Jaren but is certain he cares for Retha and is not conniving to control her or her home. He also has a strong sense that Jaren is a level-headed young man trying to do the right thing. He can't help but come to the defense of his newest friend. "Damn, y'all give the boy a chance. Jessie, when we pulled up in front of Retha's house the other day you said she needed to have a sprinkler system installed. If the boy laid up over there for the next year and didn't spend a dime you'd be calling him a "stingy motherfucker." Don't deny it, because I been married to you too long not to know you. But since he's more than willing to do things without being asked, you figure he must have a hidden plan to get in control of Retha's life. He's damned if he do and damned if he don't. Retha, tell him what you'd like him to do and when to do it but make sure you get your sisters' approvals first. You need to be calling Ida and discussing this shit with her. That's who you need to be talkin' to 'cause Jessie is not going to like the boy until he marries you." Needless to say Robert and Jessie aren't talking to each other when they climb into bed that night.

Retha takes Robert's advice to call and talk to Ida. The voice of reason amongst the Gray children, Ida never has a serious disagreement with anyone in the family. She doesn't let the drama faze her that much, whatever it is. She speaks her mind but will occasionally get very quiet if, in her opinion, the person she is speaking with is misguided. Each of her siblings, other than Andre, has called her when they have a gripe or a concern or need advice. She is truly fair-minded and doesn't take sides when the siblings have spats with each other. Ida is recently divorced and happy about it. She has no interest whatever in a new mate. She is the only thin, light-skinned member of her family. One might guess she was left on the doorstep until they see her alongside Madelyn. Ida and Maddie share the same likeness except Maddie is dark and carries more weight. Ida is also the Good Samaritan of the family. She often has people in need living in her home. Wherever she lived during her military career she had families in need, be it financial or emotional, that she adopted and assisted. Jessie used to complain that Ida set herself up for problems. These days Jessie says her sister is "doing the Lord's work."

Retha is hoping that Ida has a divine word from the Father for her right now. She is unsure where to set her boundaries with Jaren. Ida listens to Retha and says very little until she asks, "Where did you find this man and are there any more like him?"

"Come on Ida be serious. I need advice and Robert says you're the one I should ask."

"Glad brother-in-law thinks so highly of me but Retha, baby, you have to figure this out for yourself. I can't tell you what you should or should not accept from your friend. You have to decide where to draw the line. I will ask you this. Would you be taking advantage of him if he put in a sprinkler system? Would it set him back financially? I mean, would you let him control you or your home because he spends his money there? 'Cause if you are too afraid to put him in his place, money or no money, maybe you need to send him on home. And one more question. Do you need to spend more time together before you accept such a personal gift? Because, believe it or not baby, a sprinkler system is more personal than a piece of jewelry."

"Well," Retha starts to answer but Ida stops her. "I don't want you to give me the answers. I want you to consider those questions in dealing with your friend."

Retha ponders her discussions with her sisters and brother-in-law. Her reservations have nothing to do with the sprinkler system. It is more a trust issue. She does not trust Jaren to be around for long, so why get dependent on him? Retha imagines herself watching the drops of water springing from the automatic sprinklers as tears run down her face in memory of a long-gone Jaren. That settles it. Jaren does make a good argument for having the system installed, so she decides to take his advice and pay for it herself. She advises him of her decision over breakfast the next morning. Jaren is more offended than ever. "So, if you can afford to have the system installed why haven't you done it?"

"I hadn't thought about it. But it is a good idea that will save me time and money plus make the yard look better. I'm glad you thought about it because it will be a big help."

"Yeah, well you're welcome." Jaren gets up from the table and takes the newspaper out to the patio until he gets over his injured feelings.

Chapter 21 -- Palimony?

Disappointment descends on Retha like a shroud when Jaren announces he plans to spend Thanksgiving with his family back in New York. Since Retha is away from home five days and three evenings a week, Jaren has had a great deal of time to himself. On the other hand, Retha has little time alone causing Jaren to worry that she might tire of having him around all the time. The sadness in her eyes after hearing his visit is ending confirms that she wants him to stay longer.

Retha gathers her courage and asks Jaren when he plans to return. His answer is Retha's first hint of the next conflict to arise between them. "I had thought I might come back that following Monday or Tuesday but what's the sense in that when you'll be working every day after that up until Saturday night. I'll call you before I come back."

Don't want to seem too needy here. "I'll miss you Jaren."

"Me too."

Spending so much time in San Antonio with Retha and being away from his homes and family is not as easy as Jaren had thought. Retha's home is comfortable enough but all the Joe memorabilia is unsettling. Jaren spends a great deal of time alone in the house and although he is accustomed to living alone, he came to San Antonio to be with Retha. They share more time together than they would if he was in New York or Tampa but Retha works sixty or more hours each week and when she is at home she is tired. There are things Jaren could do to help and occupy his time but Retha refuses to let him spend money on her home. The finance issue is awkward for them.

Also, Jaren had no idea he would miss his family and friends so much. Almost daily calls from his mother do not help. He told his family he would be visiting with a friend in San Antonio for a while but did not discuss his plans in detail with his family, friends, or Retha because he had not been sure of his plans. He is sure now. He wants to be with Retha regardless of jobs, family, or financial issues. Jaren believes these are minor concerns and they will work through them if she cooperates.

During his trip home, Jaren plans to explain his relationship with Retha to his family. He can sense his mother's concern during each call. He wants to assure her he is okay and that Retha does not have him under some mystical spell though he isn't too certain of that himself. He needs his dad's advice on his relationship with Retha because she baffles him in so many ways.

--

"Are you in love with this woman? You plan to marry her?" Charles Daniels asks his son the evening Jaren arrives at his parents' New Rochelle home. Susan has left them alone in Charles's study for a man-to-man, heart-to-heart talk.

"No to both, Dad, but I do like her a lot. I don't plan on marrying anyone for a long time."

"Yeah, right," Charles replies, his voice dripping with sarcasm. "So why are you trying so hard to please her? I don't blame her for being leery of you."

"Look, I just want to be there with her and take care of the things she needs while I'm there. Why is that such a big deal? She should be happy I want to do things for her but she rejects everything I offer."

"I doubt this woman has any idea of the amount of money you have. You and she live in different worlds and time is the only thing that will change that. It does her credit that she's not trying to get more out of you since you seem so willing to give her whatever she wants, except marriage."

"What makes you think she wants to get married? You haven't even met her."

"She's a woman isn't she? Women usually want to marry the men they're in love with, not always, but usually. They don't resist marriage like men. I assume she cares for you as much as you do for her or your nose wouldn't be open so wide."

"I was thinking about buying my own place in San Antonio." Jaren expects his father's disapproval on this issue.

Charles rises from his seat and begins pacing the floor. After a moment he asks, "Son, are you crazy? You hardly know this woman. I thought you said she owns her own home. Why not stay with her when you visit? "

"She does, but it's small. I need more room so I can work out. I was thinking about asking her to move in with me and maybe rent her house out. Her place is nice but there's too much of her husband there. I feel like a visitor."

"That's what you are. A little jealousy there for the dead husband or do you think he's watching you make love to his wife and might get pissed off and haunt yo' ass? You need to give thought to the fact that you're turning this young woman's life upside down. What happens to her when you get bored and decide you want to move on?"

"Dad, she'll dump me long before that happens. I don't see myself ever getting tired of her."

"So after you talk her into giving up her home and moving in with you, how easy do you think it will be for her to dump you, even if she wants to?"

"I hope not easy at all," Jaren responds with a sly smile. "Listen, Retha is by no means a rich woman but she has a decent income without working. She also has substantial savings and investments. She's pretty well off. She sure doesn't need to work two jobs. I want her to quit one. She likes working her uncle's restaurant. She hates the other job."

"Yeah. That's probably the one she should keep," Charles smirks.

Jaren's father is seeing a side of his son he has not seen before. Jaren has never been prone to hasty decisions. His involvement with Retha seems to have dumbed him down.

"You ever heard of palimony, pal?"

"Yep and I'll just have to take my chances. Listen, Dad. I'm discussing this with you because I want you and Mom to know what's going on and so you can advise me on how to talk to Retha about these things. Can I get a little positive advice? All you're doing is giving me the negatives."

"That's because you're making a mistake. The simplest thing is to let her stay in her place and you visit her when your schedule allows or she can visit you when she has free time. That way, when the time comes and you or she move on, it'll be much easier. And, damn, whatever you do, don't ask her to leave a good paying job to lay up days with you. When are we going to meet this femme fatale? Bring her with you for Christmas."

"She's having a big family dinner at her home for Christmas."

"In the cracker box?"

Jaren ignores his father's snide remark. "I hate not being here for Christmas but I plan on spending the holiday in San Antonio. I hope you and Mom won't be too disappointed."

"You planning on being in shape when the season starts?"

"I'll be in shape. I've been getting my workouts more than usual. They've got several good facilities in San Antonio. Besides, what else have I got to do during the day? She works all the damn time."

"I hope you're thinking all this through, Son, all of it."

--

Charles realizes his wife will have a hissy fit when she learns her son is spending Christmas away from home with this strange woman. He wonders if he should tell Susan right away or wait until Jaren leaves. When he climbs into bed with his wife that night, she makes his decision easy by questioning him about the conversation he had with their son earlier. "You were right; he's serious," Charles tells her, not trying to allay her concerns in any way. Charles practices sledge hammer tactics when dealing with his family.

Susan pops straight up on the bed. "How serious? He's not planning to marry her!"

"Oh, he doesn't think he is, at least no time soon. I wager a chunk of his money he'll marry her and not in the too distant future. I'm surprised he's so naïve about his feelings but as I can recall I was the same way about mine before I married you."

Susan does not want to hear Charles's recollections. She has lost all sentimentality when it comes to their relationship. "I want to meet her. Please don't tell me it's the same one that was in the Army?"

"You want to spend Christmas in San Antonio?" Charles drops the bomb.

"Are you kidding?"

"That's the only way you'll spend it with your son because that's where he'll be."

Susan is ready to go and confront Jaren at that very moment. *What is he thinking to place a stranger before his own family?* The family always spends the holiday together. How can he abandon them for her? Charles grabs his wife by the tail of her nightgown and stops her planned verbal assault on their son by explaining she might make him angry and more determined to be with "the girl." Again, Charles suggests they take their daughter Rachelle and fly down to San Antonio to meet Mrs. Retha Lindo in person.

After much discussion Charles and Susan decide they cannot drop everything, abandon their holiday commitments and show up in San Antonio for Christmas dragging Rachelle behind them. After all, Jaren is an adult and hopefully Retha is not the awful spell-casting gold-digger Susan imagines. Susan has it fixed in her mind that she will size Retha up and if she isn't what she pretends to be, Susan will tell Jaren what she thinks. Even if Retha does have good intentions toward Jaren, from what Susan has heard so far, Retha is not up to the standard she wants for her son -- a female soldier restaurant worker -- not for her boy. After all, what kind of people would allow their daughter to join the Army?

Rachelle is more heartbroken than her mother when she learns her brother will be away from home at Christmas. She wastes no time confronting him. "Who are these people you are spending Christmas with? Are they more important than us?"

"I'm going to visit with a friend in San Antonio. You should come down for a few days."

This is a first. He must be getting serious. "Is this the lady in Texas you told me about at the beginning of the season?" Rachelle asks with genuine interest.

Jaren smiles because Rachelle forgets nothing. "You remember that? Yeah, she's the one. Do you remember her name?"

"No, but I remember it was unusual, very ethnic. You have a photo?"

Jaren scrolls through his phone and finds a picture of Retha and him outside Jessie's house grinning at the camera as if they share a delicious secret. He hands the phone to his sister. "Her name is Retha."

Rachelle stares at the picture and smiles. It does her heart good to see her brother does like black women, one in particular very much. Jaren is smiling with his eyes and he and Retha appear happy together. "She is gorgeous. I hope she's nice." Rachelle hands the phone back to Jaren.

"She can be, sometimes." He laughs lightly, looks at the picture for a moment and puts the phone down. Rachelle considers asking him to show the picture to their parents but doesn't. She remembers the conversation they had about skin color and thought the subject bothered Jaren more than she had expected. Rachelle is certain that if Susan sees the picture of Jaren's newest girlfriend her reaction will not be positive. It is almost Thanksgiving, not a time for stirring up confusion.

Chapter 22 -- My Sisters are My Sisters

Thanksgiving Day is a truly blessed one for the families of both Retha and Jaren. The group at the Daniel's home is small in comparison to the one Jessie and Robert entertain in San Antonio. There is an abundance of family, gratitude, food, joy, and laughter at both gatherings mixed in with healthy doses of disappointment.

Susan worked especially hard preparing all of Jaren's favorite dishes for their Thanksgiving dinner. Charles cannot remember the last time his wife put out such a wonderful meal. She invited Jaren's favorite relatives and friends to stop by and visit even if they couldn't make it to dinner. She told each of them that Jaren had expressed a particular wish to see them. She even invited one of his old girlfriends to dinner. Fortunately for Jaren, the lady declined because of a previous engagement. No matter, Susan does not care for the lady particularly but Jaren had liked her at one time and she is doing quite well for herself as a budding attorney.

It appears as if Susan's hard work is paying off because Jaren is definitely enjoying himself at home with his family and friends. So Charles and Susan are floored when Jaren announces he will leave on Friday instead of remaining the entire weekend. He had told his parents the day before that he might leave early, but he was having such a good time they were certain he would stay the weekend. His mother and sister plead with him to stay longer. Jaren is being selfish but his need to get back to San Antonio far exceeds the guilt induced by their pleas.

Charles is angrier with Jaren than he can ever remember. Jaren has never placed another person ahead of the family and his planned early departure puts a damper on the entire holiday weekend. The rest of the family is surprised and more than a little disappointed that Jaren is leaving the party early. He is always a spark at any family gathering and missed immensely when he is away. His career keeps him away a great deal and now it appears they are losing him to another family. The loss is hard to swallow. After Jaren leaves for the airport early that Friday morning, Susan goes in her room and lies awake for hours worrying about her son and his new relationship.

--

Thanksgiving is Retha's favorite holiday but she is anxious for the weekend to pass and for Jaren's return. By Thanksgiving Day, he has been gone three days and half of her heart is lonely beyond belief. The other half is overjoyed with the presence of her family. Raymond, his new lady friend, Tamera, and RJ are visiting from Houston. Jermaine, Phyllis, and their two boys are in from San Diego and Philip and Aubrey have driven back from Atlanta. Of course all of the San Antonio family and a few others from Houston are all piled into Jessie and Robert's home. Thankfully the weather allows the children and those adults who desire to spend time out of doors in the cool fall sunshine.

Raymond and the rest of the out-of-towners express considerable disappointment that Jaren is not present for Thanksgiving dinner. Both the brothers are gossips, especially Jermaine. They question everyone that has met Jaren. Each time one of them asks Retha a question that is too personal, she tells them it's none of their "damn business." Most of the other family members are more than willing to provide every drop of information they can.

When the brothers get to Sugar, he refuses to cooperate with the interrogation they have given everyone else. "Hell, I ain't no damn gossip columnist. Meet the man yoself and find out." Sugar's lack of interest is out of character. He usually loves to laugh and gossip with Raymond and Jermaine.

"Uh oh, somethin's up. Since when you ain't got nothin to say about a Negro, Unc? What is it you're not tellin? You don't like this dude or somethin?" Raymond probes further.

"Don't go jumpin' to no conclusions. I didn't say nothin' 'bout not likin' the boy. I just don't know him well enough to judge him. Let's say I'm takin' the wait 'n' see approach. Now leave me alone about it and let me finish my cake." Sugar walks away from his nephews and they do not pursue the issue with their uncle any further.

Needless to say the two nosey brothers have more questions than ever, one of which is Sugar's closed mouth, a mystery which must be solved. Gluttons for punishment, the brothers corner Jessie and ask why Sugar doesn't like Jaren.

"Who said Sugar don't like Jaren? Don't come here startin' no mess. I know Sugar ain't told Jerry Springer and Ricki Lake he don't like Jaren. He and Jaren haven't spent a good five minutes in conversation together. Sugar wants to make sure Jaren don't mess over Retha but that's all there is to that. Now leave me the hell alone."

The brothers are a little disappointed that there's not more dirt to dig up. In a pretense at making amends, Raymond leans over his older sister and tries to kiss her on the cheek. Raymond is treading in dangerous waters but cannot help himself. He is not happy unless Jessie rejects him in some small way. His eldest sister always aims to please her brothers. She places her fingers in Raymond's chest, pushes him away, and grumbles "Get off me," as she marches away in customary disgust.

To everyone's relief, Raymond and Jermaine's verbal speculation about Jaren comes to a screeching halt when he shows up at Jessie and Robert's home late the next morning with a smile on his face and more than ready to enjoy these new acquaintances.

Retha can hardly contain a squeal when Jessie calls her at work and tells her that Jaren is back in town. Her joy lessens slightly when she learns that he is off with Robert, Philip, Mykol and her brothers. She wonders what the brothers will say about her and hopes Jaren understands their sense of humor, which is warped to say the least. They had teased Retha all Thanksgiving Day about her "imaginary boyfriend." Even though they were kidding, Retha is relieved they have met Jaren or they would have continued the ribbing their entire stay.

Jaren spends that Friday afternoon out playing golf with the men of Retha's family. The guys are amazed at the preferential treatment they receive once the management of the golf club realizes who they have playing their course. Afterwards they settle in at a sports bar and shoot a few games of pool. Jermaine asks the bartender to run a tab but the owner insists on paying the tab once he realizes that Jaren is part of the group. Raymond and Jermaine are astounded at the irony. Jaren is a rich man, yet people trip over themselves to give him something for free.

Jaren is nowhere in sight when Retha gets in from work. She waits for what seems like forever but is only thirty minutes in real time and finally breaks down and calls Jessie. Not wanting to sound desperate, she starts chatting nonchalantly.

Jessie, as usual does not play along. "You looking for yo' man?"

"And why do you think that?"

"Because you never call me on a Friday evening to chat. They been gone since he landed. I hope they haven't taken him off somewhere and got him arrested along with my baby and me and Madelyn's husbands. Maybe we should disown those brothers of ours and ban them from the damn city. Sugar's been calling for 'em. They were supposed to show up at his place for a late lunch and never showed. He's mad. They should have been back by now. Come on over. They'll be here pretty soon."

"I'm tired. I think I'll stay at home."

"You better bring yo' tired behind on over here. Madelyn's doctoring up these leftovers."

Retha hears Madelyn questioning in the background. "What she say?"

"Talkin' 'bout she tired." Jessie answers Madelyn and then speaks back into the phone to Retha. "Jermaine and Raymond are not going to let you have that boy over there to yourself -- not tonight. RJ and Aubrey and Jermaine's babies have been running in here every fifteen minutes asking when they're coming back. They'll probably break down and cry if they don't get to spend some time with Jaren. They begged their daddies to take them out today -- just a waste of breath."

Madelyn yells in the background. "That's what you get for having a famous boyfriend. You should have a regular old tired nobody like the rest of us -- always showin' off."

"I'll be over in a little bit," Retha concedes.

There is still no sign of the delinquent males when Retha arrives at Jessie's home. Phyllis, Nicola and Baby Jevon, and Raymond's friend Tamera are also sitting in Jessie's family room. When the gang of men arrives, they are so jubilant that the little pique the women felt at their absence disappears.

The men are hungry. Robert and Philip grab plates and load them with leftovers. Raymond cozies up to Tamera and sweet talks her into serving him. Jermaine and Mykol declare they are not ready to eat yet but take seats at the table. As soon as Jaren can break away from the children he comes into the kitchen and grabs a plate also. He and Retha give each other friendly hellos and knowing glances but nothing else. After serving himself, Jaren joins the other men at the table.

As the kitchen and family room are adjoining, the women are privy to the men's conversation, most of which they ignore until Raymond decides to start up with his sisters.

"Man you ain't got her trained to fix your plate yet?" Raymond asks Jaren with feigned astonishment. Jaren smiles and glances at Retha in response. The sisters laugh at Raymond's deliberate attempt at starting an argument.

Robert and Jermaine have competing plans for Jaren's time on Saturday. Jaren declines both because he plans to spend the day with Retha. When Retha reminds him that she is scheduled to work her insurance job, his displeasure is obvious. Jaren realizes he should have stayed in New York until Tuesday as planned and he voices that sentiment loud enough to cause Retha to squirm.

Jermaine finds Jaren's declaration to spend time with Retha astounding. He has been married eight years and jumps at any opportunity to hang out with "the fellas" over spending time with his wife. He stares at Jaren for a moment and, as if he can't help himself, says what's on his mind. "Man, I don't get it. You wanna close up with Retha instead of hangin' out with us. Guarantee we'll show you a good time. Robert's a pretty cool guy if you can get him away from Jessie. You can spend time with Retha anytime. I can't see what you like about her anyway."

"Don't be so ignorant Jermaine," Madelyn snaps but fails to shut up her baby brother.

Jermaine proceeds to point out each of Retha's faults as he sees them. "She black, she mean, she short with big feet, got a big old butt, her hair's nappier than mine, and she talks way too much shit and always wants to give her opinion. I don't see what you like about her. I can't stand her and she's my sister."

Jaren watches Retha to determine if she takes Jermaine's mocking seriously. Based on her demeanor, she's very much accustomed to Jermaine's verbal assaults. Jessie, the keeper of the castle, does take offense and comes to Retha's defense.

"Boy if you don't stop talking like a school age imbecile and leave my sister alone."

"Yeah," Phyllis adds. "Why do you pick at Retha so much?"

Raymond chooses up sides. "That's right, stop pickin' on Retha. She ain't no worse than Jessie, Ida, and Madelyn. She's a lot nicer than Jessie. Jessie's mean as a linebacker on steroids. That's probably where Retha gets it from."

"At least I can get along well enough with my husband that I don't have to switch every year or two," Jessie retaliates drawing hoots from just about everyone in hearing distance.

"See how mean she is. Kick a man when he's down. Retha gonna be just like her when she gets old. You better run while you got a chance, man," Raymond advises Jaren. "Check out Robert. He's cowering over there in the corner. Philip too. They scared man. These women got 'em scared. My biggest blessing is that my sisters are my sisters and I never have to worry about marrying one of 'em."

Chapter 23 -- Meet the Family

Sunday is both welcomed and dreaded as it sends the last of the out-of-towners on their merry way. Sunday night brings exhaustion, indigestion, and an extra two to four pounds. Jaren and Retha's brothers took to each other like three-year-olds on a playground and Jaren is ready to take a drive up to Houston to visit with Raymond whenever Retha can get the time off.

"Seems like you'd be tired of them by now. I know I am. I love Raymond but he never wants to be with the women. He always wants to hang out. He has to be up to no good."

Jaren is caught off guard by Retha's awareness of her brother's character. Tamera is an attractive woman and seems bright and friendly, but Jaren noticed that Raymond was constantly on the hunt for new prey. "Maybe he doesn't care that much for what's her name."

"Humph. Next thing we know, Raymond and Tamera will be married and he'll be acting the same way he was acting when you guys were out. I know my brother. He makes me wanna tell women to run. I don't think he ever learned what the term faithful means. I love him but I don't think he'll settle down for a long time, if ever. He should learn from my uncle and try to do different. He just loves to love a lot of different women. Doesn't seem like he'll ever change but I hope he does."

Jaren decides to change the subject. He has asked Retha no less than three times to skip work and stay at home with him on Monday and tries one more time to convince her to take the day off. Retha explains that after any holiday weekend too many people call in sick and she won't do that unless she is genuinely ill.

So Retha is up by six the next morning, out of the house by seven in order to make it across town and be seated at her desk with her PC and phone logged on by eight. As sure as spring brings green, several of her coworkers who are scheduled to work the ten a.m. to eight p.m. shift fail to show. Retha's normal ten-hour shift is extended to twelve hours. She is exhausted when she pulls in at nearly nine that night.

Jaren is too angry to wait and discuss Retha's work schedule at a time when she might be more receptive. No sooner than she sits down on her family room sofa, he lights into her. "Retha, don't you think you're working too hard -- ten-hour shifts, way across town, overtime and almost all weekend at Sugar's?" Jaren paces the floor to relieve his frustration as he talks to her. "I can't understand why you are working two jobs. I mean damn, you have a decent income. Why not just work Sugar's? Since I've been here we haven't spent much time together. I understand your passion for the restaurant. I can relate to that. I love baseball; it's my life. But why not let this insurance crap go? You don't even like the job. It makes you miserable. You're always complaining about the company policies and how mean the customers are. Why put yourself through that?"

"My job at UP&C is not that bad. It's a good company and my manager tells me I am moving fast. The director is considering me for a lead position. I'm a bit of a drama queen but most of the time I'm just making conversation when I complain. I love Sugar's but I can't depend on the little I make there and a check from the government to live on. My home needs repairs that I should have taken care of before I left the Army and I am trying to grow my savings. I need to be able to pay for home and car repairs and vacations without using credit or touching my investments or savings."

Jaren tells himself to calm down and sit down. He waits a few moments before he speaks again. "I want you to let me take care of the things you need done to the house. You don't have to worry about the money. I have more than I can ever use in this lifetime."

Retha holds her tongue between her teeth to keep from telling Jaren that she can't depend on him to be around to take care of things for her. She would be a fool to let go of a good job because he wants to spend more time with her at the moment. Retha realizes that her future must have priority over a short-lived fling with Jaren. His season will start soon and that may be the end of their involvement.

Jaren watches her and wonders what she is thinking. "What if I put money aside for you? It'll be yours to do whatever you want with, no strings attached. Would you quit that job?"

Retha stares him directly in the face before she proclaims, "I'm not quitting my job, Jaren. I'm glad you're here but I can't quit working to be with you. Besides, once the season starts we won't be spending much time together anyway. Let's leave this alone."

Damn, this woman is hard-headed. Jaren realizes that he has to settle for what he can get from Retha for the time being. Since he must be in Tampa for a few days to attend two charitable events he asks her to visit. Fully expecting Retha to turn down the invitation, he is shocked when she says "sure."

--

Retha enjoys her first night in Tampa with Jaren and a group of his friends at a local restaurant and bar. No sooner than they walk into his Tampa home he announces with a smile that says trouble, "Hey, I've got a special treat planned for you tomorrow night." He is doing his best to hold back laughter.

"What is it?" Retha asks apprehensively.

He sits down on the arm of a sofa, draws her close, and wraps his arms around her hips. "We have a date with my family for dinner."

--

Retha is nervous about meeting Jaren's family. She has no reason to suspect that her jitters are well justified. It seems every eye in the upscale eatery is turned on the couple as they approach the table occupied by Susan, Charles, and Rachelle Daniels. Jaren, of course, is a great favorite around town, but he is not often seen escorting his dates about. Retha has made every effort to look her absolute best without overdressing. Jaren was no help with her attire. She wanted to yell at him "I AM MEETING YOUR FAMILY FOR THE FIRST TIME OUT AT DINNER. OH MY GOD!" The meeting was so unexpected and Retha had no idea what to expect. She never thought she would meet Jaren's family. She wants them to like her and hopes she likes them.

The attention they receive as they approach Jaren's family adds to her jitters and the reception from at least one member of Jaren's family keeps Retha on edge for the remainder of the evening. Charles Daniels receives her with a glimmer in his eyes and a smile on his face as if he is seeing an old friend for the first time in years. Retha notices that he and Jaren have the same open and clear eyes. Rachelle is stupefied. In her opinion, Retha is the loveliest woman Jaren has ever dated. She is too stunned to be very welcoming but does manage to squeeze out a sweet smile after cutting her eyes at her mother no less than three times. Susan's mouth hangs open, though only slightly, and she stares at Retha through the introductions. At first Retha is not sure what the problem is. She wonders if she is overdressed. She sure isn't underdressed; Rachelle has on jeans. She hears Jaren ask "What's wrong, Mom?"

"Nothing, nothing." Susan's eyes dart around as she tries to figure out how to compose herself. "That is a lovely top you have there. I'm sorry. I am bad with names. Is it Aretha?"

"No, just Retha," Retha responds with a now plastered on smile.

Retha does not want to jump on the conclusion bandwagon, but as she sits there and listens to Susan, a tiny but strong assumption starts to rope her onto that flat bed. *She thinks I am too dark.* Retha glances around the table at Jaren and his family. Rachelle has lovely brown skin but she is much lighter than Retha. Jaren and his parents are very fair skinned, high yellow people.

Susan continues to babble on, not giving anyone else a chance to speak. She is nervous. Retha notices Charles reach across the table and take his wife's hand very gently and start to pat it in an attempt to calm her down. Rachelle peeps at Retha and Jaren from under her downturned lashes, clearly embarrassed. After a while, Jaren interrupts his mother and starts to talk to his father about their joint charitable foundation, thus bringing calm to the table.

Once their dinner is served, the atmosphere at the table settles a bit more. Retha and Rachelle work up a nice discussion about school and girl stuff and find themselves sharing a few quiet laughs. Jaren reaches for Retha's hand under the table and squeezes. Retha can sense his mother tense up across the table as if she is aware that Jaren has touched Retha intimately.

Dinner with the Daniels family is the most uncomfortable night out Retha has ever experienced. She lets out a visible sigh of relief when they leave the table. Charles and Rachelle give Retha warm hugs and thank her for joining them for dinner. Susan extends her hand. "It was very nice meeting you, Aretha. I hope we have the opportunity to meet again."

"I don't think your mother likes me," Retha tells Jaren once they are back at his home.

"Why would you say that? She liked you okay. She was a little nervous tonight. I have never seen her like that before."

"I wonder why?" Retha asks.

--

Rachelle is in for a rough ride home. No one says a word when they start the ride and she hopes rather than believes it will remain peaceful. Susan is so agitated she cannot sit still. Charles stays quiet not wanting to have the inevitable discussion in front of his daughter. Susan asks rhetorically "I wonder where he found her?" After a few more moments, Susan says to Charles, "What could your son be thinking?"

"What are you talking about, Susan?" Charles asks, although he has the answer.

"I knew this girl was going to be a problem when Jaren first told me about her. So he abandoned his family on Thanksgiving for her. This girl is common. Why is he doing this? I thought he had better judgment."

"Common! What do you mean, common. She's nice," Rachelle counters from the back seat, stoking the fire as she takes up an alliance with Retha.

"Okay, I guess a word you would understand better is 'ghetto.' Does that work for you? I don't recall asking you anything, Rachelle. I am talking to your father. Just shut up and let us talk."

Charles wants to have it out with Susan for speaking to Rachelle that way but he does not side with his children against his wife in their presence. He will discuss it with her once they are behind closed doors. "What's wrong with the girl, Susan? I like her and I can tell you one thing, your son likes her a lot."

"Yeah, I bet you do like her and your son had better get over himself because we don't have people like that in our family."

Charles shakes his head. He wants to ask her what type of people she is talking about but is certain his wife will not answer.

The next day Charles walks into his Tampa home to find his wife and daughter in a full blown argument. It seems Susan is irate because Rachelle supports her brother's choice in women. Rachelle is crying rivers of tears. "Why are you two arguing about one of Jaren's girlfriends? He changes them like the weather and you both know that."

"Mom doesn't like her because she is dark. She doesn't want us to have anything to do with dark-skinned people. It's crazy. Grandma Betty is dark and she is family. That's your mother, Dad. Mom doesn't even like her. I can't wait until I finish school so I can leave this house. I just want to get my own place. Do you hate me too, Mom. I'm dark." Rachelle yells at Susan who turns and goes into her bedroom and slams the door.

--

A few days after Susan and Rachelle's blowup, Jaren's father calls and announces plans to visit San Antonio for a couple of days before Christmas. Jaren ungraciously asks Charles the reason for the visit.

"That's an odd question. If I didn't know better, I'd think you don't want us to come." Charles responds sharply.

"No, no. It's not that. I'm just surprised. I ah, I mean, you didn't say anything about a visit when I was in Tampa."

Charles is impatient with his son. "Well, to answer your question. Your mother and sister miss you a lot and want to see you. This will be the first Christmas the family spends apart and quite frankly I want to meet Retha's family. Now, if there is some reason you don't want us to come, say the word and we will change our plans."

"Yes sir. Of course you can come. But you know I'll be back and forth during the holidays so I will be stopping in."

"Well, you know as well as I do that you won't have much time for us with all those charity fundraisers and such."

Jaren knows he has lost the battle. "Let me know exactly when you're coming and I'll have Connie make your hotel reservations."

"We thought we might stay with you and Retha unless we're not welcome. Of course we don't want to intrude. If the place will be too crowded, I guess we'll have to stay in a hotel. Your mother's not too particular about hotel rooms though."

"I don't think Retha will mind. Like I told you, her house is not very big but she does have room." Jaren is a little sick in the stomach but is not quite sure why.

Adding to the increased quaking in his stomach, Susan picks up an extension and joins in the conversation. "Hi, baby."

"Hey, Mom. How's it going?"

"Good. We're so excited about coming and meeting Retha's family. Is she there with you now?"

"No, she's at work. She doesn't get in until pretty late in the evening. How's my little sis doing? What's she up to?" Jaren makes a futile attempt to change the subject.

"Rachelle is Rachelle. She can't wait to get to Texas. I suppose she expects to see horses and cows walking up and down the street or something ridiculous like that." Susan laughs. "Listen, Jaren."

"Yes, ma'am." Jaren is too stunned to fake pleasure at his family's visit to San Antonio.

"You need to check with Retha and make sure it's okay for us to stay there before we settle any plans. She might not like you opening up her home to strangers or she may not want to be bothered. I can stay in a hotel for a few nights if she doesn't want us to stay there. It won't be a problem."

Yeah, right, Jaren thinks to himself. "It won't be a problem, Mom."

"Oh good. I was dreading that hotel room. Now I won't have to worry about that."

Jaren and his parents share a little small talk; he gets the dates of their visit, and gets off the phone. "Damn!" shoots from his throat once he puts the phone down. He is certain Retha will not be happy about his family's visit. After all, he's not happy about it and they are his family.

Upon hearing the news that Jaren's family plans a visit, Retha's face goes blank as if the words did not sink in. When her expression comes to life, she asks the reason for the visit. Jaren gives her the same answer his father gave him.

"Are they staying here?" Retha asks quietly and holds her breath, praying as she awaits his answer.

"If it's okay."

"It's okay. They're welcome to stay here."

"Retha, I didn't ask them to stay here. I offered to get them a hotel."

"It's okay Jaren, but I won't be comfortable sleeping with you while they're here. That would be disrespectful."

"What do you mean? We're not children."

"Jaren, if my parents were alive and at my home, I would not sleep in the bed with a man I was not married to and I will not show your parents less respect than I would show my own. I know it's old fashioned but that's how my parents raised me."

"Your parents would care; mine don't."

"But I do. You'll have to sleep in one of the upstairs bedrooms while they're here."

"Is this punishment? Just say you don't want them to stay here." Jaren is clearly upset.

Retha takes a deep breath to keep her cool. She doesn't want to argue over his family's visit. That would be disastrous. "Jaren, why would I punish you because your family is visiting? I'm a little hesitant about their visit but they are welcome."

"I'll sleep upstairs if you sleep up there with me."

"I'm not sleeping with you while they're here. I won't."

"That's so backwards, Retha. We sleep together every night. Is it any less disrespectful because they're not in the house with us? I never heard anything so asinine."

"Well, forgive me for being stupid or asinine as you put it but that is how I feel and as asinine as it may be, I'm not changing my mind. I need to put a decent bed upstairs for your parents."

Jaren starts to protest that the beds are fine but sees an opportunity. He hates Retha's bed, partly because it is a little short for him, partly because she needs a new mattress set, and mainly because she had shared that same bed with Joe. She might have even slept in it with James Freeman. "Retha, you're probably not going to want to do this but I'm having a problem with the bed we're sleeping in because my legs are too long and I'm sure you need a new mattress set. How about we buy a new mattress set for that bed and put it upstairs and buy a new bed for your room."

"That works." She is mad at him. She goes along with him better when she is a little upset.

--

In preparation for Jaren's family, Retha goes on a cleaning frenzy and she makes him help. She wants her home to be perfect when Jaren's family arrives. Jaren suggests they hire a cleaning team but Retha doesn't respond.

There are two words to describe Retha during the days leading up to the Daniels family arrival. The first is exhausted. She has two demanding jobs. The party season is in full swing, requiring more of her time and attention at Sugar's Place. Even more demanding are her personal commitments, Madelyn and her family's homecoming; Jessie's party; Jaren back in her life full force; Thanksgiving; Tampa; preparing for house guests, one of whom may despise her;

entertaining said guests; next comes Christmas and New Year. She is haggard and Jessie tells her as much, but she cannot rest

The second word that describes Retha is excited. She has not experienced so much holiday joy since the first Christmas she and Joe spent in San Antonio with Jessie, Robert, Uncle Sugar, and the children. She gleefully anticipates putting up her tree, a nice fresh one; Noble Fir is her favorite. The tree will be the first large one she's had in four years. She plans to take out all of her old ornaments for the tree; many had belonged to her parents. She is elated Jaren has promised to be in town to help her decorate the tree. Since childhood, decorating the tree has been a favorite part of the Christmas celebration for Retha. When he was living, Joe always picked the tree. He got the best deals on trees when Retha was not with him because once Retha set her heart on a tree; she was willing to pay the asking price -- not Joe. He would haggle and once got a ninety dollar tree for thirty-five dollars.

Enthusiasm is contagious. Once Jaren gets started helping with the preparations for his family's visit and the holidays he seems to truly enjoy himself. He even shows up one evening with a set of lighted wire mesh reindeer for Retha's yard.

Jaren splits his time between San Antonio, New York, and Tampa during the time prior to his family's visit. He promises Retha he will be in San Antonio a day or two before their arrival specifically to help her put up the tree. Jaren calls the day prior to his scheduled return to tell her he will fly in with his family a few days later. Retha is surprised at the depth of her disappointment. "I thought you'd be back to help me decorate the tree," she whines selfishly.

"I wanted to Retha, but I've got too much going on here. Go ahead and decorate the tree without me."

Signs of Retha's emotions are close to the surface. Her eyes fill with water as she squeezes them shut to prevent the tears from streaming down her face. It is all she can do to keep her sobs from her voice. The weight of Jaren's heart grows in his chest when Retha asks, "Have you ever decorated a Christmas tree alone, Jaren?" They are both quiet for a moment before she adds "I'll see if Lizzie can help me."

Chapter 24 -- Santa Claus

Retha is at work when Jaren and his family arrive in San Antonio. Susan is pleased to have an opportunity to scrutinize Retha's home while she is away. Beloved possessions make a house a home with its own unique character and it is clear that Retha has many things she cherishes and has possessed for many years. Retha's home is modest, clean, inviting, and reeks of comfort. Rachelle doesn't hesitate to declare her opinion of the place. "I like her house. It's cozy. She has good taste."

"It is nice," Susan agrees. She notes that Retha does not have a Christmas tree up and asks Jaren why. Jaren had not noticed the absence of the tree until his mother mentioned it. He finds the tree standing in water in the back yard. "Damn," he mumbles under his breath.

Less than an hour after the Daniels family arrives in the River City, Jessie; Robert; Madelyn; and Elizabeth show up with a fresh carrot cake in tow to meet Retha's house guests and keep them company until she gets home. Not long after Jaren makes the introductions, he asks Jessie, "What's your sister planning on doing about the tree?"

"What tree?" Jessie looks around bewildered.

"The Christmas tree out back," he answers and directing his attention to Elizabeth asks, "Did your aunt ask you to help her decorate the tree?"

"She didn't mention it to me. I didn't even know she had a tree." Elizabeth appears as lost as Jessie.

Robert and Charles were outside getting acquainted while Charles took a few tokes on his cigar. They enter the house in the midst of the Christmas tree mystery. Robert has a piece of the puzzle. "Oh yeah man, Retha asked me to help you trim more branches off the bottom and get the tree set up in the stand. That's a big-ass tree. It's gonna take up some room." Jessie shoots Robert a "watch your mouth" look and Robert renders an embarrassed apology to Jaren's family.

Charles laughs and slaps Robert on the back having caught Jessie's chastising glance. "Tell her to cut you some slack man. 'Ass' isn't a bad word any more. They say it on the tube, now."

The three men go out in the backyard and supervise each other trimming the tree. Jaren gets the stand put together with more confusing supervision from his father and Robert. Then comes the next puzzle piece. "So where does she want us to set it?" Jaren asks.

"She said for you to decide," Robert answers with a wicked grin without looking at Jaren.

"Oh, hell no!"

"That's what I thought you would say when she told me that." Robert is suppressing his laughter.

"No matter where I put it, she won't like it. That's too much responsibility." Jaren goes inside to find Jessie in an attempt to put the burden on her but Jessie isn't much help. "She's put it up all over but she moves the furniture around to make room when she has a big tree."

Jaren has a dilemma, one of those "damned no matter what you do" dilemmas. Madelyn sees Jaren's problem and understands it well. She would not dare select a spot for the tree in Retha's house. Not that Retha will fuss or raise hell -- no not Retha. Retha will see where the tree stands and her face will say it all. Then the next day or maybe even the same day, Retha will move the tree. Madelyn knows exactly what tactic to take. "Susan, why don't you decide where to put the tree? No way will Retha complain if you pick the spot for the tree."

Susan thinks for a moment, glancing around the house for options. "She might not care for that."

"Oh she's not going to like it wherever we put it, but she wouldn't dare criticize your choice or move the tree, at least not until you leave town," Madelyn quips.

Susan has to smile at Madelyn's honesty. "Well, I was thinking it would look nice in front of that dining area window. We'll need to reposition the table though."

No one objects, so that's where the tree stands throughout the holidays. Jessie mentally commends Madelyn's move to involve Susan in the tree decision. By the time the tree is standing in front of the window everyone in the house, except Susan, is laughing and talking like one family. Rachelle asks if they should start decorating the natural beauty.

"No baby, we'd better wait for Retha because she loves decorating her own Christmas tree. She's a big kid when it comes to that," Jessie advises. Jaren hears and takes note. He never puts up a tree because he spends most of his free time during the holidays at his parent's home and they have their tree professionally decorated.

By the time Retha steps in the front door of her home, Susan and her sisters are talking easily and Robert and Charles are beer-drinking cigar-smoking buddies. Elizabeth and Rachelle are upstairs chatting and texting. The two girls are close in age and have taken to each other easily. They have decided that Elizabeth will spend the night at her aunt's house to keep her new friend entertained and they have mapped out extensive plans for the rest of Rachelle's visit. Retha loves her family; they have her back.

Susan's impression of Retha had changed after entering her home and it changed again when she met the family. Seeing Retha in her own environment gives Susan a slight twinge of guilt about her thoughts toward the young woman. She can see why Jaren is attracted to Retha. She admits to herself that Retha is beautiful "in a different sort of way" and has an unusually warm finesse about her. But Susan is certain she understands Retha's type of woman and does not trust them. Although Retha's family members seem warm and inviting, they are too simple for Susan's taste.

Retha greets the members of the Daniels family with hugs and welcoming words. After a few polite questions about their trip, Retha asks Susan and Rachelle to help Jaren and her decorate the tree later that night. Madelyn immediately jumps in and informs Retha that Susan selected the location for the tree. Retha thanks Susan and adds her opinion that the tree is in a good spot. The glances and sly smiles that circle the room do not escape her notice but she decides to ignore them.

The entire group goes to Sugar's for dinner. Charles loves the place and likes Sugar even more. Susan is mildly impressed with the restaurant. She had not expected such a large, efficiently run establishment. She is surprised to see customers waiting for tables. The service is exceptional, surpassing even Retha's expectations. As impressed as Susan is with Retha's place of business, she feels justified when she meets Uncle Sugar who, in her opinion, could be standing on a corner asking for change. She wants to pull Charles and Rachelle to the side and say "I told you so." On the other hand, Charles has found a kindred spirit in Sugar, who keeps him company on and off throughout dinner. Sugar brings Charles samples of various dishes on the evening's menu, causing Charles to do his best Andrew Zimmern impersonation and declare each dish "really good." Charles makes plans to return to the restaurant for lunch, without his family, the following day.

Mykol, Nicola and baby Jevon return home with Retha and her guests to help decorate the Christmas tree. Susan declares that she is too tired and retires for the evening and Charles soon follows. From their room they can hear music and laughter as the young people enjoy themselves. It is well past one in the morning when the house shuts down for the night.

Jaren has forgotten he is restricted from Retha's bed during his family's visit. He is dumbfounded that she will not let him sleep with her, especially since they haven't seen each other for days. He makes a production of the fact that he will sleep on the family room sofa, which is without question the most uncomfortable option available to him. There is a comfortable bed upstairs but Jaren curls up on the sofa hoping that Retha might renege and allow him in the room with her.

Jaren's father is tickled to tears when he goes downstairs for a snack and finds his son stretched out on the sofa. "What are you doing out here?"

"Don't ask," Jaren answers grumpily.

"You guys have a fight or something?"

Jaren sits up because he can tell that Charles finds his situation humorous and will not leave until he gets answers. "She says we shouldn't sleep together with you guys in the house, something to do with her parents." Jaren shakes his head in disgust and glares in the direction of Retha's bedroom.

Charles thinks for a moment as he opens the refrigerator. He considers his own daughter who had better not try to climb into bed with a man she is not married to in his home. Charles tilts his head in agreement and tells his son "She's right." He stops Jaren's attempted rebuttal with his hand in the halt position. "I know, I know it's old fashioned but right." He turns and heads upstairs with an orange and a glass of water. "Sweet dreams, son." Jaren watches his father go, punches his pillows and lies back down.

Forgetting his wife's mistrust of Retha, Charles comments with a chuckle to Susan as he climbs back into bed. "That boy's got it bad and I can see why. She's something ain't she? She's got him sleeping on the sofa."

"And why is that?" Susan asks with slight concern.

"Something about respect for us."

"What a crock," Susan comments sarcastically and turns to go to sleep.

When Jaren's family leaves San Antonio the following Monday morning Retha breathes a deep sigh. Although Susan never warmed up to Retha or her family, Charles and Rachelle were great guests, easy to please and lots of fun. The visit went better than Retha had hoped even with Susan being so aloof. Jaren is pleased that his father and sister were more relaxed and happier than he has seen them in a long time. His mother was her usual self, very engaged with him, though having little interaction with anyone else. He wonders how Retha and her family have won over his father and sister so fast. Rachelle has invited Elizabeth to New York for a visit. Charles is making plans to return to San Antonio. He has developed a great affinity for Retha's family. Jaren and his mother are put off by all these future plans. Susan hides her discomposure from Jaren because she does not want to be at odds with him. Jaren hides his reservations from everyone. He does not want his family to become too friendly with Retha and her family. Too much interaction between their families could make things very awkward when the relationship between Retha and him ends.

--

Once Jaren's family leaves San Antonio, he takes Retha Christmas shopping and insists she buy whatever she wants for whomever she chooses. Retha is conservative and spends as little of Jaren's money as womanly possible. The temptation is too great to resist all together, so her family and friends will receive more expensive gifts that usual. On Christmas morning, Jaren and Retha open their gifts from each other as if they are ten-year-olds, with the grins on their faces growing larger with each new surprise.

The season is full of family and good cheer. Retha and her sisters prepare another huge meal for the family on Christmas day. Retha holds the Christmas day dinner at her home this year. Andre and his daughters Hannah and Dora, Ida, Raymond and RJ, and of course Madelyn, Philip and Aubrey are in town.

One minor downside is Uncle Sugar's ailments, particularly his stomach. Sugar insists on eating everything though nothing agrees with him. The very foods that have the worst effect are the ones he is determined to scarf down. The sisters make sure they include foods that are the least upsetting to their uncle's digestive system but he refuses to touch these healthier culinary morsels. Within an hour of eating his dinner, Sylvia has to take Sugar home and nurse him out of his misery. He completely ignores his family's recommendations that he go to the hospital. Sugar recognizes a good case of indigestion when he has one. Another damper on the holiday is Retha's dread of seeing her oldest brother Andre who she is certain will not approve of her relationship with Jaren.

Though not large in stature like Raymond and Jermaine, Andre is a dominant presence. He holds high expectations for all the members of his family. If those close to him fail to meet his standards he tells them. His siblings avoid approaching him with bad news or any form of a request. It is not uncommon to hear them arguing amongst themselves, "I'm not gonna tell him; you tell him," with a response of, "Why should I tell him? He likes you better than me." Andre is the intimidator though he has no wish to be. He is just direct as hell with his brothers and sisters. On the occasion when, out of sheer desperation, one of them does work up the nerve to approach him with a problem, he will lay out a course of action so detailed or ask such hard questions his sibling will retrench with an entirely different perspective. Often his solutions seem tougher than the issue. Temporary solutions have no place in Andre's world. When you resolve the problem, finish it dead.

Yes, Andre is thoroughly disgusted and disappointed by the fact that his sister is involved with "this baseball player" as he refers to Jaren. He thinks his relatives are bordering on insanity by accepting Jaren without question and is amazed that the three older sisters are not providing Retha with better counsel.

Jaren has discerned Retha's dread of her older brother's displeasure and it is apparent that no one in the family wants to cross their oldest sibling. So when Andre escorts Jaren into one of Retha's spare bedrooms for the purpose of discussing a subject Jaren is sick of receiving criticism about, the younger man is prepared for battle. Andre starts off with customary small talk but gets right to the point.

"I must tell you I was shocked and surprised to hear that you and Retha are seeing each other."

Jaren laughs nervously. "I hope it wasn't too much of a shock."

"Well, yes, it was. Especially when I learned you were spending so much time together. It seems all my family was keeping it from me because no one mentioned it until I got here. That's pretty unusual for a family of gossips."

"They're pretty good people. They've taken me in like family." Jaren is offended by Andre's reference to his friends.

"Yeah, my family is full of good people, but I guess you must seem like Santa Claus to them. It gives you an unfair advantage, you know." Andre gives Jaren a direct gaze which Jaren calmly returns. "Listen, man," Andre continues. "I'm concerned about my sister. You being who you are and spending your money may or may not influence how she feels about you, but I can tell she really digs you. It's clear your plans are temporary. Maybe you should be a little more honest with her and stop turning her head with the gold mine. She's had her share of troubles. I'm not asking your plans because it is my understanding that you haven't been seeing each other very long. I wouldn't normally do this, but, in my opinion, Retha's circumstances are special. I don't want my sister used."

Jaren looks over his shoulder and stares out the bedroom window. He continues to look outside long enough to gain his composure. When he directs his gaze back toward Andre, the older man has to sit back in his chair to escape the threat of Jaren's glare. "I don't mean to be disrespectful but I am so tired of hearing this. You're not the first person to confront me with concerns that I may be misleading Retha. My own father discussed these issues with me. I hope I don't sound arrogant but I plan on doing much more for Retha than I have so far. I don't understand the big deal over me buying her a gift or the family gifts at Christmas time."

"It's not that," Andre starts to speak but Jaren cuts him off.

"Just a minute. I let you speak your mind. Now I'd like to finish. She almost had a fit because I offered to put a sprinkler system in her damn yard. People do things for each other. People give each other gifts. So what if I have lots of money? Hell, she probably spent as much or more on me for Christmas than I did her. It's not about the money with me. I'm not trying to use it to buy Retha. The money don't mean nothing. Don't get me wrong. I enjoy having it. But what good is it if I can't spend it on a person I care about? Everyone thinks I'll leave Retha high and dry one day. I promise you, I won't do anything to mistreat her. And no, I'm not planning to ask her to marry me. Marriage is not in my plans any time soon. We haven't been together long, but I do plan on being around a while longer and as long as I am with Retha I plan to do as much as I can for her."

Andre is put off by Jaren's frankness and more than a little impressed with the young man. He is not accustomed to being put in his place so directly and correctly. "Well, I guess we've both said what we felt needed to be said. I appreciate you taking the time to talk to me." Andre stands, shakes the younger man's hand, and leaves the room. He goes out on the patio to sit and reflect.

Andre holds a strong obligation to his parents and Joe to watch out for Retha. He realizes that he has no power over Retha's decisions. She will have a relationship with whomever she chooses, and it seems she is much more than a passing distraction for Jaren. Andre, deciding that Jaren may be acceptable for his sister after all, enters the house and spends the remainder of the holiday enjoying his family.

Chapter 25 -- This is Not about Jealousy

As wonderful as the weeks from Thanksgiving to the New Year were, they resulted in a significant change in Retha's life. Whether this change is to Retha's benefit or detriment depends on one's point of view. Uncle Sugar's stomach problems become so severe during the holidays that Sylvia goes to Retha and humbly pleads for more help running the restaurant. Without giving the decision much thought, Retha gives notice on her job with UP&C Insurance and doubles her hours at Sugar's.

Madelyn has departed San Antonio for Atlanta, giving Jessie much more time to focus on Retha and her affairs. "Are you sure you want to quit that good job? You're living high right now but as much as I have started to appreciate your friend, there's no guarantee he'll be around next year."

"You don't need to worry about me Jess. My manager tells me she will recommend they rehire me if I decide to return. She understands about Sugar. I'm not hurting for money. I'll do fine, even after Jaren moves on. I'm not depending on him financially."

Retha is avoiding the real issue here which is her emotional independence. Jessie is convinced Retha would not have quit her job at the insurance company if Jaren wasn't constantly pressuring her to do so. Of course Retha would make any sacrifice for Sugar and his beloved restaurant, but quitting such a good job doesn't seem necessary or wise to Jessie. She suggests Retha adjust her hours on the insurance job. Retha ignores her sister's advice. Working the restaurant is where Retha's heart lies and she wants to give Sugar's her full time and attention.

Jessie is on to something; she nearly always is. Jaren is happy about having more time with Retha but he is beginning to feel like he believes a married man might -- trapped. These are trappings of his own making but trappings nonetheless. He needs to be certain he can still do as he pleases. After all, he is still a single man. So one week after Retha quits her "good" job, Jaren comes to town for the sole purpose of informing her that he is going on vacation to Puerto Rico for two weeks with Aaron and a few friends.

"Angry" is an understatement. *How can he do this?* "You get me to totally change my life and now you're going off to Puerto Rico to be with your friends."

"Hey, I'm sorry, baby. I should have mentioned it before. Me and the guys get together and go every year before the season starts back up. It's a tradition. And what do you mean I got you to change your life? You left that job because of Sugar, not because of me."

Left hand on hip, right hand flailing, brow raised, nostrils flared, Retha attacks. "Why didn't you tell me before? I thought you wanted us to spend more time together. What the hell was I thinking? You'll be in season in no time and now you tell me that you're taking a two-week vacation to Puerto Rico."

Jaren throws up both hands and steps back as if to stop the onslaught of temper. "I didn't know it would be such a fuckin' issue. I won't go. You better now?"

Retha has sheer disbelief on her face. She can't remember ever hearing Jaren curse, other than the occasional "hell," "damn," or "shit." *What's he got to be angry about? I'm the slighted party here. I'm the damn victim. How dare he try and make me out the villain.* "Oh hell no, you go! Don't use that guilt trip bullshit on me. You go. I don't want you here if you want to be somewhere else." The guilt trip bullshit works.

Jaren wonders if Retha has any idea how far she is off base. Jaren wants to be with her all the time but he does not want to feel this way. He had not planned on making the Puerto Rico trip. He decided to go at the last minute because he felt he was losing a grip on his life. Lately, it seems everything is about Retha and him. He needs a little of his old life back, just a little.

So, he goes and, woefully, the trip turns out to be a total waste of his time. No matter how many beautiful women parade in front of him, he turns away. He applauds the ladies' efforts to cheer him up, but his mind is elsewhere.

Jaren is determined to stay on the island the full two weeks even if he is miserable. He refuses to call Retha, mainly because he does not want her to know how much he misses her and secondly she told him not to call. She was still angry when he left. She did make love with him though. He was at his Tampa home but that didn't deter Retha. She flew in with one purpose in mind. They made hot and passionate love that permeates Jaren's mind so intensely that when he closes his eyes he can see her on top of him; he still smells her. Retha was mad, not stupid. No way was she sending Jaren off to Puerto Rico for two weeks sexually deprived. She made love to him seven times in three days. She hadn't wanted to be intimate with him. She hated making love when she was angry but Ida laughingly advised her to make sure Jaren was well satisfied before he got on the plane. Retha made sure he was both satisfied and exhausted.

--

Two weeks without Jaren proves to be more than Retha can stand. She decides to go to New York to visit Aida and JJ and meet Jaren when he returns. She can't help but be childish about the Puerto Rico trip so she decides to stay with Aida instead of Jaren. She doesn't tell Jaren her plans because she wants to surprise him. She flies up early Thursday morning, one day before his scheduled return.

Aida is not nearly as happy to see Retha as usual. She is not happy to have an unexpected house guest. Retha is offended until she learns the reason for the change in Aida. Over dinner, Aida tells Retha all about her old neighbor, Mr. Breaux, who lost his wife two years earlier and is now a frequent visitor. Aida is glowing like a schoolgirl in the sun. JJ arrives in town the following day, so Retha, Aida, and Mr. Breaux spend Friday evening in Brooklyn celebrating Marta's fortieth birthday.

First thing Saturday Retha ventures over to Jaren's. Jaren has just finished a light breakfast of juice and bagels and is settling in with the sports page and *Sports Center* while waiting on Aaron so they can head out for a scheduled workout. When he hears his cell phone and the doorbell ring almost simultaneously, he answers his phone and, assuming Aaron is at the door, opens it without bothering to look out. Retha enters the apartment and follows Jaren as he walks down the gallery and enters his bedroom. She easily hears his end of the conversation and can tell by his manner of speech, pitch, and tone he is speaking with a woman.

"Yeah it was nice meeting you too. Let me ask you, how did you get my phone number?" There is quite a pause on Jaren's end before he continues, "Oh, Aaron, yeah, Aaron." Retha stands not far from the bedroom door getting angrier by the second. Jaren continues "No, no that's okay. I've got a minute or two." Jaren walks out of his room and finds Retha standing there. He does not know what he said into the phone but he is on the phone with another woman who is undoubtedly trying to hit on him and he is screwed. The young lady on the other end of the phone is stammering but Jaren can see fire shooting from Retha's eyes and smoke coming from her nostrils. "Listen. I've got to go. I don't mean to be rude but I've got to go." He hangs up on the caller. "Retha what are you doing here?" he asks as he puts the phone down. That was the wrong question to ask.

"I came to see Aida and JJ and to meet you. You didn't need to get off your call; you could have continued." Retha turns and walks back toward the gallery with Jaren in emotional tow.

"That was nothing, Retha, some woman Aaron gave my number. He shouldn't have done that. I'm gonna tear him a new one for this."

"Did you meet that woman in Puerto Rico?" Retha stops near the front door and turns.

The sudden harshness of her stance prevents Jaren from coming any closer. "Well, yes but," Jaren stammers, not understanding why he feels guilty. We can say that he is "saved by the bell" because the doorbell rings and Retha opens the door for Aaron. Aaron can tell that Retha and Jaren are in the midst of a fire storm. Retha looks like she just consumed a fire breathing dragon for breakfast and neither she nor Jaren bother to speak a word of greeting.

"I'm leaving. I can see you have plans," Retha nearly barks and shoots looks so sharp both men want to duck in order to elude the pain.

Aaron is more than ready to get away from the hostility coming from his friend and his friend's lady. "Man, you want me to call you later?" he asks Jaren.

"No, I'm leaving," Retha repeats as she heads toward the door.

"No, Retha don't leave," Jaren pleads. "Hey man, I'll call you," he tells Aaron but Retha is on her way out the door.

"I'll be at Aida's." Retha gives Aaron an up and down look, glares at Jaren and passes on words of wisdom she attributes to Wanda. "You know, Jaren, my mother always told me that you can tell the character of a man by the company he keeps." Wanda never said that to Retha, but she heard it somewhere.

Aaron feels like he has been slapped across the face. Retha is usually so friendly toward him that he always wants to see her. "Damn, man, what did I do?" he asks Jaren after Retha's futile attempt at slamming Jaren's two-ton door behind her.

"You gave some woman my phone number. Why did you do that?"

"I didn't mean no harm. I thought you liked her. What? Did Retha answer the phone or what? You couldn't play it off?"

"Man, just go. Just leave. I'm gonna have to pay for this shit a long time."

"I'm sorry, man. You want me to talk to Retha?"

Jaren's look tells Aaron to leave.

As usual Retha does not answer her cell phone and Jaren can't find Aida's home number so he tries JJ's cell phone. He gets JJ's voice mail so all he can do is leave a message. He tries Retha's cell phone again but the call goes straight to voice mail. He gets angrier with each number he dials. As he is heading out of his apartment to try and catch Retha at Aida's, JJ calls and gives him Aida's number. Speaking with JJ has a calming effect on Jaren. The men chat for a couple of minutes with light conversation about Jaren's trip, JJ's school, and sports events. They make perfunctory plans to get together and Jaren confirms an earlier promise to supply tickets to the ballpark during the season.

Retha owes a great deal of thanks to her stepson, but would never guess it by the way Jaren sounds when she answers Aida's phone. Jaren doesn't even bother to return Retha's hello. "So, when you get upset with me about something, you just walk off and don't give me a chance to explain? Is that the way it's going to be with us? Because if it is tell me now."

Retha is stunned and silent for a moment but her mind is working. *How is it that when a man messes up he is so adept at turning things around to make the woman appear to be the culprit? If he had found me on the phone with a man that I had spent two weeks with on a vacation island and the man was hitting on me, he'd be hotter than fish grease. How can he justify being mad at me? Is this a threat?*

Retha's anger flares back up like a brush fire meeting a strong summer breeze. At one point, after leaving Jaren's, she had thought she might owe him an apology. Jaren's threat squelched the apology.

"Okay, I'm giving you notice. If you think I need you to explain what I heard this morning, you must think I'm really dense. I'm not putting up with this crap."

"What crap, Retha? I don't want to argue over the phone. Maybe we need to get together and talk about it."

Retha doesn't want to hear it. "No, unh, unh. I'm going home tomorrow. Maybe I'll call you in a few days."

"So that's the way you want to play this."

"See, that's the difference in me and you, Jaren; I am not playing a game. I'll talk to you later." Retha hangs up the phone.

Jaren stares at the phone in his hand. *She's crazy. Forget her.* He heads to the gym to take out his frustration on the exercise equipment.

--

Retha does not call Jaren in a few days. Jaren does not call her. Hurt feelings abound, hearts are breaking and imaginations are producing volumes of negativity. Jaren walks into Retha's home eight days later. Neither speaks a word for several awkward moments. Retha tries not to show her relief. Soon, fear that he may have come to pick up his things drowns out all relief.

"I thought you were going to call me," Jaren asks as he twirls his keys on one finger.

"I was, but the time didn't seem right. I didn't know what to say. I still don't know what I want to say to you or what I should say."

Jaren moves away from the foyer. Retha watches him move toward her and the air catches in her chest. She is so happy to see him. She fights to bring her breathing under control as he sits down on the arm of the sofa next to her. Retha now senses the electrical sparks flying from Jaren to her.

"I don't understand why you got so mad but wouldn't let me explain."

No response from Retha. She is busy watching her fingers play with each other as if she is seeing them interact for the first time.

Jaren takes a deep breath, a sign of his exasperation. After a moment he asks, "So, are we finished, taking a time out, what?"

Retha can't answer. She gets angry at the thought that Jaren might have been with another woman. She finds her recent anger strange because when she left New York she was certain he had not been with anyone. Now, after a week with her imagination, she has her doubts.

"I didn't screw around on you Retha. I can't believe you think I did. Are you still upset about that phone call or are you using that as an excuse to stop seeing me? You don't have to bullshit me."

Retha has enough composure to speak but cannot keep her seat. She needs to distance herself from the energy flowing from Jaren before she can express herself, so she moves to the other side of the room. "This is not about jealousy. I will not be with you, if you're screwing around. You say you didn't, so why the trip to Puerto Rico? Wasn't that the purpose of the trip, for you and your pals to screw around?"

"Maybe for the others but not for me. I swear, Retha. I don't get off on screwing around. I wish I could make you believe me. I have never cheated in my life. I've dated more than one woman, but if I'm in a relationship like we have…" Jaren stops. He wonders how to convince her.

For Retha, his face says it all. The silence penetrates the room. Jaren doesn't want to say more. He doesn't want to beg. Retha exhales and heads toward the front door, grabbing her purse on the way. "You hungry?" she asks.

The couple sits peacefully enjoying their first meal together in several weeks. Paesano's is quiet for a Sunday. As they leave the restaurant, Retha casually takes Jaren's hand on the walk to the car. They share exhaustion and relief.

--

Retha and Jaren enjoy a few blissful days before he takes off for Florida and submerses himself in preparation for his upcoming season. Once the regular season starts, Retha visits New York whenever she can get away. She even travels to other cities and stays with Jaren when he has away games. Occasionally, Jaren surprises her and shows up in San Antonio for an overnight

Soon the lovers are so comfortable with each other that they decide it is time to take down another barrier in their relationship. Jaren is taking a huge step because he has never been truly intimate with a woman. He has had all sorts of defenses in place to protect him from a serious attachment. The condom has become an emotional as well as a physical defense. He has been using them so long that their use seemed natural up until now. Jaren is anxious to make love to Retha without a condom though he experiences a degree of anxiety when he and Retha decide to get HIV tests for each other.

Commitment anxiety is hardly the problem for Retha. Retha fears for her life. Sex with Jaren without a condom is that tangible for her. Jaren is much more susceptible to outside sexual activity than she is and she must trust him completely to do away with the protection. Retha has no idea of the number and variety of propositions Jaren receives, but she is certain there are many. Retha and Jaren have been tested for HIV in the past, but their decision to get tested for each other makes Retha question if she's ready for the covers to come off, so to speak. She hesitates and doesn't get tested for several weeks after Jaren shows her his results. Retha gets tested after he tells her he doesn't mind if they continue to use condoms. They celebrate! Retha and Jaren are deep in the midst of the quiet before the storm.

Chapter 26 -- The Fear Factor

While on a business trip to Wilmington, North Carolina, Andre's home, Charles Daniels meets Retha's older brother for lunch. The two men find common ground in their academic careers and enjoy each other's company. Over drinks the following evening, Andre takes to Charles when, laughingly, Charles tells him that Jaren is too confused to know he wants to marry Retha. Charles appreciates Andre's response. "He sure is spending a hell of a lot of time and money on a woman he doesn't plan on marrying." With these statements they acknowledge the other's concerns and an appreciation of the other's viewpoint. The men manage to squeeze in a couple of games of chess during the visit. By the time he leaves Wilmington for home, Charles is convinced that Retha's people are some of the best.

--

A couple of days after Charles returns from his Wilmington trip, Jaren shows up at his parents' home for dinner. Unfortunately for Jaren, his mother is out to dinner with friends, so he will dine with Charles and Rachelle, leaving him little protection from his father's queries.

"Had a good business trip in Wilmington, son. That's a beautiful old city," Charles casually informs his son over the dinner table.

As soon as Jaren walked in the door, he sensed that his father wanted to talk to him. Jaren usually enjoys having dinner with Rachelle and Charles but not tonight. There is a trap waiting and Jaren wants to escape. The friendship between his father and Retha's brother does not sit well.

"Yeah, good." Jaren does not want to encourage Charles.

"I visited a friend of mine there one time. It is a pretty city and they have some great food, beautiful gardens too. It reminds me of Savannah, where Aunt Jane lives." Rachelle joins the limited conversation. She can tell a sparring match is in the works and she is sure Jaren expects one also, but Charles doesn't, although he picked up the first saber.

"I like that Andre. That's one smart fellow there." Charles is far too goal-oriented to respond to Rachelle's opinion of Wilmington.

A simple "yeah" won't work this time. "Retha says he masters whatever he does. Did you guys make some moves on the board?"

Charles leans back in his seat as he allows his lips to spread in a wide-faced grin of pleasure. "I think I surprised him. Took him some time to get checkmate on the old man."

"You mean he beat you, Dad. I thought sure you'd show him a thing or two."

"I showed him a thing all right -- showed him how to lose." Charles laughs with more pleasure than either Rachelle or Jaren have seen since they were at Sugar's Place in San Antonio. Jaren decides this might be a good time to make his escape.

"Glad you guys had a good time and your business came out okay but listen, I'd better get going. I've got a long day tomorrow."

Jaren is truly in another world if he believes he can get away so easily. "Wait a minute. I've been meaning to talk to you, son. Let's go in the study." To Rachelle he adds, "Excuse us, Sweetie." With these words an anxious look darkens Rachelle's face as her eyes move from Jaren to Charles and back.

"What's on your mind?" Jaren sits down on the leather sofa in his father's study. Charles takes a seat in his beloved leather lounge recliner. He shifts his position in his seat in an attempt to be more comfortable. "Well, I was wondering what your plans are."

"What plans?"

"You and Retha. You plan on setting a date anytime soon?"

"Date for what? I hope you're not talking about marriage."

"That's exactly what I'm talking about. You two have been together for a while now. What's the holdup?"

"What's the hold up? There is no hold up. Retha and I have no plans to get married. Where is this coming from?"

"Don't you love Retha? She loves you. You two are good together." Charles watches Jaren and the expectation in his eyes causes his son more discomfort than his words.

Jaren is having a hard time controlling his anger. "Did you talk to Andre about me and Retha getting married?" he asks his father in a raised voice.

"Don't speak to me with that tone, boy!" Charles commands.

"What tone?"

"That tone!" Charles glares at his son.

Jaren calms his emotions. "Sorry. I'm trying to find out where this is coming from. I can't believe Retha would discuss marriage with her brother when we have never mentioned the subject to each other."

"Don't go blaming Retha. She doesn't know anything about this, neither does Andre. I'm asking you." Charles is still agitated and not letting up on his goal.

"Look, there is not going to be any marriage, okay, not now, probably never unless Retha wants to hang around a long time. I'm not in love with her or anyone else and I hope she doesn't call herself in love with me."

Jaren looks at his father, who seems stricken. He wishes he could relieve Charles's shock but decides it is best to leave things as they are. "I gotta go. I'll call before I leave on Thursday."

During the drive home Jaren contemplates what passed between Charles and him. *Maybe I should have went to San Antonio and screwed around with her a little during the off season and returned to New York without getting so close to her and her family. Maybe I should have kept her away from my family and friends. Now I understand why some of the guys keep their love lives under wraps.*

Jaren never wanted his relationship with Retha, or any woman for that matter, to take over his life. Baseball has been his first love for almost as long as he can remember; it is supposed to be his priority in life. Retha never attempts to interfere with him and baseball but she has managed to occupy the number one spot in his life. It was a mistake asking her to spend so much time with him in New York. He should have simply visited her in San Antonio. She would have been happy with that, but would he? The issue of marriage has him scared. The strangest thing is that Jaren has set all this in motion. He couldn't move slowly with Retha once he got back to her. He had to have all of her with him as often as possible. Now he realizes commitment has a life of its own and either grows or dies.

Rachelle enters her father's study and finds him staring out the window thoughtfully. "I'm not going to mention marriage to that boy again. I hope he knows that girl is not going to wait too long for him."

Rachelle agrees. "No she won't wait for him. She's waiting now because it's only been months but soon her pride will get in the way or she'll decide it's better to leave him than let him use her as long as he wants then maybe move on; she won't wait. She'll leave him and still be in love with him. That's what I would do and Retha is nobody's fool."

Charles glances at his daughter with surprise on his face. Such old words from such a young woman. He hopes Jaren is at least as wise as his little sister.

--

Soon after Charles asks Jaren about marriage, Jaren takes action to set things right between Retha and him. He only calls her twice during his series in Anaheim, Oakland, and Seattle. Retha senses things are not quite right but she's preoccupied with restaurant business. She ignores the change in his behavior and reserve in his conversations.

Jaren finds Retha waiting in his apartment when he gets back to New York. At first he is a little cool with her, giving no sign of how pleased he is to see her. He missed her as much as she missed him but he is determined to get his old life back even if he does like the new one with Retha much better. They make love with as much fervor as ever. Jaren holds Retha close to him in the bed and complains if she moves away from him for any reason during the night.

The reserve is back in Jaren's demeanor the following morning. He is quiet and contributes little to their conversation during breakfast. Just before he leaves for the stadium, Retha works up the nerve to ask if there is a problem. Jaren seizes the opportunity and pounces without thought. "I think maybe we should see other people." *Oh shit, what'd I say that for? Damn!*

Retha's breath catches in her throat. Her heart throbs loudly in her ears as her head starts to swim. She opens her eyes wide to hold back the tears but the waves are rushing to the front. Retha yells inside. *Don't cry Retha. Don't you dare cry. Oh, please don't cry.* The tears are coming. To keep from being embarrassed further and hide her pain, Retha rises from the table and responds with a mere shrug. "Sure, if that's what you want". She turns to leave the room, telling him, "I'm going to take my shower." By this time, the tears are overflowing their banks and flooding her face. *Thank God, he didn't see me cry.*

Jaren wants to follow her and take his words back. He is certain she is angry. Sitting for only a few moments longer, he decides to discuss the change in the relationship later. He needs time to think about what he should say.

Retha stays in the bathroom with the shower running until Jaren leaves for the stadium. She had planned to go to the game with Rachelle and JJ. She calls them, cancels, and boards the next plane to San Antonio.

She finds an irate message from Jaren waiting for her when she gets home but she doesn't return his call. She needs counsel. She doesn't dare tell Jessie about Jaren's latest proposal, not yet. There are two people she can confide in, Ida and Simone. She calls Ida first but gets voice mail. Next she calls Simone who listens and says all the right things and then asks a very important question. "So does he have someone in particular he wants to see?"

"I don't know," Retha responds quietly.

"You didn't ask?"

"No. I was too upset."

"You need to find out. He's bullshitting you. I know how you feel about Aaron but they're tight and Jaren is one of Aaron's favorite subjects. Jaren's not interested in anybody else. He's running scared."

"What if he's not? What if he is tired of me and wants to see other people?"

"Are you willing to have an open relationship with him?"

"Hell no!"

"If he's determined to date other people, I guess you'll have to move on. You told me a long time ago that your relationship with Jaren would not last. Do you think you can move on or will you need me to come and push you?"

"I can move on if I have to."

Simone doesn't like the resignation in Retha's voice. "Retha it won't come to that."

The friends talk a while longer until Jaren beeps through. Retha is better after the conversation with Simone. She has that "I am woman; hear me roar" feeling when they say their goodbyes.

"Why didn't you tell me you were leaving? You scared me. Rachelle told me you cancelled on her and JJ but didn't say why. I called everybody here. You don't answer your cell phone. I don't know why you have one. I was calling there one more time because I didn't know where else to call before scaring the hell out of Jessie."

"I needed to be alone. You dropped a bomb on me this morning. If things are changing between us, I need to think about what I want, how this will work for me."

Jaren is quiet on the other end of the line. He feels his body and spirit descending into a sinkhole but is too stubborn to pull himself out.

"Jaren is there someone in particular you want to be with?"

"No, no one in particular, It's just that we are too wrapped up with each other right now and I need some breathing room."

"Is there more than one person you're interested in?"

"Retha, this isn't about anyone but me and you. That's it, just us. But if I meet someone and I want to ask them out, I don't want to feel like I'm cheating on you. I don't want to feel that I should spend every free minute with you. I need some time to myself."

"Got it. Anything else?"

"Retha, please try and not be upset. I want us to keep seeing each other, just not so much. We need to back off each other a little."

"Okay. Now I need to figure out what I want from the starting point you've set. Is that alright with you?"

"I guess it would have to be," Jaren answers hesitantly.

"Okay, I'll see you later." The water is rising in its banks again and Retha's roar sounds more like a sickly meow. *I guess it's time to move on.*

Chapter 27 -- Reality Check

Retha sits down and considers her current situation. After a few days of reflection she comes to several conclusions. She is certain things are nearly finished between Jaren and her. She cannot understand why Jaren has not ended the relationship but she is convinced he will end it soon. Retha will not hang on like a leach and wait for him to flick her off in disgust. She also concludes there are two things she wants. One is to get as far away as possible from everything associated with Jaren Daniels and she wants to have his baby. Now how she will manage to get pregnant by a man she wants to completely disassociate herself from is a dilemma yet to be resolved.

I must be losing my mind. This is crazy talk. Since the thought of a child entered her head she has not been able to discard it. She is hopelessly frustrated when she acknowledges that she did not conceive during eight years of marriage, but this little ray of hope, the thought of having a baby, is the light that shines in Retha's life at present. After losing Joe, many of the tears she shed were because she never had his child. Now she is losing the only other man she will ever love. She determines she will keep a part of Jaren more valuable than memories and gifts. Joe had left her with every material need and want fulfilled. Material possessions are as useless to the broken heart as a solitary drop of water to a woman dying of thirst in the desert.

--

The first thing Susan notices is Jaren's lack of interest in anything she has to say; he is distracted. When she sees her son she realizes he is unhappy. It doesn't take her long to recognize that there is trouble between Jaren and Retha. Susan has managed to keep her poor opinion of Retha to herself and cannot help but be pleased that there may be a breakup coming. It's not that she dislikes Retha but she tells herself that the girl is bargain basement and only top shelf is good enough for her boy. When Jaren's mood doesn't get any better over the course of a few weeks, Susan is elated.

--

It has taken Dr. Jean Randolph less than six minutes to figure out that her patient has a horrible plan in the works. "Retha I always thought you were about the most level-headed young woman I know. Why would you consider having a baby under these circumstances and what makes you so sure it will happen now when it didn't happen with Joe? Have you given any real consideration as to how difficult it is to raise a child alone? You have a good family and lots of support but it can still be a daunting task. And consider how hard it is on kids when they are raised by one parent and the other is alive but not around. They wonder why that parent doesn't want them. It's bad for the self-esteem."

Retha listens to the barrage of issues and questions presented by her gynecologist. Retha has been seeing Dr. Randolph for nearly ten years and the woman still treats her like she is a twenty-year old. The foolishness of Retha's current decision may validate the doctor's behavior.

Retha tells the doctor that she has considered all these issues and several others. She tries to be honest with Dr. Randolph about her reason for wanting a child with Jaren. Dr. Jean, as Retha often calls her, always asks the hard questions. "Is this a way to try and hold on to your boyfriend because if it is you're making a big mistake? If he doesn't want you now, Retha, he could end up hating you and disowning the child. You don't want that. Women use this tactic all the time on wealthy men. It's not fair and I'm telling you, they'll portray you as a gold digger or some stupid ghetto slut or at best a very ignorant woman."

"I don't care! I don't care! I don't care! I know all of this, Dr. Jean. I want to have a baby, that's all. Joe's gone but Jaren is still here. This may not be the best situation but if I don't have a child with him I will never have one. Please, help me." Retha pleads desperately.

The doctor looks at Retha with pursed lips and shakes her head. "We'll get that IUD out and go from there. We'll need to run your labs to make sure everything is okay. You've had just about every test available and unless you have reason to think things have changed you should be fine, medically that is. But please, Retha, don't deceive yourself. He's not going to be easy to give up, especially when you're carrying his child."

The encounter with Dr. Jean makes Retha cringe. By the end of Retha's visit, her doctor who has always been so strong and assertive now shows only signs of disappointment, disgust, and defeat. She does however advise Retha, one last time, that she is making a mistake. Retha allows her doctor and friend the last word and prays she is wrong.

Retha tells no one other than Dr. Randolph about her baby making scheme. She wants no further advice or criticism. Jessie and the rest of her family would have a fit if they knew her plans. Retha hopes she can continue to see Jaren long enough to conceive. She is convinced she will get over him once she gets pregnant. Poor thing, reality has flown out the window.

After seeing her doctor and completing the necessary tests, Retha has a long talk with Uncle Sugar and explains that things aren't going well with Jaren and she needs to get away for a while. For the first time in forever, Sugar doesn't give her any lip. Retha hops the first plane smoking to Seattle to visit with Ida, leaving her cell phone and hopefully any possibility of contact with Jaren in San Antonio.

Jessie is disappointed with Retha and Jaren once she learns that Jaren has told Retha he wants to see other people. Jessie believes all this drama could be avoided if Retha would tell Jaren he can either be with her or he can date other women but he cannot have both. Jessie has no doubt that Jaren would choose Retha.

When Retha first arrives at Ida's home in Seattle, Ida wants to baby her "mistreated" little sister. Ida, like Jessie, can't understand why Retha doesn't give Jaren an ultimatum. "Retha, did you at least ask him if seeing other people means having sex with other people too? You don't want him dipping that thang in you if he's dipping it somewhere else. And listen, if he don't mind you screwing someone else you're better off without him. I guarantee you; he's not going to tell you he meant sleeping around."

Ida takes Retha on a leisurely road trip down to their hometown of Seaside, California, for an extended visit with their Aunt Reggie and her family. Retha occasionally tries to put up a good front but mostly mopes around like a lovesick fourteen-year-old. "What's wrong with her?" Aunt Reggie asks in disgust. "It's hard to enjoy y'all with her acting like the world has come to an end."

Ida gives her aunt the quick down and dirty of Retha's love life. "I did not know she was involved with that boy. Y'all should not have let her get caught up like that. She's strong or she would not have kept going like she did when she lost her parents and her husband. That Iraq thing toughened her up. She'll need all her strength to deal with this. Y'all be patient with her." Aunt Reggie makes a special effort to lighten Retha's spirits during their stay.

By the end of the trip, Ida's disgust with Retha and Jaren well surpasses Jessie's. She finds no less than five messages from Jaren on the answering machine upon their return and has had to field calls from Jessie, Jermaine and Madelyn concerning Retha's well-being. Of course Retha declares she has no interest in the contents of Jaren's messages.

Retha goes and stays with Michele for a few days and Ida is thankful for the respite. Michele is so busy with her new baby girl, Cecily, and her older children, Julia and Jordan, that she barely notices Retha's funk and is thrilled to have the company and the help. Keeping the children overnight so Michele and Sean can enjoy a night to themselves brings Retha out of her melancholy. She enjoys the children but they wear her out. When they finish with her, she is too tired to be heartbroken and slightly more upbeat when she returns to Ida's.

Retha does not call Jaren until she returns to San Antonio. Needless to say, he is not in the best of spirits when she gets him on the phone. To make things worse, she asks him if seeing other people means having sex with other people. He is nearly speechless after hearing the question. *Is she asking me this because she wants my okay to sleep around or has she been with someone?* "Why are you asking me this, Retha?"

"What did you mean when you said 'see other people'? That's not self-explanatory. Does it mean having sex with other people?"

How can he possibly answer the question? *Just say no.* "No. That is not what I meant." Jaren feels stupid. Retha is a little better though.

"I think we need to talk about this. When are you coming to New York? It's been three weeks." He sounds demanding and angry not realizing that if he expressed his honest desire to see her in his quiet voice, Retha would drop everything to get to him.

"I promised Ida I'd come back up there when I finished here."

Jaren waits for Retha to answer his question but she says nothing further. *I'm not begging.* "I'll see you when you get here."

"Bye, Jaren."

Neither Retha nor Jaren make an effort to see or talk to each other for weeks after that conversation. Jaren is determined to stick to his guns about distancing himself from Retha. If he can figure out how to keep her close enough to touch regularly without making a commitment, things will work out just fine.

The next visit with Dr. Jean is positive and the doctor seems to have accepted Retha's decision though not in agreement with it. Dr. Jean explains that it can take months to years to conceive after removing an IUD. Retha senses the doctor's hope that she will not conceive under these circumstances. She finds Dr. Jean's stance ironic since the doctor had dedicated years to helping Retha and Joe get pregnant.

After two more weeks of torturing poor Ida in Seattle, Retha flies straight to Jaren in New York. Her plan is to stay in the city for three weeks. Jaren will be on the road for eight of those twenty one days, but Retha will make the most of the days he is at home.

The couple is happier than ever to see each other. Neither mentions their recent decision to date other people. Retha makes love to Jaren each and every day he is in town. On his one travel day, they stay in bed most of the day. Retha is getting exactly what she came for, as much of Jaren as possible. Jaren is doing everything he can to make amends without apologizing or admitting that he does not want to date anyone but her at present.

On the other hand, except for the frequent hot sex, Retha is acting more like a friend than a lover. She doesn't want to fool herself like nothing has changed and fall into a false sense of security. She reminds herself that things are different between Jaren and her and that he is a man she wants to make love with but he is no longer her lover. She cooks dinner for him nearly every night but refuses to go out to dinner or elsewhere with him, not even to the store or coffee house. She will go to his games but not if Susan plans to attend. She keeps his home clean and well organized and has all his laundry done. She does these things because she enjoys taking care of him and loves him. Retha understands her behavior but not Jaren's.

Indeed, Jaren is so loving and attentive that halfway through her stay, Retha does begin to fall back into that secure place. She also begins to hear Dr. Randolph's words over and over inside her head. Retha is beginning to slip back into the realm of reality. One night as she lies next to Jaren watching him sleep, panic grips her. As much as she wants a child, she is wrong to get pregnant without Jaren's knowledge. She lies there and tries to justify her plan as the terror rises. *Have I lost my mind? I can't do this to him. I can't do this to myself. My God, what if I'm pregnant?* She gets dizzy as the reality of Dr. Randolph's words sets in. She wonders what she should do. She calms down when she remembers that she and Joe tried to get pregnant for eight years. The chance that she will become pregnant during ten unprotected days with Jaren is slim. She considers telling him that she's not using any birth control and suggesting that they use a condom but she would need to explain. She can't see herself telling Jaren how desperate she became at the possibility of losing him. She decides to take her chances for the remainder of her stay.

Toward the end of Retha's visit, she answers the phone one morning to hear Jennifer's voice on the other end asking for Jaren. Each woman is surprised and distraught to hear the other's voice. Jennifer had heard through her friend Lauren that Jaren and Retha were on the outs so she had called Jaren several weeks earlier under the pretense of asking for tickets to an upcoming game. Jaren was cordial and had promised to provide the tickets but had not shown the least bit of interest in renewing the relationship.

Jennifer is calling to confirm the tickets but does not want to explain her reason for calling to Retha. She and Retha share friendly greetings and a little small talk. She tells Retha not to bother giving Jaren a message because she will see him over the weekend. Retha is sick to her stomach when she puts down the phone. She can't ignore their situation. Jaren has warned her of his intentions. No sense waiting for it to hit her upside the head again. She tells herself she is finished with Jaren, boxes up all of her belongings and ships them to her home in San Antonio.

When Jaren comes in that night, he is surprised to find Retha out. He's gotten accustomed to coming in and finding her there waiting for him. The apartment is dark and cold. At first he assumes Retha is out visiting or shopping. Soon he realizes she has taken her things from his room and must have gone back to San Antonio. He is struck that nothing of hers is left in his room. Whether she is in town or not, she usually has more personal items in his bath than he does. He immediately checks the guest room where she keeps most of her clothing. There is not one item that belongs to Retha in the entire apartment. Jaren sits on the edge of the bed and cradles his forehead in his hands. How had their relationship become so twisted?

The following weekend, Retha sits in front of her television and watches Jaren slug a walk off home run to end the rubber game of the Wranglers versus Liberty series. She sits there dazed when the camera pans in on Jaren's family cheering gleefully alongside Jennifer and an older woman Retha has never seen before.

--

"Worrisome" is how Jessie describes Retha to Robert when she informs him her sister is back in San Antonio and seems as miserable as when she left all those weeks ago. Jessie had rested well while Retha was away, especially during the time she was in New York. While Retha was with Jaren, Jessie thought everything would be fine between the couple and Retha would show up accompanied by a glow. Jessie's heart sank when her sister walked in her front door with a faint pitiful smile of hello and not a trace of joy in her demeanor.

"Did you ask her what happened?" Robert asks in search of a ray of hope. All hope fades when Jessie renders a slight shake of her hanging head.

"You want me to call Jaren? I haven't talked to him in a while."

"No baby, we can't make them be together." Jessie pats him on his shoulder as a thank you. "I can't believe she stayed up there with him so long if it's over between them."

"Look, Jessie. I don't want you worrying about Retha. You got enough on you with Catrina."

"I'm not worried. It'll be okay," Jessie tells her husband but continues to worry. Retha is like one of her children and when Retha is unhappy, Jessie cannot help but share her burden.

--

Susan decides she must act. It is obviously over between Jaren and Retha but she can tell from her son's behavior that if Retha dials his number they will be back together. Jennifer might be the answer to the problem, at least she should help get Jaren's mind off of Retha. Once Susan decides to take action, she wastes no time. "I was wondering if I could get you to call your friend Jennifer for me and ask her if she will model in our women's club upcoming winter show. As always, we will have professionals, but the designers thought it would be a good idea to have a few more models. Jennifer is so elegant and svelte. I believe I heard her say she has modeled professionally. She would blow the designers away with her looks. Do you think she would do it?"

"I have no idea. You'd have to ask her. Do you want her number?" Jaren responds to his mother with absolutely no interest.

"Would you ask her for me? She would not refuse you. She likes you."

Jennifer might agree to help his mother but Jaren does not want to call her. No, calling Jennifer and asking for a favor is a bad move on his part. She says she wants to remain friends but old lovers make for complicated friendships.

His mother has never asked him to do anything like this before. As far as he can recall, Susan has met Jennifer twice. The first time was out to eat with a group of Jaren's friends and teammates after a game last season and the second time was the weekend the Liberty played the Wranglers. Susan had paid little attention to Jennifer during the first meeting but seemed to fall in love with the girl at the recent game and has talked about her to Jaren almost incessantly since.

Jaren, suspicious of Susan's motives, sticks to his decision. "Mom, it's not a good idea for me to call her. You can either get someone else or ask her yourself."

"I have racked my brain and I can't think of anyone else that has the style and poise of Jennifer. She is absolutely perfect."

"Ask her." Jaren is irritated with his mother. He is certain she will push and push until she gets her way.

"That's alright. Don't worry about it. We'll have to work something else out. I'll talk to you later." Susan puts the phone down hard to ensure her son knows she's upset.

The call has the intended effect. Jaren feels bad about refusing his mother such a small request. So two days later Jaren calls her and gets all the particulars to pass on to Jennifer who is more than thrilled when she receives his call. Jennifer takes Susan's information and asks Jaren to a party at her place the following week. "I'll plan to be there," Jaren responds with all the enthusiasm he can muster. *This is how the game is played; I scratch your back and you scratch mine.*

The fundraiser hosted by Susan's club is attended by her entire family. She plans to seat Jennifer next to Jaren and ensure there are lots of photos of the couple in print and on social media sites.

Unaware that her son long ago dated and lost interest in Jennifer, Susan hopes the lovely lady has what it takes to capture Jaren's attention and possibly his heart. But if Jennifer falls short, maybe all the publicity photos of the couple will keep Retha away. It sickens Susan to see the way Jaren obsesses over Retha. She knows next to nothing about Jennifer but believes whatever her background, she is a better choice for her son than Retha.

Everything in Susan's plan falls into place beautifully. Fate plays its hand by way of a couple of college girls wanting to visit each other. Rachelle has invited Elizabeth for a stay at the end of their summer break and it happens that the fashion show will take place during Lizzie's visit.

In the past, Susan has allowed Rachelle to beg off and not attend the event but not this year. "I need you girls to dress nicely and make an appearance. You only need to stay an hour or so." She does not want the young ladies at the show too long because Elizabeth might get a real sense of the nonexistent relationship between Jaren and Jennifer.

Elizabeth greatly enjoys her stay with Rachelle. The young ladies spend most of their time in the city at Jaren's apartment. He is in town but leaves for the stadium early most days and comes in when they are out. Jaren has never allowed Rachelle to stay at his place with a friend before Lizzie's visit. He treats Elizabeth like a sister and makes sure she has everything she needs and much of what she wants. Rachelle and Elizabeth understand that the special treatment is because of Retha.

The girls show up for the show, meet other guests, eat a light luncheon, watch Jennifer flirt with Jaren, and leave as soon as they can get away. Susan is satisfied. Elizabeth flies home the following Monday and does not mention one word about the event to her mother, father or her aunt. Elizabeth saw nothing to indicate that Jaren had any interest in Jennifer. The photos in the papers and on the social media sites tell a different story. There appears to be a real effort to make it seem as if Jaren and Jennifer are a couple.

--

Brenda doesn't say hello. She starts the call with, "Just tell me one thing, Re. Is that the same Barbie that was at Jaren's apartment when we were there last year?"

"What are you talking about, Brenda?" Retha answers wondering if she might be in an episode of the *Twilight Zone*. "Yeah, I'm sure that's the same ho," Brenda continues. "You gonna have to put her ass in check. She is all over Jaren. What is he thinking? You need to call him and tell him off. He don't need to let women be hanging all over him like that. He got a woman." Brenda laughs with no idea of the state of the relationship between Retha and Jaren. The photos appear harmless to her. She has seen others on Jaren's fan pages, which she follows religiously, with women all over him. She is calling because she recognizes this woman. Retha pulls up the page on her laptop and recognizes her also; it is Jennifer. Retha's heart starts to pound in her chest. She wants to get away.

--

Retha no longer has a job at Sugar's. Over the last eight months she has hired two assistant managers that perform well and work together to ensure everything in the front of the house is covered. Between Sugar, Sylvia, Jim, and the two assistant managers, Retha feels inconsequential.

She is also tired of Jessie treating her as if she is a delicate flower. She has tried to put on a happy face. That doesn't work so she tries to stay away from her sister but Jessie calls her two and three times a day. So, when Retha learns that Aida has plans to visit the Dominican Republic, Retha invites herself along on the trip. Honestly, everyone in her family is happy to see her leave.

Retha takes off and tours the country, either alone, accompanied by Aida, or one of Joe's cousins. The island offers the serenity and natural beauty she needs to rest her weary mind. She stays an entire month and wants to stay longer but the holiday season is approaching and she is obligated to get home. Also, Aida's threats to leave her behind persuade her it's time to go home.

By the time Retha boards the plane for home, the Liberty have won their second consecutive World Series and Retha is certain she is pregnant. Fear and happiness swarm around her like honey bees in a field of sunflowers. She sits very still, deep in her thoughts, afraid if she moves she may get stung and wake up from her dream or is it a nightmare? *Deceit* – that word keeps creeping in. *No, I won't be unhappy about my baby. I have wanted a child and I will not let what happened between me and Jaren steal my joy. What's done is*

done. If Jaren hates me -- Oh, God please don't let him hate me --
he'll have to hate me. God if you bless me with this child, I will be a
good mother. I will take my child to church whenever the doors
open. Please Lord, please!

Retha is ecstatic, but the hurt over losing Jaren is the other side
of the coin. She tries to be honest with herself but refuses to admit
she is clinging to a hope that if she has Jaren's child she will have a
continued connection with him. She is a desperate woman and does
not care. She wants her baby even if she never sees or speaks to
Jaren Daniels again.

The glow is back. Jessie and Robert are satisfied to see Retha so
happy and content. The pain of losing Jaren and Retha's longing for
him grow more intense each day but these emotions are well hidden
by the joy of her pregnancy.

--

Jaren cannot understand how Retha has moved on so easily. He
hasn't heard a word from her in weeks. She didn't return his phone
calls before she left the country and was gone a week before JJ told
him where she was. He did not know she was back in country until
after Thanksgiving. Jaren imagines Retha decorating her Christmas
tree alone or even worse with someone else and he gets angry. His
family offers him no solace. Rachelle is full of questions about
Retha. He can't play the situation off any longer.

Charles is hands off when it comes to Jaren and his love life. The
one time he interfered he screwed things up royally. Susan is pleased
Jaren is no longer seeing Retha but hates for him to be unhappy. She
tried to get him to invite Jennifer for Thanksgiving Dinner. If stares
could bludgeon, Susan would have needed emergency care.

Jaren has realized that his mother was trying to separate him and
Retha with the charity fundraiser at her club. There were cameras
everywhere and later photos everywhere with all kinds of innuendo
about him and Jennifer. There is no telling what Elizabeth went back
and told her aunt. Jaren finds it hard to believe his mother could be
so conniving but when Rachelle showed up with Elizabeth, Susan's
intent became clear. He stayed and put on a good show for the crowd
and the camera when he wanted to walk out with his sister and
Lizzie. But Jaren understood that the charity was the important thing
that day, so he remained at the event, signed autographs, and smiled

for the cameras as long as he was needed. The reason he has not been more upset with Susan is because he was the one who caused the breakup with Retha, not his mother.

--

Nearly all of Retha's ambivalence about her pregnancy has faded. She finds her solace in the fact that she is having a baby. It is the most beautifully fulfilling thought as long as she doesn't bother to put in the complete picture of her circumstances.

Jessie bursts out crying when Retha gives her the news. At first Retha fears Jessie is crying out of disappointment. Then she sees that Jessie is laughing along with her tears. "I have wanted you to have a baby of your own for so long so you can stop borrowing my children," Jessie laughs as the tears stream down her cheeks. She calls Robert at work and places calls to Madelyn and Ida to share the news. Retha puts a damper on the joy when Jessie asks if she has told Simone and Brenda. "Not yet. Simone talks to Aaron all the time and Brenda can't hold water down. I don't want this to get to Jaren."

"He doesn't know? Retha baby, you got to tell him."

"I'll tell him when the time is right. He thought I still had an IUD, Jessie. I don't know how he'll take this. If he doesn't want to get married he sure doesn't want a child."

"Retha!" Disappointment reeks through Jessie's voice. "You got to tell him anyway."

"I will when the time is right."

No one likes Retha's decision to keep her pregnancy a secret from Jaren. Robert is so upset he barely speaks to Retha for a few days and fusses at his wife nonstop for a full week. "What she think? She think she the only one capable of loving or wanting that child because she's a woman? Where you women get this idea that you and the baby are the only ones that matter? The man don't have no say. We men we get left in the cold if the woman decides that's how she wants it. It's not right. That boy deserves better. I'm ashamed of my sister-in-law. I never thought I could get this mad at her. I should call Jaren and tell him; that's what I should do."

Jessie doesn't say a word while Robert expresses his anger. Robert makes a good point but they have to respect Retha's decision. Jessie isn't worried that Robert will tell Jaren about Retha's condition though she wishes he would. Robert loves Retha far too much to betray her but he is so mad at Retha that he is mad at Jessie also. He wants Jessie to make Retha tell Jaren about the baby. Jessie remembers her uncle's words well over a year ago, describing her sister's stubborn character. "Cain't nobody make that girl do what she don't want." This is true of most people and it definitely fits Retha. All Jessie can do is advise her sister and she has done that. Retha is the one that must do the right thing.

Chapter 28 -- Sweet Sugar

"Jessie, is Retha there with you?" Sylvia sobs frantically into the phone.

Jessie stands up from the kitchen table where she and Retha have been sharing quiet cups of tea. "Yeah, she's here. What's wrong?"

"Can you guys come to the hospital? It's Sugar. We had to bring him in because he was in so much pain. It's not good Jessie. Can you guys come down here? We are at The Baptist."

"Which one?"

"Northeast Baptist. You guys hurry, okay."

Fear and nausea attack Retha all at once. The telephone conversation was clearly not good. She dreads what Jessie has to say. "They took Sugar to the hospital. It's his stomach again. Sylvia wants us to come down there."

A tearful, red-eyed Sylvia meets them in the hallway of the hospital. Nathaniel is making a futile attempt to comfort his brother Gerald who is sitting in a chair sobbing.

"We've been here almost all morning. The doctor got the test results back late yesterday. Oh Jessie!" Sylvia falls into her niece's arms.

"What did the doctor say?" Retha is losing patience with her family. Jessie cuts her eyes at Retha whose eyes are now filling with tears. Jessie is trying to hold on but it's becoming more difficult with each moment.

"It's his pancreas. Not an early stage. There is nothing they can do, just give him pain medication to make him comfortable. The doctor says Sugar waited too long to get help."

"It was those damn cigarettes," Nathaniel declares.

"Uncle Sugar stopped smoking years ago." Retha rejects Nathaniel's premise.

Gerald stops sobbing long enough to get in the conversation. "He did stop all together for a while but it wasn't long before he started back up at home. He didn't smoke around y'all because Jessie would give him such a hard time. He wouldn't listen to us, never does." Gerald's anger is apparent.

"Sylvia tell you how long he's got?" Nathaniel asks his cousins. When no one answers he tells them what they don't want to hear. "One to six months. Doc says he might not last three months."

222

Jessie nor Retha want to believe their uncle is dying. The sisters sit down in the waiting room and don't move until Robert arrives ten minutes later. Robert goes directly in to see Sugar.

"Where them nieces of mine?" Sugar asks.

"Oh, they'll be here after a while."

"I'm supposed to believe you got here before either of them. They don't want to see me do they? Scared I might see how scared they are for me. Tell 'em to come on in here and pray for me. I need all the prayer I can get 'bout now."

Robert gathers everyone into Sugar's room and they all hold hands as Jessie leads them in a good old fashioned family prayer. They pray and cry out to God for healing. This prayer is difficult for Jessie. She can't shake the feeling that a physical healing is too much to ask of God. She knows God can heal Sugar, but will He? The cancer is far along. Jessie feels a spiritual healing is the only healing God will hand down at such a late stage. She knows she is wrong for thinking this way and questions her faith. She is supposed to believe and ask the Lord for the desires of her heart, and right now that desire is that God spare her uncle's life and make him whole physically as well as spiritually. She can't ask; it seems futile. Later, she acknowledges that she didn't ask because she didn't believe God would answer her prayer -- not that God couldn't do what she wanted but that he wouldn't.

--

No sooner than Retha walks in her front door, Jaren calls. They have spoken only two times since she abandoned him in New York months ago. He wants to visit for Christmas. Retha cannot turn him down. She wants to see him. "If you want. When are you coming?"

"Tomorrow," Jaren answers to Retha's dread.

--

Retha gets more nervous with each moment leading up to Jaren's arrival. She is following Dr. Jean's orders to stay off her feet and having a hard time keeping down food. Jaren will know she is not well. She calls Robert and asks him if he told Jaren her news. Robert swears he hasn't talked to Jaren in nearly a week. Retha is surprised to hear that the two men have talked at all. She does not question Robert about their conversations because he won't divulge their discussions. She hardly sleeps at all in anticipation of Jaren's arrival.

Retha calls Dr. Randolph early the next morning and asks her if sex is out of the question. "No, but tell your ballplayer to be very gentle -- softball no hardball and stay off your feet. Now let me go back to sleep."

--

Whipped Dog best describes Jaren's spirit when he arrives in San Antonio. Well, not quite. He is angry and does retain a degree of resistance. His dominant mind tells him to do whatever it takes to get back with Retha. His Angry Resistance interrupts and calls him a "pussy." Angry Resistance tells Jaren that if he surrenders to his desire for Retha, he has lost the war. She will triumph over him for the rest of their lives together. Thus far Whipped Dog has overpowered Angry Resistance.

Once Jaren arrives in San Antonio, Retha does her best to help Jaren's resistance grow stronger. Jaren had no idea Retha possessed such a cold distant side. She has little to no conversation, no touching, no eye contact, smiles, nothing to give him any hope. Within an hour of his arrival at her home, Jaren wonders if he should have come.

As Retha expected, Jaren recognizes that she is not well. She seems to have lost weight and is exhausted. She hates to use Sugar as an excuse for her appearance and condition but does. She also explains that she has a female condition and must stay off her feet for a few weeks to get her strength back.

"Why didn't you call me or have Jessie or Robert call? I talked to Robert a few days ago. He told me you were fine, just tired."

"I am fine. I haven't discussed my medical issues with Robert. I told you I have female problems."

When Jaren has an opportunity, he asks Jessie about Retha's medical condition. Jessie tells him not to worry. She explains that Retha is having the problems most women experience when they reach her age. Jessie's explanation sounds flaky to Jaren, worse than Retha's. He has never heard of any problem females have at age thirty-three.

Things get no better between Retha and Jaren and his hope for a reunion diminishes. Retha lets him sleep with her but stays on her side of the bed. She used to sleep so close to him that at times he had to wake her to keep from being pushed onto the floor. Now she doesn't seem to want him near her. If he tries to embrace her, she pulls away as if she's repulsed by him. She hardly looks at him and their conversations are about other people and things. They don't discuss their future. Jaren can see no point in trying. He'd have to be an idiot not to see that she doesn't want him around any longer. He understands that she is upset about Sugar but that is hardly an excuse for her behavior toward him. He doesn't understand why she allowed him to visit her.

--

"I'm sure glad you back, man." Sugar treats Jaren to a huge smile and even manages a weak hug. "That Retha, she's a good woman but just like her motha. I'm surprised she didn't run you off long before now. All them girls and Andre, Wanda and Donald did a good job with the lot of 'em, 'cept that Raymond and that Jermaine. They're my favorites. Them two are like me." He laughs thinking about his nephews and coughs a little before continuing. "You take good care of Retha. That's my baby and she sure does love you."

Jaren sees no sign that Retha loves him but does not challenge Sugar's assertion. He and Sugar "shoot the breeze" as Sugar would say for more than an hour. Jaren's visit does more to take Sugar away from his illness than any so far. Jaren shares stories about his team, the coaches and manager he would normally not tell. Sugar tells Jaren about his days in "The Nam" and how he wanted to be a ballplayer when he was young. Sugar also talks about Sylvia and his children. At one point he shifts his position trying to secure a modicum of comfort, becomes very serious and looks Jaren straight in the eye. "Listen, I don't mean no disrespect toward your family, but that mama of yours don't like Retha and Retha knows it. Don't you let her mistreat my girl. I mean that."

Jaren cannot believe Sugar is telling him about his mother's dislike of Retha. He is not insulted or injured by the allegation because it is only confirmation of his thoughts on Susan's behavior. Susan is usually all in his business but has not once questioned him about his breakup with Retha.

Jaren gives Sugar a promise to take good care of Retha but is not sure he can keep the promise. After visiting nearly an hour, he leaves to find the doctor to ensure everything possible is done for Sugar. Sugar's oncologist assures Jaren that more money will not heal Sugar. She tells Jaren Sugar will be taken home and a hospice nurse will visit daily. Around the clock nursing may be advisable at some point, but the doctor does not recommend such extensive nursing at this time. Jaren speaks with the social worker and provides his phone numbers so hospice can contact him when the doctor recommends the private nursing. He discusses Sugar's care with Robert and Jessie but doesn't broach the subject with Retha.

Christmas is not nearly as memorable as the first Jaren spent with Retha's family. That Christmas was a short year ago but so much has happened since. It appears Jaren is spending his last Christmas in San Antonio. Jaren is the only out of town guest because most of the family believes they will need to be in San Antonio in the very near future to honor Sugar. They will all want to forget this Christmas.

On the eve of his planned departure, the day after Christmas, Jaren sits and waits for Retha to return home. After a while he starts to worry because he has no idea where she is. He calls Retha's cell phone and realizes she left it in the bedroom when he hears it ringing. He calls Jessie who hesitantly informs him she has no idea where Retha could be. Jaren fights back his anger. He told Retha he planned to leave early the next morning and it is the ultimate in cruelty for her to stay out on his last night in town. When she walks in, well after midnight, Jaren confronts her. "Listen, what the hell is going on? If you didn't want me to come why didn't you say so?"

"You have things here. For all I knew, you wanted to get your things?"

Jaren is disgusted with Retha's meager response. *Cold bitch.* Whipped Dog is dead and gone. Angry Resistance is strong and powerful. "What is your problem? I come here to see you and you treat me like shit. You're always playing little childish games. In case you don't know it, you're not a child, Retha. You're a grown woman who should have the courage to say what's on her mind."

Retha stops dead in her tracks. She can't believe Jaren is speaking to her in that tone. *What does he expect? He's the one that wanted to date. He wanted to be free of me.* Anger grips Retha. She does not want to speak words she may regret; she leaves the room.

Jaren follows her down the hallway talking to her back. "Don't you walk away from me when I'm talking to you. When did you get up on this damn throne? You don't dismiss me like that." He follows her into the bedroom.

Retha remains silent, causing Jaren more frustration as he watches her put away her things.

"So I guess you don't want me around anymore. Okay, that's alright. I'm sure I can find someone who doesn't mind having me around. I might find someone that even enjoys my company."

Crap hitting the fan is an understatement. "You damn right, I don't want you around any longer. All you do is make me miserable. I got everything I want from you. So you take your tired ass to whoever it is or they are that enjoy your sorry ass company.

Damn where did that come from? "So you want me to leave?"

"Isn't that the plan? Yes, I want you to leave. I got what I need from you." Retha is seething. It is remarkable that she's not frothing at the mouth.

Once again Retha said she got what she wanted from him. Jaren knows there is a hidden meaning by the way she threw the comments out. "What did you get from me Retha or is that another one of your childish secrets? You like to play games and keep secrets like a little girl. I guess it would ruin your fun to tell me what you're talking about. You go ahead and keep your secret. I don't even care."

"You know what? You're right. I shouldn't keep secrets. I think I'll tell the world the first chance I get. I'm pregnant. You are going to be a daddy. You happy now? That's what I wanted more than anything and that's what I got. I don't need anything else from you. You performed your service."

No sooner than the words spill out, Retha wishes she could swallow them back or at least the malice that accompanied them. Sorry will not do and her remorse does not go deep enough to warrant a full-fledged apology. She does not regret being pregnant?

Mixtures of emotional waves rush from Jaren's brain to his heart and back. Anger, excitement bordering on joy, and confusion are dominant. Anger is at the forefront. Jaren is not sure how to respond but anger takes on words of its own. "What the hell do you mean, you're pregnant? I hope you're bullshittin' me. This had better be another one of your fuckin' games."

Retha goes mute again. Jaren can tell she is not lying. His anger subsides but he wants answers. "When did this happen? I thought you were on birth control. You did this on purpose, didn't you?"

Retha calms down considerably. She cannot maintain her anger because there is no justification for it. She is the villain. She is hurt and ashamed. Jaren's words are like rocks being pelted against her frail body as she slumps down onto her bed. She feels dirty, like a sleaze that intentionally set up a rich young man for her own purpose. Money, baby, or marriage – whatever her purpose, what she did was low and deceitful. Jaren had trusted her and in turn she tricked him; she didn't give him a choice. The film that covered the vision of her mind has been pulled back allowing her to see her actions through the eyes of others. Still, her words do not quell Jaren's anger. Instead she speaks words that injure him more. "Jaren, I'm not looking for anything from you. This may be hard to believe but you never even have to see this child. I didn't get pregnant to trap you. The baby is all I want."

At this moment, Jaren understands the emotions that might cause a man to hit a woman. He grabs his bags to leave. "You know what Retha? You're one selfish heartless bitch. I never would have expected this from you." He glares and waits for a response, hoping Retha says something to calm the storm tearing him up inside. When no sound passes her lips and she refuses to look at him, he leaves.

Retha sits there and listens until she hears the door slam, then runs to the bathroom and slings herself over the toilet bowl just in time to release the remnants of the junk she ate at Charmaine's house earlier.

--

"I have a big secret Uncle Sugar. Do you want me to tell you now or do you want me to tell you when I come back tomorrow?" Sugar is running Retha out of his room for the day. Lately, she stays longer than he likes and he is tired of her company.

"Tell me when you come back tomorrow. It'll give me something to look forward to."

"What time do you want me to come tomorrow?"

"Come early so I won't have to wait too long to hear yo' secret." Sugar starts to laugh but flinches in pain and stops.

Retha kisses him on the cheek and asks him the same question they all ask before leaving and gets the same answer they all get.

"Prayer, that's all I need is prayer."

When Retha arrives at the hospital the next day, Sugar is sitting up much straighter in his hospital bed. She can tell he is waiting for her, not anyone else. She hands him a couple of magazines, *Sports*

Illustrated and *Jet*. She starts chatting with him about things in general, torturing him. Sugar gets annoyed with her. "What is this mess? Stop playin' with me. I been waitin' all mornin' for you to show up with this big secret. Now, what is it?" Retha is worried that maybe her secret isn't good enough. Uncle Sugar has grandchildren and has been around kids all his life. How excited can he get over another Solomon baby?

"You have to promise to keep my secret from everybody. You, Robert, and my sisters are the only ones that know."

"You mean not even old big mouth Brenda knows?" Sugar asks with a grin.

"Nope, not even old big mouth Brenda."

"Well it better be good. What is it? You getting married again?" Sugar watches Retha out of the corners of his eyes with a wry smile. That puts a damper on her secret for sure. That is what she should be telling before what she is about to divulge. She hopes her uncle will not be too disappointed she is having a baby without a husband or the child's father.

"This is much much better. I'm having a baby, Uncle Sugar."

Sugar looks at her for a moment and then with much effort pushes himself up straighter in the bed before asking, "You adoptin'?"

"No! I'm having a baby."

"Glory be to God! Come here girl and give me a hug." Sugar reaches for his niece with all the energy he can conjure up.

He holds her close and when she pulls away Retha can see his eyes are watering. For the first time she sees a resemblance between him and Jessie.

"So you and Daniels did it. Why you keepin' it secret from him and his family? He's got a right to know."

"I just found out for certain yesterday. I'm going to tell him when he comes back; make a big to do over it," Retha lies a little. She doesn't want to upset her uncle. Retha wants him to believe all is well but Sugar knows Retha and Jaren are in rough waters.

"Well don't wait too long. Men are funny. He'll start to question if he's the daddy if you wait too long and wonderin' why you kept it a secret. I tell you somethin' else Retha, you makin' him miss out on somethin' he's gonna want to share in. This ain't yo' doin' alone. You need to be fair to him."

"I will Sugar, I will."

"How far along are you anyway?"

"One month." She lies again.

"Congratulations, Retha. You been wantin' yo' own child for a long time. That's gonna be one lucky baby cause you gonna make a damn good motha and that Jaren is gonna make one hell of a fatha. He's a good man. Got a good fatha too, though his motha ain't worth a damn. I know she been givin' you a hard time. Don't think I don't know what's going on." Sugar takes Retha's hands in his. "You listen to yo' old uncle. I appreciate all you done for me -- you, Jessie, and Robert. I don't know that I could have made it without y'all and you puttin' that money in the business. That was good of you girl and it was a real help. You done good by me but that's not what I'm tryin to tell you. It's gonna be alright. It's gonna all work out in the end. I told Jaren something I didn't need to tell him, to take good care of you. He will and you better take good care of him too.

"I will, Unc," Retha barely whispers loud enough for Sugar to hear.

This visit is the best Retha has with Sugar. From that day on he slips deeper and deeper into the well of his illness. As sure as the sun sets and rises his condition worsens each and every day. Before long he is too weak to talk much or fuss much for that matter.

--

Jaren enters his parents' New Rochelle home just as they have finished dinner. Rachelle is home for Christmas break so it's a good time for a family meeting. The family is not expecting Jaren and is surprised and relieved to see him. They had no idea where he spent Christmas which made theirs the worst ever. He did call on Christmas Day but when Charles asked him where he was he just said he would be home soon. That was three days ago.

"Jaren!" Susan rushes to throw her arms around him and holds on as if she hasn't seen him in a great while. "Where have you been? I have been so worried?" Rachelle falls in behind her mother to hug her brother also. Jaren's absence has caused Rachelle to shed tears on more than one occasion. Charles does not rise from the table but sits and stares at his son waiting for an apology. Charles is pretty sure Jaren spent Christmas with Retha, but he has not shared his thoughts with his wife or daughter because he was not certain. All he told them was that Jaren was fine wherever he was.

"I'm sorry. I didn't mean for you to worry about me. That's why I called." Jaren joins them at the dining room table. "I need to talk to all of you. It's important."

"What has happened?" Susan asks in a panicked voice.

Jaren ignores her. "I spent Christmas with Retha." He notices his mother panic for real and speaks to her. "Don't worry, Mom. We are not back together." Susan is shocked and ashamed that Jaren is aware of and openly acknowledges her feelings about his relationship with Retha. Jaren continues. "Her Uncle Sugar is dying; he doesn't have long. It's pancreatic cancer."

Susan can't help herself. "On my goodness. How are Retha and the family doing?"

"They're okay. Sugar is the one dying," Jaren responds sarcastically.

"I'm sorry to hear that, Son. He is a nice old guy; loves his family." Charles's mood has mellowed.

"Yeah, well." Jaren lowers his eyes for a moment before he continues. "Dad, remember when you asked me about marrying Retha and I told you I was not getting married anytime soon."

"Charles, you didn't?" Susan glowers at her husband with bug eyes.

"I am sorry about that, Jaren. For the first time I might have pushed you in the wrong direction. I know you overreacted to that talk."

"You damn right, I overreacted." Jaren smiles slightly. "You were trying to tell me what you thought was right. I wasn't ready to hear it. I ran her off. Now she's pregnant."

"What?" comes from Rachelle. "Pregnant?" comes from Charles. "That bitch. I knew she was no good!" comes from Susan. All eyes turn to Susan.

"You never liked Retha did you, Mom? You never wanted me to be with her. Why is that? Did you dislike her from the start because she's dark?"

"That has nothing to do with why I didn't like her. I knew she was common. I told your father and Rachelle that girl did not belong in our family. Her family is ghetto. That uncle of hers…" Susan catches herself, ashamed that she was about to speak harshly of

Sugar. "Well, I'm not going to say anything because he is ill, but I knew she was no good the moment I laid eyes on her. She acted like she was so in love with you but no sooner than you breakup, she goes off and gets herself pregnant. You can't get involved with people like that, baby. You need to try and find people that have the values we raised you with," Susan adds with satisfaction written all over her being.

Tears are running down Rachelle's face and Charles has covered his with his hands. Jaren looks at his mother as if he has never seen her before. "I hated to believe this about you, Mom but you are so wrong." He turns his gaze to Rachelle and says "I am sorry I didn't believe you. I couldn't wrap my mind around something so cruel happening in our family." Jaren stands and turns to his parents. "You are going to have to fix this. I will not have a child of mine growing up around people who treat him or her different because of the way he or she looks." He moves to his sister and takes her hand. "Rachelle, I love you and you are the best sister a brother could wish for. I am prejudiced when it comes to you, but you are so beautiful and don't you let anyone ever make you believe that you are not." Jaren sits down and consoles Rachelle as she sobs into his shoulder.

Charles and Susan sit and watch their children in shameful silence.

Once Rachelle stops crying, Jaren gets up to leave. Before leaving the room, he stops, turns around and says "No, Retha and I are not getting back together, but you need to congratulate me because I am going to be a father."

--

Sugar went straight from the hospital to a hospice care center. Sylvia proves to be a devoted wife and tries to spend as much time as possible with Sugar but she also has the children. Jim and the assistant managers are running the restaurant. Jessie puts in time at the restaurant and helps Sylvia with her kids. Retha tried to help at the restaurant but Jessie and Robert insist she follow doctor's orders and stay off her feet. Everyone tries to sit with Sugar and since Retha is the one who must stay off her feet; she is with him several hours each day.

One day Retha enters the room to find a nurse sitting in attendance. At first Retha assumes a charitable organization provided the nurse. She is even more surprised to learn that her uncle has around the clock nurses. When Jessie tells her that Jaren is paying the tab, she is brought to tears. She wants to call and thank him but decides it is best if she doesn't. She fears hearing his voice will make her long for him more. Retha loves Jaren more with every passing day and she wants to move through the pain of their breakup and the emotions associated with him.

To everyone's joy, Sugar gets better after the nurses start caring for him. Hope begins to rise because he seems to be gaining a little strength and is talking again. The family laughs and teases him that he is better because a couple of the nurses are real babes. Sugar laughs back and says a couple of them are real dogs with voices deeper than his and hair on their faces, referring to the male nurses. One evening Jessie, Sylvia, Robert, Retha, and Gerald meet in Sugar's room for prayer and bible study. Sugar participates with so much fervor and enthusiasm that they all leave with uplifted hearts.

Retha wakes before daybreak the following morning to the ringing of her phone. She answers to hear Jessie on the other end telling her that Uncle Sugar is dead. Retha gets into her car, drives to Jessie's, and together they ride to Sylvia's. They find Sylvia sitting at the kitchen table drinking coffee. They are all cried out, making Sugar's death all the sadder. Retha wants to cry but it is as if she has no more tears to shed. She wants the world to cry for Sugar, loud and hard. He deserves a wailing cry.

Chapter 29 --Apologies and Confessions

Retha awakes the morning of Sugar's funeral to overwhelming exhaustion. It is as if she has a yoke about her neck. She wishes her uncle was still alive but is relieved his suffering is over and thankful he did not suffer long. The members of the family are all staying strong for each other but Retha isn't sure how much longer she can hold out. She wishes the tears would flow. She has tried to cry during times when she is alone but nothing comes. She yelled, stretched out on the floor and pounded her fist but not one tear flowed. Retha, the crybaby, cannot cry.

She worries about her baby with this extreme burden of depression that has engulfed her heart, mind, and soul. She hopes relief will come once Sugar is buried. It has been six days since his death and each day has been torture. Watching Sylvia's mourning grow deeper and seeing Jessie, Robert, Nathaniel, and Gerald stressed out with all the planning and coordination and caring for the children and Sugar's business affairs makes Retha pray for the end of the day. She knows from the past that once the day is over the healing will begin. Retha's own efforts to help cause Jessie to become agitated and worried.

Retha's morning sickness is worse than ever but there is no way she can sit the day out. Family and friends have been arriving for two days. Every family house in San Antonio has guests. Many of the family members are coming from Houston and will not need a place to sleep overnight. Mykol has volunteered to pick up Simone and Brenda from the airport so Retha can drag herself over to Sylvia's to help get the kids ready for the service. She is relieved to find Elizabeth there helping with the children. Elizabeth gets one glimpse of her aunt and sends her home. "Go home, Auntie Retha. We got this. Justin got himself and Billy ready so I just need to check them out and make sure they're not too greasy or ashy and comb their hair. I got Bertani bathed and I'm dressing her now. We're almost finished. Try to get more rest before the service." Retha doesn't argue. She checks on Sylvia, who appears to be fine, before returning home to get herself dressed.

--

"Re, are you pregnant?" Brenda yells after seeing Retha for less than thirty seconds.

"Is it so obvious? I thought you guys might not be able to tell."

Brenda grabs Retha in a suffocating hug then jerks Retha away from her and holds her at arm's length with a serious expression. "It is Jaren's ain't it?" Leave it to Brenda to make her friend laugh when she wants to cry. "You laughing but we don't want no broke-assed Negro's babies around here, not when we can have little millionaires. I bet Jaren is too happy."

"Let's not talk about Jaren today, okay?" Retha pleads.

Brenda gives Retha a hard stare. "You did tell him about the baby didn't you?"

"She said she doesn't want to talk about Jaren today, Brenda. We are here to support her so maybe we could respect her wishes for today." Simone tries to stop Brenda's prying.

"Well, I'm gonna expect some answers tomorrow," Brenda compromises.

Retha and her friends arrive at Jessie's just in time for Retha to climb into a limousine with other family members for the ride to the church. Brenda and Simone follow in Retha's car. The small church is packed. Sugar's funeral probably breaks the church attendance record. He'd be proud. The service goes along smoothly until Bonnie, one of Sugar's many ex-wives, starts to weep loud enough to be heard throughout the church. Crying at a funeral is contagious. Sylvia begins to cry a little louder than Bonnie and Sylvia's children join in. Before long the service comes to a complete halt in order for the mourners to calm down. By the time the service ends there is barely a dry eye in the place. Those that aren't crying because of loss cry from the extremely sorrowful music the organist plays along with the melodic moaning of the soloist. There are many Sugar stories, all cleaned up real nice and respectful. It is hard to get a sense of the true Sugar, the one everyone liked so much because he was so mean, sometimes raunchy and direct. The minister's eulogy portrays Nathaniel Solomon Sr., aka Sugar, as nothing less than a saint and in the minister's eye's Sugar may have been since he was one of Sugar's longest and most faithful customers. The graveside ceremony is not nearly as dramatic though those closest to Sugar have a hard time leaving him to his internment.

The repast is served in the church dining room. While sitting there gazing at the food and praying she can keep it down, Retha looks up and sees Jaren and Aaron for the first time. "Ouch! What's wrong with you girl?" Madelyn jumps as Retha reaches under the table and squeezes her thigh hard. Her eyes follow Retha's and she understands why her sister pinched her. "You just now seeing him? He's been here since we walked in. Wipe your nose; you're sweating."

Retha can hardly believe Jaren is in attendance at Sugar's Homegoing. She wonders why he hasn't said anything to her? She watches Jaren mill around the room and talk to different friends and family. Retha is self-conscious about her appearance which is disheveled and sickly. She might have spent more time on herself if she had known he was coming. Robert must have contacted him but why didn't he or Jessie tell her Jaren might attend the service?

Retha's heartbeat increases with anticipation. She contemplates what she will say to him. She considers telling him all about the baby, not here at the church, but maybe she can get him alone. She decides to let whatever happens happen. She waits for him to approach her but he never does. She catches his eye at one point and smiles but he just stares at her for a few moments and turns his head away. As the time passes and Retha realizes that Jaren does not plan on speaking to her, it takes all her strength and focus not to break down. Retha is not alone in her distress. Her family and friends expect reconciliation between Jaren and Retha when they see him at the funeral. They watch the couple as if they are the main event on a Saturday night boxing venue. All are greatly disappointed.

Most of the family and many of their friends pile into Jessie's home after the dinner at the church but Jaren and Aaron do not make an appearance. Not one person mentions Jaren to Retha. Everyone is downright sorry for her. She has never looked so poorly, not even after Joe's death. Retha's appearance is attributable to several things including Sugar's illness and death but mostly it is the time she spends gagging over her toilet bowl. Fruits and vegetables are the only foods she can tolerate. She has not lost any weight but she has not gained one pound either. Her weight has been redistributed to her child, making her appear almost skeletal. Retha's pregnancy and pitiable appearance make her usually over-protective family hyper-protective.

Andre had spoken with Jaren after the funeral and thanked him for the service he provided Sugar and the family by hiring the nurses. Their conversation had been amicable but at that time Andre assumed Jaren would attempt to reconcile with Retha. When Jaren doesn't show up at Jessie's and Mykol informs Andre that Jaren said he was flying out immediately after the repast, Andre is furious. He wants to call Charles and tell him to keep his son away from Retha. But, of course, Jaren hasn't approached Retha in weeks.

Andre is frustrated and needs to act, so he complains to Robert. Robert looks at him long and hard before giving his opinion. "Jaren is going to do right by Retha. Don't you worry about that. The reason he was here today is because of her. I'm not saying he hasn't been foolish but as far as I can tell now, Retha is the one throwing a wrench into that wheel. All she's got to do is move that damn wrench." Andre greatly respects Robert's opinion, so he decides to join the rest of the family on the sidelines.

Retha remains at Jessie's home as long as possible. She stays until her body makes her leave. If Brenda and Simone were not in town, she would go upstairs and climb in one of the girl's beds but her friends are tired also. It has been a long day and she wants to get a bath and go to bed. She tries not to think about Jaren. She wonders if he is visiting with Jeremiah or if he flew back to New York. The situation is bad because not one person has mentioned Jaren to her, not even Brenda. As Simone drives the ladies home, Retha wonders if she will ever see him again. Envision her shock when they enter her home and find Aaron stretched out on the sofa. Before she can catch herself, she hears her voice asking for Jaren. Aaron points down the hallway leading to her bedroom.

That old queasiness Retha gets whenever she is going to see Jaren after a long separation wells up. She goes into the kitchen for a glass of juice to settle her stomach and returns to the family room where she sits down and starts chatting with her guests. Brenda and Simone stare at her as if she has lost all reason.

Aaron isn't sure what is happening. The whole day has been a mystery to him, starting out with Jaren's behavior toward Retha. When Jaren asked Aaron to accompany him to San Antonio to attend the funeral, he explained that they would stay overnight at a hotel. Once the funeral ended Jaren declared he wanted to return to Tampa right away, then later announced that they would stay over after all but not at a hotel, at Retha's. "I'm just along for the ride, bro," Aaron responded. So here he sits awaiting the outcome of the day's journey and comforted that Simone and Brenda appear as lost as him.

Retha continues to ignore her friend's curious glances until Ida and Andre arrive. The newcomers are surprised to see Aaron and also simultaneously ask for Jaren. They get the same response Retha got but this time three hands point down the hallway. Ida and Andre look at Retha as if to ask "So why are you out here?"

Retha takes a deep breath and gets up and parades down the hall mumbling, "I guess I'd better go check on him."

The room is dark when Retha peeps in and she can't tell if Jaren is awake, so she goes into the bathroom and takes the world's fastest shower and dresses for bed. She starts to leave the room then decides to do what she wants and climbs in the bed with Jaren getting as close to him as possible. He opens his arms and wraps them around her before she realizes what's happening.

"Hey," he greets her.

"Hey."

"How are you doing?"

"I'm fine what about you?"

"I've been waiting here for you a long time. I came in, took a shower, watched television and fell asleep. I was beginning to wonder if you were ever coming home."

"I didn't know you were here. I was surprised to see Aaron when I came in."

"Would you have come home earlier if you knew I was here? I started to call you at Jessie's and ask you to come."

"I would have come. I was afraid you had gone back to Tampa or New York."

Jaren chuckles sarcastically. "Like I could leave here without talking to you."

Retha doesn't respond. They lie there sensing each other and before long Retha starts to cry. She tries to hold back her tears but can't. Jaren has never known Retha to cry before and isn't sure what's causing the tears. He assumes her tears are for Sugar but wonders if they are the accumulated tears from the last few months that they have been apart. He has wanted to cry so many times himself since the separation. Retha doesn't know why she is crying. These aren't Uncle Sugar's tears. Other emotions have been on the edge for so long and Jaren's chest and shoulder seem to be the place the tears from these emotions want to rest.

"Thank you for what you did for my uncle, Jaren."

"You're more than welcome. I'm sorry about Sugar. I know he was very important to you."

"I couldn't bring myself to call. I said terrible things and I didn't think you'd ever want to see me or talk to me again. What I did was wrong Jaren – getting pregnant. It was not an accident; I intentionally got pregnant. I pray you can forgive me." There is dead silence. After no response from Jaren, Retha continues. "I'm glad you came. I wanted to see you."

"Why?"

"Because I like looking at you. You're my screen saver, remember?" she answers.

Jaren reaches over, turns on the light, and turns on his side to face Retha. They lie there looking at each other for a while before he speaks. "You have beautiful eyes. It's been months since I've really seen your eyes. I miss you Retha."

Once again, Retha's eyes began to fill with water. Jaren leans forward and kisses her. His mouth tastes better than she remembers and she doesn't want to let him go.

"Retha, I want you to tell me something and please be honest."

Retha doesn't answer. She is afraid of what Jaren may ask and even more worried about her answer. She has been so warped in her behavior toward him.

"Retha."

"Yes."

"Are you sick? Is everything okay with the baby?"

"No, I'm fine, just never ending morning sickness. It comes and goes but mostly stays around. Jessie says she was the same way with Mykol."

"No Retha, there is something else going on. You don't look well. You're not even acting like yourself. I want you to tell me and please don't lie to me."

Retha is at a loss. She can tell he is upset; his voice is quivering.

"I'm pregnant and tired and upset over Sugar and us."

"Don't lie to me, Retha! Are you seeing a doctor regularly?"

"Well, yes."

"I want to talk to the doctor. What's his name or her name?"

Agitated, Retha pulls away from Jaren and sits on the side of the bed. "Jaren, I'm seeing my OB doctor regularly. She's probably tired of me; I bug her so much. The baby is fine and I'm okay. Why so much concern all of the sudden? I haven't heard from you in weeks. Do you get this excited about all the women you date?" Retha must resolve this issue. No matter how she tries, no matter that Jaren is lying in their bed next to her, no matter that he tells her he misses her, no matter. She cannot be satisfied with even the possibility of sharing Jaren with another woman.

"That's not fair and you know it. I care what happens to you. Retha, I care for you more than anyone in this world but you told me you didn't want me around anymore. You said you didn't need anything else from me, dismissed me like I was crap you flush down the toilet. Do you have any idea how I felt when I left here? You think I should have called you anyway to find out how my baby is doing? Yeah, I should have but I was hurt and I was mad. To love someone as much as I love you and be sent away like that – well, let's say it took me a while to get past my anger. I had to convince myself you wanted me here. When you walked in this room, I didn't know if you were going to tell me to get out or what. You have no idea how relieved I was when you climbed in this bed with me."

Jaren moves to Retha's side of the bed and takes her in a strong embrace. It has taken two years for Jaren to say he loves her. She wants to be happy but has those old reservations. Are these just words? As sweet as these words sound and as much as she enjoys hearing them, if they carry the same old "afraid of commitment" attitude, nothing has changed. Jaren often behaved like a man deeply in love but never enough to commit and Retha wants him completely.

After a few moments, Retha suggests they join the others in the front but Jaren wants to stay in the room with her. She insists so they make a brief appearance but return to the bedroom within half an hour. Their guests have no intentions of leaving until things are resolved between Retha and Jaren and are having a great time entertaining each other.

Once back inside the room, Jaren starts to disrobe Retha. She asks him to turn off the lights but he wants them on. "I want to see you, all of you. It's been so long since I've been close to you. Let's leave the lights on." Jaren and Retha take their time and gently share the most exquisite "softball" make up sex. Retha hates to make Jaren hold back but in the end she has to get on top to prevent him from being too rough with her.

The baby is moving like never before and Retha is better than she has felt in weeks. She realizes she needs Jaren as much as she wants him.

When she comes out of the bathroom and climbs onto the bed, Jaren tells her, "We need to have a serious talk."

"About what?" Retha asks, taking in the concern on his face.

Jaren doesn't answer right away. He walks around to her side of the bed and pulls her into a sitting position with her legs hanging off the side. He kneels down in front of her, places his head on her chest, and proceeds to have his talk.

"I've wanted you since the day I first saw you. I wanted you so much that it scared me because I had to change my life to be with you. I told myself that my life was perfect and couldn't get any better. Things got heavy so fast between us that I felt I needed to slow the relationship down. I wanted things to cool off between us a little because it was like I couldn't move without you and I didn't want to. I wanted to be with you all the time. It wasn't you pushing; it was me. I couldn't help myself. I tried to get as much of you as I could but I got scared. When I made that stupid comment to you about dating other people, I didn't want that. I haven't been with anyone else. I've loved you for a long time Retha. I hated to admit it to myself. It seems everyone knew it except me."

"Not me," Retha says almost belligerently.

"I get upset about the time I wasted when I could have been with you. You really had no idea how much I loved you?"

"No, Jaren; I didn't. I knew I loved you very much."

"So why didn't you ever tell me?"

"Because I didn't want to run you off and besides, if I told you how much I loved you I would have wanted you to love me too and you wouldn't have told me you loved me. I thought you did but I wasn't sure."

"Do you still love me?" he asks.

"Very much."

Jaren takes Retha's hand and places an object in it. "Will you marry me? If you love me, will you marry me?"

Retha is stunned. A marriage proposal exceeds her sweetest dreams. She is content to have Jaren with her. Crying and laughing at the same time, she opens the tiny box to reveal the ring he has had custom made for her. It is lovely.

Jaren watches her with quiet anticipation, still waiting for an answer. Retha blows her nose, cries and laughs while looking from him to the ring and back several times. "Are you sure you want to get married, Jaren, and that you just don't want to get back together?"

"Retha, we need to get married and live together. No more of this living apart crap, not another day."

"Before I answer I want you to consider something."

Jaren is disappointed. Retha stands up and asks him to stand up also. He stands looking bewildered as she takes his hand and places it on her stomach. The baby is moving around like a contortionist on speed. Jaren jumps as if electricity has passed through his body. He looks at Retha with a wrinkled brow and fear in his eyes. "What the hell! Retha, is that the baby?" He asks placing his hand back on her stomach. Retha watches the awe sweep his face before he lights up with a smile.

"Look at me, Jaren."

Jaren pulls his eyes from his hand resting on Retha's swollen belly and looks in her face.

"What I did was not right. It was deceitful and conniving. Can you forgive me for that? I don't want to start a marriage if you resent me or act out of a sense of obligation because I'm having our child. If you are asking me to marry you because of the baby, it's not necessary. We can continue to see each other as long as I don't have to share you."

"Retha, I had that ring with me when I came at Christmas. I thought about returning it when I got back home but engraved custom jewelry is a little hard to sell." Jaren smiles and then becomes serious. "I know what you did Retha and maybe I should resent you for getting pregnant but I don't. I love you too much for that. I'm happy about the baby but I wanted you long before I learned you were pregnant. I could never resent you. I'm as much to blame for our problems as you. To be honest, I'd have to say I started them. I offered you a relationship I didn't want and refused to admit it. I've been angry about not being a part of my child's life from the very beginning. I want to see your stomach grow. I need you with me. I want us to move on with our lives as a family."

--

Susan, Charles, and Rachelle know Jaren is in Texas. They pray he will bring Retha back home to Tampa with him and things will be right, again. After Jaren confronted his family, Susan apologized to Rachelle, Jaren, and Charles. She sat Jaren and Rachelle down and explained her behavior with Charles listening in. "I am not trying to justify what I did or how I acted. I need to explain. I was raised my whole life to feel superior because I was light-skinned and had a light-skinned family. My parents never told us that we were better than dark-skinned people but their actions showed us how they felt. We were not allowed to associate with dark-skinned people, even if they had money." She pauses and looks at Charles with love in her eyes, love Charles has not seen for a long time. "I fell in love with your father at college the moment I laid eyes on him, but he had a girlfriend named Regina and he loved her. I did everything I could to come between them and stole your father from that girl." Susan has to stop for a moment and take a breath. "Your father loves me but he had to grow in to that love. He never stopped loving Regina. Every time we see a nice looking black woman with dark skin and about Reggie's height, your dad looks for her."

"Don't Susan." Charles interrupts his wife. "We don't need to bring all this up now."

"Yes, we do. Jaren said we have to fix this and I have to be honest to resolve my problems. I have hurt my beautiful girl who I treasure more than my life." Susan looks at Rachelle and holds her gaze for a moment before looking at Jaren. "I will do whatever it takes to make things right. I always believed I would have to pay for breaking up Reggie and your father. I tried to be a good wife but I fell short. When I saw Retha who is so like that girl I remember, I was shocked. I almost thought you introduced her as Regina. I hated the idea of her having you. I felt like – I don't know – like Regina was taking Charles." Her tears are flowing freely now. "When I saw Retha, I saw Reggie. I am not making an excuse kids and I promise I will do better. I hope Retha will forgive me. I am so happy about my grandchild."

--

Jaren keeps Retha up talking most of the night. It is obvious to him that Retha cannot fly back and forth between New York and Texas as she has in the past. He asks her to move to Tampa with him for spring training and then to New York. Retha balks a little but when he asks her if she wants to be separated from him for weeks at a time during the season she relents.

Jaren insists on meeting with Dr. Randolph and gets an appointment the next afternoon. Embarrassed, Retha goes along with him. Dr. Randolph is thrilled for Retha who is without question one of her favorite patients. Retha goes in to see the doctor alone for an examination and fidgets under her friend's questioning. "So you were wrong about him weren't you Retha? He wasn't ready to get rid of you after all."

"I guess not," Retha answers quietly, smiling with her eyes turned down.

"You didn't trap him did you?"

"No. He says he had the ring before I told him about the baby. It was my Christmas present."

"Good for him. Otherwise, you would always wonder if he married you because of you or the baby. Now you know. He's pretty impressive -- better than on TV," the doctor smiles.

The doctor is pleased Retha seems less frail than on her last visit. When Jaren joins them in Dr. Jean's office it is clear he has been reading up on what to expect during pregnancy; he asks all the right questions. Dr. Jean gives the couple the names of obstetricians in New York and Tampa she recommends highly. By the time they leave her office, she understands why Retha loves Jaren and is certain they will take good care of each other and their child.

No sooner than Retha gets home, her sisters, aunt, sister-in-law, and niece pull her to the side for advice. Ida is very serious as she begins. "Retha, you know there are many women who wish they were in your shoes." Retha doesn't respond but waits receptively for the lecture to continue. "I mean, we want you to realize that this marriage may be a little harder than you might expect," Ida goes on. "You've been married before but this marriage will be very different because as fine a man as Joe was you didn't have to worry about the celebrity thang. Women will be falling all over themselves to get to your new husband."

"That's right," Madelyn adds. "And listen, you were very young when you married Joe and pretty much went along with whatever he said or wanted. You've changed and you've been on your own for a while now. Marriage is not the easiest thing in the world and when you have two grown people trying to make joint decisions it's hard. You will both have to do a lot of compromising to keep your marriage strong, most likely more than the rest of us because we don't have to worry about that dynamic career or all that money."

"I wish I did have to worry about all that money," Phyllis adds causing everyone to laugh and thankfully lightening the mood.

"Retha, baby, we want you to be strong and prepared for less than the fairy tale. Your marriage is not going to be easy all the time but you and Jaren love each other and have gotten through some pretty rough struggles. He's a good man like his father. I know he is. He comes from good people. I never mentioned it before but Charles Daniels and I were at college together and spent a good bit of time with each other. Charles is a very good man. There isn't anything we can say to completely prepare you for the road ahead but we want to pray with you." Retha's Aunt Reggie has the last word.

The women stand and form a circle as Jessie leads them in their request to the Father for a blessed union.

Retha and Jaren marry two weeks later in a very small church ceremony followed by a large reception in San Antonio. They set up residences in New York, Tampa, and San Antonio and three months later they give birth to one of the world's most darling baby girls. They name her Morning after Retha's Great Great Grandmother and often call her Sugar Babe.

~~~

Thank you so much for reading *Romancing Retha*. I hope you enjoyed the novel as much as I enjoyed writing it and that you will take a moment and visit your favorite retailer's site and leave a review for fellow readers. Be sure and look for my upcoming novels and share your thoughts and comments on the *Cinda's Books* Facebook page.

Thanks again!

About the Author

Cinda Brea is a native of the city of Carthage, Texas, located in the East Texas Piney Woods and grew up in the city of Seaside on the beautiful Central California coast where she attended Monterey Peninsula College. Cinda is retired from the United States Army after 22 years of service. She has degrees in culinary arts and restaurant management from St Phillips College in San Antonio. She is the wife of one, mother of four, grandmother of four, great grandmother of two pooches, a family member and friend to many. She and her family make their home in San Antonio, Texas. *Romancing Retha* is her first novel.

Novels by Cinda Brea

Friends No Longer
Sylvia's Solace
Romancing Retha

Contact Me
www.Cindabrea.com
*follow on Facebook at https//www.facebook.com/***Cinda's**
Books
or via email to: cindabrea@gmail.com

www.ingramcontent.com/pod-product-compliance
Lightning Source LLC
Chambersburg PA
CBHW031720170626
46808CB00005B/1824